FINAL DEPLOYMENT
AN ASTRA MILITARUM NOVEL

More tales of the Astra Militarum from Black Library

OUTGUNNED
A novel by Denny Flowers

ABOVE AND BEYOND
A novel by Denny Flowers

SIEGE OF VRAKS
A novel by Steve Lyons

KRIEG
A novel by Steve Lyons

MINKA LESK: THE LAST WHITESHIELD
An omnibus edition of the novels *Cadia Stands, Cadian Honour, Traitor Rock* and several short stories
by Justin D Hill

SHADOW OF THE EIGHTH
A novel by Justin D Hill

HELL'S LAST
A novel by Justin D Hill

THE FALL OF CADIA
A novel by Robert Rath

CREED: ASHES OF CADIA
A novel by Jude Reid

DEATHWORLDER
A novel by Victoria Hayward

LONGSHOT
A novel by Rob Young

KASRKIN
A novel by Edoardo Albert

CATACHAN DEVIL
A novel by Justin Woolley

STEEL TREAD
A novel by Andy Clark

VOLPONE GLORY
A novel by Nick Kyme

WITCHBRINGER
A novel by Steven B Fischer

VAINGLORIOUS
A novel by Sandy Mitchell

WARHAMMER 40,000

FINAL DEPLOYMENT
AN ASTRA MILITARUM NOVEL

R S WILT

Black Library

A BLACK LIBRARY PUBLICATION

First published in Great Britain in 2025 by
Black Library, Games Workshop Ltd., Willow Road,
Nottingham, NG7 2WS, UK.

Represented by: Games Workshop Limited – Irish branch,
Unit 3, Lower Liffey Street, Dublin 1,
D01 K199, Ireland.

10 9 8 7 6 5 4 3 2 1

Produced by Games Workshop in Nottingham.
Cover illustration by Dan Watson.

Final Deployment © Copyright Games Workshop Limited 2025. Final Deployment, GW, Games Workshop, Black Library, The Horus Heresy, The Horus Heresy Eye logo, Space Marine, 40K, Warhammer, Warhammer 40,000, the 'Aquila' Double-headed Eagle logo, and all associated logos, illustrations, images, names, creatures, races, vehicles, locations, weapons, characters, and the distinctive likenesses thereof, are either ® or TM, and/or © Games Workshop Limited, variably registered around the world.
All Rights Reserved.

A CIP record for this book is available from the British Library.

ISBN 13: 978-1-80407-658-3

No part of this publication may be reproduced, stored in a retrieval system, or transmitted in any form or by any means, electronic, mechanical, photocopying, recording or otherwise, without the prior permission of the publishers.

This is a work of fiction. All the characters and events portrayed in this book are fictional, and any resemblance to real people or incidents is purely coincidental.

See Black Library on the internet at

blacklibrary.com

Find out more about Games Workshop
and the worlds of Warhammer at

warhammer.com

Printed and bound in the UK.

For Brian.
We will play.

For more than a hundred centuries the Emperor has sat immobile on the Golden Throne of Earth. He is the Master of Mankind. By the might of his inexhaustible armies a million worlds stand against the dark.

Yet, he is a rotting carcass, the Carrion Lord of the Imperium held in life by marvels from the Dark Age of Technology and the thousand souls sacrificed each day so his may continue to burn.

To be a man in such times is to be one amongst untold billions. It is to live in the cruelest and most bloody regime imaginable. It is to suffer an eternity of carnage and slaughter. It is to have cries of anguish and sorrow drowned by the thirsting laughter of dark gods.

This is a dark and terrible era where you will find little comfort or hope. Forget the power of technology and science. Forget the promise of progress and advancement. Forget any notion of common humanity or compassion.

There is no peace amongst the stars, for in the grim darkness of the far future, there is only war.

PROLOGUE

He did not trust himself to sweat.

The air of the senate chambers was stagnant and stiflingly hot as General Hurdt marched into position before the governor's dais. He sucked on his teeth, fancying he could draw fresh fluid from the mean yield of his parched salivary glands, and not for the first time that day craved a sip of water.

It had been fifteen hours since he had last permitted himself a drink, knowing that the morning's schedule would not provide him with an opportunity to relieve himself. He was to be at the forefront of his division throughout the day's celebrations. His bearing and the wear of his uniform would be painstakingly recorded and scrutinised. The assembled luminaries and their attendant courtiers, gossips and lickspittles would spend weeks afterwards dissecting even the smallest imperfection – there was no place for human weakness before the great and the good of Rilis. Even celebrating the return of their honoured sons and daughters from a war waged across the stars, the assembled potentates relished any fault they could scent with their powdered noses, or pluck loose with their long, avaricious fingers.

Sweat could betray him. The meanest trickle from his forehead would draw scrutiny, and too soon. So too could it unman him, serving as an inopportune, personal reminder of the frailty and human weakness the gathered leaders so despised in others but revelled in themselves.

He could not afford the luxury of weakness at such a time as this, and so he rose above it, bearing the heat and scrutiny for the sake of Rilis and his Third Division. Just as he had borne the rehearsals for this ceremony, twelve hours a day for a week in the sweltering heat, he would bear this. Only perfection would do for the world's highborn, who claimed to represent the rest of Rilis' sons and daughters.

To his left, his division's colours drooped in the lifeless air, the gold-fringed sky-blue flag emblazoned with the armoured track and lightning bolt emblem of the Third Rilisian Heavy Division. Behind him stood his two surviving regimental commanders at the heads of their reconstituted command squads, their standards equally motionless.

Survivors of Captain Dorran's company of Stygians occupied the gallery above. Faceless in their black carapace armour, they were inert as statues, save for the humming of the capacitor backpacks powering the hellguns they held across their chests.

Hurdt suppressed a shudder. Though their supreme discipline remained unwavering, none of these Stygians had returned from Oranesca's depths unchanged. The Third Division itself had lost more than half of its complement beneath the orbital bombardment – that any of his command survived at all might appear the divine will of the God-Emperor made manifest.

The general knew better. Engineered by Dorran, the method by which the Rilisian forces had achieved their salvation from the depths of the collapsed hive city was something Hurdt had not yet come to terms with.

Summer had come early to Vytrum, and the rest of his division stood in formation outside, enduring the day's oppressive heat in full regalia. Despite the baking sun above, Hurdt found himself envying them the breeze on their faces. There was no such respite for him beneath the glaring lumens of the chamber and the covetous scrutiny of the lord governor and the assembled senate.

Hurdt wished for even the slightest breath of air where he stood beneath the sweltering lights illuminating the Dais Aquila and its lectern of black stone and burnished gold from which the governor presided. The general was no longer a young man, and though he appeared far younger than one fast approaching his first century, years and war had taken their ineluctable toll. Unable to sweat, he found himself silently praying for relief as he waited for the eternity it seemed to take for the senate to assemble.

Despite the headache pounding in his forehead, Hurdt stood at stiff attention, sweltering in his full panoply – ochre breastplate and pauldrons, trimmed in Imperial gold, atop his brown leather greatcoat and drab floxwool uniform beneath. Polished and restored since his return to Rilis, his power sword hung upon his left hip, while his bolt pistol rested in its buffed holster of brown leather, its grip angled for speed draw, upon his right.

Above, limp tapestries lolled like parched tongues from the vaulted ceiling. Grim bas-reliefs and carved effigies depicting the final, contorted moments of Imperial saints and martyrs leered from the chamber's walls, with every inch of space that might otherwise remain blank seemingly embellished with skulls both graven and real.

The skulls filled his sight, displacing the grinning, simpering assembly gathering before him. Skulls covered everything, more ubiquitous in the gallery than representations of the aquila itself. They watched expectantly, the dark hollows of eyes delineative of the Guardsmen he had left in the smoking pit of Oranesca Hive, waiting to see how their general acquitted himself.

The darkness of their eyes swallowed him, carrying him below.
Darkness.
Crushing, soaking, screaming darkness.
Darkness, like a dead weight on his chest, as the world collapsed.

Hurdt glanced about, fearing for a moment that he had fallen faint. He remained on his feet at the centre of the senate audience chamber. All about him was as it had been before, save that now the governor was addressing them.

He wondered how much he had missed.

'...ultimately crushing the Enthan Schism, bringing the God-Emperor's righteous justice and restoring the light of true faith to that once-benighted shrine world!' said Armitage Montcomme, lord governor of Rilis and Ganspur. Montcomme beamed from his lectern, centuries of juvenat treatments rendering his visage a taut rictus that appeared ready to snap free of his skull at any moment. Montcomme's scarlet robes rustled, his liver-spotted scalp gleaming in the harsh light as he raised his arms in thanksgiving. 'We rejoice that Rilis continues to enjoy the blessings of the Golden Throne, thanks to the glorious efforts of General Hurdt and his division.'

'Half,' Hurdt said.

'Eh, what?' Montcomme asked, lowering his hands. He still grinned, despite his confusion, and Hurdt wondered if the lord governor remained capable of any other expression.

'I've only half a division, my lord governor. The rest lie beneath the rubble of Oranesca Hive, where our noble allies, the Fire Angels Chapter of the Adeptus Astartes, buried them.'

'Indeed,' Montcomme stammered, wrong-footed by being

forced off-script. 'It's, uh… it is a miracle which returned you to Rilis', uh, bosom! The… the blessings of the Throne–'

'The Throne blesses Rilis with children enough to die where you decree, in the Emperor's name, my lord,' Hurdt said. 'The Throne blesses the children of Rilis with thrifty minds and skilful hands, then sends the fruits of their labours as far afield as Hydraphur to feed the hunger of a war machine as insatiable as it is uncaring.' He grinned. 'The Throne certainly blesses you, my noble lords, with such means and comfort as the sons and daughters of Rilis and Ganspur could scarce imagine from the luxury of their field cots! If such are the blessings of the Golden Throne, my good lord governor, then we, the children of Rilis, have had our fill of them.'

The assembled senators murmured amongst themselves in agitation. This confrontation had not been on the programme.

'Surely,' Hurdt continued, 'the God-Emperor Himself smiles upon you, you assembly of craven jackals!'

'The martyrs–' Montcomme spluttered.

Hurdt scoffed. 'Isn't that what you always call us, irrespective of where we die fighting and who kills us?'

Hurdt drew his bolt pistol.

Montcomme's expression of surprise was only momentary, before Hurdt shot him in the face.

The Stygians in the gallery above opened fire on the senate before the governor's headless corpse had time to reach the ground. Hotshot las-fire burned through the assembled senators' finery as if it were insubstantial as smoke.

General Hurdt holstered his bolt pistol and left the Stygians to their work. Turning on his heel, he marched back out the way he had come in, leaving the crack of las-fire and the screams of Rilis' masters echoing behind him as he rejoined the remains of his division outside.

He really needed a drink.

ONE

FROM STRENGTH COMETH WILL

I

Norroll was first out, as usual, plummeting from the edge of space.

The Valkyrie fell away rapidly, thirty-eight miles above the planet, as Norroll plunged through the upper atmosphere at speeds high enough to crack the sound barrier. He grinned beneath his rebreather, his carapace armour protecting him from low pressure and murderously cold temperatures as he made his descent, unmarked, towards his objective below. He relished the opportunity – such drops had been uncommon since his departure from his old Aquilon squad two years earlier.

Departure. That was one way to understand it.

'*Norroll, report.*'

Transmitted through the clarion vox-net, Tempestor Traxel's order, delivered in his customarily clipped, stentorian tone, reached Norroll as clearly as if they were seated next to one another.

'Just lost in thought, sir.'

'I'd be concerned about that if you could think.'

'You'll doubtless be pleased to know that I've been reflecting upon my pre-mission reading. Nice and clear up here, boss. Orbital ring's beautiful, this time of day.'

'I'm glad you're enjoying your sightseeing tour.'

'Thank you, Tempestor.'

'Now do your job.'

The northern continent's central plains stretched out beneath him, a dustbowl of dun ochre intermittently broken by broad thickets of tangled, drab olive scrub and crisscrossed by barren red-orange rivers meandering lifelessly across the flatland. The largest of these rivers, the Zholm, was home to some of Rilis' finest orchards, the culmination of a desperate initiative to renew an environment ravaged by millennia of overmining and rapacious industrial production. Generations of farmers spent their lives attempting to coax life from the planet's appallingly polluted soil.

As cleverly as the planet's leaders had packaged it, Norroll was not fooled by the pale attempt at renewal – Rilis was a war world. Every child born, every scrap of ore grubbed from the soil, was earmarked for the Departmento Munitorum; the planet's restoration took whatever pittance remained.

If the collective illusion of working for some notion of a better future ensured the Rilisians looked forward to their tithe quotas, so be it. Despite his general indifference to such things, Norroll found the concept novel.

'Status at objective?' Norroll voxed.

'Unknown,' Replendus, the eradicant's vox-operator and newest member, replied. Norroll hardly knew the Scion at all, save that he had been remanded to First Eradicant for some manner of tech-heresy or other during an operation with his previous squad. Replendus had just replaced Trooper Lo, who had been killed

during the cleansing of the Vero Salient. Lo had himself replaced Trooper Ochuthi, who had been killed by a sniper on Antarill. Ochuthi had replaced Actis, cut down six months earlier by blood-mad murder-cultists on Tecerriot.

First Eradicant was hell on vox-operators.

'Xi-Three-One's Taurox Prime is transmitting,' Replendus continued. *'Strong signal. Encrypted, but zero data.'*

'Lights are on, but nobody's home.'

At seven miles high, the atmosphere thickened and Norroll began to spin, reducing his headlong terminal velocity to around one hundred and eighty miles per hour. The entirety of the front spread out beneath him – the Zholm River, like fresh blood slowly oozing across a dry and blackened scab, wended across a battlefield six miles deep and nearly twenty miles long. Serried lines of broken trenches and reinforced earthworks scarred the length and breadth of the battleground, separated by the ample swathes of blackened earth, churned and heavily cratered, that delimited no-man's-land. Thick mustard-yellow clouds of dust blended with billowing plumes of suffocating black smoke to create an impenetrable smog that boiled upwards from directly beneath him, obscuring all detail in his landing zone.

He checked his position relative to Xi-3-1's Taurox Prime on his slate monitron, the portable data-slate mounted to his armour's right vambrace. 'Six point three-five miles above objective,' Norroll reported into the vox. 'Winds have blown me a bit westward, so I'll have to make up the difference on foot.'

Unlike the sophisticated grav-chutes Norroll had employed with the Aquilon squads, his current unit – a pair of suspensor fins mounted on either side of his backpack – allowed for little in terms of steering. Though eradicants were more tactically flexible than either a standard Tempest squad or the Aquilons, such flexibility carried drawbacks of its own.

'What do you see?' Traxel asked.

'Battlefield specs look pretty much as reported from up here, but I have zero visibility on the dropsite due to obscuration from smoke and dust.' Norroll keyed a rune on his data-slate. 'I'm deploying Actis.'

'Throne, Norroll,' Bissot sighed. *'Don't call it that.'*

The reconnaissance servo-skull uncoupled from its mount on his backpack. A large augur display was fixed to the skull's right hemisphere, and its right socket was now a repository for a plan position indicator. Considerably more powerful than a conventional auspex scanner, Actis was connected directly to Norroll's capacitor unit, feeding power to the variety of sensory apparatus studding its cranium. A snaking network of steel-banded cables slid into a series of sockets in Norroll's armour, interfacing with his data-slate and his helmet's visual display.

'Eight hundred feet,' Norroll announced. 'Deploying grav-chute.' Seven blips arrayed across his optical heads-up display. 'I've got seven marks in the landing zone.'

'Noted,' Traxel acknowledged. *'Neutralise and continue mission. We jump on your mark.'*

Dropping silently through the cloud, Norroll primed a frag grenade. Setting it for a five-second fuse, he tossed it towards a cluster of four blips to his left and drew his monoblades.

Actis' augurs fed data directly into the tactical array in Norroll's omnishield helm, marking the troopers with outlines of green light. As he plunged through the smoke, Norroll's descent was unobserved, the faint buzz of his grav-chute obscured by the crackle of armoured vehicles burning nearby, distant volleys of artillery and the panicked shouts from the four troopers when the grenade plunked onto the ground amidst them.

'Begin jump.'

Even before he landed, he was on them, his right monoblade

slicing into the unprotected area between chinstrap and flak collar of one as the left slipped between the base of the skull and first vertebra of another. Withdrawing the blades, Norroll landed in a crouch, using his legs as springs as he redirected the force of his landing, pistoning forward into a third trooper before the first two hit the ground. Norroll eviscerated him, thrusting one blade between the trooper's belt buckle and flak armour and cutting upwards and sideways with a flick of his wrist, then plunged the second blade through his trachea, just to be certain. Orienting on the four other Guardsmen as he shoulder-rolled over the disembowelled trooper, Norroll came up on one knee, sheathing his right monoblade and drawing his hotshot laspistol.

The grenade exploded, spearing through the remaining four troopers in a squall of fragments. Cut down by shrapnel, the two nearest the blast fell outright, while a third was seriously injured.

Norroll dropped the furthest, least injured of the troopers with four quick shots from his hellpistol. Giving the wounded trooper no time to react, Norroll charged him, opening his throat with a monoblade and ducking aside before the blood had time to spurt from the wound.

Norroll sheathed the blade and drew a locator beacon from one of his belt pouches, then thumbed it active, dropping it next to the man he had just killed. He shot the two troopers who had been injured by the grenade's blast between the eyes and ran on.

'Dropsite secured and marked. Moving to objective.'

'Any chance those were friendlies?' Durlo asked.

'We weren't formally introduced.'

Norroll sprinted into the smoke, using Actis' augur readings to orient on the objective. Hefting a corpse as he passed, he tossed it atop a barrier of rusting triple-strand razor wire and leapt into the area beyond.

Sensing anti-personnel mines, the servo-skull pinged a warning.

Norroll dropped a second locator beacon before zigzagging through the minefield, guided by the overlay in his heads-up display.

'Minefield at beacon two,' he reported. 'Recommend diverting around – it's too big for Durlo to disable a path through.'

'Acknowledged.'

Near a bend in the river, Norroll noted structures emerging from the dense haze of dun smog. Cautiously approaching the complex, he found it little more than ruins, its buildings reduced to burned-out shells and debris by artillery fire. Accompanied by the low droning of flies, the foetor of death seeped through his respirator's filtration system, lingering noxiously in the breathless atmosphere with a reek like rotting fish and faeces. Corpses in their dozens littered the ground, identically uniformed and armoured in Departmento Munitorum-standard flak, so it was impossible to determine whether this had been a battle between two indistinguishable forces or a one-sided massacre. They were bloated and flyblown. Norroll knew from experience that these soldiers had lain there for no less than three days.

The largest building in the complex, perhaps once a grand home or farmstead, had apparently been used as a makeshift headquarters – a company guidon yet leaned by the main door, its banner drooping languidly in the lifeless air. With no traps evident, Norroll took no further time to investigate the area, stepping over the mouldering carcasses of the dead on his way out. Ducking through a breach in the property's low stone fence, he continued onwards.

At the edge of a quarter-mile-wide swathe of artillery-pitted no-man's-land beyond the former headquarters and its garrison of corpses, Norroll came upon a series of earthworks. Banked up behind nests of barbed wire, the hastily built emplacements provided cover for the tanks and other armoured vehicles overwatching the area he had just passed through.

Its armour melted like wax by a melta weapon, the turret of a lone Leman Russ protruded above the edge of the embankment, its rusting Punisher gatling cannon still trained on the killing fields below it. Norroll cleared the dirt bulwark, skirting the edge of the fortifications. Corpses surrounded the tank, though Norroll could not determine whether they were crew or attackers. The engine compartment gaped open, what remained of its contents scattered on the ground around it, rifled through and plundered of any useful, or valuable, components.

He checked his wrist-slate, verifying his route across what Actis' augurs indicated were a series of abandoned trench networks. According to his maps, Xi-3-1's Taurox Prime was only slightly over two hundred yards away.

'Just dropped beacon three at the end of no-man's-land, where the trench network starts. I'll drop the last when I reach the objective.'

'*Acknowledged.*'

Closing the vox-link, Norroll felt the hairs at the back of his neck stand on end. He sprang to his feet and sprinted towards the nearby trench system, diving in head first as the Earthshaker round exploded twenty yards ahead of him. Shaking himself free of displaced dirt, he slithered through the layer of muck coating the trench's bottom on his belly, crawling through the murk towards a nearby dugout.

Norroll surged into the earthen shelter as a round of follow-on fire struck the edge of the trench network where he had entered, rolling against the near wall to protect himself from the blast. He was in a small dirt-floored bunker, approximately three yards square, its walls reinforced with flakboard. An old iron-framed bunk bed, its mattresses stained with mud and blood, stood along the rear wall, while a small folding desk and chair lay overturned in the corner on the dugout's far side. Loose wrappers, food tins and lho stubs littered the dirt floor, but the only thing of real value Norroll found inside was cover.

Listening for any additional follow-on fire, Norroll poked his head out of the dugout, sending Actis floating up over the edge of the trench as he reviewed the servo-skull's readings.

'What in the hells are they firing at?' he breathed. The likelihood of his detection, especially under these conditions, was low to the point of absurdity. Stinking mud caked his carapace, recolouring it from the 36th Xian Tigers' ferric oxide green to dingy Rilisian ochre.

'First Eradicant, have you been noticed?'

'Negative,' Replendus responded. *'Why?'*

'I just took indirect fire.'

'That was you? Have you been detected?'

'Unlikely, which makes me wonder what they were shooting at. Keep your heads down.'

Norroll cut the link. He vaulted free of the trench and continued at a run, listening for any further indication of indirect fire. The recon trooper sprinted between trenches and bypassed pillboxes, laspistol extended as he kept to the cover of burned-out vehicles and other heaps of battlefield detritus. A north-easterly breeze whispered between the trenches, clearing the smoke marginally and improving his visibility through the dust and smog to around ten yards.

Naturally, this meant that the enemy had a better chance of seeing him as well. Setting Actis' augurs for longer range, he picked up his pace.

Ahead, a trooper peeked over the lip of an embankment. Norroll shot him in the head and leapt the ditch without breaking stride. He dropped into a controlled roll down the opposite side, gaining speed on his descent before throwing himself back into his sprint.

Norroll hugged the ground, picking his way between a pair of dead Chimeras, their armour blasted open by artillery fire. Three corpses lay on and around the back ramps of the infantry transports, uniformed in the standard Departmento Munitorum-issue drab green fatigues and Rilis' characteristically mustard-coloured flak armour of every dead body he had encountered on the battlefield to this point. Bumper numbers, stencilled on the front and rear of each Chimera, indicated that they belonged to the First Battalion, 212th Rilisian Mechanised Infantry Regiment, though Norroll had no idea which side of the civil war the 212th was on. Clearing each vehicle, he found the crews slumped dead in their seats, their corpses riddled by las-fire. He secured medi-kits and several ration tins from the Chimeras before moving on.

Actis' readouts indicated that the objective lay nearly thirty yards east of his current position. Use of bio-agents in the area in the recent past had garbled the servo-skull's ability to identify life signs, so Norroll proceeded cautiously, hunched over as he jogged between available areas of cover.

Fifteen yards closer, and he encountered more corpses in Rilisian green and ochre like the rest. Most were relatively whole, splayed haphazardly over soil recently cratered by artillery fire. He noted at least sixteen of them, though he hazarded that their proximity to the artillery splashes made an accurate count difficult. Their right shoulder pads, like the Chimeras he had just scouted, marked them as belonging to the 212th Mech. Rolling one over, Norroll observed the reddish blotches of livor mortis on his face. Unlike the others, this one had been shot in almost the dead centre of his chest, penetrated through by a high-powered las-bolt. The body was still limp and slightly warm, likely dead for under two hours. The closer he got to his objective, the more the casualties appeared to have been cut down by hotshot las-fire.

As Norroll slipped between the dead, Actis' augurs scanned the corpse of a nearby Tempestus Scion. *Rale, Jovian – Trooper First Class, Tempest Squad Xi-3-1*, scrolled across Norroll's slate monitron, followed by a monotone flatline. Selecting this data, he transmitted it to his squadmates in First Eradicant and received a ping of acknowledgement a few seconds later.

He found Rale's corpse half buried beneath the bodies of the Rilisian Mech. His armour's oxide-green carapace and dull steel edging were nearly obscured by the blood of his killers, and his clarion vox-array had been torn free of his back and riddled with las-fire.

The smog parted, and Norroll saw the Taurox Prime's turret, its dual gatling guns and storm bolter aiming idly in his direction from behind a low earthwork. The armoured transport was still running, the berm sheltering it surrounded by the remains of shredded Guardsmen.

He dropped the fourth locator beacon.

'First Eradicant, I have eyes on the objective.'

'Acknowledged,' Replendus replied. *'Proceed with caution. We're entering no-man's-land.'*

Actis located two more Tempestus Scions between the dead 212th troopers and the Taurox. Isardo and Noku. Norroll looked around at what must have been more than two score dead troopers surrounding his fellows and their vehicle.

He had known Isardo since the Scholam Tempestus on Sindral-Gamma. While they had never been as close as Norroll had been to Actis, he remembered Isardo as a faithful and diligent comrade, if never exactly a friend.

Norroll climbed over the earthwork, clearing the area around the Taurox as he approached from the vehicle's front left. Behind it lay two corpses, both shot neatly between the eyes. The troopers were clad in matt-black carapace armour, Cadian pattern, over black fatigues. He dragged the closest one into the area between the left rear track and the embankment and rifled through the man's pouches. There was nothing to identify him, though he had ample supplies of grenades and hotshot laspacks to supplement Norroll's back-mounted capacitors. As Norroll stripped both corpses of anything useful, Actis' scanners identified two more Scions, Trooper Anche and Tempestor Ezl – and the servo-skull's augurs indicated the Tempestor yet lived. A blood trail, still fresh, led from the two black-armoured troopers around the Taurox's rear.

Norroll's chest tightened – given the carnage surrounding the Taurox, he had no hope to find any of the Scions alive. 'First Eradicant, Norroll. On objective. Tempestor Ezl is still alive.'

This time Traxel responded directly. *'Status?'*

'Contact to follow.'

Norroll stepped over the troopers, carefully following the blood trail around the corner, where he found the rear hatch standing open. Inside, Trooper Anche hung limply in the gunner's cupola, blood pooling beneath her on the deck below. Readying himself, Norroll cleared the far side of the vehicle and sprang around the rear corner of the Taurox, stopping short as he found a hotshot laspistol aimed directly between his eyes.

Tempestor Ezl sat propped up against the Taurox's rear track unit. Blood flowed from a broad rent in his lower cuirass, staining his olive drab fatigue trousers red-black and soaking into the thirsty ochre dust beneath him. His right hand held his laspistol steadily on Norroll's face, while his left attempted to hold in his innards.

'Where in the hells did you come from?' the Tempestor hissed, instinctively putting up his sidearm when he identified Norroll.

'Trooper Norroll, Tempestor. First Eradicant.'

'Traxel's outfit?'

'Aye, Tempestor.'

'That figures.'

Unsure whether he had just been insulted, Norroll voxed his squad. 'I've located Tempestor Ezl, but he's badly wounded. Daviland, I could really use you here.'

'Estimate we'll be there in four minutes,' Daviland replied.

'How long?' Ezl asked.

'Four minutes, Tempestor.'

'Thanks. I've been off comms for a while.' He tapped his damaged helm with the side of his laspistol. 'No vox.' He held up his right vambrace to display its shattered screen. 'No slate, either. Blocked a chainsword.'

Multiple pings sounded as Actis' sensors picked up contacts to the south-east. Still too distant to show up on his heads-up display, Norroll's slate presented several large blobs of green blips, representing at least three sizeable formations closing on their location. While Actis' long-range bio-augurs remained fouled, the servo-skull's movement prognosticators functioned perfectly.

'Enemy infantry inbound. Estimate at least a platoon, approaching on foot from south-east. Three hundred and fifty yards and moving cautiously, but steadily,' Norroll called into the vox. 'First Eradicant, any way to pick up the pace a little bit?'

Norroll raised his laspistol as Bissot rounded the front corner of the Taurox at a dead sprint with Daviland on her heels. The gunner stopped, bracing her hotshot volley gun against the corner of the front fender as she faced south-east into the ochre cloud of dust and smoke.

Daviland passed Bissot and slipped down next to the wounded Tempestor, raising Ezl's omnishield visor and opening his respirator. The Tempestor's dark skin was ashen and sheened with sweat, and his bloodshot sclera made the deep brown of his irises seem nearly black. Despite the mauling he had taken, he was fully conscious. Bright red blood dripped down Ezl's chin and onto his plastron, mingling with the darker blood that leaked steadily from his ruptured abdomen.

To the east, a series of explosions rumbled through the yellow smoke. Norroll checked his wrist-slate. The green blobs on his indicator array shifted position rapidly, breaking into a series of smaller pips spreading out in all directions. Explosive readouts populated the screen at the inbound enemy's location, where they had apparently stumbled upon a minefield.

Daviland lifted the Tempestor's chin and ran an oxygen tube up his nose. Ezl never flinched. 'I'm going to move your hand, Tempestor,' she said, taking hold of his bloodied left gauntlet.

'Don't bother…' He paused.

'Daviland, Tempestor.'

'Daviland,' Ezl repeated. 'Don't bother, Medicae-Adept Daviland. Save your gear for someone who can use it.'

'Right now, Tempestor, that someone is you,' Daviland said, trying to pull his hand away.

Ezl resisted, locking his arm in place and keeping his hand pressed vice-tight against his wound. 'Don't make me strain much harder, Daviland, or I'll end up squirting my guts out on you.' His eyes narrowed as he fixed his gaze on hers. 'When a Tempestor tells you to save your gear, trooper, it's not a suggestion.'

Daviland relaxed her grip. 'Understood.'

Ezl slumped back against the rear track guard with a sigh. 'Good. Now where in the hells is Traxel?'

'Here,' Traxel said, rounding the corner of the Taurox at that moment. 'And my orders to Daviland were to keep you alive, whether you liked it or not.'

Ezl scoffed through bloodstained teeth. 'Wouldn't have a drink for us, would you?'

'Fresh out, I'm afraid,' Traxel answered, kneeling next to Daviland. 'You've looked better.'

Ezl's grim chuckle degenerated into a hacking cough. 'It's hard,' he wheezed, coughing up pinkish phlegm, 'going out amongst the beautiful people. What are you doing here?'

'Reinforcing Xi-Three-One.'

Ezl grimaced. 'Yesterday, I'd have told you to push off.'

Norroll reviewed his wrist-slate. 'We might want to get Tempestor Ezl into the Taurox,' he said. 'Enemy infantry's closing. Replendus, Durlo, are the guns reloaded yet?'

'Almost,' Durlo replied. *'Clearing a jam.'*

Ezl wiped blood from his mouth with the back of his gauntlet. 'Listen – the situation on Rilis is worse than the initial assessments. These Rilisian traitors are motivated, they're well trained, and they have a serious axe to grind with this world. The Third Division took down the planetary militia in three days. They're also almost impossible to distinguish from the loyal Rilisians, so that's a persistent challenge.' He winced, swallowing hard, and attempted to clear his throat. 'The biggest problem is the Stygians. Elite infantry. Last time they attacked as a unit, they killed the senate, then eliminated the enforcers in their own precinct house. Since then, we've only seen them supplementing the traitors' infantry squads...' He trailed off, his breathing shallow.

'What assets do we have?' Traxel asked.

Ezl coughed hard again. 'Two loyal Rilisian regiments, pieced together after the traitors struck. One's here in the Zholm with the handful of Militarum forces from off-world who answered the distress call, just as we did. No coordination. Different units using different vox encryption.'

'So, they can't talk.'

'Won't. They can communicate in the clear just fine, but the enemy's listening. Beats them back every time they try to put something together.' Ezl's eyes closed slowly as his head sagged forward.

Daviland rolled his head to the side and injected a dose of stimm into his neck.

The Tempestor jolted awake, his eyes flaring angrily. 'I thought I told you–'

'You can't tell us what we need to know if you're dead, Tempestor,' Daviland said.

Ezl nodded weakly. 'Fair.'

'Where is the other regiment?' Traxel asked.

Ezl worked his slack lips back to life. 'Other regiment's back east, towards the capital,' he said. 'They were trying to dislodge an enemy strongpoint in the mountains, open it up for ground movement, since the enemy controls the skies – not that there's anything flying any more. Nobody's heard from them in months.'

His eyes rolled up as his head fell backwards, his helmet banging against the track guard. He began to spasm, his body struck by a spate of sudden convulsions as he vomited dark blood all over himself.

'Help me hold him steady, Tempestor!' Daviland urged. The two Scions strained against the seizures, desperately trying to hold Ezl still as Daviland struggled to clear the bloody ejecta from his mouth. She readied a syringe, wrestling to keep the afflicted Tempestor steady enough to administer the compound.

Ezl went slack, hissing out a long breath. His spasmodic twitching subsided as quickly as it had struck. Daviland pressed the syringe into Ezl's artery.

Without warning, Ezl snatched Daviland's wrist with his blood-soaked left hand. Twisting her arm away, he fixed her with a fierce glare. 'How much of that are you planning to waste on me?' he snarled, before coughing a stream of red-brown bile from his mouth.

Traxel waved Daviland off.

Ezl nodded his thanks. 'I split the squad. Kept half of us with the Taurox, shoring up a weak point in the Imperial line here. The other half went south, under Commissar Fennech.' He spat, at the same time trying unsuccessfully to push his intestines back in through the gash in his belly. 'Resistance was heavy, but enemy capabilities in the area were light. Seemed like a good idea at the time.'

Traxel visibly tensed at the mention of the commissar's name. 'Where is Fennech now?' he asked.

'Continuing his assessments.' Ezl shrugged weakly. 'Almost half of my Scions survived eradicant detail before they came to me, so those are the ones I sent with him. With you already deployed when he got to Sindral-Beta, and Second and Third Eradicants destroyed, it seems he decided my squad was the next best option.'

'My sympathies.'

'As to where he is...' Ezl spat a wad of bloody phlegm into the dust. 'No idea. Too far out of range for slates or intra-squad vox. We lost clarion when Rale died. We were on our way to link up with Fennech and the others when the artillery started falling. We buttoned up behind an earthwork, hoping to ride it out. Mad bastards assaulted us through the barrage!'

He slumped back limply, breath wheezing out between his lips.

'Twenty yards!' Norroll shouted.

Traxel rose, chainsword revving as he adjusted the throttle.

Ezl fixed Traxel with his feverish gaze. 'Find the loyalists and you'll find my squad. Find them, though, and you find Fennech.'

'Tempestor Ezl,' Daviland said, withdrawing her reductor pistol from its holster, 'do you desire the Emperor's Peace?'

Exhaling, the wounded Tempestor seemed to deflate. With eager eyes and a wan smile, Ezl nodded weakly. 'Now you can use your kit on me, Daviland.' He looked up at Traxel. 'Been an honour,' he said.

'Emperor light your way, Tempestor,' Traxel replied. 'The honour's been mine.'

Daviland removed Ezl's helmet and pressed the reductor pistol to the Tempestor's left temple.

'If you're lucky,' Ezl wheezed, 'Fennech's already dead.'

Daviland fired, driving a heavy-gauge piston through Tempestor Ezl's skull with enough force to liquify his brain, killing him instantly.

'I've never been that lucky.'

II

Daviland holstered her reductor pistol and sealed her medi-kit before unslinging her lasgun. Beside her, Traxel took a step closer to Norroll. There was no need for orders. What came next was ingrained at the core of each of them, honed to muscle memory by decades of training and reinforced by unshakeable hypnotic conditioning, until it was as reflexive as breathing.

At ten yards, the first hint of the approaching infantry appeared, indistinct phantoms in the umber fog. As soon as they were visible, Bissot opened fire, roiling the smoke as her hotshot volley gun tore into the formation's front.

'Taurox moving. Clear zero to one eighty fore. Mark,' Replendus voxed.

Daviland and Bissot moved away from the personnel carrier's front as Norroll and Traxel withdrew from its rear, both pairs repositioning on either side of the Taurox as Replendus pivot-steered right to face the enemy. Tempestor Ezl's remains slumped to the ground, rolling back to face the sky as his corpse collapsed into the divot left by the right rear track.

The Taurox pivoted back and forth, grinding Ezl's remains into the dirt as the twinned hotshot volley guns mounted to either side of the vehicle strafed the enemy, sending the troopers diving for whatever meagre cover they could find. The turret traversed, swinging in the opposite direction. With a shrieking whine, the twin six-barrelled cannons spun up and vomited fire, scything down nearly a dozen traitors.

Durlo's voice crackled across the squad vox. *'Taurox weapons function check complete.'*

Bissot whooped above the roar of her hotshot volley gun, cutting down enemy troopers as they fled the Taurox's blistering firepower. Fed by the capacitor she wore on her back, her weapon could fire nearly three hundred rounds without need of a recharge, and countless hours spent on practice ranges and the battlefield had honed her skills to ensure she made the most of every shot. Desperate for cover, the traitors received no respite.

The Taurox continued moving, its guns sweeping across the Guardsmen, pummelling them as they sought to flee. Left, and they escaped into Bissot's line of fire; right, into Traxel's and Norroll's blades.

To Bissot's rear, Daviland fired her lasgun more selectively, picking off any survivors that managed to escape the enfilade they had unwittingly stumbled into. Though her hellgun's ammunition capacity equalled Bissot's, the weapon was unable to match the volley gun's rate of fire.

Bissot raked shots over the troopers who had fallen to the ground. A las-round struck her in the upper right of her chest plastron, staggering her slightly and disrupting her merciless sweep.

With an irritated grunt, Bissot opened fire again, irritably singing a psalm. Daviland had learned that it was her equivalent to cursing.

*'My refuge and my fortress,
God-Emperor, my soul entrust,
He calls on me, and I shall answer,
In wrath I grind His foes to dust.'*

What began as a massed assault of thirty enemy troopers swiftly degenerated into a panicked rout, and the eradicant gave no quarter. Their weapons blazed as they culled the traitors who had already begun to retreat.

Some few rallied – shouting a challenge, one of the troopers rushed the Scions, swinging his hatchet at Traxel. Redirecting the axe with the flat of his chainsword, Traxel fired his plasma pistol into his opponent's belly. The trooper's torso exploded in a flash of superheated mist, carrying his head and limbs away on the blast wave.

The champion's death was the final blow to the traitors' morale. Unable to withstand more, the enemy broke utterly. Hemmed in by the eradicant on both flanks, the survivors retreated hastily in the direction from which they had come.

The Taurox roared forward, still firing, its armoured tracks crushing the fallen traitors into the dirt. The Tempestus Scions advanced on its flanks, Bissot and Daviland to the left, Traxel and Norroll on the right, giving the enemy no choice but flight.

Actis' sensors pulsed a warning across Norroll's wrist-slate. 'Replendus,' he called. 'Minefield ahead.'

The enemy troopers halted. In their haste to flee, they had retreated to the edge of the very minefield they had stumbled into on their way to engage the Taurox earlier. They had been able to deviate around it then with minimal casualties. Pursued by the eradicant and unable to bypass it, they faltered in the face of their predicament.

'Make the traitors clear it,' Traxel growled.

Still firing, the Taurox lumbered forward.

With the devil behind them and the deep blue sea ahead, the traitors tried to swim.

After halting briefly to allow the Tempestus Scions back inside, the Taurox sped away from the minefield. The enemy troopers had done such an admirable job of clearing the mines that the armoured transport had no difficulty following them through. Leaving the broken remains of the traitor platoon behind, the Scions continued east. The breeze had shifted north, increasing steadily and dispelling much of the ochre smog that had heretofore occluded the battlefront.

Daviland sutured a gash on Norroll's right thigh, the dermal stapler whirring as it drew the edges together tightly and covered them with a transparent membrane of synthetic skin to seal the wound and speed recovery.

Blood caked Norroll's short beard where it had sheeted from his broken nose, and a livid bruise was spreading just above his right temple, beneath his close-cropped copper-red hair. Norroll wasn't what Daviland would call handsome, at least not by her estimation of it, and his appeal was not in the least improved by the swelling and severe bruising that accompanied the rightward cant of his nose. His otherwise pasty face was liberally dusted with freckles and marred by old scars.

Daviland took a firm hold of his nose and snapped it back into place.

Norroll made no response, which Daviland found surprising in itself. She had expected some manner of inane reaction and found herself inexplicably disappointed when he failed to give one.

Perhaps he was not as incorrigible as she believed.

Over the past six months, Daviland had exhaustively detailed First Eradicant's aberrant behaviours in her assessment logs, and Norroll, in her estimation the most fundamentally broken member, generated the preponderance of her data. From the reports she had read, his proclivity for independent operation, bordering on recklessness, saw him remanded to the eradicant an astonishing two years earlier. Hypnomatic suggestion and enforced chemical mindscaping seemed hopeless, and his contumacy appeared contagious – Norroll and Bissot perpetually strove to outdo one another, bickering like children on-mission and off. The recon trooper might have seemed a simple glory hound to Daviland were he not the most singularly effective hunter and close-in killer she had ever encountered amongst the Tempestus Scions. That he managed to survive for two years in an eradicant was noteworthy, but thriving in such an environment was practically inconceivable.

Almost as inconceivable as Tempestor Traxel's wilful inattention to the anomalous behaviour of his subordinates.

Norroll stared straight ahead, his tawny eyes glassy as he chewed absently on a mouthful of grey protein supplement, paying Daviland no heed as she worked. He had fallen into a hypnogogic trance almost the instant he sat down, speeding recovery from his excursion across no-man's-land and the subsequent battle. Unconscious but aware, Norroll had followed Daviland's instructions to remove his helmet before lapsing back to inactivity, periodically biting chunks off the foul-tasting vat-grown protein roll he held – something Daviland knew was always preferable to eat while trancing. Norroll's eyes, bruised by his broken nose and the suction cups that secured his helm's multispectral array to his face, stared at nothing as his head rocked gently with the Taurox's ponderous motion.

Above Daviland, the transport's turret traversed, panning side to side, front to back, at random intervals as Durlo's unstinting vigilance kept them from being taken unawares. Lacking support from other vehicles to cover their travel, the demolitions trooper did it all himself, periodically glancing at the data coming in through the augurs mounted in Norroll's servo-skull. Durlo minded their surroundings with one hand on the guns' controls, while the other fiddled incessantly with a gold thronepiece.

Daviland sat down beside Bissot, who likewise stared ahead vacantly in a trance. Tall, olive-skinned and heavily muscled beneath her armour, the volley gunner wore her black hair cropped in a short, utilitarian cut, to not interfere with her helm. A tattoo was visible above the edge of Bissot's collar – a small black Imperial aquila above a line of High Gothic script reading: *Be just and fear not.*

Silence between missions, something once so normal when she had still served with the 55th Alphic Hydras, had become odd to her since her reassignment to First Eradicant. The marked eccentricities of the eradicant's Scions had become Daviland's normal. Surrounded by the constant low rumble of the Taurox's tracks and the tinny whir of the turret's hydraulics, she found herself missing her squadmates' repartee.

She reached into one of her belt pouches and took out a small metal token, the likeness of a white enamelled shield with a simple red triangle at its centre. The triangle, the symbol of the 55th Alphic Hydras, represented Mount Charax, her parent regiment and true home.

Daviland had felt herself greatly honoured when Commissar Fennech had recommended she be transferred from the Alphic Hydras to the Xian Tigers to aid in his assessment of the eradicant formations there. Transfers between Militarum Tempestus regiments were nearly unheard of, and she was even more honoured to discover that her regiment would serve as the basis upon which 36th Xian's eradicants would be evaluated and potentially restructured. Such an honour made the harrowing journey she faced during the nearly three years crossing the galactic gulf seem a worthy endeavour, despite the myriad horrors of warp transit. In the beginning, the honour alone was nearly enough to silence the overwhelming sense of alienation she felt upon her assignment to this new regiment.

Daviland ran her thumb across the sigil's bevelled top edge, then glanced to the yellow disc of the Oculus Tigris now emblazoned on her left knee. Six months later, and she remained with the Xian Tigers and First Eradicant's seemingly incorrigible Scions, with no sign of ever being returned to Mount Charax.

The last embers of her great honour long since extinguished, she wondered if she missed the banter between her new teammates in First Eradicant because it filled, however shallowly, her ever-deepening well of estrangement.

Traxel sat next to Replendus in the Taurox's cab, navigating as the vox-operator manoeuvred the armoured gun truck across the artillery-scarred ground and broken trenchworks. The transport rumbled through the ruins of a village, crunching piles of rubble beneath its grav-assisted tracks. The few remaining villagers fled, wretched apparitions retreating into the cover of their ruined homes as the Taurox passed. Durlo panned his twin gatling cannons across wan faces peeking furtively from shattered windows.

It was an example of what remained of the Zholm valley's farmers and orchard-keepers. Deemed unsuitable for service to the regiments or to the thronging labour crews on the industrial moon of Ganspur, the war had reduced the villagers to refugees on their own world, huddling in what remained of their homes or in tumbledown encampments at the edges of the battlefield. Unable to differentiate friend from foe, they feared both sides of the conflict, hiding from everyone and sheltering against the fighting and bombardments. Reeking piles of uniformed corpses and scavenged military gear mouldered at the village's edge, grim testament to how its inhabitants managed to survive amidst the ruins.

Though Replendus gave the villagers as wide a berth as possible, Traxel appeared to pay them no heed whatsoever, the bruised lids of his hooded eyes focused on the map display before him.

Above Daviland, Durlo's golden thronepiece glinted in the Taurox's low light, flitting back and forth across the knuckles of his left hand as he operated the turret controls with his right.

She glanced at Traxel in the cab, suddenly angry at the Tempestor's negligence in ensuring these talented yet obviously damaged Scions received the psychochemical and hypnotic treatments that might restore their places in the line. Time and further degradation would only make the process more painful and less likely to succeed – failure would necessitate execution or servitor conversion.

Daviland tried to convince herself that the uncharacteristic flash of dismay she suddenly felt was because squandering such talent was grossly wasteful, as Fennech had once said.

'Why do you do that?'

'Do what?' Durlo asked. He rolled his hand from side to side, never looking away from the turret's targeting display as the coin flitted back and forth between his gauntleted fingers.

Daviland tilted her head to the side, unsure whether he was joking.

'With the coin?' Durlo closed his fist on the thronepiece, opening his hand again to display an empty palm. Legerdemain was yet another of Durlo's peculiarities. 'Something to do, I suppose.'

'You don't have enough to do?'

Durlo shrugged. The coin reappeared and resumed its dance across his fingers.

Replendus drove the Taurox up an embankment, concealing

the tall vehicle behind a berm overlooking the river below as the sun sank towards the horizon. Looking out through a side viewport, Daviland watched the foul, sulphuric waters of Zholm River meander, rust red and treacle slow, across an area that had once been farmland at the edge of a forest. Blackened stumps of trees gave way to the ruined vestiges of civilisation.

Rising from his seat, Traxel headed towards the rear of the troop compartment. With a nod to Daviland and a clap on the side of Norroll's head, the Tempestor exited the Taurox's rear hatch. Following Traxel, Norroll and Daviland crawled to the edge of the breastwork to look out across the river valley.

Las-fire flashed in the growing twilight on the far side of the river below, the whip-crack release of each round reaching the Scions a split second after each pulse of red and white.

Norroll pulled a set of magnoculars from a pouch at his side and scanned the area below.

'Tempestor Ezl said there were other Imperial forces on Rilis?'

'He did,' Traxel said.

'Here.' Norroll handed the Tempestor his magnoculars.

Below, a pair of troopers fired from behind the cover of an earthwork, the crisp white of their peaked caps and trousers standing in stark contrast to the red-piped cobalt of their jackets. Their gold epaulettes and buttons, black boots and silver belt buckles faintly glistened in the twilight. The two troopers provided covering fire for four others struggling to weld a heavily oxidised steel plate over a rent in a Chimera's hull. Blast scoring and las-impacts marred nearly every surface of the vehicle, leaving what little remained of its original matt black almost entirely obscured beneath a caked ochre layer of Rilisian dust.

The Chimera's multi-laser spat las-bolts over the two troopers to its fore, lashing at the unseen enemy beyond them with strobing flashes of energy.

'Iron Guard,' Traxel said, handing back Norroll's magnoculars. 'Back to the Taurox. Time to lend a hand.'

Crawling back down the embankment, the three Scions embarked the gun truck.

'Replendus,' Traxel said as he knelt behind the driver's seat, 'are you receiving any vox-traffic from the Mordians below?'

'Not sure, Tempestor. Everything I pick up is encrypted. I was trying to break the ciphers while you were outside, but no success yet.'

'Set clarion to broad-spectrum jamming and broadcast my voice in the clear.'

'Sir, if they can hear you in the clear, so can the enemy.'

'That's the idea.'

Replendus bent over his vox-array, now connected to the Taurox's onboard vox-mount. Adjusting dials as he muttered the catechisms of actuation, he toggled a series of switches up and down repeatedly, cursing as he argued with the machine's recalcitrant spirit. A rune below the set's antenna flashed red. He lit a small scented votive and placed it atop the vox-assembly with a mumbled prayer. Soon, the scent of promethium and myrrh filled the Taurox's cab.

The red light below the antenna continued to blink.

With a frustrated hiss, Replendus pulled a servo-skull from his pack. Taking hold of the heavy-gauge vox-fill cable, he flicked back the spring-loaded green steel fill connector sheathing with his right thumb. Hissing the Savant's *Benediction for Meaningful Connectivity* between his teeth, he licked his left index finger, using his saliva to wet the interface's gasket ring to ensure the Omnissiah would bless the seal. After blowing thrice across the thirteen golden tines that would couple the skull to the vox-set's service connector, he carefully linked the cable assembly to the prepared steel interface plug on the vox. Pressing firmly, he twisted the connector sheathing clockwise. Checking its fastness, Replendus spoke the invocation to kindle the servo-skull's spirit.

A green light blinked in the skull's right socket, flashing rapidly. Its onboard cogitators whirred as it introduced itself to the clarion's machine spirit. A garbled stutter broke from the vox, squealing as Replendus twisted a pair of dials. He mumbled a quick prayer as he adjusted another knob.

The servo-skull's cogitators clattered like a maglev train, the light in its orbit blinking erratically. With a shuddering clank and a sudden whiff of ozone, the construct fell silent. A few seconds later, its lamp stopped blinking and became a steady, solid green glow. With a pop, the red light below the vox-array's antenna blinked off.

'Your will is done, adept of the forge,' the servo-skull intoned, its monotone voice distorted by crackling static. 'May the Omnissiah bless your endeavour.'

'Handy you had that servo-skull,' Bissot said, leaning over Replendus' seat with interest. 'Where did you come by it?'

Replendus hitched a thumb over his right shoulder, towards Durlo.

'Did you nick that from a tech-adept?' Bissot gasped.

'I didn't *nick* it, Favae,' Durlo said indignantly. 'I don't *nick* things. And nicking things from the Adeptus Mechanicus gets your gear cursed. I found it.'

Bissot snorted. 'Lucky find, then.'

Its strength boosted by the Taurox's power supply, Replendus' clarion vox-link stepped on all other stations in range, overriding them as it broadcast Traxel's voice over all frequencies across the bandwidth.

'Soldiers of the God-Emperor, this is First Eradicant, Thirty-Sixth Xian Tigers, Militarum Tempestus. Mordian force on the eastern bank of the Zholm, identify yourselves.'

The Mordian troopers across the river turned suddenly, momentarily halting their hasty repair as Traxel's voice burst through their squad's vox-systems. Ahead of them, the exchange of fire briefly ceased altogether, both sides taken aback by the unexpected transmission that broke across every vox-feed.

'First Eradicant?' a guttural voice crackled back in heavily accented Low Gothic, the response as much a question as a reply. *'This is the Eight-Hundred-and-Thirty-Second Mordian.'*

'Hail, Eight-Hundred-and-Thirty-Second Mordian,' Traxel said. 'We are due west of you across the river and en route to your position.' He swatted Replendus' shoulder.

The vox-operator disengaged the brakes and gunned the engines. Black smoke belched from the exhausts as he hit the accelerator. The gun truck climbed over the berm, rapidly picking up speed as it rolled down the hill towards the river.

'Acknowledged, First Eradicant,' the heavily accented voice said. *'We see you.'*

Across the Zholm, the Mordians cheered. Plumes of black smoke roiled skyward as a trio of Chimeras rumbled back to life behind the shelter of their earthworks.

The Taurox plunged into the Zholm, plumes of red-stained water spraying in its wake as it thundered across the riverbed. Accelerating as the transport burst free of the water, Replendus steered the armoured vehicle up the opposite bank, the Taurox's four independently powered tracks easily taking it over the rise.

'Replendus, take us between those two enemy Chimeras,' Traxel said, indicating the ochre transports the Mordians had been engaging. 'Get behind them, then cover us while we deploy.'

First Eradicant's Taurox rumbled past the rightmost Mordian Chimera with its improvised armour plating, the quad-tracked gun truck easily outstripping the battered infantry fighting vehicle as multi-laser fire was exchanged anew. Crimson streaks strobed across the battlefield, flashing like lightning in the darkness as they stitched across the enemy's armoured transports.

The eradicant held their fire. Optimised for an anti-infantry role, the Taurox Prime's side-mounted hotshot volley guns and gatling cannons were nearly useless against a Chimera's armour. Las-fire and heavy bolter rounds peppered the Taurox, gnawing at the vehicle's frontal armour like scree-gnats upon the shaggy hide of the beast that was its namesake, and just as easily ignored. Opening the throttle, Replendus outpaced the other two Mordian Chimeras, weathering enemy fire as it roared between the two enemy transports Traxel had indicated. Pivot-steering around once it was behind them, the Taurox opened fire with hotshot volley guns and a hail of gatling fire, chewing into the armoured vehicles' lighter rear armour and keeping the enemy buttoned up inside.

Caught between the Mordian Chimeras and First Eradicant's Taurox Prime, the enemy vehicles pivoted and opened fire. Heavy bolter and multi-laser rounds hammered the gun truck's front armour.

Bissot and Daviland charged out through the Taurox's left side hatch, already firing before they hit the ground as Traxel and Norroll plunged out through the hatch on the right. Screened by Durlo's and Replendus' covering fire, the Scions transcribed a broad arc around the Chimeras' flanks. Once behind the transports, Daviland and Norroll tossed krak grenades onto the vehicles' upper hatches, blowing the doors down onto the infantry within. Billowing smoke, the Chimeras' rear hatches dropped, disgorging the panicked, disoriented survivors straight into the eradicants' fire.

Daviland and Norroll each tossed frag grenades into the gaping troop bays and got clear. Detonating with a tremendous bang within a split second of one another, the grenades killed the vehicles' drivers, turret gunners and the assistant drivers manning the bow-mounted heavy bolters – the method was unspectacular but effective.

Less than two minutes had passed since First Eradicant's assault on the Chimeras began. Their enemy eliminated, the Scions re-embarked the Taurox wordlessly, their return to the vehicle coordinated by reflex by a life of deep hypnotic conditioning, relentless drilling and merciless training. Sealing the hatches behind them, the Tempestus Scions moved to locate their next targets.

Bissot assisted Durlo with reloading the gatling guns' ammunition hoppers. By the time they were finished, the eradicant was already in position to dismount and engage again.

III

Atebe scanned the installation through the scope of her Ryza-pattern/226B hotshot long-las. She stretched out across a long branch in a tall daekki tree, all but invisible beneath the canopy of spade-like leaves and the enveloping folds of her cameleoline cloak.

Below her, the traitor 212th Mechanised conducted a rapid mass resupply at the Rilisian militia's mostly derelict Kiemchek Ridge Depot. Located several miles behind the forward lines, distance and obscurity had spared the depot from the devastation to the west.

Vehicles underwent emergency maintenance in crumbling motor pools, while the regiment's casualties were laid out for triage on the cracked pavement and patches of weed-choked grass surrounding the depot's dilapidated medical facility. Full-bellied cargo-8 supply haulers were mobbed by squads of filthy, bedraggled troopers in search of ammo packs, rations and water. The furtive, haunted glances of the troopers' hollow eyes and their tight grips on their lasguns spoke of horrors witnessed, even before their return home to Rilis.

Her eye pressed against the rubber cup on her scope's rear aperture, Atebe focused on a pair of figures at the edge of one hastily cleared motor pool. Officers – Rilisians made them easy to spot with their brown leather greatcoats under their dark mustard flak armour. Even the lieutenants, who boasted no greatcoats, were marked by the light khaki trousers they wore beneath their olive drab jackets. Easy for the troops to identify at range, but easy for everyone else, too.

The pair she watched were engaged in a heated argument. She adjusted her magnification, zooming in on the officer to the left and subjecting him to minute, if rapid, scrutiny. Hypnotically implanted information, rooted in her mind before deployment, flashed into her conscious thoughts. The Rilisian order of battle, heraldic data and high-value target profiles populated in her forebrain with far more clarity than they could have if she had tried to memorise the details herself.

The officer wore his gleaming silver Imperialis rank insignia mounted on his epaulettes and a blue-and-gold braid draped over his right shoulder. A colonel – regimental commander, by the green tabs on his shoulder boards – holding his helmet in his left hand. He was tall, lean and clean-shaven, as all Rilisian troops were, with close-cropped black hair greying at the temples. Though his skin was darker and more aged than in the picts, the mole on the left eyebrow, the scar marring the bridge of his flattened nose and half a dozen other facial markers ensured that Atebe now knew Colonel Dashrek Gruenner's face as intimately as she knew her own. Fresh bandages, already soaking through with blood, covered the right side of his face. Gruenner was fourth on her list of high-value targets.

He argued with an older man, another senior officer, who

had his back to Atebe. Shorter than Gruenner and considerably stockier, his responses were unambiguously negative. Even from behind, she could make out the twin silver starbursts on the dark blue shoulder boards of his greatcoat. Even though he was facing away and wearing a helmet, fifteen physical markers identified him as Major General Oleg Hurdt, commander of the Third Rilisian Division, Mechanised Assault.

Hurdt was the primary target on Xi-3-1's priority kill list, and the crosshairs of Atebe's long-las were fixed on the back of his head.

'I've got eyes on General Hurdt,' Atebe whispered, the tip of her index finger resting lightly on her trigger. Reflexively, she released her breath, consciously slowing her heart rate. The sense of separation between her and her long-las blurred as she entered a semi-trance known as the Killstate.

'You're certain?' Trooper Quisse's voice crackled over Atebe's vox-link. Quisse, who had served as Tempestor Ezl's second-in-command in Xi-3-1, was the senior trooper in their detachment – while Commissar Fennech was in overall command, he had been called away for an urgent conference over the vox several minutes before.

'Hurdt *and* Colonel Gruenner,' Atebe confirmed. 'No question. I've got a shot lined up.'

'Take it,' Quisse ordered.

'You will hold your fire.'

The voice, unequivocal despite its conversational warmth, broke onto the vox-link.

Atebe instinctively raised her finger from the trigger as the voice shocked her from the Killstate. 'Commissar,' she breathed. 'I thought you were on the regimental channel.'

'I am monitoring both.'

'I have General Hurdt and Colonel Gruenner in my sights, sir.'

She bit her lip, her inbuilt, instinctive desire to eliminate two of the highest-priority targets on her implanted target list conflicting with Commissar Fennech's order.

'Noted. And you will hold your fire.'

'We're unlikely to get another opportunity like this, commissar.'

'Agreed. However, we've had a significant breakthrough on our end, and the senior ground forces commander has ordered that we and our comrades in Attack Battalion hold fast as the Hundred-and-Thirty-Ninth coordinates their attack. Hurdt and Gruenner have been marked for capture and future interrogation.'

'Sir, I could fatally disrupt the enemy chain of command now. They'd never have a chance against any coming assault.'

'I have already had this conversation with Colonel Zheev, Trooper Atebe. Our orders are set beneath an incontrovertible seal.'

Atebe let out a breath, still watching Hurdt through the scope of her long-las. Orders overrode instinct every time.

'Acknowledged, commissar.' She paused. 'Do you wish for me to return to your position?'

'No. Remain where you are and await orders. Fennech out.'

Atebe took a deep, sulphur-laden breath. She had fought all manner of foes during her years as a Scion. Two years before, she had spent almost three gruelling months assigned to an eradicant, and her time in the kill-squad had scoured her clean of almost all remaining emotion. She sometimes considered her time in Second Eradicant as an inoculation, as the exposure to so much horror and privation inured her against feeling much of anything afterwards.

Fennech was something else. There was a distance to him – a coldness beneath the layers of unfailing politeness and propriety. Even the perfect intonation in that warm, paternal baritone of his deeply unsettled Atebe. She had watched him execute discipline-lax soldiers with the same bland disregard he displayed when killing the enemy, devoid of malice or regret. It was as if he had compressed every solitary particle of his humanity into a tiny kernel, then buried it in the darkest, most frigid corner of his soul he could find.

Finally exhaling the breath she had been holding, she resumed her watch on the depot, relieved that her current position limited her exposure to him. She had few emotions left to lose.

Leaning over Traxel's shoulder, Norroll watched Kiemchek Ridge Depot's outer perimeter expand through the Taurox's front view slits with the fervent anticipation that always preceded a major engagement. He grinned beneath his respirator, delighted at the opportunity to once again participate in a full-scale battle, rather than the solitary and clandestine operations which had been his sole meat and drink since being consigned to First Eradicant. It was life as a Scion was meant to live it, and his heart thundered with the joy of it.

Glancing around the Taurox, he knew he was not the only one so profoundly stirred by the promise of bringing death en masse to the God-Emperor's foes. There was an electricity in the air, an urgency that grew amongst the Scions as their objective drew ever closer. Even Traxel was not immune to the excitement and leaned forward in his seat in anticipation.

Norroll was grudgingly impressed by the speed with which the motley of loyalist formations had come together following First Eradicant's contact with the Mordians – experience had taught him to expect quite the opposite. Such coordination amongst disparate Militarum forces was difficult under the most ideal of circumstances, with jockeying between commanders often crippling efforts before marshalling even got underway. Norroll suspected that a fervent desire for payback had much to do with the willingness with which the loyalists committed themselves to the assault and enthusiastically submitted to Colonel Zheev's lead.

A barrage of artillery streaked overhead as the Xian Tigers breached the traitors' first predetermined fire zone, the rush of the shells' flight momentarily audible even above the noise of the Taurox. An Earthshaker round splashed down behind and to the left of the transport, the blast wave of its detonation buffeting the armoured truck on its tracks. Shrapnel rang like a gong against the Taurox's hull.

Chaos erupted across the vox. 'Bear and Cold Steel Battalions, Hundred-and-Thirty-Ninth, and Two-Hundred-and-Twenty-Second Krieg Separate reporting multiple losses from indirect,' Replendus said, though they could all hear the reports over the Taurox's speakers.

'They're a more tempting target. Let them draw the enemy's fire,' Traxel said indifferently. 'Keep well ahead of them and get inside the artillery's effective range.'

A shell detonated under fifty yards from the Taurox's fore. Debris peppered the gun truck's front, shattering the viewport in front of Traxel. Replendus jinked to the side with a curse.

'Forward,' Traxel said. 'You will not divert laterally again.'

'Tempestor, aye.'

Despite Replendus' apparent misgivings about plunging headlong through an artillery barrage, the vox-operator's contributions to the Imperial mobilisation had been nothing less than astonishing. With the aid of his servo-skull, Replendus had transformed the eradicant's Taurox Prime into a mobile retransmission station, using his clarion vox-array to push a clear signal to every loyalist position along the front. His efforts to unify and distribute the proper encryption djinni across the formation permitted the disparate loyalist forces to communicate securely for the first time in months. As a result, the revanchist Imperial force roared on-line across the plain towards Kiemchek Ridge on a multitude of tracks, daring the enemy's fire.

Norroll smirked – if such ingenuity didn't get Replendus out of the eradicant after this deployment, nothing would.

First Eradicant travelled well ahead of the Imperial formation, their Taurox easily outpacing the Chimeras of the Astra Militarum infantry and Cold Steel Battalion's ageing Leman Russ battle tanks. Traxel had remained deliberately aloof during the attack's coordination, though he worked to ensure the eradicant remained at the assault's fore. Though he monitored the constant stream of loyalist vox-traffic, he refused to participate in it, reserving sole command of his Scions for himself.

Traxel had likewise remained silent any time Commissar Fennech's voice crossed the vox, never commenting on the commissar's recommendations to the senior ground forces commander. From a tactical perspective, Norroll was perplexed by this – First Eradicant's mission was to locate and reinforce Xi-3-1, or what remained of it, and that made encountering Fennech inevitable. On the other hand, any who had ever met the commissar on Abstinax could readily understand Traxel's reticence to make contact. Nothing unified the Scions of First Eradicant so much as their mutual loathing of Commissar Fennech.

The battle cannons of Cold Steel Battalion's Leman Russ battle tanks roared, tearing through the thin defensive screen of Chimeras and infantry that the 212th had emplaced ahead of the depot.

Thunder rumbled across the traitors' front lines as an Earthshaker barrage briefly turned night into day. Called in by Attack Battalion's forward observers under Commissar Fennech, the artillery batteries of the 139th's Firepower Battalion hammered Kiemchek Depot, throwing the enemy into utter disarray as the Imperial force tore towards the installation's front and flanks.

Staggered by the unexpected cannonade, the enemy fell back,

seeking to reconsolidate before the loyalists managed to collapse the gap between them. As the Imperial formations drove forward, Firepower Battalion shifted fire, shelling the traitors' flanks and rear echelon, further disrupting the enemy's movement and hemming them in as they attempted to retreat. Unable to escape through the back gate and incapable of reconsolidation, the enemy rapidly lost coherency, scattering into smaller cells which sheltered behind whatever cover lay closest. Commanders screamed orders into the vox, urging their forces to turn and face the loyalists, only to be cut down by sniper fire that lanced from the daekki grove above the depot's left flank.

Hurtling ahead of the loyalists, First Eradicant burst through the gates of Kiemchek Ridge Depot. Behind them, the Iron Line of the 139th Rilisian Mech, the Krieg 222nd Separate and the 5228th Tallarn rammed through the facility's decrepit perimeter defences. The loyalist forces slammed into the enemy's forwardmost formations like a sledgehammer, crushing infantry beneath their tracks as they drove a wedge through the traitors' line. The Chimeras' multi-lasers flashed above the tumult of heavy bolters and the blaze of heavy flamers, scouring the traitors as the eradicant's Taurox unleashed hell in rending torrents of bullets and hotshot las-fire.

Covered by bursts from the gatling cannons and Bissot's volley gun, Traxel leapt from the Taurox, tearing into the shellshocked press of enemy infantry. His plasma rounds bored corkscrewing contrails through the smoke, explosively vaporising their targets as the Tempestor's chainsword decapitated, gutted and maimed any who found themselves too close. The very air about him lay thick with the sharp, coppery tang of aerosolised blood as Traxel butchered with a master's efficiency and singularity of purpose, his chainsword's snarling mono-edged adamantine teeth parting armour, flesh and bone with ease.

Norroll swept to the Tempestor's right, monoblades flashing in the light of exchanged multi-laser fire as he plunged through a squad of troopers, the press of bodies too thick for them to effectively retreat into their Chimera. The 212th's troopers, battered and starving after more than two months of grinding trench warfare, were unable to match the recon trooper's consummate murderousness as he bowled through them.

Slinging her lasgun, Daviland sprang past Bissot's keening volley gun, engaging the enemy with laspistol and dagger. She weaved between them, using her opponents' momentum against them to deflect attacks struck against her onto their comrades.

What began as an assault rapidly degenerated into a slaughter. It was battle as First Eradicant liked it best – a merciless cull with no quarter given. Precise application of unremitting violence sent the foe reeling, desperate and incapable of effectively striking back. Carapace armour shrugged off any attack that managed to get through the Scions' defences, while a lifetime of close-combat training ensured that any answering blow struck would be their opponent's last.

The Tempestus Scions' remorseless extermination of whatever enemy troopers lay in their path proved contagious – thirsty for revenge upon the traitors after months of bloody deadlock, the Imperial loyalists stormed from their Chimeras, cutting down any who stood before them. With the heretics unable to mount a successful defence or counter-attack, it could only be a matter of time before the perfidy of the 212th Rilisian Mech was permanently expunged.

High above, a throaty vibration shuddered the night, cutting through the blaze of heavy bolter fire and the artillery barrage to the rear. Tossing a frag grenade into a Chimera and getting clear, Norroll looked up.

'Oh, shit.'

* * *

It plummeted through the night sky, riding a plume of smoke as it descended from the heavens like a comet. The roar of its powerful engines shook the firmament itself as it passed, its hull still glowing orange from the heat of atmospheric re-entry. While Norroll had never seen one in person before, he had no doubts about what he was looking at, and it was coming right for them.

Its meteoric descent drowned out even the din of battle as it hurtled towards Kiemchek Depot on a column of fire. Dumbfounded, the combatants gaped upwards at the doom roaring down on them like a blazing spear hurled by the hand of a wrathful god.

'Drop pod incoming!' Norroll shouted into the vox, scrambling away to join the eradicant in their seamless withdrawal. They disengaged from combat, retreating towards the depot's perimeter to put a safe space between them and the most likely point of impact.

The awestruck Guardsmen in the thick of battle were not so fortunate. Traitor and loyalist alike were flash-incinerated by the pod's engines in the split second before the entry vehicle smashed into the pavement.

Norroll dived behind the Taurox as the shock and heated overpressure from the cataclysmic impact hurled Guardsmen in all directions. Raising his head, he hazarded a glance around the track at the fuming craft.

The drop pod bore little resemblance to the ones Norroll had seen in the picts. Five thick, talonlike struts jutted from each corner, penetrating deep into the pavement around it like dreadful bladed claws. With the whine of hydraulics and the grinding of gears, the blackened pod rose up along its blade struts.

Traxel picked himself up from where the drop pod's impact had thrown him down and crawled next to Norroll. He peeked around the Taurox's track as the oculus hatch on the drop pod's base spread open, staining the roiling smoke with red light.

Three figures dropped from the hatch and landed heavily on the ground below, their massive boots crushing pavement that yet smouldered from the heat and force of their arrival. Yellow eyes gleamed through the swirling smoke and dust of their touchdown. Though obscured, there could be no mistaking what they were. Silhouetted in the dull red light cast from their drop pod above as the fumes about them cleared, they appeared inhumanly large and bulky, rendered even more massive by the power armour they wore. They separated wordlessly, moving swiftly across the drop zone with cool assuredness, harbouring no fear of mortal violence. Their fists bore weapons of a scale never intended for human hands.

A motionless silence, pregnant with foreboding, engulfed the battlefield. The dazed combatants, traitor and loyalist alike, scarcely dared to breathe for fear of drawing the attention of the terrible power which had landed amidst them.

'Astartes,' Traxel whispered.

'Angels!' a Guardsman gasped, rising unsteadily from where he sheltered next to Colonel Zheev's command Chimera. 'The Angels! Bless us, the Angels of the Emperor have come!'

One of the three Space Marines turned in his direction, chaincannon shrieking as the weapon's rotary barrels spooled up. Flame belched from its muzzle as it vomited a torrent of high-calibre rounds, strafing across the Guardsmen in the Chimera's shadow and shredding them into indistinguishable masses of riven meat. Muzzle flare backlit the Adeptus Astartes, glinting from plates of pitted, weathered iron edged with tarnished brass. Against the sable black of his left pauldron, the gunfire reflected upon the grimly stylised likeness of a skull forged of dull iron.

Behind him, a second Space Marine charged Cold Steel Battalion's

Leman Russ command tank, targeting it with a lascannon mounted to the servo-rig on his armour's power pack. The warrior covered the ground with unimaginable speed, the servo-arm mounted to his back gyroscopically stabilising the massive anti-armour weapon and allowing him to fire on the run. The las-bolt, dazzlingly bright in the darkness, speared through the tank's turret ring. Terrifyingly nimble for something so large, the Space Marine weaved around the damaged command tank, deftly sidestepping the fire from one of its sponson-mounted heavy bolters. He mag-locked a melta bomb to the engines then sprinted towards the next tank in Cold Steel's line without pause.

Even compared to his brothers, the third Space Marine was something vomited from the nethermost depths of nightmare. Forward-curving horns sprouted from his battle helm, and the left half of his power armour was twisted and encumbered with protruding bony growths. His left arm ended in a fused mass of ceramite, flesh and claws, from which extended a keening blade that rippled like the madness of the Great Rift in the night sky above.

An unfamiliar sensation, as if his heart were being gripped in an icy vice, clutched at Norroll's chest. As he tore his gaze from the malevolently glowing blade, the sensation passed, leaving only kaleidoscopic afterimages flickering in his vision. Swallowing hard, he looked to Traxel.

'Orders, Tempestor?'

Traxel stared ahead, transfixed, as the twisted Space Marine loped forward on mismatched legs into a mass of prone Guardsmen, firing his bolt pistol. It howled in gleeful abandon, its blade paring through flak armour as if it were nothing.

'Looking for guidance here, Tempestor,' Norroll hissed through clenched teeth. He raised his laspistol and took aim at the Space Marine.

The las-bolt struck true, sparking against the twisted Adeptus Astartes' plastron. The abhorrent Space Marine continued onwards without pause, running down the Guardsmen fleeing before him.

Kiemchek Depot was aflame. Smoke belched from the burning wrecks of Chimeras and Leman Russ tanks, enveloping all beneath a choking pall of toxic fumes. All pretence of command and control lost, Guardsmen from both sides bolted, shrieking in breathless, aimless terror as they attempted to escape the broadening kill-zone. Las-bolts flashed in the gloom, loosed into the flickering dark at random by trembling hands until their power packs ran empty.

The Space Marines orchestrated the firestorm, shaping the chaos around them as if it were the function of some mathematical formula they had solved before the battle was even joined. The cold calculus with which they culled all before them was merely an operation, the only output of which could be their victory. They strode through the destruction, invulnerable and implacable, the loyalists' fire pattering from their armour as ineffectually as rain. All about them, explosions blossomed in the night, their tumult joining with the screams of the dying to thunder across the battlefield like the laughter of dark gods.

'We need to go,' Daviland called, sprinting from the far side of the Taurox with Bissot close behind. 'You and Bissot get in the Taurox, I'll handle the Tempestor.'

Durlo opened fire on the warped Heretic Astartes with the Taurox's gatling cannons, spraying fire across both Imperial and traitor troopers to bring it down.

'Daviland...' Norroll began to protest.

'Go! I'll take care of him.'

With a muttered curse, Norroll followed Bissot through the Taurox's rear hatch, leaving the Tempestor and medicae-adept outside.

* * *

Atebe adjusted her scope, dialling back the light sensitivity so the chaincannon's flash wouldn't blind her. Finding a happy medium, she scanned the Adeptus Astartes gunner, trying to find a weak point in his armour to exploit.

There were few enough to choose from. The Space Marine's enormous brass-edged pauldrons provided ample cover for the weaker armour covering his throat. She panned across the series of cables snaking like steel dreadlocks from the back of his battle helm, considering them insignificant. In profile, his two-handed grip on his chaincannon locked the iron-layered plates of ceramite in position, giving her no real targets on his upper body. Scanning lower, she found that he wore a mail skirt, covering the weaker, flexible areas at his hips and the backs of his knees.

She had no doubt she could penetrate the mail with her hotshot weapon, but the las-round's effectiveness would be blunted, making it less likely to penetrate the soft armour or cause any significant damage. Scanning back up to his head, she brought her crosshairs level with his eyeline and focused on the side of the augmetic targeting eyepiece mounted to his helm. He was bound to shift fire, so she waited for him to turn and give her a shot.

She had been displaced twice already during the assault, forced from her hides both times by counter-sniper fire from the Stygians below. They had even managed to tag her, and though her carapace had taken the worst of it, one round had creased her left thigh. The pain was negligible enough, but the Stygians' persistent interruptions made it difficult for her to assume the Killstate.

The Space Marine chaingunner ceased firing, taking a knee as the hoppers mounted to his backpack cycled fresh ammunition to the weapon's belt feed. She followed him down, then back up as he opened fire again.

Patience, patience.

A lull in the Stygians' volleys gave her the window she needed.

The Adeptus Astartes turned right, slowly and steadily, as he raked his torrent of fire across the troopers in front of him, uncaring which side they were on.

The large augmetic scope over his right eye glowed red in the darkness, targeting the troopers before him. Like the mail skirt, a shot there would likely be wasted.

Fingertip on the trigger with the barest pressure, she waited.

He kept turning, cruelly methodical as he scythed down ranks of Guardsmen.

Another inch, and the centre of his left eye-lens lay between her crosshairs. Almost unconsciously, her finger tightened.

A Leman Russ exploded, the magnesium-bright detonation of the melta bomb blinding her as she fired.

She refocused, momentarily disoriented by the sudden glare through her scope. Blinking away the strobing afterimages as best she could, she saw the Space Marine gunner was still standing.

He was looking right at her, the red glow of his targeting system narrowing as he found and marked her. The brass-edged vox-grille that covered the lower half of his face glowered at her in an overexaggerated snarl. Her las-bolt had left a smouldering dent in the centre of his helm's forehead, her shot fouled when he had glanced to the explosion behind him.

Still smoking, the six barrels of his Reaper came up spinning, right in the centre of her scope.

Atebe dived from the daekki tree as chain-fire chewed through her position, sending a mist of toxic white sap spraying in all directions. She hit the ground hard, and the branch she had been lying on collapsed heavily atop her. Milky sap rained down, burning the exposed skin of her face and right eye, forcing it shut. Ignoring the searing acid, she pried herself free of the branch and moved, long-las in hand as she sprinted towards the hill's edge, a hail of bullets following at her heels.

She could almost feel the Adeptus Astartes' targeting reticule burning between her shoulder blades. She pelted headlong for the cover of the hill, knowing he could take her down at any moment, her carapace useless against such a volume of fire. The rounds followed in her wake, raking towards her – teasingly, breathtakingly close, but never quite close enough. She fought to keep her eyes open as daekki saplings exploded all around, filling the air with a blinding haze of sap.

The sadistic bastard was milking this out.

Atebe leapt for cover, throwing herself over the hill's edge.

The sound of chain-fire still echoed from the kill-zone, but it had changed.

On the other side of the hill, First Eradicant's Taurox Prime pelted the Traitor Astartes with twin gatling fire.

'Tempestor!' Daviland shouted. 'Come on!'

Traxel looked furtively to his left and right, head jerking as he responded to a threat only he could see. Norroll and Bissot dodged past, into the armoured cover of the Taurox, but he didn't notice them.

Daviland could practically feel where he was. From the moment the traitor drop pod had disgorged its cargo of Heretic Astartes, as soon as she saw his reaction, she knew that he was back on Tecerriot, fighting for his life against the Space Marine headsman.

Above her head, Durlo blazed gatling fire, peppering the Adeptus Astartes chaingunner with twin torrents of bullets and forcing him back into the cover of an abandoned Chimera.

The 139th Mech and its allies were hastily pulling back, limping away from the kill-zone without any semblance of order. Engines roared as the loyalists fled westward, chased by throngs of wailing survivors too slow to embark or too unlucky to find space on a vehicle.

'I'm not moving until you move him, Daviland,' Replendus voxed from the cab.

Daviland shook Traxel's shoulder. 'Tempestor!' she shouted into his ear. 'We have to go!'

His augmetic left hand twitched on his plasma pistol, shaking it back and forth with erratic, jerking movements.

Not shaking it – *parrying* with it. His left hand had been his sword hand before he lost it.

'Traxel!' she roared, smacking him hard in the side of his helmet. 'Get moving, Scion!'

Shocked back to the present, Traxel raised his plasma pistol, suddenly disoriented when he found himself someplace other than where he'd thought he was.

Daviland crouched in front of him, hands raised, her helm's optics glowing with faint green light.

Traxel lowered the pistol, breathing heavily. 'Daviland?'

'Come on, Tempestor,' she said, grasping him by the forearm and dragging him to his feet. 'Into the Taurox!'

'Where are–?'

'They're already in the Taurox. Get in!'

Scores of corpses lay spread before the gun truck like some hideous, bloody field, ripe for harvest. Traxel hesitated, puzzling at the scene before him.

'We're not on Tecerriot, Tempestor!' Daviland said, yanking him into the Taurox. Another Leman Russ exploded off to their left, the force of the detonation blasting its turret into the air. 'We're in a world of shit on Rilis! Now screw your head on straight and move!'

Half dragged by Daviland, Traxel staggered into the Taurox and fell, crawling across the film of Trooper Anche's blood encrusting the deck.

Behind him, Norroll pulled the hatch shut.

'Replendus, get us out of here!' Norroll shouted.

The Taurox rumbled, knocking Norroll and Bissot off balance as Replendus jolted it into reverse as fast as he could coax its engines. Churning the dead beneath its tracks, the Taurox lurched backwards from the kill-zone. Replendus brought the vehicle around in a swift pivot, facing west as it took off after the fleeing loyalist Chimeras.

Durlo traversed the turret to the rear, the roar of his covering fire interrupted by a series of heavy clanks. 'I'm dry!' he called. 'Bissot, help me reload!' He unfastened from his harness and dropped into the troop hold.

Norroll knelt next to Daviland. 'What's going on?'

Daviland flipped up Traxel's visor. He blinked rapidly as the suction cups affixing it were forcibly pulled from his eye sockets.

'Not now!' she said impatiently, shining a light into each of Traxel's eyes before roughly pulling off his helmet.

'I'm fine,' Traxel said, trying to push her away. A jolt from the Taurox knocked him backwards.

Daviland ignored him and rubbed a disinfectant wipe over his throat. She drew a syringe and a phial of an opaque, pearlescent liquid from her medi-kit.

'What is that?' Norroll asked.

'Obluvarine.' Daviland drew a tiny measure of the fluid into the syringe. Timing the rocking of the Taurox, she injected it into Traxel's neck.

'The mindscaper?'

'Blessed Emperor on Throne of gold!' Replendus shifted the Taurox into reverse as he laid down withering fire with the volley guns. 'He's coming! Durlo, get those damned cannons reloaded!' The eradicant pitched sidelong, slamming into the bulkheads as Replendus swung the rear of the Taurox around, furiously weaving away from whatever pursued them.

'Almost,' Durlo said, pulling himself back upright. Uttering a hasty prayer against jamming, he struck the feeder actuator and cycled the hoppers to armed.

'Go down, Throne damn you! Go down!' Replendus snarled from the driver's seat. The Taurox rocked back and forth, sending the eradicant frantically grasping for handholds. Thumbs on the volley guns' triggers as he struggled to evade, Replendus loosed a staggering volume of las-fire into the night.

The las-bolt pierced the front of the cab, lancing through Replendus and sizzling past Durlo's raised arm to punch straight through the Taurox's turret ring. The gun truck lurched to a sudden halt as the vox-operator's torso burst, spraying the interior of the cab with steaming viscera.

'Bissot, drive!' Norroll shouted.

Unbuckling Replendus' belt harness, Bissot dumped the sizzling lower half of his body to the floor and threw herself into the seat. Hastily wiping steaming blood from the cab's shattered armaglass viewport, she strained to see what was happening outside.

The Traitor Astartes with the lascannon had already turned away. A las-bolt streaked from his weapon, killing another vehicle as he moved on, ignoring the disabled Taurox behind him.

Bissot thumbed the volley guns' triggers. She clicked them again and again, humming irritably to herself when they didn't respond. 'Volley gun controls are dead!'

Behind her, Durlo clambered back into the turret. Gripping the controls, he tried to traverse the guns to face the Heretic Astartes. The turret jolted, kicking an inch to the left before stuttering back and forth erratically between gear teeth. Releasing the controls, he glanced down at the steam hissing through the holes burned through both sides of the turret ring, then to his left arm, where his sleeve still smouldered over his bicep.

'Turret guns inoperative,' he said, indifferent to the burn and how close it had come to taking his arm off.

'Can we still move?' Norroll asked.

Bissot hit the accelerator and the Taurox lurched backwards. 'Yes.'

'So, move! Get us out of here, Favae!'

Beginning with the chorus of *Blessed be the Martyrs*, Bissot gunned the engine, swinging the gun truck around in its own radius. The exhausts belched plumes of black smoke as Bissot shifted gears, accelerating First Eradicant away from the kill-zone.

IV

The Taurox skirted the edges of what Daviland supposed might loosely constitute a convoy, cloaked by the haze of ochre dust billowing in its wake. While the cloud obscured much of the landscape around them, it served as a smokescreen, concealing the actual location of the convoy's vehicles as they travelled south through the deserted farmland that lay along the western front.

There was little organisation in the Imperial withdrawal. Following their panicked retreat, the surviving vehicles had simply headed west, then south as fast as they could, leaving any possible survivors remaining at Kiemchek to the mercy of the Space Marines. The vox was silent, the loyalists' recently acquired ability to communicate amongst themselves seemingly forgotten as the sundry units attempted to put as much ground between them and the nightmare at the depot as possible. Their destination was southward, as far as the Scions knew, for they had no further information.

Bissot drove along the outermost edge of the loose formation – twice already she had narrowly avoided collisions with Chimeras, which had broken down along the route and were now concealed by the dust cloud. She had been half singing, half grumbling hymns beseeching a measure of the Emperor's boundless patience since the last close call.

A third immobilised Chimera materialised out of the dust directly ahead and dropped its back ramp.

'Idiot!' Bissot snarled, swinging the Taurox around the crippled transport and narrowly missing the rapidly disembarking Guardsmen. She leaned forward in her seat, grinding her teeth, and attempted once again to clean Replendus' blood from the cracked view slit.

Daviland and Durlo sat on the benches lining the sides of the Taurox's troop compartment, while Norroll sat on the deck opposite them. The entire vehicle reeked of spilled blood, ruptured offal and the early stages of rot.

Seated beneath the turret ring, Durlo patched the scorched sleeve of his carapace armour with a heavy-gauge needle and wire thread, patiently drawing the small-arms-resistant fabric on his left bicep shut. His carapace was no longer void-hardened, but it would still be able to protect against most terrestrial extremes. He flexed his arm, nodding at his handiwork with satisfaction, and leaned back against the Taurox's bulkhead.

'Why did you inject the Tempestor with a synapse cleanser?' Norroll asked, chewing on a protein lozenge. He had scarcely taken his eyes from Traxel since awakening from his restorative trance.

The Tempestor slumbered on the deck behind Bissot, under the influence of the obluvarine Daviland had injected him with. Traxel breathed deeply, his body occasionally twitching or shaking as the mindscaping compound scoured his brain.

'Trying to shake loose some aberrant thoughtforms,' Daviland said. 'Back there, when those Space Marines attacked, he froze. He's a detriment if that happens the next time we encounter them.'

Norroll swished a mouthful of water from his canteen to rinse away the protein compound sticking to his teeth. 'What happened?'

'I think he was back on Tecerriot.'

'Tecerriot?'

'In the Colosseum Imperial six months ago, fighting that Astartes executioner.'

Norroll swallowed the last bite of protein lozenge and took another sip of water.

'And you think, what? That these Astartes last night prompted some kind of flashback?'

The medicae-adept sighed. 'Yeah.'

'I didn't think that happened with Scions,' Bissot said from the driver's seat. 'Intensive hypnomatic therapy after every mission's supposed to wipe out memories like those.' She looked behind her into the troop compartment. 'Do you think that's what this is about, Daviland? That we've not received re-enlightenment since before Tecerriot?'

'Maybe,' Daviland said. 'Six months is a long time. Possibly too long to rely on autohypnotic rotes.'

Norroll leaned forward. 'Can he hear us now?'

Daviland shook her head. 'Not in any way that would be meaningful to him.'

'So, what exactly happened to him?' Durlo asked.

'I don't know.'

Norroll grimaced. 'But you think an encounter with a Space Marine was enough to break decades of hypnotic conditioning?'

Daviland unscrewed her canteen's cap and took a sip. 'That's my theory, yes.'

'Groxshit,' Norroll said acerbically. He gestured at the unconscious Tempestor. 'You're telling me that the single greatest Tempestor in the Thirty-Sixth Xian Tigers is broken because he survived the fight of his life?'

'Yes,' Daviland said. 'Despite your hyperbolic summary, I believe that severe trauma, coupled with a long-term lack of deep-level re-enlightenment, has resulted in the degradation of Tempestor Traxel's psychobehavioural architecture.'

Norroll rolled his eyes. 'Well, if it's only the degradation of his psychobehavioural architecture...'

Daviland scowled.

'And you hope for what, Daviland? That a dose of obluvarine can fix what a lifetime of dedicated hypnotherapy and rotes couldn't manage?'

'What else can I do? I don't have a hypnomat in my medi-kit, Norroll. Even if I did, I forgot to pack a tech-priest to use it. I don't know to what extent the obluvarine will work, if it does. But it's our only option, and better than nothing.'

'Better than him freezing up if we encounter them again,' Bissot said. 'Stop acting like a child, Norroll.'

'You're the one acting like a bloody child!' Norroll spat back.

Bissot snorted a laugh.

'Gry...' Durlo said, trying as always to mediate between the two. 'Please.'

Norroll shook his head angrily, his swollen lower lip accentuating his petulance. 'Groxshit,' he repeated, resentfully crossing his arms over his chest.

The flat bitterness of nutri-paste, accompanied by the coppery tang of blood, was the first thing Norroll noticed as he slipped from his trance. The dull throbbing in his nose was next. The pain was inconsequential, so he ignored it. The nutri-paste was an altogether different form of unpleasantness, and he wished he could just as easily convince himself the lumpen gruel tasted like something other than sodden, vaguely salty cardboard.

Replendus' mortal remains lay wrapped in a blood-soaked shelter half in the centre of the Taurox's passenger hold. Any gear that could still potentially be used by the squad had been set aside – not that there was much. The lascannon had obliterated the Scion above the hips, leaving only his head and legs intact.

Norroll took a pull of water and swilled it around his mouth. His broken nose was enough to keep the scent of rot from his nostrils, but it failed to fully eliminate the flavour of the nutri-paste.

Daviland sat across from him, her unfocused eyes staring directly at Norroll without really seeing him. Quite at odds with the dirt and blood caking her carapace armour, Daviland's pale skin, with its dusting of freckles beneath her almond-shaped eyes, made her look more like a courtier than a warrior. Only the white, blade-thin scar disappearing into her tightly plaited dark auburn hair on the upper-right corner of her forehead hinted at her bloody vocation.

Daviland was foreign to Norroll. Her origins in the Alphic Hydras, her Ultramarian peculiarities and accent – to say nothing of her spying on them for Fennech – made it difficult for him to fully trust her.

His trance had bled away his rancour from earlier – though Daviland's assessment of Traxel had aroused Norroll's choler beyond his conscious control, remaining angry with her was counterproductive to the mission. Rotes deeply imprinted within his psychological architecture expunged the hindrance, clarifying his mind and restoring purity of purpose. The scholam taught every progenius that purgation was the most effective means of dealing with the undesirable, whether emotional or otherwise, and provided them with the means to do so.

Beside Daviland, Durlo stared off towards the ceiling, his dark eyes gazing without intent. Already the largest and most physically imposing Scion in the eradicant, Durlo's physique was further bulked by the ablative demolitions suit he wore over his carapace. A thick burn scar dimpled the left side of his face from cheek to jaw, blanching his mahogany skin.

Glancing down to where Traxel still lay unconscious on the Taurox's deck, Norroll slipped back into his restorative trance.

It had started to rain. Torrential downpours quickly transformed the dusty plains into a mud-slicked flatland, stripping the limping convoy of its dusty canopy. Having slogged along at the edge of the Imperial retreat, the eradicant's Taurox now idled at the corner of a broad field, denuded by armoured treads. The cloudburst had formed pools of oily muddy water about the rutted turf and showed no sign of letting up soon.

In the cab, Bissot drummed her fingers vexedly on the controls. Her exasperation seemed to grow by the minute as the eradicant waited towards the back of a line of Chimeras at the edge of a makeshift motor pool. Vehicles stood abandoned about the area at irregular intervals, rapidly evacuated by their crews as they hastened with their dead and wounded to impromptu facilities established at the field's edge.

Traxel sat next to Bissot in the cab. He wore the dark green beret of the 36th Xian, the badge representing the Oculus Tigris upon crossed downward-pointing silver daggers over his left eye. Despite Traxel's outward calm, Norroll noted a marked agitation in the Tempestor – his dark, hooded eyes flitted from vehicle to vehicle, person to person, straining to pierce the obscuring deluge outside.

Norroll looked through a view slit, likewise attempting to catch a glimpse of the black greatcoat or peaked cap he was certain his commander sought. He felt a momentary pang of shame when he found himself relieved to find nothing.

Nearly two decades on, and Fennech still held them in his iron grip.

The Scions were on their feet as soon as the vehicle stopped, devoid of true sleep's disorientation or sleepiness as they shook free of their trances. Donning their berets as their Tempestor had, they followed him through the left side hatch and into the sheeting rain.

The muddy field serving as the 139th Mech's motor pool was large enough to easily accommodate three hundred vehicles. Barely one hundred had escaped Kiemchek Ridge. Non-ambulatory wounded who had been recovered from the rout were dragged or carried out of their vehicles on stretchers and placed beneath the dripping roof of a hastily erected tarpaulin shelter to keep them from the worst of the rain. The wounded who were able to move unaided milled aimlessly, waiting for the limited number of available medics to finish their triage and treatment of those more seriously injured.

Mechanicus adepts in the pitch-black robes and crimson plate of Stygies VIII conducted triage of their own, accompanied by silent entourages of mind-wiped, cybernetically enhanced servitors. The tech-priests swept over the field, pushing aside clots of Guardsmen in their haste to perform the sacred rites of maintenance and repair on the regiment's damaged vehicles.

The dead, mostly those who had died en route, were laid out in an area well clear of the crude shelter of the makeshift medical facility for eventual materiel reclamation and disposal. Rain seeped through their uniforms and pooled in the craters of open wounds, staining the ochre mud beneath them a thin, rusty red.

Lasgun slung over his right shoulder, Durlo carried Replendus' remains to the mortuary area. He lowered the carcass to the ground and returned to his teammates without fanfare.

First Eradicant continued to the Rilisian command centre, navigating the makeshift structure's rusting plasteel corridors, silent but for the hollow thudding of their boots on the floorboards and the creak of sodden press-wood. Guardsmen along their route pressed against walls or ducked up adjacent corridors, eager to avoid the grim-faced Scions as they made for the facility's principal assembly room.

The auditorium lay beyond the threshold of the rusting plasteel blast doors which belonged to the command centre's original structure, making it the only room in the complex that looked like it belonged in a proper military facility. Dull bulkheads of bare plasteel, buttressed by a skeleton of adamantine struts to solidify its physical structure, hardened the compartment, which was in appearance not unlike the strategium on a small Naval void-craft.

Colonel Mercheverant Zheev, the senior ground forces commander, stood behind a slowly rotating wire-frame hololithic display representing Kiemchek Ridge, rendered in bottle-green light. Zheev leaned on a steel rail, flanked by an officer on either side, a lieutenant colonel and a major by their rank insignia.

Zheev looked up from the display when the eradicant entered. 'Tempestor-Eradicant Traxel,' he grumbled around the thin, three-inch length of lakrish root he held in the centre of his downturned mouth like a cigar. 'The man who united the loyalists and convinced me of the wisdom of a full-on frontal assault. I'll admit, I'm pretty damned impressed – since you showed up we've lost as many men in three hours as we did in three months.'

A tall man with a perpetual frown and a bulbous nose, Zheev seemed to slouch beneath the weight of his carapace armour. His brown leather greatcoat was shabby and dishevelled, looking like he had been sleeping in it for months – he very likely had. His black hair gave an impression of youthfulness that had long ago ceased to exist anywhere else on him.

'Tempestor will do, colonel,' Traxel said, refusing to acknowledge Zheev's intimation of fault.

Zheev scowled. 'These two gentlemen standing up here with me are some of the Iron Line's iron officers, serving as battalion commanders as well as regimental staff.' He indicated the officer to his right, a stern, grey-haired man who wore a red sash across a gleaming silver cuirass proudly displaying the Imperial aquila in gold. 'This is Lieutenant Colonel Sahn, Firepower Battalion commander and my master of ordnance.'

He indicated the officer on his left – a handsome, younger man with a head of thick, close-cropped auburn hair, wearing the customary brown leather greatcoat of a Rilisian field-grade officer. 'And this is Major Raff, Attack Battalion's commander and my quartermaster.'

Zheev chewed his lakrish root. 'Bear Battalion's commander, my adjutant, hasn't joined us yet. I gave Lieutenant Colonel Sarring an important task and she's doubtless still at it. My Cold Steel Battalion commander, Lieutenant Colonel Calando, was one of those killed in action last night.'

Traxel nodded his understanding, if not his sympathy. 'Despite our losses, our assault at Kiemchek forced the enemy to reveal his hand.'

'That's an exceedingly optimistic way to view losses I would conservatively refer to as catastrophic.'

Traxel was undeterred. 'The enemy has shown that it has thrown its lot in with the Archenemy, sir. That alone should ignite the flames of righteous retribution amongst you and your men. With preparation, we can locate and eliminate the Traitor Astartes directly and strike the head from this rebellion.'

'"Ignite the flames of righteous retribution"?' someone beneath

Zheev's command dais scoffed bitterly. 'I don't think we need Space Marines to do that, once you tin soldiers showed up.'

Traxel ignored him, his attention still on Zheev.

A junior officer pushed through the rabble of Guardsmen towards the Scions.

'Let it go, lieutenant,' Zheev cautioned.

'No, sir. I won't. This one here,' he said, closing on Norroll. 'Handsome fellow with the monoblades. Glory boy here dropped on my platoon two days ago, out on the edge of no-man's-land. Killed six of our troopers. Nailton, the only survivor, said he tore them apart.' The lieutenant was half a head shorter than Norroll, the tip of his nose barely an inch from the recon trooper's chin.

Norroll stared past him, his tawny eyes inert.

'I've read the report, lieutenant,' Zheev said. 'It was a regrettable incident, but these things happen in the fog of war.'

'"Fog of war"? Really, sir? You're going to give me that "regrettable incident" crap, too?'

'I am, because it was,' Zheev said. 'You are out of line, Lieutenant Dormichel. Stand down.'

'I see, sir,' Dormichel said, nodding. 'It's true that a few men killed by friendlies on the edge of no-man's-land is no cause for retribution. But are you telling me you're going to stand for the absolute slaughter they walked us into last night? Colonel Sarring is still running the butcher's bill–'

'Lieutenant,' Zheev said, his voice betraying his tension. 'For your own safety, step away from the Tempestus trooper.'

Dormichel looked into Norroll's lifeless stare, his hand resting on the pommel of the bayonet sheathed at his hip, face pale with anger. 'Don't worry, colonel. I'm so far beneath a noble Scion of the Imperium like him, he doesn't even notice me.' He flicked the button of the sheath's fastening strap. 'Maybe he'd like to see how it feels, being gutted like a fish.'

Norroll remained still, his gaze unfocused. The lieutenant was no threat, but he was curious what the young officer would do.

'Lieutenant Dormichel!' Zheev shouted. 'You are relieved of your duties until–'

The bolt pistol's report exploded across the confines of the command room as Lieutenant Dormichel's head detonated, spraying blood and brain matter over Norroll's face and the back of Traxel's head and neck. No few Guardsmen in the auditorium started as the shot rang out. A handful dived to the floor, seeking cover.

None of the Scions reacted. Blood dripping down his face, Norroll didn't even bat an eye – discipline forbade it.

Commissar Fennech loomed over Norroll, his face impassive as an alabaster effigy's. He held his bolt pistol loosely at his side, almost casually, the muzzle angled towards the ground.

'Forgetting oneself on the field of battle, however well intentioned, jeopardises the mission, Cadet Norroll,' Fennech said. 'If the God-Emperor smiles, it is only the transgressor who pays the price for indiscipline.' He raised a white-gloved finger admonishingly. 'I have learned, however, that the Emperor rarely smiles.'

The obsidian sands of Abstinax faded away as Norroll tasted fresh blood on his lips. He had no need to turn to know who had executed the incensed lieutenant.

Commissar Fennech stood in the doorway behind the Scions, smoking bolt pistol gripped in his white-gloved hand. The report still echoed from the plasteel walls. Holstering the bolt pistol, the old man limped forward, steadying himself on a cane.

The Scions stood aside as Fennech hobbled between them with uneven steps. He leaned heavily upon his stick, balancing on it as he clopped unsteadily across the floor on prosthetic wooden feet. He halted between Norroll and Traxel, standing over the headless corpse without so much as a downward glance.

He was, in many respects, quite different from the iron-handed martinet who had ruthlessly tutored the Scions of Abstinax on the virtues of discipline and sacrifice. Beneath the panoply of a decorated Imperial commissar, Fennech was an old man, his body destroyed by decades of battle in unstinting service to his God-Emperor. He wore a simple patch of black leather over his left eye, and only the nub of his ear's external tragus remained in the scarring that stretched the skin taut across his skull's left hemisphere. A power sword lay scabbarded on his right hip, though he would find it difficult to draw – the empty left sleeve of his greatcoat was neatly folded and pinned beneath the gold-tasselled epaulette that extended over the space where his shoulder used to be.

The commissar declined his head in a curt, respectful nod. 'Forgive the interruption, colonel,' he said affably. 'Pray, continue.'

Zheev removed the lakrish root from his mouth and quietly spat out a tiny splinter of wood. Like the Scions, the colonel had not reacted to the sudden execution, though he had visibly paled.

Norroll took conscious leave of the situation, lapsing into the Rote of Unimpeachable Calm. By the third iteration, his heart rate began to slow.

Lieutenant Colonel Sarring limped as she sprinted across the command centre. She splashed through the standing puddles that covered the floors, trying to ignore the searing ache throbbing in her augmetics' anchor points. Already late due to the casualty reports she had been compiling for Colonel Zheev, the unmistakable discharge of a bolt weapon echoing through the ramshackle structure had quickened her pace. Her teeth clenched as she struggled to bite back the pain spearing down her spine, a persistent reminder of her leading Cold Steel Battalion's Armatura Company to victory over the aeldari, fifteen years earlier.

She wondered if someone had got inside again. It had proved easy enough for the traitors before, slipping past sentries unimpeded because they were Rilisian like them.

No. Not any more, they weren't.

The scent of bolt propellant wafted through the open blast doors of the auditorium, mingling with the odour of blood and faeces when she got inside. The door was bottlenecked by a group of four Tempestus Scions in filthy green carapace armour and green berets, barring her way to the command dais. Beneath their heavy boots, blood seeped towards her, spreading as the thin layer of water on the floor rendered it less viscous.

She slid to a halt on the water-slicked decking, almost losing her footing.

Struggling to maintain her balance, Sarring gripped the door's heavy plasteel frame, nearly dropping her sheaf of reports. Righting herself, she instinctively checked the bundle of parchments, shuffling them together and tucking them back in the blue folder she carried. Embarrassment pushed panic, but not pain, to the side.

A one-armed commissar wearing an eyepatch watched her with detached curiosity, before favouring her with a thin smile that was less than reassuring.

'Tempestor,' Zheev called, 'kindly have your Scions stand aside so Lieutenant Colonel Sarring may pass.'

Sarring thought she noted a strained tremulousness to the colonel's voice – a mean hint of disquiet breaking through his perpetually affected air of nonchalance. She glanced to Sahn and Raff next to him, wondering if they noticed it as well, but they seemed absorbed in their own apprehensions.

The Scions parted in silent unison, forming up along either

side of the entryway like some grim honour guard lining Sarring's way. The moment they moved aside, she saw the headless corpse of a lieutenant, his blood soaking across the floor and splattered across the wall.

She swallowed thickly, and hoped he hadn't been one of hers.

Sarring could feel the thrum of the capacitor units attached to the Scions' backpacks, feeding power through thick cables to their high-powered lasguns. She kept her eyes on the lieutenant's body as she passed, careful not to make eye contact with the Scions, who reeked of blood, death and ozone.

She accidentally glanced up at the Tempestus trooper to her left as she stepped over the corpse – blood and chunks of brain and bone stuck to the Scion's bruised face and short ginger beard, congealing on his chin and dripping down his cuirass. He was quite tall and powerfully built, with light red hair and inanimate tawny eyes. A pair of monoblades lay sheathed on either side of his belt buckle, and Sarring suppressed a shiver.

She recognised him by his panoply, as it had been described to her by the sole survivor of a squad from Dormichel's company. The Scion had slaughtered her troopers and moved on before they had even been able to react.

Zheev had asked her to forget about the incident – asked, not ordered. The Old Dog had called it a regrettable error resulting from the confusion of battle, but she hadn't been able to let it go. Nailton, the survivor, was a boy pulled out of his basic Militarum training to fight the traitors, not so much older than her own son.

Still looking at the Scion's bruised, bloody face and his bland auburn stare, Sarring realised that he probably couldn't have cared less which side of the war her troopers had been on.

Sarring turned away, her gaze falling on dark eyes every bit as spiritless as those of the Scion who had slaughtered her men. She recognised him as a Tempestor by his three rank chevrons. He was bald and clean-shaven – haggard, severe and dusky-skinned, his weatherbeaten face and scalp crisscrossed by scars and burns. Blood had spattered across the back of his head and over his left shoulder, though like his subordinate, he appeared perfectly indifferent to it.

The squad's vital signs pulsed across the data-slate mounted to the Tempestor's right vambrace. Many of her troopers had told her, in conspiratorially hushed tones, that the Militarum Tempestus cut its Scions' hearts out and forced them to wear them in metal boxes on their wrists. While the wives' tale had always sounded ridiculous to Sarring before, she now found her attention fixed upon the Scions' heart rates pulsing across the slate.

Sarring tore her eyes away from the Tempestor and his vambrace. Cold, cold bastards, these Scions.

Trying not to rush as she ascended the command dais, Sarring offered her folder to Zheev.

'Apologies for my lateness, sir. It was a bit of a struggle collating the reports. There are contradictions–'

'Just give me the basics.'

'The basics, sir?' Sarring said, her voice for Zheev alone. 'We're sinking. Everything we lost in the three months leading up to the assault on Kiemchek Ridge amounts to just under half of what we lost last night. Balt's battalion is hanging on by its fingernails, and Cold Steel Battalion has been rendered almost completely non-mission capable. What we have left–'

'Throne, I know what we have left,' Zheev said. 'Cooks. Balt's supply clerks. Your personnel orderlies, Euri. Vox-operators. Three companies of artillery, half of it wrecked, and what's left of their complement of mounted security. Seven barely operational tanks. Some scouts. Enough shattered infantry platoons to make up maybe a whole battalion and a half, if the Emperor smiles on us. A few captains, a handful of lieutenants, some sergeants, and you, Balt and Archie. Am I missing anything?'

Sarring shook her head. 'That's about the size of it, sir. The presentation I made detailing that basic summary presents it with a little more colour. It's only sixteen pages long.'

Zheev snorted cheerlessly through his nose. 'Fortunately, we have our allies,' he stated loudly, facing the assembly.

A tiny smile tilted the edges of Sarring's lips. The Old Dog's theatrical bombast meant he was starting to sound himself again.

'Our allies,' Zheev said, 'whom we can finally communicate with, thanks to the will of the God-Emperor, and the exceptional efforts of Captain Grosht of the Eight-Hundred-and-Thirty-Second Mordian and Tempestor Traxel of the Thirty-Sixth Xian Tigers.'

'That is so, sir,' Sarring said under her breath, 'but we are having a bit of difficulty coordinating with our allies, our ability to communicate with them notwithstanding. The disparate methods of warfare, standard operating procedures–'

'Which brings us all here,' Zheev interrupted. 'Emperor knows, our lack of coordination over the past months has been hugely detrimental and kept any of us from mounting a meaningful strike against Hurdt's traitors. Some forces here prefer mechanised assaults. Some like rolling with the punches before swinging back. And don't get me started on the Krieg…'

Zheev waved at the small delegation from the 222nd Krieg Separate below. 'No offence intended, Major Gunvaldt.'

'None taken, sir,' the Krieg officer replied impassively, his voice distorted through his respirator's voxmitter. 'I understood it as a compliment.'

'My intent is to get us all on the same sheet of music, especially considering our losses. Our scouts have reported the Two-Hundred-and-Twelfth has displaced from Kiemchek Ridge and is moving eastward, towards Vytrum,' Zheev said. 'After the drubbing we suffered last night, coupled with the past three months along the Zholm, we cannot fulfil our oaths to the Throne as discrete formations any longer. As senior officer of this regiment and acting senior ground forces commander on Rilis, I am reorganising the Hundred-and-Thirty-Ninth Mech and its allies into a combined regiment.'

The Astra Militarum forces below the command dais glanced amongst themselves. Some nodded to one another in silent acknowledgement of the fact as it was, while others accepted the notice without external response.

'Major Gunvaldt,' Zheev snapped. 'Please step up to the command dais.'

Gunvaldt separated from his subordinates without comment or ostentation, passing through the assembled Guardsmen and officers to ascend the dais, stopping just as he reached the top of the stairs.

'As seniormost officer among our allies, I'm appointing you as commander of Cold Steel Battalion, One-Hundred-and-Thirty-Ninth Mechanised Infantry,' Zheev announced, indicating a spot next to Major Raff on the grated steel deck of the platform the 139th's commanders stood on.

'In addition to this duty,' Zheev continued, 'you will serve as the Hundred-and-Thirty-Ninth's chief of planning and operations. The Two-Hundred-and-Twenty-Second Krieg Separate will likewise fold into Cold Steel Battalion, as will the remnants of Lieutenant Basharaneh's Five-Thousand-Two-Hundred-and-Twenty-Eighth Tallarn and Lieutenant Carritz's platoon from One-Thousand-Seven-Hundred-and-Twenty-Fourth Catachan.' His pronouncement complete, Zheev thundered his regimental motto: *'Iron Line!'*

The battle cry stuttered through the assembled Astra Militarum like a slightly damp string of firecrackers, the still unfamiliar motto spreading patchily across the auditorium until it had risen from each disparate faction with varying degrees of enthusiasm.

Satisfied enough with their reaction, Zheev nodded. 'Dismissed.'

The assembled Astra Militarum forces departed, passing by the Scions who silently lined both sides of the command room's entrance. When the last of the assembled Guardsmen had left, the blast doors ground shut.

'Tempestor Traxel,' Zheev said. 'A moment. I have something special for First Eradicant.'

V

Daviland watched the rotating image representing Kiemchek Ridge Depot fizzle into green haze with a stutter and a tickle of static. Servitors burbled nonsensically as they received freshly cogitated data for hololithic in-load, their monotasked minds rapidly building a fresh structure from the jade light.

The image of the new facility was not terribly different from the representation of Kiemchek Ridge Depot that it had replaced. Sixteen squat warehouses took up nearly the entirety of the installation's quadrangular structure, divided by a broad central avenue and tributary roads which connected the facilities together. The base was walled, but insignificantly fortified, with a guard tower overlooking each corner of the perimeter.

'This is Pokol Armoury,' Zheev said. 'The largest planetary militia resupply facility on the continent and the most mission-critical piece of land we own. Pokol is the sole source of fresh munitions, ordnance and materiel that we still have control of, and the enemy wants it. It's located thirty-seven miles to the north-east of here, just west of the Foretrak Range.'

'You don't wish us to accompany the Hundred-and-Thirty-Ninth in your attack on the traitors, colonel?' Traxel asked.

'Oh, I would,' Zheev admitted. 'I wish I had another unit of Tempestus Scions on Rilis. I wish I had ten, but if you wish in one hand and shit in the other, you'll see which one fills up first every time.

'Intelligence had been monitoring a few enemy raiding parties in the vicinity. They've been preying on the local farmers, mostly, but also making probing attacks against the company guarding the facility. We anticipate that it's too big a prize for them to resist for long, and desperation will force them to commit to attacking the armoury with a large enough force to overwhelm its defenders. I need First Eradicant to shore up the line.'

'And if the enemy doesn't show up?' Traxel asked. 'How reliable is your intelligence that the heretics will attack?'

'It's just shy of airtight, as far as I'm concerned. The enemy raiders have been getting more brazen, of late, and they seem more willing to risk larger skirmishes. We received reports of enemy artillery moving north from Kiemchek just this morning, so we anticipate–'

'Sir!' a lieutenant called from behind one of the cogitator stations beneath the command dais.

'Not now, Bartlin,' Zheev said.

'Sorry, sir,' Bartlin said, 'but the clouds have cleared. We've got restored orbital imagery over Sector West.'

'A weather report's certainly important enough to interrupt me when I'm talking to the Tempestor.'

'The drop pod, sir,' Bartlin said, hovering over the trooper working the cogitator.

Traxel's glare immediately fell upon the lieutenant.

'You've got my attention,' Zheev said.

The map of Pokol Armoury disintegrated amidst the mumbling of the hololith's attendant servitors. Lines coalesced from the haze of green light and refined into a three-dimensional terrain map of an area covered in denuded ridges. Boxy structures of unknown use squatted atop the mountains depicted on the western edge of the area. A ring of anti-air platforms sat inside the perimeter walls, dispersed evenly around bare, fortified zones to maximise cover against aerial insertion. The flanks of the easternmost ridges had been stripped of vegetation and planed smooth, all cover replaced with an interior of barricades, redoubts and automated pillboxes. The ridge fortifications appeared designed to funnel any attackers who managed to penetrate the perimeter into the valleys between, where broad, obstacle-laden kill-zones had been established. Square markers punctuated the terrain, representing emplacements of automated sentry guns, configured to permit redundantly overlapping fields of fire for maximum lethality with minimal expenditure of ammunition. The network of battlements and gun-studded bastions meandered between the ridges, broadening and contracting as they first encouraged, then restricted, movement through the area in a never-repeating maze.

Daviland was hardly an expert in strongholds, but it was immediately apparent that 'overkill' seemed an insufficient description for what they saw in the projection. There was an absurdity to the defences, an unconstrained obsessiveness with superfluous fortification and lethality that defied sensibility. No sane mind could design such a labyrinthine stronghold, let alone implement it.

'I don't see the drop pod,' Sahn said.

'Wait, sir,' Bartlin said, shaking the shoulder of the trooper at the cogitator.

Seated at his terminal, the trooper's fingers tapped furiously across the cogitator's runepad. The servitors gabbled as the data refined, zooming in on the image of a boxy three-storey structure brooding atop the tallest ridge. The drop pod sat on a landing platform outside the facility.

'Pull back,' Zheev said. 'I don't recognise where this is.'

The image shifted, zooming out to allow a view of nearly half the continent, east of the Zholm River.

'Foretrak Gap military facility,' Zheev breathed. 'Throne, I couldn't recognise the place with the forests gone!'

'What is the Foretrak Gap military facility?' Traxel asked.

'In older times it guarded the only major ground thoroughfare between here and the capital, Vytrum, through the Foretrak Range.' Zheev shrugged. 'There are others, of course, but the gap is the most direct route. It wasn't exactly abandoned, but it was obsolete long before my time. The planetary militia used it for training, sometimes. They still had a garrison there, back when I was a kid. Mostly for show.'

Like the ridges leading up to it, the area around the Foretrak Gap's main facility had been stripped of vegetation for hundreds of yards in all directions and fortified with an even greater obsessiveness than the rest of the complex. Short of an air assault, which the region's overwhelming air defences rendered an effective form of suicide, the chances of an infantry attack making it to the Foretrak Gap's principal installation were negligible.

'How long ago was this?' Zheev asked.

'Twenty-three minutes, sir.'

'That is where we need to be, colonel,' Traxel said, his eyes devouring the hololith's details.

'No,' Zheev said. 'We've had an entire regiment, the Three-Hundred-and-Seventeenth Light, working to take the Foretrak Gap almost since the war broke out.'

'What is the status of their siege?'

Zheev closed his eyes wearily. 'We don't know. We've heard

nothing from them since just before the traitors began their bombardment of the Zholm.'

'Which makes it likely the regiment has been destroyed,' Traxel said. 'First Eradicant can infil–'

'I said no,' Zheev said. 'Foretrak Gap is not the priority. I need everything available to me so we can hit the Two-Hundred-and-Twelfth while it's running, before it reaches the Foretrak Gap and slips through to Vytrum. I've already given up my sole undamaged line company to defend Pokol. Keeping that armoury out of Oleg Hurdt's hands is of tantamount importance to our efforts – otherwise, I wouldn't be ordering you to go there.'

'Colonel, we can cut the head from this apostasy now if we take this–'

'Where does Tempestor-Eradicant fit into the Imperial Munitorum manual's rank structure?'

'It is the equivalent to major,' Traxel replied, 'depending on regimental nomenclature.'

'Precisely. And I'm the equivalent of colonel in damn near any nomenclature you like, Traxel. Is my meaning in any way obscure?'

'No, colonel.'

Zheev nodded. 'Look, Traxel,' he scoffed, rubbing his weary eyes. 'I'm not trying to break your balls here. First Eradicant's presence is deeply, deeply appreciated. But I need us to have an understanding. I need your team to reinforce First Company Attack while the rest of the Hundred-and-Thirty-Ninth breaks the Two-Hundred-and-Twelfth. Once both of those objectives are accomplished, we'll meet at the Foretrak Gap. We need to take it anyway before we move on to Vytrum, so you'll get your crack at it.'

Traxel's expression was unforthcoming. 'I understand, Colonel Zheev. Our preparations begin immediately. I would like to requisition some supplies prior to our departure.'

'Balt,' Zheev called to Major Raff. 'Escort First Eradicant to your supply area and give them what they need.'

'Yessir,' Raff said, already clanging down the stairs.

'Don't be too generous this time,' Zheev cautioned.

Five more Tempestus Scions in the steel-trimmed green carapace of the 36th Xian Tigers joined Fennech just outside the auditorium. They stood in formation behind the commissar, silent and glassy-eyed, their weapons held across their chests.

Fennech regarded First Eradicant from behind his long, acute nose, his hollow face all cheekbones and creases. He smiled thinly, his scarred lips stretching above his pointed chin in a veneer of polite cordiality which drowned in the sunken depths of his remaining glacial-blue eye.

'Kindly forgive my physical frailties, Tempestor,' Fennech said. 'Three months on Rilis left my augmetics badly in need of repair, I'm afraid.' He tapped both shins, his cane clopping hollowly on the wooden limbs. 'Even my legs. The tech-priests have assured me that they will have them back to me before the day is out, though, so I'll be on my feet in no time.' He sniffed, rolling his eye in momentary introspection. 'So to speak.'

Traxel nodded, but remained silent.

Norroll glanced at the bolt pistol that hung in its well-used, lovingly maintained leather holster on the commissar's hip. For an instant, he was on Abstinax again, trudging through the black sands of shifting obsidian and breathing the toxic, sulphur-laden air. Blood and pain, wading barefoot through the razor sand…

'And Medicae-Adept Daviland,' Fennech said, and this time the smile nearly went all the way to his eye. 'It pleases me to see you again. It has been far longer than I would have liked.'

Daviland smiled at him – genuinely smiled. Norroll thought it was the first time he had seen her face really light up since he had known her. 'For me as well, commissar,' she said, with a respectful dip of her chin.

'May I present Tempest Squad Xi-Three-One?' Fennech asked. Norroll was beginning to find the commissar's unflagging formality stultifying.

The first trooper came forward, extending his hand to Traxel. He had somewhat watery brown eyes and an unfortunately weak chin. He was sunburned from too many days out without a helmet beneath Rilis' relentless summer skies, and his skin was peeling.

'Dja Quisse, Tempestor Traxel,' the Scion said. 'Acting Tempestor, Tempest Squad Xi-Three-One.'

'I know who you are, Trooper Quisse,' Traxel said without taking the proffered hand. 'I am familiar with all of you. With the death of Xi-Three-One's Tempestor, I assume responsibility for you in his stead. Let me be the first to welcome you to First Eradicant. Now fall in.'

Quisse's look of unvarnished surprise would not have been out of place had Traxel sucker-punched him. In a way, perhaps he had.

The Scions formerly belonging to Tempest Squad Xi-3-1 parted to allow the Tempestor to pass. They stood at attention, eyes straight ahead, rifles to chests – Rybak and Akraatumo stood along the left wall, Quisse, Atebe and Phed along the right.

Norroll and the rest of First Eradicant followed behind the Tempestor. Save Rybak, with whom he had long shared a mutual antipathy, Norroll had never personally met any of the others before.

Rybak held his active plasma gun over his chest, the weapon's magnetic accelerator coils rippling with a brilliant blue-white glow. He wore the Decus Iason in gold, the highest award for marksmanship offered by the Departmento Munitorum, inlaid upon his carapace's left pectoral.

Akraatumo stood to Rybak's left. A burly, barrel-chested Scion, Akraatumo was more heavily built than Durlo, but shorter. He stared straight ahead, lasgun held in a light grip, his wide-spaced dark eyes vaguely focused on a trickle of water that dripped down the wall opposite him.

Across from Akraatumo was Atebe, a sniper by her long-las and the ghillie camo-cloak draped over her carapace armour. Her blonde hair was tightly braided into twelve cornrows, the gold striking against the deep umber of her skin and the dark brown of her eyes. Unlike Rybak, Atebe wore no honour markings – her skill with her long-las was apparent in the almost casual familiarity with which she held it.

Next to Atebe stood Trooper Phed. Right out of the Scholam Tempestus, Phed's beret was creased with a fastidiousness that Norroll was certain would make Daviland jealous. His skin was the colour of oiled chestnut, and he had high cheekbones and dark eyes which appeared intently focused upon Akraatumo's nose. Phed held his lasgun in a grip so rigid it seemed he feared it might escape.

'Durlo,' Traxel said. 'Wait for Major Raff and accompany him to the supply area. The rest of you, with me.'

'Tempestor,' Daviland said, 'I request to accompany Commissar Fennech to the medicae, to help reinstall his augmetics.'

Traxel regarded Daviland through heavy, bruised eyelids, his expression as forthcoming as a stone mask's.

'Do so,' he said, then turned and strode down the corridor.

The newest inductees into First Eradicant fell in behind their predecessors, marching through the dripping, ramshackle hallways as they made their way out of the command centre and back to their Taurox Prime.

'It is good to see you again, commissar,' Daviland said, smiling. She walked on his left, slowly on account of his uncertain, shuffling gait, though she made no offer to assist him.

'And you, Medicae-Adept Daviland,' Fennech said with a thin

smile of his own, albeit one bereft of true warmth. His eye, a striking blue, was the sole spot of colour in the pale, papery skin beneath the visor of his peaked cap.

'I wanted to apologise, commissar,' she said.

Fennech raised his remaining eyebrow, though Daviland couldn't ascertain whether his expression corresponded to raising both brows or cocking one.

'Why would I require your apology?'

'My report on First Eradicant, sir. From the Tecerriot incident.'

'Was there something you failed to include in your account?'

'No, commissar. But six months' further observation have made it clear that my initial assessment was incomplete.'

Fennech's brow furrowed, puckering the scar tissue marring his forehead. 'Initial reports are always wrong.'

Daviland felt her face flush at the blunt admonishment and was suddenly glad he was not looking at her.

'What was lacking?' Fennech asked.

'The Scions of First Eradicant are broken, as is their Tempestor.'

'This is not news.'

'I've further reports for your review.'

'I shall do so on our way to Pokol,' Fennech said. They had finally reached the command centre's medi-bay, and the commissar shuffled to a free examination table. 'Give me the long and the short now. Especially concerning Traxel.'

A hooded genetor, swathed in the black robes of the priesthood of Stygies VIII, approached, attended by a trio of medicae servitors. The glistening, rubberised surface of its hermetically sealed form creaked as it moved.

Daviland fell silent, unwilling to continue in the tech-priest's presence.

'Commissar Fennech.' The tech-priest's voice rasped through an integrated respirator that obscured its features entirely. 'Omnissiah be praised, your augmetic components await reinstallation and actuation.' It looked at Daviland, noting the bar of white decorated with a winged golden helix which bisected the green of her left pauldron, vambrace and gauntlet. 'And you brought a medicae-adept to assist.'

Daviland worried that her presence might be construed as an insult.

'That should speed the process,' the tech-priest said.

Daviland bowed. 'I would be honoured, honoured magos...'

'Zerkhan. I do not stand on ceremony, though your designation would simplify our exchange.'

'Daviland.'

'You are familiar with the installation of augmetics, Daviland?'

'Yes.'

'Prepare the insertion sites at the intermedial femoral and tibio-femoral junctions.'

Assisted by the servitors, the medicae-adept and tech-priest worked in silence for nearly an hour as they rebuilt the commissar. Under their ministrations, Fennech transformed from a one-armed, one-eyed cripple with truncated legs to a partially completed sketch of a man. Though his digestive tract and onboard pulmonary systems had not yet been fully reinstalled, he was looking considerably more complete.

'You have something you wish to say to the commissar, Daviland,' Zerkhan said as it disconnected Fennech from the temporary external respiratory unit the commissar had been carrying.

'I-'

'The persistent licking of your lips - thirteen times in the last two minutes - coupled with your heightened body temperature and raised respiration rate, indicates pronounced agitation. I do not believe you are nervous about this procedure. Neither do I believe that you have anything relevant to say to me. Speak.'

'I'm not sure…'

'Speak,' the genetor repeated, not raising its head as it mounted an audio receiver to Fennech's skull. 'You may be assured that whatever you say interests me not in the slightest.'

Fennech, his head held immobile in a servitor's grip while Zerkhan moved to install his augmetic eye, grunted his assent.

'Tempestor Traxel suffered an episode during the Adeptus Astartes' attack on Kiemchek,' Daviland said.

'An episode?'

'One I would describe as a post-traumatic event.'

'Interesting,' Fennech said. 'And opportune.'

Daviland looked up from rethreading the subdermal power cabling to Fennech's lower augmetics. 'Opportune, sir?'

'You are familiar with the fancifully named Scholam's Gift?'

'Of course, sir,' Daviland said. 'Thanks to decades of deep mindscaping, where lesser soldiers might wet themselves from terror, a Tempestus Scion feels anticipation and satisfaction – enjoyment, even. The longer they survive, and the greater the dangers overcome, the more deeply they feel it. Over time, they may even develop a craving for it.'

'I believe this Scholam's Gift is the genesis of Traxel's intransigence,' Fennech said. 'It whispers in the deepest corners of his mind. He cannot stop and has no desire to.'

'After missions,' Daviland said, 'Scions are to submit to obligatory re-enlightenment.'

'And when was the last time any in First Eradicant submitted to these obligatory sessions?'

The shake of Daviland's head was nearly imperceptible.

'Regrettable,' Fennech said without the slightest hint of melancholy. The servitor released its grip on his head, and the commissar flexed his neck. 'Ordinarily, such problems could be served by the direct application of a bolt to the skull, but Traxel's uninterrupted string of successes have ensured his star waxes ever brighter in Lord General Trenchard's eyes – especially after Tecerriot. Say what you will of the man, but Traxel gets results.'

'Yes, sir.'

'Per my recommendations, and thanks in no small part to your reports, Thirty-Sixth Xian's eradicant formations are being shifted from the regiment proper to the Scholam Tempestus, as they are in the Fifty-Fifth Alphic Hydras. It is a change I expect the whole of the Militarum Tempestus will one day embrace.'

Daviland felt a quick flash of pride. 'That is excellent news, commissar.'

'To appease the lord general, command of the Scholam Tempestus is being given to Traxel.'

The blush of pride paled as suddenly as it had appeared. Daviland's lips parted in quiet amazement.

'This episode, as you called it, marks a singularly appropriate time for Traxel to be retired from active service and settle into a comfortable semi-retirement. His experience will doubtless benefit the next generation of Xian Tigers.'

'Is Traxel aware?' Daviland asked. 'Of the position waiting for him at the Scholam Tempestus?'

'He is. I daresay he is not at all pleased, but he cannot continue as he does now. If Traxel will not take the Scholam Tempestus, his only recourse is death.'

Daviland swallowed her sudden, unexpected dispiritedness. 'What if he suffers another episode when we encounter the Adeptus Astartes again?'

An icy grin crept across Fennech's lips.

'That evaluation you will leave to me.'

The supply crates and ammo cans the Scions sat upon shifted ever so slightly as the Taurox powered into a deep crater which had shattered the eastbound highway's surface. Durlo had outdone himself in his resupply efforts, enlisting the aid of the entire eradicant to help him lug it all back to the vehicle. They perched atop their spoil in silent trances, save for Traxel and Quisse in the cab and Fennech and Daviland on either side of the rear hatch.

Norroll manned the twin gatling cannons. He had volunteered for the first shift in the hatch to give the others a chance to trance along the way, but Daviland had opted to use the time to catch up with her old mentor.

Norroll sat at chest defilade in the turret, traversing it to and fro at irregular intervals, panning across a waterlogged landscape that was gradually more rolling and densely forested than the broad flats that lay along the Zholm. The recon trooper had patched his servo-skull into the Taurox's power supply, extending its augurs to a horizon-wide sweep that the onboard generator in Norroll's backpack could never match. The radial display mounted to the skull's right side swept around every two seconds, giving them advanced warning of any enemy or potential obstacles that lay in their way. An identical readout played on the Taurox's cab, giving Quisse ample time to react to any threats as he drove.

At the back of the Taurox, Daviland and Fennech faced each other on opposite sides of the Taurox's rear hatch, each sitting atop several layers of hastily piled supply crates. Beneath the visor of his peaked cap, the commissar's augmetic left eye emitted a dim glow that gave the pale, papery skin of his face a ruddy tint in the low light of the troop compartment. The reinstallation of his bionics had restored Fennech's missing left arm and his mobility. A power fist of glossy black durasteel, trimmed in scarlet and adorned with a golden Imperialis, rested on his left knee. He wore his carapace armour's gleaming black cuirass and pauldrons over the oiled leather of his greatcoat, another Imperialis proudly displayed in the centre of his plastron. Like his greatcoat and cap, Fennech's visible armour plates were edged in scarlet.

Norroll couldn't hear them over inter-vox, which likely meant they were talking over a private channel – ordinary conversation was rendered unintelligible by the grinding of the gun truck's tracks and the roar of its engine.

Traxel sat in the cab, poring over the printed topographic map he had spread across the Taurox's front instrument panel. He compared their location on the map to the gun truck's navigational display.

'Right here,' he said as the Taurox approached an intersection. Quisse complied, and the Taurox headed east.

'Is there a problem, Tempestor?' Daviland asked over the squad's inter-vox.

'No. Why?'

'I thought Pokol Armoury was practically due north from the command centre,' she said. 'Are we diverting?'

'We are not going to Pokol Armoury,' Traxel said. 'We are going to the Foretrak Gap.'

'Have we received new orders?'

'No.'

Norroll smirked. Typical Traxel.

'Tempestor,' Daviland began, 'our orders–'

'Our standing orders,' Traxel said, turning to look back at her, 'are to break the back of the insurrection on Rilis by the most expeditious means available, short of causing irreparable damage to the world itself. Those are the orders given to us by Tempestor-Prime Bassoumeh, passed directly from Lord General Trenchard himself. Having allied themselves with a Traitor Legion, the apostasy of the Rilisian traitors is incontestable. As Traitor legionaries are not magnanimous with their power, we assume that they are at the centre of the rebellion and are the gauntlet holding the traitors' leash. Their elimination is our highest priority.'

'I am not disputing our standing orders, sir,' Daviland said. 'Has our change of mission been coordinated with the Hundred-and-Thirty-Ninth?'

'It has not, because there has been no change to our mission.'

Daviland paused. 'We have our orders from the senior ground force commander, Tempestor. We're expected at Pokol.' She glanced over to Fennech, whose expression betrayed nothing of his thoughts.

'Don't look to Commissar Fennech for support, Daviland,' Traxel said. 'He does not command First Eradicant.'

'The Hundred-and-Thirty-Ninth will need to divert a formation from their main force to secure–'

'We cut the head from this insurrection by eliminating the Iron Warriors,' Traxel said, and his tone indicated that was the end of the discussion. The eradicant remained silent for several minutes afterwards.

'You make a fair point, Daviland,' the Tempestor finally said. 'Given the scope of potential disciplinary and doctrinal violations inherent in my intent, I would have your input, commissar.'

Norroll could practically feel how much it galled Traxel to make such a request. The Tempestor had done his best to studiously ignore Fennech since the commissar had joined them. While he was a maverick, Traxel was no fool – flouting the senior ground force commander's orders in the presence of a commissar would have already seen most officers earn a bolt through the skull. It was a prudence Norroll had never yet encountered with him.

Prudence, or fear.

Fennech collected his thoughts for several seconds before replying. 'I agree with Medicae-Adept Daviland, Tempestor. I find abdicating Colonel Zheev's orders, which he understood you to accept in good faith, distasteful. Not giving the Hundred-and-Thirty-Ninth time to appropriately respond to our absence will very likely result in the loss of many faithful Imperial souls at Pokol, and may likewise result in the armoury's resources falling into the traitors' hands. I don't believe we will fully understand the magnitude of our delinquency's impact until the after-action reports and butcher's bills are compiled.'

Daviland straightened up in her seat.

'I have taken this into account,' Traxel said. 'My failure to coordinate with the senior ground force commander has been considered within this mission's risk matrix. I have deemed it an inappropriate use of our time to argue the point with Colonel Zheev, as he proved unwilling to accept my position before. Moreover, having such a discussion over the vox, post facto, bears too great a risk of information leakage that the enemy could exploit.'

Fennech flexed the thick fingers of his power fist. 'You are correct, Tempestor Traxel. Despite my stated misgivings, I support your decision to divert to the Foretrak Gap. As you said, our orders come from the lord general himself. As Rilis' contributions to the God-Emperor's war effort are critical to military operations across the segmentum, our course is clear.'

Daviland said nothing further.

VI

They ground eastward for several hours, stopping only to refuel using the blitz cans requisitioned from the 139th. Behind them, the sun set, casting the forested ridges ahead in brilliant gold. The curve of the orbital ring above had become stark and bright in the sun's reflected light, bisecting the darkening skies to the south-east.

They encountered no other living soul along the way, and though such a situation might lull an ordinary soldier to relax his guard, it only served to make Norroll uneasy. He swept the gatling cannons across abandoned lots and yards, searching for threats as they rolled past another seemingly deserted town. He checked Actis' augurs but noted no motion pings or active power sources in the vicinity. Nevertheless, Akraatumo, who had replaced Quisse as driver, kept the Taurox at a manageable distance – no point wasting resources on an avoidable firefight.

It had been the thirteenth such abandoned village they had skirted around since their departure from the Zholm valley. There were no signs of fighting here, nearly a hundred miles removed from the polluted, artillery-churned wastes of the battlefield they had left behind. Every farm, residence and business visible from the road bore the signs of long-term neglect. Fields stretched along the rolling hillsides and narrow valleys surrounding the town, fallow and overgrown. Crumbling low walls of grey stone, discoloured by russet mosses and dull brown patches of lichen, demarked the fields' borders. Impenetrable masses of thorny hedge and unmanaged thickets of daekki and quaroak trees sprouted near the walls' edges, creeping to infiltrate the broad, weed-choked wastelands of unkempt farmland. Weeds strangled the remains of small garden plots and sprouted through cracks in the rutted pavement. The doors and windows of every weather-stained, plastek-sided building had been boarded up with plates of flakboard.

Norroll had volunteered for a second shift in the turret, ostensibly because he preferred to read the terrain with his own eyes rather than rely solely upon Actis' augurs. In the cab below, Akraatumo drove, while Rybak had relieved Traxel on command and navigation – and Norroll had no desire to talk to Rybak.

He intensified his scan on the surrounding terrain as darkness fell. Every structure, tree stump or scarp of rock along their route could potentially conceal an enemy position, and every bit of roadside detritus might hide a booby trap. His senses corroborated Actis' readings – there really was nothing here. He took a long draw on his helmet's feeder pipe, sucking in a mouthful of gritty, vaguely salty nutri-paste, unsettled by the calm.

Actis pinged.

Norroll glanced at his augur feeds. 'Akraatumo, stop!' he called down from behind the gatling cannons.

The Taurox clattered to a halt, shifting the Scions forward as the supply crates they sat upon slid towards the cab.

'Status, Norroll,' Traxel requested.

'Got a ping from Actis.' He reviewed his slate. 'Active power source, metal. One-fifty yards, bearing six-six.'

'Size?'

'Small. If he hadn't caught it, we might have missed it.'

'Check it out,' Traxel ordered. 'Durlo, go with him. Atebe, in the turret.'

Norroll disconnected Actis from the Taurox and waited for the few seconds it took for the servo-skull to connect to his power supply and data feeds. Durlo was already unsealing the portside hatch as Norroll released his security harness and dropped into the crew bay. A few more seconds and the Scions were out, low-crawling across a field with an abundant crop of weeds and briars in the direction indicated by Actis' augurs. They slipped forward by turns, advancing between grassy mounds and thickets to avoid detection, covering one another as they moved through the thick vegetation and heavily furrowed soil.

Norroll scanned the area indicated by Actis with his magnoculars from beneath the concealment of a knot of brambles. Less than fifty yards away, a Tarantula sentry gun pivoted back and forth on its squat four-legged base, concealed beneath a canopy of camo netting. It was emplaced at the top of a low steel-frame tower just inside the edge of the forest, ten to twelve feet off the ground. Its machine spirit endlessly sought targets for its twin heavy bolters through the small rectangular aperture atop it, which housed its optics and sensors. The centre of its mass was a metal block, featureless and blunt, the aquila once bolted to it roughly pried off.

'Tarantula, boss. Heavy bolter configuration,' Norroll called back to the Taurox.

'Just one?'

'Just one here. We'll probably find more entertainment up that hill.'

'Likelihood of tripping an alarm if we engage it?'

'Low,' Durlo replied from his position. 'Communication with the slaved servitor brain that controls a Tarantula is one-way. Tell it to point and shoot, and it will search for targets until the stars go cold.'

'Atebe, can you see the turret?' Traxel asked.

'No, sir.'

'Norroll, light it up.'

Norroll fished out a black metal tube from his right cargo pocket. He unscrewed the end cap, flipping it up to form an iron sight that he used to aim at the turret. He pressed a rubberised red button on its base, projecting an intense beam, invisible to human sight, that marked the turret.

Though human eyes could not perceive the beam, the Tarantula's sensors took note of it immediately. Its turret swivelled to target the source, bringing its heavy bolters to bear on Norroll.

Norroll was moving the moment he saw the turret spin in his direction, unconsciously reacting to the threat with reflexes honed over a lifetime's training and combat experience. He tore across the thicket as he displaced, powering through the tangle of knotted growth and thorns that clutched at his armour as he threw himself to the ground near Durlo's position.

A flash of red light speared across the field, followed a split second later by the crack of Atebe's long-las. A shower of sparks burst from the Tarantula's sensor array as the turret began to fire, shredding the hedge as it churned the ground where Norroll had been an instant before with a flurry of large-calibre mass-reactive shells.

Blinded, the turret responded in the direction of attack, swinging towards the Taurox and firing wildly in erratic sweeps.

Durlo laid down covering fire, rapid-firing at the Tarantula as Norroll crawled up beside him.

'Did you know it would be able to see the marking las?' Norroll asked.

Durlo continued to fire. 'Nobody asked.'

A second shot from Atebe's long-las struck the turret in the centre of its flat frontal assembly, the high-powered round boring through armour plating and shredding the surgically mutilated servitor brain housed within. The heavy bolters went immediately inert.

Norroll picked himself up from the ground, rising to one knee behind the grassy rise he sheltered behind, cautiously watching the turret as the thin plumes of smoke trickling from its bolter muzzles dissipated. Checking his augur display after his visual sweep, he thumped Durlo on the top of his helmet and jogged back to the Taurox, still bent low as he continued to hug the available cover.

Blodt walked the perimeter of his fortress, crushing the cushion of pine needles into the soft soil beneath his armoured boots. He held his chaincannon in his right hand, using his left to steady himself as he clambered up a narrow plasteel ladder to walk along the interior battlements.

Beneath him, his bodyguard of four armoured servitors milled about the base of the ladder. One attempted to follow, nearly losing its balance beneath the weight of the heavy bolter replacing its right arm at the shoulder.

Loiter, Blodt pulsed, and the servitors formed a perimeter about the ladder's base.

He could have overridden their standard movement protocols, limiting their combat engrams in favour of greater surefootedness, but he didn't feel like reprogramming them again when they reached the top. He didn't need them up here now, and he enjoyed having the time to survey his domain privately.

He looked westward across the bare ridges of the Foretrak Gap and smiled beneath the brass-fanged vox-grille of his snarling Sarum-pattern faceplate, thinking proudly on the past three months' toil. Foretrak had been the perfect spot for him to put his concepts into practice, and with the labour of the thousand serfs he had brought down from Ganspur, he had made it a reality.

The regiment of Imperial Guard which had wandered into the Gap at the beginning of the civil war had been a veritable godsend – their efforts to displace him proved invaluable to the never-ending refinement of his design. Blodt had made no direct effort to eliminate the survivors, preferring to keep the rats trapped in his maze, where they could continue to provide more data for his unending improvements.

Another group had entered the Gap two hours earlier, triggering the passive augurs on the western end as they blundered forwards. They were only eleven strong, merely a squad, but had already made it past the first ridge's defences entirely intact.

Blodt heard the juddering fire of his automated turrets two valleys away. Rapt, he closed his eyes and listened to the pulse of heavy bolters and autocannons in the dusk – rising legato transitioned to prolonged staccato and back again in a never-repeating symphony of war.

The prospect of testing his design against a seemingly more competent force, and the improvements that would follow, electrified him. Blodt intended to watch the progress of these newcomers quite closely.

'*Numus,*' his brother called over the vox.

'Not now, Shomael,' Blodt said irritably. How typical of Zelazko to interrupt him at a time like this.

'*What are you doing?*'

'Assembling fresh data.'

'You have missed your deadline again,' Zelazko said. *'What delays your transmission of the plans for the Fortress of Iron and Lead?'*

'Refinement, brother,' Blodt replied, smiling as a distant explosion stilled another of his turrets. 'A new force has penetrated the eastern perimeter and nearly taken the first ridge. I will need to refine the particulars before my plans are ready for transmission to the Warsmith.'

Zelazko's silence was indication enough of his displeasure.

'Alert the garrison,' Zelazko said after a pettish pause, *'and return to Vytrum. This obsession of yours disrupts our timetable.'*

'As you will, consul,' Blodt said with a chiding formality. 'On the morrow, then.'

'On the morrow, brother,' Zelazko said. *'No further delays.'*

Blodt savoured the sound of renewed gunfire as Zelazko cut the link. His auto-senses flashed an alert indicating the intruders had crested the first ridge.

'Perhaps I focused too heavily upon larger-scale engagement?' he mused. 'Bogged down by their own casualties, it took nearly three days for the Three-Hundred-and-Seventeenth to get that far. This smaller unit seems to fare far better. Curious.'

The Iron Warrior smiled. He had no intention of alerting the garrison at the top of the next ridge – he would play this game out as he would in absentia and test the strength of his design on its own merit. If the intruders somehow managed to breach the Fortress of Iron and Lead itself, he would deal with them personally.

Blodt hummed to himself as he climbed back down the ladder. In his hearts, he hoped they might make it that far.

First Eradicant trudged up another ridge, dispersed between the trees across a hundred-yard front. The emplacement of Tarantula turrets had increased steadily, and in variety, as they continued to push east through the mountains. Night and camouflage netting obscured the sentry guns – a nearly disastrous early encounter with a multi-melta turret saw them abandon their Taurox at the edge of the fortified zone in favour of continuing on foot. Concealing their vehicle in a defile, they had divided into two fire teams of four Scions each, one under Traxel and the second under Fennech, with Norroll and Durlo scouting ahead and Atebe providing mobile, long-range support. The low-light optics of their omnishield helms cast aside the night, allowing the Scions to see their surroundings clearly – despite this, the turrets had been emplaced and concealed with great skill and cunning, making them difficult to spot.

Dragons' teeth tank traps studded the ground between the Scions and the next ridge, combining with a network of reinforced plascrete barricades to create channels for any vehicle that had managed to make it this far. The narrow paths created by this hazard-striped network of barricades bent at ninety-degree angles before switching back in the opposite direction. No tank in the Imperial arsenal could take such a corner at speed, and any armoured vehicle making the turn would need to stop, back up, adjust position, and turn again, considerably slowing ingress. Lascannon and multi-melta turrets had been emplaced at minimum stand-off beyond the barricades, ensuring those that risked slowing enough to make the turn would be vulnerable to the turrets' anti-armour fire. Any infantry who survived would then have to brave the heavy bolters.

Unencumbered by a vehicle, the eradicant clambered over the barricades, avoiding the multi-meltas and slipping past the heavy bolter emplacements. The Tarantulas were readily fooled by loud, visible distractions, which allowed the Scions to creep past. They only destroyed the turrets when there was no other way forward – though bypassing the Tarantula guns was time-consuming, it was more efficient, and less dangerous, than reducing them individually as they came upon them. The eastern sky was already beginning to lighten as the Scions cleared the second valley, their entire night spent picking their way through the fortified labyrinth.

They found the burned-out hulks of five Chimeras clogging the switchback choke points, the gaping wounds that had killed them edged in a fringe of resolidified metal droplets. Their crews had fled into the complex, seeking cover from the heavy bolters and assault cannons that rose in staggered positions on either side of the route, above the barricades. These unlucky souls remained where they had been cut down, their mostly skeletal corpses cratered by mass-reactive fire and shredded by storms of solid shot. As the column of vehicles had penetrated this far into the complex, it stood to reason that the vehicles closest to the rear were the first destroyed, leaving the foremost to press onwards. The lead Chimera had made it considerably further than the others, as the multiple anti-armour strikes riven into its armour attested.

There was a creatively vindictive cruelty behind the defensive network's design, the strange artistry of a perverse genius that had stepped far beyond simple security and wandered into fertile fields of mania. Each turn teased the enemy forward, baiting them with tantalising morsels of success, daring them to risk another advance and cheat death again. There was no going backwards once committed, and at every turn the only chance for survival was to continue – the entire maze was built on weaponised hope.

He was unsure what manner of troops they were, but they were well equipped, determined and resourceful.

A pair of them, accompanied by a servo-skull, crawled along

the edge of a reinforced embankment. They picked their way around an ambush kill-zone he had been particularly proud of, one scouting for traps and the other marking them as they found a way through. Signalling their fellows, they crept beneath fields of enfilading fire with a spider's patience.

A sniper, rendered nearly invisible by her cameleoline cloak, provided overwatch from the canopy of trees above, distracting and destroying the automated defences as the others moved forward. He had not even noticed her at first.

He rubbed the dent in his helm's forehead and chuckled. He remembered her.

Movement on the eastern edge of the kill-zone caught Atebe's attention, but by the time she had reacted to it, it was gone.

'Something moving to your east, Norroll,' she voxed. 'Outer edge of the engagement area.'

'What?'

'Gone now. Just stay aware. Might be something else out there.'

Norroll scoffed. *'At this point, I'd be more surprised if there weren't.'*

Durlo accompanied Norroll forward once again, searching for booby traps as the recon trooper scouted and marked the sentry turrets' positions using his wrist-slate. Atebe remained cut loose from the main formations to scout about the eradicant's rear and flanks. Concealed beneath the folds of her cameleoline ghillie cloak, the sniper provided overwatch for her fellows, twice eliminating sentry turrets that had been too baffled beneath auspex-scattering camo netting to appear on Norroll's augurs. She stalked back and forth behind the fire teams like a ghost, slinking to the right flank to screen one team, then left to screen the other, bringing the improved range and sight capabilities of her long-las to bear wherever needed.

Atebe slung her weapon as she clambered up into a daekki tree. The forests became increasingly sparse as they approached the main facility, the mountainsides and valleys between them increasingly stripped of cover. Even given the number of Tarantulas they had been forced to destroy as they progressed, the enemy made no indication that it had detected them. They encountered no patrols as they went, and neither manned guard towers nor emplacements barred their path. The Scions still cleared the defences when they were unable to divert around them, but it seemed the eradicant could have established a base here and no one would have been any the wiser for quite some time.

Taking the near ridge posed little problem for the Scions – the area defence provided a relatively clear route of ascent, broken by broadly spaced automated turrets and barricades which beckoned them forward, seemingly inviting them to the top. They had managed to make the climb without serious injury, reducing any sentry guns they encountered thanks to Durlo's sabotage and Atebe's precision fire. The eradicant diverted around the narrow switchback pathway of vehicle kill-zones whenever possible, avoiding the armour-reducing turrets above and enfilading fire of the heavy bolter and assault cannon turrets within, sticking to individual heavy bolter turrets when available.

The second ridge had proved murderous.

It was night when they began their advance, and it was night now – though it seemed that there had been at least one period of daylight in between. Fighting for their lives through fields layered with automated turrets, choke points, lethally equipped cul-de-sacs and all variety of minefields and traps made any attempt to tell time impossible.

The labyrinth channelled intruders along a pre-set course, pulling any who sought to cross it from task to task and from pitfall to pitfall, each subsequent leg of the journey more perilous than the last. Yet in each section there lay a chance at salvation, an apparent flaw in the design providing an ever-narrowing opportunity for victory. Each such deficiency carried the maddeningly tantalising promise of certain victory, if the attacker could simply conquer the next stage. The Foretrak Gap's defences were no simple lure, however – they were a marriage of lethal skill and design, consummated by an inhuman sadism.

Despite their avoidance of the vehicle routes lining the way, the Scions sheltered within one now, barely a hundred yards beneath the complex that lay atop the ridge. They rested between the avenue of barricades, taking advantage of the opportunity to recover for the next push. Searchlumens swept the hillside beneath the complex, their powerful beams illuminating the bare earth that surrounded it.

Although they had avoided death, none of them had escaped unscathed. Daviland sealed wounds and braced injuries as she prepared to fortify the Scions with a cocktail of anti-inflammatory compounds and chemical stimulants. This elixir, vitalotox, accelerated their healing processes while banishing all notion of pain or exhaustion. But though the infusions would keep the Scions functional, alert and combat ready, the medicae-adept's balms and tinctures were not without cost.

'I have my reservations about administering this so early on,' Daviland said, filling a syringe with the murky, peach-coloured compound. She knelt next to Bissot, cleaning the injection site on the gunner's neck. Bissot's armour was pockmarked with battle damage, armaplas and ceramite ablatives cracked down to the plasteel frame beneath in some places. Blood seeped through her flakweave fatigues.

Daviland hesitated as she prepared to administer the injection. 'We risk serious metabolic and psychological side effects, which will compound with each subsequent dose I administer. Vitalotox should only ever be used as a last resort.'

'When will it start to adversely affect mission capabilities?' Traxel asked.

'One dose is manageable. After three doses, maybe four, depending on the Scion, you risk permanent debilitation or death.'

'Per day?'

'Per mission. Without access to a full medicae, there is no way I can hope to counteract the systemic damage.'

'Noted,' Traxel said. 'Every one of us was hit by turret fire or shrapnel during our ascent, more than once. The battering we've sustained is slowing us down.'

'Our armour took the brunt of it,' Daviland said. 'I've patched up the worst of our injuries, and I have sufficient stimms on hand. We can push through the pain and–'

'We must maintain our momentum if we are to confront this compound's master,' Fennech said. Of all of them, the commissar appeared the least worse for wear – somehow, his boots still gleamed in the moonlight. 'That we have survived thus far is a testament to the training and skill of the Emperor's Scions. We need every advantage if we are to have any hope of prevailing. Victory in the Emperor's name is purchased with injury and death. It is worth the risk.'

'My greatest concern,' Daviland continued, 'is the sense of invulnerability and subsequent rash behaviour these compounds can produce, even after one dose.'

'Trust to discipline, medicae-adept,' Fennech said. 'Such temptations are as naught before the might of indefatigable will.'

Daviland kept any remaining reservations to herself as she administered the compound to her squadmates. This was the second time she had found herself at odds with both the Tempestor and the commissar since their departure.

'Could you stop chewing for three seconds?' she asked Norroll as she prepared to inject the vitalotox. 'Hard to hit the mark with your jaw moving so much.'

'Sorry,' Norroll mumbled, his mouth full of a sweetly musty brick of cake Durlo had acquired from the Rilisians. 'This isn't actually too bad.' He offered her a wedge of it. 'Tastes like… I don't know what, but it tastes like something. It's a nice change.'

'No, thanks.' Daviland jabbed the syringe into his neck.

Daviland moved on to Quisse, the final Scion to receive the injection. His head was tightly wrapped in bandages, and blood had already stained through the gauze covering his missing right eye. He stared ahead vacantly in a hypnotic trance, pushing aside shock and pain with mental rotes. He accepted the vitalotox without comment, though he flexed his neck and released a shuddering breath afterwards.

Daviland crept back over towards Traxel, where the Tempestor conferred with Norroll, Durlo and Fennech.

'It's a barracks facility,' Norroll was saying. 'It appears to pre-date the rest of the defences here. Minimally manned, possibly home to the garrison Colonel Zheev mentioned.'

'It is hardly a weak point,' Fennech said.

'If it's a barracks, it means that it houses people, commissar,' Durlo said. 'Its interior defences should be negligible compared to what we've encountered so far, especially if it's minimally manned, as Norroll's augurs indicate.'

'If,' Fennech said. 'Augurs are hardly infallible and can suffer from all manner of interference.'

'There are four manned sentry towers with two guards each,' Norroll said. 'Plus an interior guardhouse with a quick-reaction force, likely around one squad. The fence is heavy-gauge steel mesh, but it's unpowered. Should pose no problem to cut through.'

'The guards in those towers have likely been watching us

progress since we left the previous ridge,' Fennech said. 'They know we're here.'

'They've not sent the guard force to investigate,' Traxel noted.

'Meaning?'

'They don't like braving the defences any more than we do.'

'Likely not. They could be hoping we opt for a glorious frontal assault, which means they can pick us off from the safety of their fortifications. Regardless, their inaction is our advantage.'

'According to Actis, the group in the guardhouse is sleeping,' Durlo added. 'Norroll could likely enough sneak in and slit the throats of the entire force there without anyone being the wiser. At any rate, we found the flaw in this length of the defences. Every two minutes, the searchlumens' sweep pattern leaves a fifteen-second gap. Watch.' He pointed to the central area before the perimeter fence and held up his hand, waiting.

The searchlumens swept across the installation's frontage, four beams slowly panning over the hard-packed, lifeless soil. The ones situated on the towers at the far ends of the fence slid across the ground, outwards to inwards, their beams merging and separating with the light of another pair of lamps located closer to the fence's centre as they moved in the opposite direction.

'There,' Durlo said as the central lumens began to roll outwards once more, leaving a darkened patch of ground five yards wide. 'We breach, silence the towers and slip out the other side.'

The pronounced downturn of the commissar's mouth spoke to his dissatisfaction.

'Simple as that?' Fennech asked incredulously.

Durlo nodded.

Traxel looked at Durlo and Norroll, then jerked his head at the perimeter fence. The two Scions clambered over the barricades and slipped off towards their objective without another word.

Traxel rallied First Eradicant in the shadow of the fortifications.

'Fire teams as before. Slip through the blind spot in teams of two – gunners point, team leads trail.' He pointed at a sentry tower where a Tarantula turret still smouldered. 'Atebe, you're our eyes above. Stay in that sentry tower and await my call before moving forward. Do not engage unless I say otherwise.'

'Tempestor, aye,' Atebe acknowledged before melting into the shadows. Within a few paces, the folds of her cloak had rendered her all but invisible.

'Breach team in position,' Durlo voxed.

Bissot, Daviland and Akraatumo – the latter carrying the eradicant's clarion-vox – formed up around Traxel and slung their weapons. They clambered over the barricades, then low-crawled through any available cover as they crept towards the blind spot.

Bissot and Daviland stopped at the outer edge of the search-lumen-illuminated zone, muscles primed as they waited for their opportunity. The inner lumens swept out towards the guard towers, opening a hole in the curtain of light. They rushed the gap, Bissot leading, Daviland trailing, as they sprinted to the perimeter fence, diving to the ground five yards from Norroll and Durlo's position.

Norroll gave a brisk thumbs-up without turning towards them. Two minutes later Akraatumo and Traxel followed, then Rybak and Phed, and finally Quisse and Fennech.

The demolitions trooper clipped the fence links in quick succession, opening a gap nearly three feet high. On either side of the breach, Bissot and Daviland spread the edges, peeling an opening wide for the eradicant to slip through one by one before climbing through themselves and closing the wire.

Durlo clamped the breach shut – his hasty repair wouldn't withstand any degree of scrutiny, but would pass a cursory glance at night.

The first fire team slipped off, making their way to the north towers while the second team headed south. Norroll drew his monoblades, starting towards the guardhouse with Durlo in tow.

Daviland followed Bissot, creeping along the edges of the garrison facility's buildings as they approached the north-east guard tower. She had slung her lasgun and drawn her pistol and blade.

The guards in the tower talked and laughed. Daviland could smell lho smoke.

She crept up the tower's plasteel stairs. Her movements flowed smoothly into each other to evenly distribute her weight with each step, ensuring her approach was nearly silent. Her mind and body harmonised, slowing her respiration to make the least noise possible. It was as natural to her as breathing, or killing.

Daviland approached slowly. Four steps separated her from the guards. They faced north, away from her, but were more engaged in passing the time telling stories than manning their post. She focused on the one on the right, at the area at the back of his neck between helmet and flak collar. He was half a pace behind the storyteller, chuckling as he exhaled a plume of lho smoke.

She crossed the gap in an instant, instinctively driving the point of her blade between the second and third vertebrae, as she had done many times before. She had already withdrawn it before the guard on the left knew she was there, plunging the blade beneath his jaw and sweeping it forward through his throat in a spurt of crimson. She grabbed him as he clutched at the gaping wound, dragging him down to the metal decking. She held him tight, restraining him until he was dead.

Rising, she signalled Bissot, slipping back down the stairs as quietly as she had stolen up. She lost nothing by stealth.

From the west, the ringing crash of metal on metal shuddered through the still. Across the compound, Traxel ascended the guard tower's stairs three at a time. He had not drawn his chainsword, but held his Scion blade in his hand, the dagger flashing as it reflected the glow of the searchlumens.

Up in the guard tower, Daviland could see Akraatumo reeling against one of the steel walls, the vox-operator knocked back by a blow struck with tremendous force.

Bissot and Daviland pelted towards the north-west tower, stealth ignored in favour of speed. Another clang was followed by a solid, cracking crunch. They were still fifty yards away when Traxel bowled head over heels back down the stairs.

A figure loomed over Akraatumo, his brutish profile bulked by armoured shoulder pads and a crudely patched helmet. The attacker's face was masked by a steel ring mesh, and bladed spars jutted from where it had been bolted to his right pauldron. He raised his heavy club above his head as he readied a crushing, killing blow.

The blow never fell as the brute's head detonated, his battered helmet flying as the whip-crack of Atebe's long-las snapped through the air.

More las-fire cracked from the south a moment later, flashing in the dark. The charge and release of a plasma gun and the sharp bark of a bolt pistol answered.

Emergency klaxons wailed and rotating red emergency lumens flashed to life around the perimeter. Daviland staggered, momentarily blinded as the lumens on the fence pivoted inwards, the sharp white light momentarily overloading her optics' night vision.

'Thy munificent wrath!' Bissot hissed, shielding her eyes against the sudden glare.

More las-fire popped to the south as Daviland and Bissot reached Traxel. Rising, the Tempestor waved them off, sending them after Akraatumo with an impatient gesture, and drew his chainsword and plasma pistol.

Akraatumo slouched against a tower wall, his cuirass cratered and his helm cracked open along the left side. Quickly opening her medi-kit, Daviland unsealed his face shield and optics, prying his eyes open to examine them. Without a word, she removed his helmet and fastened a small, concave disc resembling a white skullcap to the top of his head. A series of wires extended from the device, which Daviland plugged into the medi-slate mounted to her left vambrace.

'Emperor's grace, it had to be the vox-operator again,' Bissot muttered, covering Daviland as she worked. 'Durlo's right – that vox-set's accursed!'

Headless, Akraatumo's attacker was splayed on his back, the tank's gear shaft he had been using as a club still clutched in his lifeless hands. The other guard was slumped over the tower's wall, his throat cut by Akraatumo's Scion blade.

'Team two, status,' Traxel called from below.

'We're being overrun. A platoon just came at us from the central building,' Quisse reported, his lasgun cracking over the vox.

'Go with the Tempestor,' Daviland told Bissot. 'We'll be along shortly.'

Bissot ran down the stairs, her steps vibrating the guard structure. She joined Traxel behind the cover of a low rockcrete barricade.

'Atebe, what do you see?' Traxel asked.

'Confirm Quisse's assessment, Tempestor. Looks like two squads headed your way. Mortar and heavy bolter teams setting up.'

Panicked cries burst from the centre of the complex as Atebe opened fire, her long-las momentarily throwing the advancing enemy into disarray.

Daviland had cleared out a large blood clot forming on Akraatumo's brain and installed a steel plate to replace the shattered section of skull above it. She had been forced to administer a second dose of vitalotox, as simple stimms were insufficient to revive him. With two doses in such short order, she risked severely overtaxing his system, to say nothing of the psychological effects.

Akraatumo's eyes snapped open, gleaming feverishly. He shivered, as if from cold, though his skin was flushed and sheened with sweat. 'Let's go,' he said, practically leaping to his feet.

'Wait,' Daviland said. 'Give yourself a moment to adjust.'

'I'm fine,' he said. He swayed dizzily and threw out his arms to steady himself.

Daviland handed him his helmet. 'Put this on and get a hold of yourself.'

Akraatumo turned his helmet over in his hands. 'Damn,' he said, looking at the fracture in its side. 'Got me good, eh? No wonder I feel a mess.'

He kicked the headless corpse of his attacker.

Beneath them, Traxel, Bissot, Norroll and Durlo had already departed to engage the enemy. The stuttering shriek of Bissot's volley gun echoed back to them.

'Just put your helmet on, screw your head on straight and follow me,' Daviland snapped, leaping back down the stairs.

VII

An uncanny silence, gravid with myriad possibilities, had fallen over the garrison complex. All sounds of battle ceased, from shouted commands and the cries of the wounded to the relentless discharges of lasguns as they crackled like fire in the air. The world around seemed frozen, a moment to be admired, suspended in resin fashioned into a keepsake by the hands of gods.

Dust clouds bloomed, rapidly gestating from the seeds of mortar shells in sprays of sparks and shrapnel. Crimson blossoms burst to life in the air from flesh turned over by las-fire. Flashes of light and heat flared all around, each pulse a brief, new dawn.

This was always Norroll's favourite part – how time crawled treacle slow as battle was joined, each moment an eternity to be savoured. He let slip his conscious mind, riding a wave of perfectly harmonised instinct forward into the enemy. His awareness expanded, gleaning the angles of the lasgun muzzles arrayed before him and the position of the gunners' fingers on the triggers, slipping between streaks of las-fire as he advanced. That he was unable to avoid them all was of no concern to him – his faith in his armour was absolute as las-bolts splashed across his carapace. He rolled with each impact, heedless of pain as he reached the enemy's front line.

This was life as it should be lived – a pageant of instinct, action and reaction, devoid of fear, remorse and doubt. There was neither future nor past in this moment, only the crystalline clarity of the here and now.

Norroll grinned behind his faceguard, relishing the shock on the Traitor Guardsmen's faces as he ploughed through their fire. He ducked beneath the fusillade, bringing them down with his laspistol as he slid across the pavement. Another instant and he was amongst them, cutting, kicking, killing.

Not far away, Norroll noted that Traxel had not been so reckless. He kept himself a hard target, holding to cover as he sprinted between barricades and barriers. Traxel crashed into the traitor line some ten yards to Norroll's right, his entire focus on hampering the enemy's ability to regroup and respond. His chainsword growled, severing limbs and opening throats as his Wrathfire-pattern plasma pistol discharged streaks of white-hot fury, hissing as it vented steam between each lethal round.

Bissot and Durlo remained in cover, each holding position behind the low barricades that blocked vehicle access to the compound's interior. Wordlessly, they operated in tandem, Durlo covering the space to Norroll's right while Bissot's volley gun chewed through troopers to Traxel's left. Flak armour proved scant protection from hotshot rounds, making nearly each shot a kill.

Despite the punishment, or perhaps due to the layout of the garrison complex, the traitors refused to fall back. They took cover behind their fallen comrades, the rear ranks moving forward to engage the Scions. Chunks of carapace armour burst outwards as the enemy laid down withering fire.

'Fall back!' Traxel called, disengaging from the traitors beneath the aegis of Bissot's covering fire.

Norroll fell back as well, his right blade slicing free of a throat in a gout of blood as he retreated towards Durlo. He dived behind the barricade, rolling up onto a knee next to the demolition trooper.

'Are you alright?' Durlo asked.

'Fine,' Norroll answered, sheathing his right blade. He drew his laspistol and opened fire.

'It's just, well… your leg.'

Norroll glanced at the deep gouge midway down the inside of his left thigh. Dark blood pulsed from the meat of the ragged wound, staining his fatigues as it sheeted down his leg.

'What was in that injection Daviland gave us?' Durlo asked, still firing into the enemy.

'No clue, but I like it.' Norroll slumped back onto his rump. He sheathed his left monoblade, transferred his laspistol to his left hand and applied pressure to the wound with his right. 'Sorry. Little lightheaded.'

'Daviland,' Durlo called. 'Where are you?'

'Shepherding Akraatumo your way.'

'Can you pick it up a bit? Norroll's hit pretty badly.'

'On it. Let's go, Akraatumo.'

'Team two, status,' Traxel called from his position beside Bissot.

'Not good, Tempestor,' Rybak answered. *'Commissar Fennech got us pushing forward, but they keep coming. Quisse is down. Phed is covering the commissar, but they're about to be overwhelmed.'* The vox-link remained open, and he muttered a curse. *'Where are these guys coming from?'*

'Commissar, Phed, fighting withdrawal to Rybak's position and defend,' Traxel ordered.

'Acknowledged,' Fennech confirmed.

'Funny,' Norroll said. 'I thought telling a commissar to withdraw got you shot.' He had set down his laspistol and was pressing on the wound with both hands. Blood oozed between his fingers.

'Shut up and rote,' Durlo said.

Norroll thought better of arguing. Clasping both hands tightly over the wound, he began the Rote of Unimpeachable Calm, rapidly falling into a trance that would slow his respiration and reduce the flow of blood.

It also made him useless in combat. Durlo ducked behind the barricade as las-fire cratered rockcrete inches from his head. He popped back up and resumed fire. 'Any time now, Salenna,' he muttered into the vox.

'Pinned down, be with you in one,' Daviland answered. *'Akraatumo, drop!'*

A mortar exploded a few dozen yards behind Durlo and Norroll's barricade. Norroll's sense of time shifted again, but this time, instead of the world seeming to freeze, he did. His mind stilled, leaving him awash in an immaculately icy calm, an island of imperturbable serenity amidst a raging sea of madness.

Daviland leaned over him, suddenly there, working on his leg as Akraatumo and Durlo kept the enemy suppressed. Norroll's head lolled to the side, towards the Tempestor's position in front of the next building. Bissot's flurry of volley rounds ensured the enemy was reluctant to sweep in and overrun their positions, but she had become more methodical with her fire. Traxel was behind her, replacing her volley gun's capacitor batteries with one of his own so that she could keep the traitors at bay. It was only a matter of time, Norroll knew. The enemy was probably repositioning, flanking around the buildings to catch them in a crossfire.

Quite suddenly, Norroll wondered if this had been how it had ended for Tempestor Ezl – overrun, overwhelmed and outmatched by sheer force of numbers.

'Fennech was right,' he said to the servo-skull hovering left of Daviland's head. His voice was still strong, which he took as a positive sign. 'Easy to trick the augurs. Not your fault, Actis. Could happen to anybody.' His field of vision had narrowed, so that it seemed he viewed Actis through a low-quality telescopic sight.

Akraatumo's lasgun whipped over his head as the vox-operator opened fire on the enemy approaching from the rear. Durlo maintained fire forward, and Norroll could hear the shriek of Bissot's volley gun and the *thump-hiss* of Traxel's plasma pistol.

Streaks of red lanced through the smoke above, flashing on Actis' gleaming cranium. Daviland pressed down on Norroll, shielding him with her body. He could feel her jolt against him with each las-bolt that struck her from behind.

'Courage and honour,' someone mumbled. Through consciousness dulled by shock and rendered placid by rote, Norroll realised he was the one speaking. 'Courage and honour.'

Mortar fire thundered all around, accompanied by the booming roar of heavy bolter fire echoing between the buildings. Time was up.

Norroll closed his eyes. This wasn't how he had envisioned dying, but he supposed it was as good an end as any. He smiled, prepared to meet his God-Emperor.

Atebe sat on a heavily cratered rockcrete barricade, chewing on a lakrish root as she cleaned her long-las. The fog had mostly cleared, and the late-morning sun shone brightly overhead. She looked east, where the orbital ring curved out from the edge of the horizon to bisect the brilliant blue sky.

She dragged the tip of her tongue between her teeth and spat out a tiny splinter before putting the length of root back in her mouth. It had a pleasantly sweet taste which increased as she chewed on it, and she had quickly learned that it gave her nutri-paste an almost palatable flavour. She understood why Durlo had nabbed a stock of them back at the Rilisian base.

A bag of blood substitute and two other bags of some clear fluid or other lay next to her atop the barricade, their contents draining through tubes into Norroll's arms.

'You're not the God-Emperor.'

Atebe looked down at Norroll, who squinted up at her from the pavement at her feet.

'What makes you say so?' she asked.

'Less golden radiance than I had been led to believe.'

Atebe ran a dirty hand over her tightly braided blonde corn-rows. 'Are you sure?'

Norroll shrugged. 'And you look like Atebe.'

She shrugged back.

Norroll glanced around perplexedly. 'So, we're not dead?'

Atebe scoffed. 'Norroll's awake,' she announced over the vox.

Norroll started to sit up.

'No, no, no. That's exactly what I was told to not let you do.' Atebe got off her seat on the barricade and gently pushed Norroll back down. She rolled back on her haunches. 'Being stupid bought you a reprieve, so stay there and enjoy it.'

'Stupid, how?'

'When is single-handedly charging a platoon not stupid?' she asked.

Norroll opened his mouth to say something, but didn't answer.

'Deny all you like, I watched you do it. Impressive display of violence. But these' – she thumped on the barricade behind her – 'are here for a reason.'

Norroll sat up, waving Atebe off when she moved to push him back down. Akraatumo and Quisse both lay unconscious only a few feet from him, their intravenous feeds set atop a nearby windowsill. He looked around, taking in the extent of the damage. The buildings on either side of the avenue were ravaged, the drab grey of their rockcrete facing pockmarked by las-fire and cratered by heavy mass-reactives. The pavement to the north bore the scars of mortar fire, marred by shallow impact craters and the thin, shrapnel-carved lines radiating from their centres like tiny suns.

Norroll began to stand up, and Atebe once again tried to push him back down.

'I'm fine,' Norroll said, though she knew he was lying. He wobbled unsteadily as he rose, his left leg refusing to move properly. Steadying himself on the barricade, he looked at the crust of rust-brown blood that had soaked all the way down the inside of his left leg and over his boot. He pulled open the tear in his fatigues to investigate.

A large patch, like a sheet of black rubber, had been sealed over the wound, puckering the skin that surrounded it. His leg had been cleaned all around the patch, though blood still crusted the skin further down. He gave a low whistle. 'How are we not dead?'

'The other regiment, the one Colonel Zheev mentioned.'

'They're still here?'

Atebe nodded, hitching a thumb over her shoulder. 'Dining facility. Tempestor and Commissar Fennech are with the commander. The rest of us are gathering supplies or, in my case, babysitting you.'

Norroll stamped his left foot. Grabbing the bag of blood substitute and whatever it was in the other two, he began to step around her, limping on his stiff, numb limb.

Atebe stepped in his way, blocking him.

He put his hands on her shoulders. 'Atebe...' He gave her a gentle shove, knocking her off balance. He grinned stupidly, then started jogging away.

'Norroll!' Atebe called, running after him. 'Don't be bloody childish!'

The door to the dining facility had been blown inwards, so Norroll charged straight in as fast as his limping gait allowed him, Atebe on his heels.

Window glass littered the floors. The tables nearest the door had been overturned and used as cover, their laminated fibre-wood surfaces chewed by las-fire. Shattered pict-viewers lay in the corners of the room, fallen on the floor or stuttering on their wall mountings. Coagulating blood streaked the terracotta tiles like tributaries leading to a broad confluence at the doorway, marking where the dead had been dragged out for cataloguing, equipment recovery and disposal.

Traxel, Fennech and three Rilisian officers looked up from where they conferred at a dining table near the far wall, the Tempestor's glare fixing both intruding Scions where they stood.

'Forgive the interruption, Colonel Mawr,' Traxel said stiffly, paying Atebe and Norroll no further mind. 'Pray, continue.'

All three officers wore heavily stained camo cloaks draped over their shoulders, tattered but still serviceable. Beneath the stains and burns on their left pauldrons, Atebe still managed to make out their unit designation, the 317th Rilisian Light. They had obviously been wearing the same stained, faded uniforms for weeks, if not months, and had darned and patched them multiple times.

Their commander, Colonel Mawr, took a noisy slurp of steaming recaff. 'Where was I?'

'Runners, sir,' one of his officers answered.

'Runners. Right.' He reached for the steel carafe and poured a fresh cup. 'As I was saying, as soon as we learned of the Adeptus Astartes' presence, I sent runners to contact Zheev's regiment. Apparently, none of them made it.'

'When was that, colonel?' Fennech asked.

'Not long after we got here. Maybe two, two and a half months ago?'

'They were still developing the fortress' defence system,' one of the other officers added. He was a spare man with dark, bloodshot eyes and a thin ring of grey stubble above his ears. 'Seems to enjoy putting his personal touches on the setup. Walks around the perimeter when the spirit moves him, just taking it all in. That chaincannon of his, plus the four gun servitors in his orbit, keep us at a distance.'

'How many other Space Marines have you noted?' Traxel asked.

'Two others,' Mawr answered. 'But only the one with the chaincannon is always here. The others come and go. There's also one with a lascannon he carries around on some kind of servo-rig.'

'He's the one who seems to be in charge,' the other officer added. 'Chaingunner steps to when he's visiting and escorts him around.'

'There's also…' Mawr took a loud swig of recaff and gulped it down. 'There's another one.' He licked his lips nervously, apparently unwilling to elaborate.

'The twisted one,' Fennech said.

Mawr nodded. He fished around in the breast pocket of his greatcoat until the third officer offered him a bag of tabac and lho paper.

'Forgive me, colonel, but why would you need to send runners to notify Colonel Zheev's regiment?' Atebe asked.

'No signals get in or out of the Gap,' Mawr replied. He sucked in another steaming mouthful of recaff with a hissing slurp, apparently indifferent to its heat.

'Why not?' Traxel asked.

'Some system the Adeptus Astartes has,' Mawr said. 'Seems it's part signal array, part air defence network, run from the main fortress. It consists of three mast towers, laid out equilaterally around the Gap. It's shut down all overflight around the capital region, and the only signals that get in or out are the ones he wants. Like us. We can't get out. Neither can you, now that you're in.'

'No?' Fennech asked.

'Letting you escape would ruin his fun.'

'With the garrison eliminated–' Traxel began.

'He never needed the garrison to defend the Gap, Traxel – automated turrets and traps do most of the work for him. And it gets worse the closer you get to the fortress.'

'You and your men have managed to survive,' Fennech said.

Mawr flicked his lho-stick across the room and rose with a grunt. 'Follow me.'

Daviland kept watch over Akraatumo and Quisse as the eradicant followed Mawr back down the mountain the way they had come, cautiously making their way past destroyed sentry turrets and reduced obstacles. The journey down the ridge took considerably less time and blood than had the way up – the tang of burned plastek and ozone still lingered about the wrecked Tarantulas.

They slogged through sucking, ankle-deep mud, the ground soaked by water seeping from a nearby spring, quickly obscuring any hint of passage. A small rusty pool lay at the valley's edge, its surface faintly disturbed by the water that continually bubbled into it from the spring below.

Mawr stopped at the pool's edge and looked back. 'Good thing it's summer,' he said. 'It was considerably colder when I found this place.' Taking a deep breath, he plunged into the water.

He bobbed back to the surface. 'Come in, and stay close,' he spluttered.

Norroll waded in first, followed by Traxel and the others. Daviland came last, following Akraatumo and Quisse to ensure they didn't get misdirected under the water.

Daviland broke the surface in a cavern beneath the ridge. The Scions had already activated the monoscopes mounted to their left shoulders, sending narrow beams of light spearing through the darkness.

'Keep moving forward, so the rest can get through,' Mawr said. His voice betrayed the barest hint of a shudder, soaked through as he was with cold water and standing in the eternal chill that reigned beneath the mountain.

They made the journey in relative silence. The route was not direct, nor could it simply be walked. They wended through caverns, often having to remove their backpacks to squeeze between tight gaps, or along narrow tunnels scraped and scoured by the passage of flak armour. Daviland wondered just how Mawr had ever managed to find a way through the meandering warren of caves, or how he came to discover them in the first place.

She had been in caves before, but never anything on this scale. It was another world, lightless and completely alien from the one they had left. Despite the oppressive darkness, the caverns were far from silent – the network lived, grew and breathed all around them.

'Lights out,' Mawr whispered. 'We're here.'

The Scions' monoscopes went dark, leaving the Imperial force submerged in tenebrous gloom.

They picked their way forward, following the path by a faint glow that grew steadily as they moved towards it.

The light came from another small pool near the cave wall. It radiated from beneath the stone itself, reflecting on the slight ripples undulating across the surface.

'End of the line,' Mawr said. 'You'll never know how glad I was when I first found this place. I'd been wandering around down here for days.'

They exited the cave network in much the same way as they had entered, through a small, spring-fed pond on the opposite side. The mid-afternoon sun glared overhead, dazzling in its brilliance. Daviland squinted, momentarily blinded, before clearing a path for the Rilisian troopers behind her. She crawled from the spring and up a bank of damp ochre clay onto the flat valley floor. As they left the pool, Daviland realised there was no other cover – the entire valley, and the ridge beyond, had been scoured of vegetation. Away from the spring, they low-crawled across a lifeless flat, baked powder-dry by the summer's heat.

On the one hand, such exposure made the area's defence systems and fortifications terribly obvious; unfortunately, it left the Imperials reliant upon the very systems built by the enemy for cover. Here, the bastions seemed more of a lure now than ever. The loyalists were entirely unprotected, easy targets for whatever defences screened their advance through the Space Marine's killing fields.

Mawr's command squad crawled past the Scions, joining their commander at the front of a formation that crept like an oil stain across the bare valley floor.

'Be ready to move,' Mawr whispered. 'Clear the trench line and head east, up the mountain. There are gun mounts on the far side. We'll cover you.'

Norroll had released Actis, the servo-skull hovering just above the recon trooper's left ear as he crawled forward. He pointed at an area on his vambrace slate, where Actis' augurs painted a rough framework of the enemy's near defences.

Traxel nodded, sending Norroll and Durlo forward.

Norroll's augur reads populated across the Scions' slates monitron.

He followed up with a message, his assessment scrolling across their vambraces in blocks of green runes.

This is going to be ugly.

The thunder of heavy bolter emplacements began within seconds of the first fire team beginning its ascent.

VIII

'*Recognise the enemy's cravenness as he cowers behind his walls and automata!*' Fennech's powerful voice carried across the vox. '*Neither will protect him, for we bring the Emperor's judgement!*'

The ascent through the Foretrak defences had become a blur of fire, dust and smoke, punctuated by exploding ordnance and the shrieks of rent metal. Daviland scarcely noted the pain and weariness that seemed to throb across every nerve, or the blood soaking through her fatigues on her left thigh and bicep.

First Eradicant had left Mawr's beleaguered regiment behind below, not far above the valley's edge. The Guardsmen had intended to draw the enemy's fire from the Scions and had done so admirably.

Through bone-deep pain and fatigue, the commissar's exhortations drove them forward. His rhetoric unlocked a myriad of deeply ingrained prompts within their psyches and dragged them to the fore, pushing the Scions beyond fear and pain.

Whether they liked it or not, Tempestus Scions always gave their best when working alongside a commissar, their natural fortitude and skill amplified by the fervour of the black-coated morale officers' bombastic proclamations. Even Traxel fought harder for Fennech's rallying cries, his zeal magnified by deeply engrained psychological conditioning.

Akraatumo dragged Daviland free of a reinforced breastwork, hurling her to the ground and dropping next to her as heavy bolter shells sizzled through the air scant inches above them. The hissing rush and *whoomp* of Rybak's plasma gun from below stilled the turret and the two sprang forward, dodging across an open field. Akraatumo primed his last frag grenade, tossing it through the gun slit of a bare plascrete pillbox as the assault cannon within spooled up. The explosion stilled the turret, and he and Daviland ducked inside.

'Wrath is your fortitude!' Fennech's voice boomed above the din.

Daviland risked a glance at her wrist, checking the eradicants' vitals as they scrolled across the medi-slate on her left vambrace. Their massively accelerated respiratory rates were to be expected and did not concern her. She looked for exceptions to the uniformly high heart rates. She had already treated both Bissot and Phed on the way up, patching wounds they had sustained during the advance, though again their carapace armour had taken the worst of the damage. Akraatumo, one of her primary concerns, was holding up remarkably well, as was Norroll – it seemed their near-fatal experiences at the garrison had done much to dislodge the sense of invulnerability brought on by the vitalotox.

Quisse, on the other hand, was a concern. There was an irregularity to his vitals, and his injuries had notably slowed his reaction times, exposing him to a greater volume of fire than the others. Twice, she had risked heavy fire to inject the battered Scion with cocktails of stimms and pain balms, as a second dose of vitalotox could prove detrimental in his state. Though he was struggling, he assured her he was still in the fight.

For her concern, Daviland had been knocked off her feet by a direct hit to her cuirass from a heavy bolter shell.

'Endure, as the Emperor has endured these ten thousand years!' Fennech bellowed as his power fist shredded the support struts of an automated gun platform. *'Next to His, your pain is as nothing!'*

Daviland sprang to her feet, compartmentalising the pain as she sprinted forward. The commissar's exhortations drove her up and onwards, much as they had when she had first met him.

'Let's go,' Akraatumo said, bent double as he bolted out of the bunker. He was almost immediately greeted by a salvo of heavy bolter fire. He dropped to his knee and fired, high-powered las-rounds boring into the Tarantula's featureless frontal glacis.

Daviland added her fire to his and the turret went inert. They were close – Norroll's marker flashed on the cracked crystalflex of her vambrace display. Over the next rise, and they would be at the edge of the fortress itself.

She set her last grenade for impact detonation and primed it, casting it at another sentry gun emplacement to her right. The heavy bolter turret burst in a plume of oily black smoke and shrapnel, its guns stilled at once as Daviland and Akraatumo vaulted into the fortified trench that ran along the outside of the fortress' western perimeter wall. They crawled along the bottom, through standing puddles of rank ochre mud, their surfaces dancing with oily rainbow slicks. Turret fire ineffectually strafed several feet above their heads, their automated systems firing blind at the Scions' last observed location.

'Why put in a defensive trench around the perimeter of a fortress wall?' Akraatumo mused, shouting over the massed turret fire.

'Last ditch for troops defending the bastion?' Daviland suggested.

'Or a reward for attackers who made it this far,' Norroll said, breaking into their conversation. *'It's like he wants us to make it inside.'*

'That doesn't make sense,' Daviland said. 'Why would he allow that?'

'Boredom?' Norroll suggested.

Akraatumo dragged himself through puddles of stinking mud as chunks of dirt rained down on them. 'Since when does anything the Archenemy does have to make sense, Salenna?'

Daviland had no answer.

Ahead, Bissot sat with her back against the rust-red iron of the bastion wall, screwing a replacement barrel onto her overheated volley gun. The rest of the Scions huddled along a twenty-five-yard stretch of trench line, dispersed so a single attack had less chance of killing them all. At the centre, Durlo mag-clamped a constellation of krak- and melta-charges to the wall's surface.

'We're rats in a maze to him,' Norroll said as Daviland and Akraatumo approached. 'He monitors us, watches what we do, measures our reactions, our responses. He's choreographed our entire assault, pulled our strings and watched how we danced the whole way.'

'He won't find us wanting,' Fennech pronounced. 'He will rue the day he sought to test the might of the Militarum Tempestus.'

'Fall back to minimum safe range,' Durlo called. 'Breach on my signal.'

The Scions complied, wordlessly peeling away from either side of the cluster of explosives that lay affixed to the iron-faced parapet.

'Breach!' Durlo called.

The moment they were clear, Durlo blew the charges. The central melta mine reduced the reinforced wall in an instant, near-solar temperatures rendering it to slag as the surrounding shaped charges ruptured it. The wall burst inwards, spearing white-hot iron into the space beyond.

The Xian Tigers plunged through the gap and into the darkness on the other side, charging through molten metal and the shattered wall of rockcrete that lay beneath it. Bissot and Rybak cleared both sides of the breach, sweeping the interior area as the other Scions pushed past them.

They stood in a narrow, curving corridor. The lights at their entry point had been blown out by the breaching explosion, the wall opposite scoured and pocked by shards of glowing plasteel and rockcrete. Lumen strips on either side of the opening dangled from the ceiling for several yards, flickering intermittently amidst the sparks arcing from their power cables.

The corridor itself was circular, its curvature obscuring what might lie beyond. The floor was covered in square tiles of mottled dark green laminate, their placement periodically broken by black tiles at regular intervals. Lengths of conduit ran in tightly bunched assemblies along the corners of the ceilings and floors, ranging from thickly insulated pipes to thin tubes of black enamelled steel. The reinforced rockcrete walls were painted a pale aqua green and generally unadorned, save for the yellow warning signs and white directional placards which provided their guidance in square black runes. According to the nearest, they were in the section of the corridor designated 2-Delta.

There were no visible defences along the passageway, giving the Scions a moment to take a knee and recover somewhat. Bissot and Rybak covered either end of the eradicant, providing security for their squadmates as Daviland moved among the Scions, paying particular attention to Norroll, Akraatumo and Quisse.

Daviland approached Norroll as he released Actis to scout ahead.

'What are your augurs reading?' Traxel asked, following her.

'We seem to have a reprieve for as long as we stay here, or until somebody comes for us,' Norroll said. A map scrolled across his vambrace as the servo-skull scanned and logged everything along its route. 'This looks like the outermost ring of some kind of shelter. Actis is sweeping the whole level and should be coming up behind us shortly. There are junctions and compartments along the inside, towards the centre. No discernible defences.'

'He's waiting for us to catch our breath,' Fennech said mildly. A long, shallow gash marred his cheek beneath his right eye, already black with clotted blood and dirt. His carapace armour and refractor field had shielded him from the worst of the damage outside. Despite slogging through the mud and blood with the rest of them, the commissar's leather greatcoat and boots somehow still maintained their shine.

Norroll's tongue clove to the roof of his mouth. It happened every time Fennech came near or addressed him, plunging him back into the fears and vulnerabilities of his childhood.

It was the same for the others. Norroll wondered how Traxel remained so aloof. Of all the Scions who had encountered Fennech at the scholam, Traxel seemed least affected by the air of menace the commissar engendered.

'It is possible, commissar,' Traxel said.

Norroll smirked beneath his respirator as the realisation struck him.

Traxel was unfailingly polite in his discourse with Fennech, which was in itself remarkable. Over two years, Norroll had come to know the Tempestor as a habitually blunt soul, entirely devoid of non-regulatory courtesy. Contrasted against his natural deportment, this alien formality accentuated the depth of the fear Traxel bore for his old discipline master. Decorum set a hard distance between the two, keeping Traxel as far from Fennech as he could manage, while still giving him a means to navigate his fear.

Norroll pushed the observation aside for later consideration and internalisation. 'There's a large energy source towards the centre of the facility,' he said. 'Likely the main reactor.'

'If we shut it down, we stand to shut down the signal dome,' Traxel said as Actis floated past him, returning to Norroll. 'Mark it as our secondary objective. Any sign of the Space Marine?'

'No, Tempestor. He could be anywhere.'

'Daviland?' Traxel called.

'Two minutes, Tempestor,' Daviland called back as she tied down a dressing on Durlo's outer right thigh.

'We move in one,' Traxel said. He turned back to Norroll. 'Scout ahead, mark defences and find us a way to that power source. It stands to reason that the Iron Warrior will be close by it.'

'Aye, Tempestor.'

'And Norroll?' Traxel added. 'Nothing stupid.'

'No promises, Tempestor,' Norroll scoffed. Blunt, indeed.

Norroll crept down the curving passage, laspistol and monoblade at the ready, heart pumping in anticipation of meeting an enemy his augurs told him wasn't there. He marked the first junction on his slate and turned down into another corridor, identical to the first but for its orange-painted walls. Sentry guns were mounted to the ceiling, ten yards inside the corridor on either side of the junction, their turrets describing a slow, lazy circuit.

'Multi-laser turrets on either side of the junction for reduction,' he whispered into the vox.

'Understood.'

First Eradicant filed into the junction behind him. Traxel crawled forward on Norroll's signal, observing the turrets for a moment. He traced a half-rectangle in the air with his index fingers, then brought his hand down in a diagonal chopping motion.

Durlo shook his head, flicking his hand horizontally to indicate he was out of demolitions equipment.

Traxel signalled Bissot and Rybak forward.

The turrets were synchronised so that one covered the junction when the other faced down the hall, but there was a brief, exploitable delay in coverage between them. The Scions leapt into the corridor when they would both be in the turrets' blind spots, Bissot left and Rybak right, angling their weapons up and firing. Bissot stilled her turret with a volley of hotshot las-fire, while Rybak's plasma gun destroyed the other in a flash of fire and shrapnel.

Norroll led the Tempestus Scions deeper into the complex.

The automated turrets were a recent addition to the network of concentric corridors, which had apparently been built ages before with the intention of carrying on military operations in the event of a catastrophic surface war. Each junction between the coaxial hoops of corridor could be sealed by heavy durasteel airlocks, which proved impervious to repeated strikes from Commissar Fennech's power fist. The Scions were forced to weave up and down through multiple layers of the complex, often doubling back as they found doors which had previously been open now closed.

Norroll leaned against a blast hatch, staring at his wrist-slate. They had wandered through the entire bunker twice, and Actis had led them here, to the bottom of the fourth sublevel, each time. He tore open his faceguard and took a deep breath, tasting the ozone in the processed, heavily recycled air. He hissed the breath out in frustration.

'Here,' he said, rapping on the door. A red placard, marked with the black-and-white-partitioned skull-on-cog symbol of the Adeptus Mechanicus, advised: *Warning – Plasma reactor. Failure to observe proper rites before opening hatch could incur the Omnissiah's wrath.*

'We've been here before,' Phed said.

'No, we haven't. We were on the other side before. I marked the wall. Core vault, level five. Actis led us here because the reactor is behind. The damned. Door!' He punched the door three times for emphasis. He roared in frustration, not pain – like all Scions, Norroll had been striking steel plate at full strength in conditioning exercises since before he was a teenager.

'There's no other way in?' Durlo asked.

Norroll shrugged. 'No idea. Maybe there's another. We just have to wander through the never-ending bunker again for Emperor knows however long until we find it.'

'It'll probably be closed, too,' Rybak grumbled.

'How many plasma flasks do you have, Rybak?' Durlo asked.

'Two. Why?'

Durlo held out his hand. 'Give them to me.'

'I have five shots left on this flask.'

'Overkill. You only need one,' Durlo said, pointing to the gold marksmanship badge on Rybak's left pectoral.

'Durlo, no–'

'Give him the flasks, Rybak,' Traxel ordered.

Rybak pulled two plasma flasks from his belt pouches and slapped them roughly into Durlo's hands.

'I'm also going to need your dynamo and capacitor batteries.'

'What?'

'You're the only one here besides the Tempestor with capacitors and no lasgun,' Durlo explained.

'Give it to him, Rybak,' Traxel said. 'You can lug mine around if you still want to carry the weight.'

'No, Tempestor. Thank you.'

Durlo helped decouple Rybak's gear from the frame of his backpack, then hauled the capacitor unit and plasma flasks to the door. Shrugging off his own backpack, Durlo opened his toolkit. 'You may as well get comfortable. This will take some time.' He paused. 'I also recommend everybody clear out of the immediate area, just in case something goes amiss.'

'Is there a large chance of that?' Traxel asked.

Durlo shrugged. 'The fellow who taught me this died while he was demonstrating it to me, but I view that as more an example of what not to do.'

'You've tried this before, though?' Bissot mumbled around a mouthful of dry nutri-wafer, her faceguard hanging open.

'No, but I understand it in principle well enough.'

The Scions retreated without another word, leaving the demolitions trooper to his work. The quiet clinking and snipping of Durlo's labours trickled down the corridor to them, and Norroll gnawed on a strip of freeze-dried grox meat as he patched his fatigues, occasionally catching individual words and muttered fragments of prayer from Durlo.

Daviland took advantage of the time to check up on the Scions, who busied themselves with weapons maintenance, eating and meditation. Fennech cleaned his bolt pistol, the components delicate in the thick fingers of his power fist as he ran a wire brush down the barrel.

'Helmets on, get down!' Durlo called down the hall. 'Also, prayers would be appreciated.' He gave them a short time to ready themselves. 'Ready in three… two… one…'

A moment later and he charged into the midst of them, ducking around the bend in the passageway and dropping low.

The heat wash from the explosion seared down the corridor, accompanied by a thunderous blast of overpressure that buffeted the Scions where they crouched. A roiling mist boiled along the passage, laden with the chemical stink of burned plastek and the sharp tang of superheated metal. They picked themselves up, their rebreathers filtering the metallic particulate from the air. Warning klaxons howled from within the reactor room.

Durlo's makeshift explosive had bored a hole through the bottom centre of the door, the uncontained plasma reaction evaporating an area of nearly three feet square and reducing the edges of the rent to glowing slag. The reinforced rockcrete floor beneath the door had likewise been rendered to incandescent slurry. The tiles nearest the door had been boiled away, and even the ones several feet away curled up from the floor, blackened and blistered. A cloud of white mist hazed through the hole, sizzling as it contacted the superheated material and leaving a crust of blackened crystals in its wake.

'Keep clear of the mist,' Durlo said. 'It will freeze you solid.'

Phed eyed the tendrils of mist coiling around the base of the door warily. 'What is it?'

'You'd have to ask the tech-priests,' Durlo admitted, 'but I had expected it. It's a countermeasure for the reactor, to keep temperatures from getting too high. It should stop when the internal temperature drops enough. Norroll, have Actis monitor the temperature of the reactor room. We'll be able to get inside when entry would be survivable.'

'What happened to my generator unit?' Rybak asked.

'Thank the Emperor for your respirator, or you'd be breathing it,' Durlo said.

The destruction of the plasma reactor plunged the fortress into unbroken, caliginous darkness. Despite this, First Eradicant unerringly navigated the bunker complex, their helms' low-light filters harnessing the scant illumination emitted from their weapons' status lumens and vambraces to cast the world in hues of static-laden green. They ascended rapidly, the turrets which had vexed them in their progress earlier rendered inert by the blackout, using the markings Norroll had left earlier and Actis' augurs to guide them ever upwards. In short order, they achieved the complex's first sublevel and began the circuit through the outer rings.

Akraatumo pressed his helm's right earpiece. 'Vox is operational,' he reported, unhooking the clarion's handset from where it lay clipped to his belt. He toggled the switch on the handset twice, one long, one short.

'Get me on their regimental command net,' Traxel ordered without breaking stride, his boots ringing on the steel stairs.

'Tempestor, aye.' Akraatumo scanned through the frequency list on his vambrace. 'Three-Hundred-and-Seventeenth regimental command net up.'

'Any station on vox, this is First Eradicant. We are inside the fortress,' Traxel called.

'First Eradicant, this is Cinder Zero,' one of Mawr's battalion commanders announced. *'We're in pretty rough shape, but comms came up the same time the turrets went inoperative. Colonel Mawr is down and Major Drossa is dead, but we've got that Astartes bastard in our sights! We're hitting him with mortar fire, but he's still up.'*

'Understood,' Traxel said, as Durlo and Bissot forced the plasteel security doors. 'We are entering ground level of the main complex.'

'Heads up, First Eradicant,' the officer said. *'I think he heard you. He – the Space Marine – has disengaged and is heading your way.'*

'I confirm, Cinder. See if you can soften him up.'

'With pleasure.'

Las-fire sizzled through the doors, perforating the steel and stitching across Durlo's and Bissot's carapace. The Scions went low, ducking beneath the fusillade that speared through the door and left fingers of daylight spilling into the darkness.

'Get that door open!' Traxel ordered.

Durlo and Bissot shouldered forward into the hatch, las-bolts pelting from their armour as they ineffectually battered at it.

'Move,' Fennech said. Sparks of white-hot energy crackled across his power fist as he wound up, driving the massive gauntlet into the lock mechanism. The security door exploded from its hinges with the force of a bomb, flattening the black-armoured volley gunner who had been raking it from the other side.

Fennech's bolt pistol barked, its deadly payload of mass-reactive shells cracking across the chest and head of the nearest Stygian. 'Forward, Scions of the Imperium! Forward! In the God-Emperor's name, let none survive!'

The security door was situated in the rearmost corner of a broad, open atrium that held the Foretrak Gap facility's original main entrance. The ceiling-high walls of stained glass in all the windows and main doors had been blown inwards by mortar fire, carpeting the graven basalt of the lobby's floor in glinting shards. Any furniture that might have once occupied the space had been removed, leaving the chamber wide open and devoid of cover – a double-edged sword, as the five Stygians who defended the room discovered.

The Scions bounded through the bottleneck at the security door and into the atrium beyond as the wrathful commissar drew the bulk of the Stygians' fire. Clearing the door, they instinctively peeled off in two teams. The leftmost team, with Durlo at the head, moved along the atrium's far wall, while Bissot led the other team right.

'Pincer!' the Stygians' sergeant warned from her position behind where the volley gunner struggled to his feet. Her hotshot laspistol blazed, striking Durlo in the left shoulder and spinning the Scion into the wall. 'Split fire!'

Fist sparking, the commissar leapt towards the reeling Stygian he had fired upon, a shower of las-fire sparking from his carapace and refractor field. He swung his crackling, outsized fist in an uppercut that struck the man in the sternum, lifting him into the air as his upper body detonated in a shower of blood, viscera and shattered carapace. The Stygian's legs continued upwards, striking the ceiling before dropping to the tiles in a bloody, disarticulated heap.

The atrium's Stygian defenders responded in good order, going low to present a reduced profile as they exchanged hotshot las-fire with the Tempestus Scions. The volley gunner rolled into a prone position, knocking Phed down as he and another gunner raked fire across Bissot's team. The Stygian sergeant engaged the second team of Scions, supported by a trooper with a vox-unit on his back.

Despite their discipline, the odds were stacked decisively against the Stygians. Devoid of cover, the volume of fire from the Scions was overwhelming. Salvoes of highly charged las-bolts chewed inexorably through the defenders' black plate. Against the far wall, Rybak's plasma gun discharged with a howl and a whooshing thump, its searing projectile catching the nearest enemy trooper in the centre of his chest, obliterating his entire midsection in a rush of pink mist. In less than half a minute, the atrium's defenders lay still, cut down by the deadly crossfire.

A brooding silence settled over the atrium, a stillness so absolute that even the mortar fire outside seemed to cease. Traxel rose to his feet, taking stock of the fallen enemy and the injuries to his own squad.

He had no sooner risen than a stream of tracer fire, shot rapidly enough to appear a solid beam, raked the atrium, punctuated by the tumult of massed heavy bolter fire. A heavy bolter round struck Quisse beneath the sternum, nearly cutting him in half as his carapace ruptured, while the stream of solid shot caught Phed in the side as he rose and tore out through his abdomen. Shrapnel spanged from the Scions' armour as a mortar round exploded just outside, kicking up a cloud of dust.

The lord of the fortress entered the chamber, his massive boots of iron and ceramite crunching on shattered glass as he racked his enormous rotary-barrelled chaingun. He thumbed the power button atop the trigger grip, setting the weapon's barrels spinning with a high-pitched whine.

IX

Blodt strode from the dust cloud, untroubled by the mortar barrage following in his wake. Smoke belched from the barrels of his Reaper chaincannon as his armour's automated hoppers cycled the ammunition in the drumlike magazines on his back. Sunlight flashed on the black-and-yellow hazard stripes embellishing his plastron, right pauldron and left greave. Scratches shone brightly on the dull iron casing and aged brass edging of his ancient war plate, where shrapnel had scoured it down to grey ceramite beneath its skin of metal. The augmetic scope which covered nearly the entire right hemisphere of his battle helm's domed crown glowed an infernal red through the settling dust.

The massive warrior was flanked by four servitors, their right arms replaced by smoking heavy bolters. They had been heavily modified, their bodies plated with thick slabs of iron which had been bolted directly to their augmented skeletons. Their heads were likewise encased in iron, targeting optics glowing balefully from stylised skull masks resembling the badge the Iron Warrior wore on the sable field of his left shoulder. They held their fire, waiting with lobotomised patience as their master reloaded.

Blodt had been listening to the loyalists' transmissions since they breached the western cordon, marking each so that he knew them by name and function, even if he did not yet know what they were. The green-armoured Imperial troopers fled before him, scrambling to reach the stairwell they had only recently left as his chaincannon's spinning barrels vomited fire. One pitched headlong down the stairs in an uncontrolled spin, bowling over two others as a high-velocity round struck his backpack.

'Fall back to the central control facility!' their leader shouted, sprinting down the stairs. He pulled two of the fallen to their feet as a volley gunner dragged their medicae forward and down the passageway.

The eradicant, so he had heard them call themselves, fled – the gunners formed a rearguard as they made for the level's centremost chamber. They cleaved to the walls as they ran, keeping themselves out of the open centre of the corridor.

The Iron Warrior and his servitors pursued, occasionally raking the Scions with quick bursts of fire to keep them invested. Employed as a prod, the judicious use of a Reaper chaincannon was a powerful motivator. He activated his auto-senses' preysight as he followed them into the lower fortress, banishing the darkness beneath a riot of heat signatures and motion sensitivity.

'Numus, the signal dome has collapsed. What is happening?'

Blodt sighed. Zelazko's timing was terrible, as usual.

'Merely a test, brother. Don't trouble yourself.'

'You still have not transmitted the plans.'

'I am in the process of compiling new and comprehensive data,' Blodt said. 'I will forward it shortly.'

'Shall I send Matebos?'

Blodt ground his teeth. That hurt.

His irritation got the better of him as he raked fire across the loyalists with unintentional accuracy. The one who had shot him at Kiemchek collapsed beneath his fusillade, forcing him to intentionally pull the rest of his shots so that her fellows could drag her clear – he had something special in mind for her, and he would be remiss if he allowed a moment's choler to spoil it.

'Have I ever failed you, Shomael?' Blodt asked indignantly.

'Numus…'

'If submitting the Warsmith an incomplete assessment is sufficient for you, brother, then I will do so immediately – with an addendum that I was provided with inadequate time to sufficiently test my design and my requests for deferral went *unmarked*. I am certain he will understand.'

That shut him up.

'Just finish what you're doing and get me that data,' Zelazko said sourly. *'We are rapidly falling behind schedule.'*

The link fell silent.

Blodt grinned. It was so easy to vex his younger brother when he was yoked to a schedule. For years, Blodt had been saying that Zelazko should relax and enjoy the moment – just as he was now.

He released another salvo of chain-fire after the loyalists, humming merrily to himself as he pursued them deeper into the complex.

Assisted by Actis' augurs, Norroll led the eradicant through the winding labyrinth of the fortress' sub-complex. The entire level was blacked out, forcing the Scions to rely upon their night filters to see. They dared not activate their monoscopes for fear of making themselves more obvious to the Iron Warrior, though the darkness did not appear to impede him in the least.

The blast door to the central control room lay partially open, the mechanism operating it having apparently failed at some point in the past. Fennech grasped the edge of the door, wrenching at it with powerful hydraulic fingers in an attempt to close it behind them, but the enormous hatch was stuck fast. The enemy's ponderous tread echoed down the corridor, forcing him to abandon his endeavour. The doorway, too narrow for the Traitor Astartes to fit through, was hopefully impediment enough.

Another sound carried down the hallway – a low, rhythmic bass throb, barely audible above the thudding footfalls following them. It was an unidentifiable, uniquely strange sound, reminiscent of the chugging of a faulty promethium combustion engine, that grew louder with the enemy's approach.

Norroll had the impression that the Adeptus Astartes was herding them, rather than trying to kill them outright, as another salvo roared from the chaincannon. Distorted by the Space Marine's voxmitters, the bass hum began again.

Norroll realised the hum was exactly what he thought it was – despite the absurdity of it, the Iron Warrior was humming to himself, his vox-speaker picking up and enhancing the low sound.

'He's enjoying this!' Norroll exclaimed, suddenly incensed at the realisation. 'We're a happy diversion to him!'

The control room was circular, maintaining enough workstations to outfit an entire regimental staff. A large circular platform lay in the very centre of the room, approximately three and a half feet higher than the rest of the workstations that radiated out from the walls. They concealed themselves in the dark behind ancient graven lecterns of dark stone and waited. Rybak and Bissot flanked the door, while the rest of the eradicant arrayed themselves around the central platform.

The humming stopped as the Iron Warrior and his formation of servitors halted outside the blast door. Slowly, the door ground open, groaning and juddering. Metal shrieked against metal, followed by the heavy pop and hissing crumple of bursting pneumatics as the Space Marine wrenched it open.

Bissot opened fire, spraying the Iron Warrior with las-fire that stitched glowing divots across his armoured chest and shoulder. One of the servitors returned fire, fist-sized bolter shells splintering the desk she sheltered behind. The volley gunner threw herself out of the way, snarling as she crawled behind the shelter of another desk with her right hip lacerated by a detonating mass-reactive.

Rybak rose from behind a desk, plasma gun at his shoulder, and narrowly avoided being cut in half by heavy bolter fire. Like Bissot, he dived for cover as the desk he sheltered behind was smashed to flinders.

The Traitor Astartes climbed up onto the platform. His servitors ranged out to the far edges around him, covering the space where First Eradicant sheltered below. The ironclad menials opened fire at even the slightest movement from the workstations beneath them, the darkness no impediment to their enhanced vision as they forced the Scions to keep their heads down. As awkward and clumsy as the gun servitors' movements initially appeared, they operated as one. Slaved to the will of the Adeptus Astartes, the constructs functioned with uncanny synchronicity, as if their master wielded their weapons with his own hands.

Screened by the flawless perimeter of his servitors, the Space Marine carefully opened a steel panel next to the central command terminal. Entirely unperturbed by the Scions, he squatted down, chaingun angled towards the ceiling. He hummed to himself as he worked on something, daring the eradicant to brave his unblinking servitors. Lights flared across the console as nearby cogitator systems clattered back to life. The Traitor Astartes rose, carefully replacing the panel before tapping a series of commands onto a cogitator runepad with his left hand.

Generators around the facility shuddered to life with knocking ticks, the whine of their dynamos increasing in pitch until it became a smooth, flat drone. An instant later, the lights kicked on across the entire level.

The Scions recoiled, momentarily blinded by the glare as their optics cut out to clear their night filters.

The Space Marine took his chaincannon with both hands and depressed the power stud, spinning up the barrels before raking a quick salvo across the desks below. Daviland and Traxel went prone as the hail of bullets shattered the desks above them.

'I am impressed you made it so far,' the Traitor Astartes said. 'Exploiting the little gateways I left in my defences is not something many have been able to manage.' He ripped off another burst, this time over Atebe's and Akraatumo's heads. 'Surviving an Iron Warrior's fortress for as long as you have is admirable.' His steps thumped heavily across the raised platform. 'I am curious – I have never seen servants of the False Emperor like you. Are you Solar Auxilia, or whatever passes for them in this benighted epoch?'

Norroll glanced down at Actis' readings. He had deployed the servo-skull into the upper reaches of the room before the Iron Warrior's arrival to develop a comprehensive image of what they fought, and the Space Marine had thus far overlooked the construct. His vambrace scraped the ground as he scrolled through the augury data and one of the servitors opened fire, the heavy bolter shells missing the recon trooper by a hand's span.

The Iron Warrior sighed, a low, static-laden growl from his vox-mitter. 'I don't expect you to answer,' he said, strafing the tops of the desks. His servitors joined in this time, sending chunks of splintered stone and shattered cogitators spinning about the room. 'Sometimes, the mystery is preferable.'

'That's it,' Norroll whispered to himself. The servitor on the right side of the podium nearest the door and another on the opposite edge fired slightly out of sync with the others. It wouldn't be immediately obvious, but Actis' sensors detected a brief, exploitable lag.

'Atebe, Rybak,' Norroll called over the vox, 'Actis has picked up a deficiency in the servitors nearest you. If I draw their fire, can you bring them down?'

'Yes,' Atebe answered.

Rybak scoffed. 'Certainly.'

'Good. We move in–'

'No,' Traxel said. 'Maintain position.'

'Tempestor,' Norroll protested. 'I've analysed the data three times. Two of the servitors are damaged. There is almost half a second's lag between when the first servitors start up and those two begin firing.'

'And I stand to lose three Scions at once if things don't go to your plan.'

'Are we to hide behind these desks and wait for them to shoot us?'

'No, we wait for them to run out of ammunition – which, if you haven't noticed, they are squandering on intimidation.'

As if to reinforce Traxel's point, the Iron Warrior and his servitors opened fire again. Daviland grunted as a heavy round fragmented the stone lectern she sheltered beneath and burst against her left pauldron.

'Atebe, Rybak… Moving in three. Two. One.'

'Norroll…'

Norroll leapt to his feet and sprang out from beneath the desk, almost immediately diving for cover once again as the servitors pivoted to open fire.

Mass-reactives ploughed through the workstations above him, blasting overturned stone pews to flinders as they tracked him.

Rybak jumped out of cover as the servitor nearest him pivoted after Norroll, bringing the plasma gun to his shoulder and taking aim in a single, smooth motion. He squeezed the trigger, releasing a plasma bolt into the side of the servitor's ironclad skull. The construct's head detonated like a bomb and Rybak ducked back beneath the desk, his plasma gun venting steam.

Atebe leapt up on the opposite side of the room. The second servitor's lifeless left eye filled the centre of her sight aperture. The high-powered las-round punched through its skull, halting its torrent of heavy bolter fire immediately. It tottered for a few seconds before collapsing heavily onto its back.

Before she could duck back behind cover, the Iron Warrior raked chaincannon fire across her chest, kicking her backwards. She collapsed in a heap beneath the withering storm of shells.

'You, again,' the Space Marine grumbled.

Norroll exploded forward, exploiting the gap in coverage left by the two destroyed servitors. He drew his monoblades, hurling himself at the Iron Warrior and latching on to the hulking legionary's backpack. He sliced through the Reaper cannon's power feed cable with his right blade, protected from the remaining servitors' fire by his proximity to their master. Norroll braced himself against the Reaper cannon, seeking leverage to stab the other blade through the flexible armour beneath the Traitor Astartes' right armpit.

Before he could drive the blade home, the Iron Warrior hurled him off. The chaincannon crashed into Norroll's sternum, sending him spinning over desks and through cogitators. The Space Marine levelled the Reaper and depressed the trigger, but nothing happened. Not wasting time pondering the problem, he launched himself at the stunned Scion, smashing desks aside as he powered forward.

The plasma bolt struck the Iron Warrior in the left side of his chest. Fired on maximal power, the round punched straight through the Space Marine's power armour, flash-cooking the flesh and organs beneath. Trapped by the war plate, the burst of pressurised steam within the Traitor Astartes' body vented through the weak point under his left arm, blowing the limb free in a churning cloud of vaporised blood.

Rybak ducked down beneath cover, plasma gun steaming, the last of its fuel spent.

Even then, the Iron Warrior did not fall. Transhuman flesh and blood laboured to overcome the catastrophic harm that would have killed an ordinary man ten times over. The Traitor Astartes staggered but remained upright, roaring as he searched for the source of this affront.

Fennech and Traxel were on him simultaneously, taking advantage of the chaos to slip inside the legionary's defences. As the massed fire of the Tempestus Scions brought down the final two servitors, who remained mind-locked in place, Traxel struck at the wounded Space Marine from behind, his chainblade shredding through the soft armour on the Iron Warrior's right hip and deep into flesh and bone.

The Traitor Astartes snarled, backhanding the Tempestor with a vicious blow from his chaincannon. The strike hurled Traxel through the air, sending him sliding on his stomach off the platform and into the shattered remains of the workstations below.

The Iron Warrior's targeting eyepiece exploded, snapping his head back as a point-blank round from Fennech's bolt pistol struck home. The wounded Space Marine rolled with the strike, using the weight of his heavy weapon as a counterbalance as he angled it towards the commissar.

Fennech blocked the chaincannon with his crackling power fist. The impact shattered the Reaper with a thunderclap of energy, sending the weapon's multiple barrels and furnishings exploding free of the Iron Warrior in a flash of arcing white sparks and twisted barrels that took his lower arm with it.

Even the loss of his second arm below the elbow did not seem to deter the furious Adeptus Astartes, who struck out at the commissar with a vicious kick, every mote of the transhuman warrior's being channelled into offensive action. Fennech dodged backwards, losing his cap as he narrowly managed to avoid a strike that would have staved in his sternum.

The Traitor Astartes staggered as Traxel clambered back onto the platform, repeatedly firing his plasma pistol at the Space Marine. The chaincannon's backpack-mounted ammunition hoppers ignited in a fireball, tearing the pack free of its moorings and pitching the Iron Warrior forward.

In the absence of the mini-reactor powering his armour, the crippled Space Marine struggled beneath the weight of his own war plate. He stumbled, attempting to right himself on legs suddenly transformed into dead weights, without the benefit of arms for counterbalance.

Lightning arced from Fennech's power fist as he drove it into the Iron Warrior's head, smashing it against the snarling brass faceplate with an explosion of dazzling force. The arcane technologies at work within the gauntlet crumpled ceramite and adamantine like parchment as the Traitor Astartes' skull burst.

Headless, the armoured corpse pitched backwards with a heavy crash, buckling the surface of the platform beneath its weight.

Fennech retrieved his cap, carefully dusting it off before setting it back on his head.

'There is nothing as wretched or hated, in all the worlds, as a traitor,' he stated to the disarticulated corpse at his feet. 'May your faithless soul languish eternally.'

Below, the eradicant picked themselves up from the ruins of desks and administrative equipment, shrugging free of their cover as they verified the servitors were indeed dead. Norroll grunted as he rolled over and sat up. Thanks to the vitalotox, he still felt little enough in the way of pain – probably a good thing, considering his body was not moving as it was supposed to.

Daviland rushed to where Atebe had fallen, any concern for her own wounds rendered secondary to the well-being of her squadmates. The sniper struggled for breath, her armour rent across her chest from pauldron to pauldron. The stream of high-powered bullets from the Reaper chaincannon had churned a swathe of the ablative top layers to powder, but the plates beneath had held. Atebe bled from beneath both her arms, superficial wounds that had scorched through the ballistic cloth and creased the flesh beneath. Daviland's cursory examination yielded that several of Atebe's ribs were broken, but there was no major internal damage.

A flatline droned across the Scion's slates monitron. 'Can you manage?' Daviland asked, helping the sniper sit up.

Atebe nodded. 'Go. I can manage,' she said breathlessly.

'Remember the Rotes for Clear Mind and Sound Body,' Daviland advised as she rose. 'Quisse and Phed,' she said urgently as she rushed past Traxel.

The Tempestor nodded, his attention fixed on the Iron Warrior's corpse. 'Bissot, Durlo, go with her.'

'Salenna, wait,' Bissot called as she and Durlo rushed after the medicae-adept.

'The Three-Hundred-and-Seventeenth is reporting that they destroyed the drop pod, Tempestor,' Akraatumo stated. 'They've restored comms with the Hundred-and-Thirty-Ninth. Foretrak's defence systems are wholly inoperative, and air defences are offline as well.'

Traxel nodded his acknowledgement again as he approached the Traitor Astartes' remains. 'Excellent shot, Rybak,' the Tempestor said.

'Thank you, Tempestor.'

Norroll regarded Traxel quizzically – he was moving as stiffly as a servitor, his eyes looking at nothing but the massive armoured corpse.

'Well done, Tempestor,' Fennech said, the faintest smile stretching his thin lips as Traxel approached. 'There are few who can boast of surviving an encounter with one of the Traitor Astartes, and fewer still who may claim to have done so twice.'

Traxel made no reply. He stopped next to the Iron Warrior, staring at the heavy plastron that curved protectively over the traitor's chest and abdomen. The Tempestor's left hand, the augmetic, trembled slightly as it gripped his plasma pistol. Sheathing his chainsword, he reached up with his right hand and raised his helm's optics before unsealing his respirator. He lifted off his helmet and dropped it heavily to the floor. The Tempestor's dusky skin was ashen and sheened with sweat, his dark eyes alight with a furious hatred behind the creases of dark, puffy flesh ringing them.

Traxel's plasma pistol flashed up. He fired three bolts into the Iron Warrior's corpse in quick succession before the trigger clicked empty.

TWO

FROM WILL COMETH FAITH

X

Dumbfounded, Norroll watched Traxel immolate the Iron Warrior's remains.

'Tempestor Traxel!' Fennech snarled, his heretofore icy demeanour slipping in light of Traxel's inexplicable action. 'What is the meaning of this?'

The Traitor Astartes' torso had burst open, the surface layer of iron glowing where it skinned plates of shattered ceramite. Thick clouds of steam rose from the gaping chest cavity, meat and organs laid open and roasted by the plasma rounds that had struck it at point-blank range. The slightly sweet scent of cooked flesh mixed with an unidentifiable spiced odour and the tang of burnt metal and ozone, strikingly noxious in its combination as it permeated the control room.

'Tempestor Traxel!' Fennech repeated angrily. He raised his bolt pistol but did not take aim. 'Explain yourself!'

Traxel drew a deep breath of the reeking steam that boiled from the Traitor Astartes' splayed chest. He closed his eyes and remained in place, stock-still and silent, for nearly a minute as he breathed in the ruin of his enemy. Without a word, he turned on his heel and marched towards Norroll.

'That went better than expected,' Norroll said as the Tempestor approached.

Traxel's right arm jabbed forward with blinding speed, striking Norroll in the mouth with the pommel of his chainsword. Even with the protection of his faceguard, the blow hit the recon trooper so unexpectedly and so hard that it dropped him to the ground. Traxel placed a furious kick into Norroll's ribs, sending him sprawling, then drew back and kicked him again.

Now Fennech took aim. 'That is enough, Tempestor,' he said. His icy composure had returned, his words delivered with the deathly solemnity of a promise.

'Tempestus Trooper Norroll, stand at attention!' Traxel barked, heedless of Fennech's threat.

Norroll rose to his feet in unconscious obedience, snapping to attention with the reflexive speed of one whose entire lifetime was filled with dreadful punishments for any real or imagined failure or act of noncompliance.

'The rest of you will submit to Medicae-Adept Daviland, or requisition supplies with Trooper Durlo if you require no aid,' Traxel said. 'You are dismissed.'

The Scions filed from the control room without comment, leaving Norroll with Traxel and Fennech.

'You as well, Tempestor,' Fennech said without looking at him.

Traxel glared at the commissar with vitriolic hatred. Norroll knew the commissar had killed men for less.

To his astonishment, Fennech did nothing.

The Tempestor rapidly regained his composure, his fury bleeding away beneath the yawning muzzle of Fennech's bolt pistol. For a moment, Traxel appeared equally nonplussed by the commissar's inaction. He masked his confusion quickly, but it had been enough for Norroll to notice.

Traxel sheathed his chainsword and holstered his plasma pistol, then turned with ingrained obedience and stalked from the room, leaving Norroll, to his horror, alone with Fennech.

'Everything I have read about you is true,' Fennech said to Norroll once the Tempestor left. 'Yet those reports do you no justice.' He leaned against a desk and crossed his arms, holding his right elbow in the palm of his oversized left fist. 'But do not misapprehend – this isn't about you, Trooper Norroll. It's about him.'

Norroll stood as if rooted to the spot. His muscles tensed painfully – his blood seemed to boil in his veins as his guts froze. He struggled to keep his knees from trembling as all the rotes he had ever learned for calm trickled from his grasp.

Fennech appeared not to notice Norroll's discomfort. Lost in thought, he picked up a broken runepad that dangled over the edge of the desk by a length of black wire. He turned it over in his hand, examining it as if the gaps in the keyboard might somehow hold a message, then set it down on the desk behind him. 'There's something very wrong with you, though, isn't there, Trooper Norroll? And with Bissot's maternal hero worship and self-destructive tendencies, and Durlo's tics and kleptomania – yet I would hazard they are both progressing better than you. If they survive this deployment, I expect they should be restored to regular duty with full honours.'

Norroll stared straight ahead, unbreathing and unblinking. His vision blurred and he nearly collapsed to a sudden lightheadedness.

Fennech stepped away from Norroll, who risked a gasp of breath. 'Why am I telling you this?' he sighed, seemingly to himself. 'You have spent two years in an eradicant, and somehow managed to survive it all. Do you know what they say about you back at the regiment, Trooper Norroll? "What's wrong with him?" they say. "What has he done to be permanently assigned to an eradicant?" What are they talking about, Tempestus Trooper Norroll? What *is* wrong with you? And why does Tempestor Traxel tolerate it?'

'Permission to speak, commissar,' Norroll said.

'The questions weren't rhetorical.'

'I'm reckless, sir. Headstrong. I take risks beyond what are required for mission accomplishment and I question orders.'

Fennech shook his head. 'Behaviour is correctable by means both subtle and gross. The underlying issue is not so simple.'

'What is the underlying issue, sir?'

'Beyond your wilful nature, impulsive tendencies and your penchant for blatantly ill-considered insubordination?'

Norroll gulped heavily. Allowances, he recalled, had to be made for misfires.

He stood ankle-deep in the obsidian razor sands of Abstinax, a child gaping up into the cold blue eyes of death as another child's blood dripped down his face.

'Every report I have read marks you as exceptional,' Fennech said. 'Having now witnessed you in action myself, I can comfortably say you are the most proficient Tempestus Scion I have ever encountered.' The commissar paused. 'Does that surprise you?'

Norroll thought better of responding.

'Dedication, competence and lethality are requisite to all within the Militarum Tempestus, Norroll. May I call you Norroll?'

Norroll's voice cracked. 'Yes, sir.'

'You possess an inquisitive mind, a talent for critical thought and a knack for nonlinear problem-solving that unsurprisingly put you at odds with Militarum Tempestus protocol. The drill abbots at the scholam, in their wisdom, typically make examples of progenia so inclined early on, but you were seemingly cunning enough to conceal your gifts.'

'This is my problem, sir?'

'No, it's Traxel's,' Fennech said flatly. 'His pet problem, in fact. He's had two years to correct your behaviour or speed you to the God-Emperor's bosom, and has done neither. I believe you suspect why.'

'Because I'm highly proficient but incorrigible, sir?'

'Because you are his useful idiot, Norroll,' Fennech said. 'And your loyalty to him blinds you to his selfish use of you. Duty demands he remain with First Eradicant until one of you is dead or he declares you redeemed. As such, he need never accept promotion and relinquish the position of Tempestor-Eradicant to you, his ordained successor.'

Norroll gawped at Fennech for several long seconds. Blood drooled through his respirator's filters.

'Do you really think Daviland's reports are the only ones I read, Norroll? Traxel has recommended as much to Tempestor-Prime Bassoumeh directly – and not recently, either.' Fennech scoffed. 'About your taking the eradicant, that is, not his promotion to Tempestor-Prime of the Scholam Tempestus.'

'The Scholam Tempestus?'

'Everything you say to me is a question, Norroll,' Fennech said vexedly, 'so I will ask you one of my own. How could so brilliant a Scion possibly be as obtuse as you are?'

'Too many blows to the head from Drill Abbot Antrydigm's hammer?' Norroll suggested, though he immediately regretted it.

To his surprise, Fennech laughed.

'Drill Abbot Antrydigm. I had forgotten him.' The commissar's grin went cold as suddenly as it had appeared, telling Norroll that he had not forgotten. 'But, no. Your trouble, Norroll, is that you are uncomfortable being what you are. Do you know what I think?'

'No, commissar.'

'A statement, finally,' Fennech said. 'I think, Norroll, that decades of training and mindscaping have impressed the model of the perfect Scion into your head, and you realise how far short you fall of that ideal. You question yourself no less than you question everything else. You strive to impress to distract everyone, yourself included, from what you perceive are your glaring inadequacies as a Tempestus Scion. Your occasional displays of compassion and common humanity, as I have read and observed, are frankly inconvenient – we of the scholam serve humanity by being set apart from the common mass of them, Norroll. It is base folly to play at anything otherwise.'

Norroll's chin drooped almost imperceptibly, but Fennech noticed.

'Worse still, you appear to bear your heterodoxy with a perverse pride. The origins of this complex of yours are immaterial to me. More vexing to your superiors, I expect, is that this pride appears to make you even more operationally effective. A common point between you and your Tempestor, who is similarly, as you say, highly proficient yet incorrigible.'

'I fail to see how my striving to be a better Scion rewards me with condemnation,' Norroll said with a taciturn growl. Fennech's apparent familiarity had opened a font of contempt within him, and he was surprised at how easily it flowed free.

'Because you have not been condemned, Norroll!' Fennech snarled, brandishing a white-gloved finger. 'As punishing as conditions in an eradicant can be, no Scion has ever been assigned to one as punishment. Never. You think this a punishment? I can re-educate you on the nature of punishments, if you like.'

Norroll ignored the threat. 'Then why send Scions to an eradicant at all? Why not just convert us to servitors or condemn us to bloody arco-flagellation?'

Fennech's cold eye narrowed dangerously as his hand twitched towards his holster.

Norroll realised he had badly misread the commissar's favour and overstepped his forbearance. He closed his eyes and made peace with the God-Emperor.

After several seconds, Norroll risked opening his eyes. Astonishment vied with relief – though the commissar yet held him with his frosty glare, he had not drawn his bolt pistol.

'Contrary to what you believe, Norroll,' Fennech said, his voice quiet, 'eradicants are not gaols to weed out the nonconformists within your ranks – they are the forges which temper unconventional Scions into weapons fit for the Emperor's hands. Your recklessness, your recalcitrance and your tendency to question orders and courses of action may have been what got you assigned to First Eradicant, but they are not the reason Traxel kept you all this time. Had he not been so selfish, you would already be a Tempestor.'

Norroll sighed. 'What would you have me do, commissar?'

'See things as they are, Norroll, not as you wish them to be,' Fennech said. 'One way or another, this is Traxel's final deployment with First Eradicant. He will either take command of the Scholam Tempestus on Sindral-Gamma afterwards, or I will kill him. If the God-Emperor smiles, the Xian Tigers' eradicant formations will fall under Tempestor-Prime Traxel, and you will remain under his command as First Eradicant's Tempestor. Otherwise…'

Norroll risked a scoff. 'I suspect we don't just return to the regimental line.'

'No,' Fennech said softly. 'You do not. And there is no "we", Norroll. Just you.' He raised a hand, cutting Norroll off. 'Traxel's command of Xi-Three-One's Scions is provisional. He will release Durlo and Bissot after this mission. Replendus is dead, and Daviland has always been free to go, as far as anyone was ever concerned. Like Traxel's, your fate after this mission depends entirely upon you.'

Norroll ground his teeth. The guttering ember of his contempt flared again, fuelled by the commissar's arrogant certainty. He rejected Fennech's suppositions – Norroll had spent two years under Traxel's unforgivingly harsh command, pushed harder and for longer than any Scion. During that time, he had followed Traxel into one hell after another, and none in all the 36th Xian could hope to know the Tempestor better. Fennech's notion that he was merely Traxel's stooge was nearly enough to make him laugh.

Except, it didn't.

Fennech was telling the truth. Blinded by his loyalty and admiration, Norroll had allowed Traxel to lead him by the nose for two years, goaded onwards by the meagre hope that the next mission would surely be his final deployment in First Eradicant. In refusing to let go, Traxel had failed them both – and in so doing intertwined his failure with Norroll's.

Norroll's hands balled into fists. The lord general and the Tempestor-Prime had mapped out his future as surely as they had mapped out Traxel's. Fennech's presence indicated that their sufferance had reached its end.

'As things stand,' Fennech said, 'your promotion to Tempestor is already approved by Tempestor-Prime Bassoumeh, pending Traxel's departure. The time for doubt has passed, Norroll.' He sniffed. 'Be ready.'

Norroll stood silently brooding as Fennech waited, watching him with indulgent patience. After several minutes of immobility, Norroll heaved in a deep breath, then puffed it back out with a long sigh.

'Meditate on your failings,' the commissar said. 'You are dismissed.'

* * *

Norroll trudged back up the steel stairs that led to the fortress' main level and through the bullet-riddled steel doors. Daviland laboured over Phed on the blood-soaked tiles, transforming the atrium into a hasty field surgery. The trooper was clearly conscious but unmoving, his teeth clamped down on a bite splint as he stoically bore what could only be unspeakable pain. Daviland worked, her bloody hands wrist-deep in the gaping hole in Phed's abdomen. Several intravenous bags lay atop two chairs that had been stacked atop one another, feeding their compounds into Phed's veins. Atebe, the only Scion in the eradicant besides Daviland herself who had not received a vitalotox infusion, stood next to the medicae-adept, assisting Daviland as best she could during the grisly surgery.

Next to them, Rybak stripped Quisse of any salvageable gear, not that there was much left. The Iron Warrior's chaincannon had ripped Quisse in half, tearing the Scion into two across his midsection and severing both his arms. His backpack's dynamo and capacitor batteries were unrecoverable, as were his shattered slate monitron and most sections of his carapace armour. Rybak rifled through Quisse's belt pouches, stowing anything useful. He removed Quisse's Scion dagger, momentarily drawing the blade halfway from its sheath to regard the gleaming, razor-sharp steel. Rybak glanced up as Traxel and Fennech exited the stairway, resheathing the dagger and clipping it to the side of his backpack.

Norroll halted beside Daviland, allowing Traxel and Fennech time to pass out of the atrium. He wanted to keep as much distance from them as possible.

'Do you need my help?' he asked the medicae-adept. Receiving a curt shake of her head in reply, he walked to the shattered doors. Splinters of multicoloured glass crunched beneath his boots as he looked out into the late-afternoon glare.

Just outside, Traxel squinted eastward, towards Vytrum, far

beyond the curve of the horizon. The Tempestor massaged his augmetic left hand for reasons Norroll could not conjecture.

Fennech stood beside Traxel, utterly composed in the uneasy silence, his right hand resting at the small of his back.

'We just killed one of the Heretic Astartes,' Fennech said. 'You know the others won't let that go unanswered.'

'I know,' Traxel said. 'They'll hit us with everything now.'

'Then we must be prepared for anything.'

'We must be prepared to *do* anything, commissar,' Traxel said. 'Though few, these Iron Warriors are the Emperor's fallen Angels. They are unlike any other foes which cling to the darkness behind the Imperial firmament. An entire regiment could not dislodge one of them from this fortress in three months. It will take another regiment to draw out the rest.'

'What do you suggest?'

'Akraatumo, have we heard anything from the Hundred-and-Thirty-Ninth?'

'Aye, Tempestor. Colonel Zheev has been in direct contact with what's left of the Three-Hundred-and-Seventeenth, and I gather he is not at all pleased that we did not support at Pokol. Why?'

Traxel nodded. 'Announce to the Three-Hundred-and-Seventeenth, so the Hundred-and-Thirty-Ninth can hear us, that we are departing Foretrak and intend to resupply at the academy supply depot, en route to Vytrum.'

'Aye, Tempestor.'

'You intend to use the Hundred-and-Thirty-Ninth as bait?' Fennech said. His effort to keep the shock from his voice was admirable, but he did not manage to conceal it all.

Traxel scoffed. 'You expect the Iron Warriors will face us in honourable single combat, commissar?' he asked. 'Alone, they would probably just wipe us from the board with artillery, but if the Hundred-and-Thirty-Ninth arrives almost simultaneously to exact retribution for our dereliction at Pokol, they will be forced to commit more assets, just to be certain. Anger means applying overwhelming force – the Third Division and Stygians besides, for we just killed one of the Space Marines' own and smashed his fortress. Overwhelming force means lots of things get lost in the confusion, which includes us. Keeps us in the fight long enough to eliminate the Traitor Astartes.'

'The potential destruction of the Hundred-and-Thirty-Ninth is unimportant to you?'

'Their purpose is to die for the God-Emperor, commissar,' Traxel said. 'Why should I care?'

'Such acumen will serve you admirably as the prefect for the Scholam Tempestus, Tempestor,' Fennech said advisedly.

'How is Phed, Daviland?' Traxel called back into the atrium, sidestepping the commissar's comment.

'Apologies, Tempestor, but I really can't talk now,' Daviland said. She screwed something together in Phed's midsection. 'I need time and space to work.'

Traxel nodded. 'Commissar, if you would accompany me, we will link up with the others when they return.'

Fennech followed Traxel across the mortar-scarred earth outside. Norroll followed a slight distance behind them, still keeping his distance.

The air was thick with the cloying reek of burning promethium. The Iron Warriors' drop pod smouldered where it had toppled over on its nearby landing pad, destroyed by what could only have been some manner of melta weapon. Rilisian troopers fired on the crippled assault craft, their shots pocking the armoured hull as they used the Iron Warriors' skull insignia for target practice.

Heat haze rippled over the hard-packed, dry ground. Squinting in the glare of sunlight, Traxel drew his canteen and took a sip of water.

Norroll watched the Guardsmen at the landing pad defacing the fallen drop pod. The troopers who were not engaged in the vandalism wandered aimlessly, silent and looking somehow bereft. Norroll would have expected a sense of jubilation from them, but there was none.

'After three months of hard fighting and survival, they now find themselves adrift, unsure of what to do next,' Fennech noted, as if somehow overhearing Norroll's thoughts. 'I should like to speak to them before we depart, Tempestor. They have won a great victory here today, but their role in this war is not yet finished. I expect they will be annexed into the Hundred-and-Thirty-Ninth, before it moves on Vytrum. I feel compelled to restore their purity of purpose.'

'Of course, commissar,' Traxel agreed neutrally, though Norroll fancied he caught a glimmer of relief in the Tempestor's voice.

Fennech went to rigid attention, clicked his heels together and offered Traxel a clipped bow. He tramped down the hill towards the landing pad, leaving Traxel and Norroll on the ridgetop.

Norroll watched Traxel in silence, dreading the Tempestor's acknowledgement while finding himself simultaneously wishing for it. After several minutes, he began to wonder if Traxel was even aware he was there.

It was likely immaterial to him – Traxel was Traxel, after all, and Norroll had already received acknowledgement enough from him that day.

Turning away, Norroll returned to his fellows inside, leaving the Tempestor to his solitary thoughts.

XI

Hurdt paused inside the threshold of the Stygians' strategium and saluted. He received no response – not that he had expected any.

Zelazko stood at the centre of the hololithic display, his gleaming armour suffused with cold green light as he simultaneously analysed schematics, assessed astronomic travel distances between Rilis and no fewer than six other systems west of the Great Rift, and monitored the ever-updating flow of data cascading in from Ganspur. The only sounds in the data node were the grinding whine of Zelazko's reactor pack and the intermittent nonsense burbled by the servitors operating the hololith.

Hurdt took his place at Captain Dorran's right – seemingly mesmerised by Zelazko, the commander of the 25th Stygian appeared not to notice. Dorran's breach of protocol irked the general somewhat, though he thought better of making an issue of it in Zelazko's presence.

Hurdt held no illusions as to how Dorran and her company of Stygians felt about him. He knew many of them were becoming increasingly vocal in their belief that the general's insistence on acting openly against the Imperial tyrants was to blame for the ongoing civil war.

He was introspective enough to understand their perspective – Hurdt's insistence on overtly eliminating the governor and seizing control of Vytrum was the precise genesis of the conflict. Had he worked with greater secrecy, there was a chance that he could have got Zheev and Mawr to come to their senses without bloodshed. He had never expected they would take things so far.

Hurdt scowled. Had he taken the Stygians' counsel, they would still be beneath the yoke of Imperial tyranny on Rilis. He had been right then, and posterity would hold that he remained so.

Still, he knew he had to tread carefully – though they were but few, Dorran and her black-armoured terror troops were heavily favoured by the Iron Warriors, and such support was not something Hurdt would challenge lightly.

He straightened his leather greatcoat, a habitual gesture betraying his irritation, and absent-mindedly rubbed the winged-skull emblem of the Imperialis yet emblazoned across the ochre plastron of his carapace armour.

He dropped his hand as if he had burned it, glancing about the chamber to see if any had noticed. The golden Imperialis was an uncomfortable reminder of the sacrifices Hurdt had made to secure victory on Rilis, and he sensed that he still had far to go. He feared the elimination of the world's Imperial authorities was hardly the nadir of their fall before they wrested Rilis from the Imperium's grip.

If siding with the Iron Warriors was the price which ensured Rilis' people could live in freedom, then it was worth the cost. He would deal with the Traitor legionaries when it was advantageous.

Dorran watched the Iron Warrior with rapt intent. She had frequently expressed her awe for Zelazko, especially in his capacity to absorb and process the fathomless inflow of information which continually bombarded him. The Adeptus Astartes only moved to shut off certain feeds or bring up new ones with the wave of a hand or the flick of a finger. Dorran admired him greatly, and not just because Zelazko and his brothers had rescued the Rilisians from the dank pit they had been left to rot in, deep within the bowels of Enth – indeed, Hurdt was beginning to feel the degree of her admiration was rapidly degenerating into something of an obsession.

The general stood on her right, hands clasped behind his back and still scowling, for Dorran's lack of acknowledgement yet vexed him.

He realised he was staring at the Stygian captain again. Her baptism in the reeking effluent of Oranesca's underhive had twisted her into a ghoulish caricature of the proud officer she had been. Her flesh had been rendered cold and waxen, bleaching her skin an anaemic, lifeless white. Her hair had likewise become chalky and lustreless, colourless strands wisping like cobweb from her scalp. Tears perpetually streaked her cheeks, dripping incessantly from unblinking, rheumy orbs which had sunk into creased sockets bruised black.

From the corner of her eye, Dorran noticed Hurdt's stare.

'Is there something on your mind, general?' she asked with contrived innocence.

Hurdt glanced away quickly. Looking at Dorran for long was never comfortable, especially when she knew he was staring.

He noted the slow grin spreading across Dorran's pallid lips with disgust.

Zelazko continued his evening's status review from Ganspur. Though he was proportionately gigantic, the Iron Warrior's features lacked the slab-like transhuman brutality Hurdt had come to associate with Adeptus Astartes in his past dealings with them. This lack did not serve to humanise him in any way, but rather accentuated the opposite – Zelazko's features appeared flawlessly symmetrical, one side of his face mirroring the other with such uncanny perfection that it seemed manufactured, rather than innate. His eyes, a brilliant, honeyed amber, hungrily absorbed data, consuming every bit of information available as a flame might devour the fuel in its path and become a conflagration.

Unscarred despite countless years of war, Zelazko's immaculate visage had earned him the moniker 'The Unmarked' from his brothers. Zelazko himself seemed to view the title with distaste, as if it were a double entendre too obscure for Hurdt to understand. Blodt particularly seemed to delight in the nickname, mocking Zelazko with it as he might tease a younger brother.

Bathed in the glowing green light of the hololith, the Iron Warrior's stillness rendered him even more mythic, a stature forged of iron and gene-wrought flesh. The servo-arm mounted to the right side of his armour's backpack gripped a massive lascannon furnished in immaculately gleaming bronze and burnished iron, its hazard-striped muzzle cowling aimed skyward. Zelazko wore a bolt pistol on his left hip, while his bronze-embellished chainsword lay mag-locked to his right, the blade's housing also emblazoned with hazard stripes.

The hatch at the far side of the room hissed open on well-maintained pneumatics as Sylera Dvart, Zelazko's tech-priest, entered. Dvart was a gangling, reed-thin shadow wrapped in mouldering robes stained nearly black by oils and other, less identifiable fluids. She drifted into the room, scuttling forward on the clicking, multitudinous assemblage of steel armatures replacing her legs, bowed almost double by the weight of the bulky apparatus moored to her spine. Twin servo-arms sprouted from either side of the burbling, crackling banks of machinery, their pincer-like callipers bedecked with a motley of esoteric tools that seemed to defy function. Three servo-skulls bobbed serenely above her head, tethered to the hardware on her back. She leaned heavily upon the haft of a massive axe, the smile of its blade a twisted homage to a toothed cog.

'Shomael,' Dvart said, her unaltered voice quavering with a crone's reedy tremulousness. 'A moment.'

'I cannot be disturbed, Sylera,' Zelazko said calmly, still focused on his data feed. 'I am behind schedule as it is.'

The tech-priest's bank of optical augmetics shifted, clusters of lambent green whirring as they refocused beneath the folds of her hood. 'I would not disturb you were it not important.'

Dvart represented what she referred to as the True Mechanicum, though any distinction between that organisation and the Martian priesthood was moot to Hurdt. Dvart devotedly heaped scorn upon the Adeptus Mechanicus with the zeal of a true schismatic and had even initiated a purge of the more senior tech-adepts on Ganspur before Zelazko had intervened. From what Hurdt could gather, Dvart and Zelazko had been together for an unfathomable span of time, and while the general recognised that the Iron Warrior appeared to value Dvart's counsel more than any other, the tech-priest's zealotry occasionally put the pair at loggerheads.

Zelazko paused his data feeds. 'Very well. What can be so important for me to risk my Warsmith's ire?'

'Your brother Numus' signal dome has collapsed.'

'I know. It appears the Three-Hundred-and-Seventeenth has finally shown its mettle. I warned my brother of the risks he was taking with his entertainment.'

'Not just the regiment,' Dvart said. 'Another force accompanied them. One not known to us.'

'They are called Tempestus Scions,' Hurdt volunteered. 'A small force of them arrived on Rilis at the start of the revolution.'

'Tempestus Scions?' Zelazko murmured. He turned to Hurdt. 'Ah, yes. The ones who are like Captain Dorran's Stygians, but not.'

'That is the common view,' Hurdt admitted. 'The Two-Hundred-and-Twelfth wiped out their command structure before the assault on Kiemchek. These must be the survivors.'

'What of them?' Zelazko asked, turning back to Dvart.

'The Foretrak Gap has fallen,' Dvart reported. 'These Scions and their allies in the Three-Hundred-and-Seventeenth breached the automated defences and have taken the fortress.'

'What of the garrison?'

'We expect they were culled.'

'And Blodt?' Zelazko asked. 'What of my brother?'

'We suspect…' Dvart began. 'We do not know. Yours was the last transmission from him we received.'

Anger twisted the pristine mask of Zelazko's features, quickly followed by an expression Hurdt had not expected from an Adeptus Astartes – concern.

'Numus?' he called into the vox-transmitter in his gorget. 'Brother, respond.'

Zelazko glared into the diffuse green light of the hololith, a nagging sense of trepidation bleeding from him as seconds trickled past. Every eye in the room focused on the immobile Iron Warrior in dreadful anticipation.

Zelazko's disquiet ultimately evaporated in the foundry heat of his anger.

'Blodt,' Zelazko snarled. 'Answer me, damn you!'

Hurdt found himself paralysed, afraid to so much as exhale beneath the awful fear radiating from the Space Marine. Even trapped beneath Oranesca's crushing darkness at the height of an orbital bombardment, he had not experienced such elemental terror as this.

Dorran was likewise rooted where she stood, rendered static beneath the horrible weight of Zelazko's menace, the Adeptus Astartes' spell over her momentarily broken.

Zelazko was a blur, his armoured bulk moving so rapidly it was nearly impossible for human eyes to follow as he leapt from the dais. The head of the rightmost hololith servitor seemed to vanish in a spurt of oily blood, the action so sudden and so fierce that Hurdt scarcely had time to register it. Tiles shattered as the Iron Warrior mashed what remained of the servitor's steel-shod skull into the floor, over and over.

He was up again before Hurdt was even conscious of it, tearing another of the servitors free of the hololith and snapping its spine over his knee. He grasped the spasming construct, beating it against the dais until it came apart. He tore the last servitor free of its moorings, hurling it across the room and into a bank of cogitators. Zelazko rounded on Dorran and Hurdt, his lascannon snapping up on its servo-armature, whining as it drew power from his armour's reactor.

Dorran flinched. Hurdt remained rooted in place.

It seemed somehow fitting for it to end like this.

'Shomael.'

Zelazko halted and looked to Dvart, breath sawing from between his clenched teeth.

'My brother is dead.'

'And this display will not bring Numus back,' the tech-priest said. She swept across the floor towards Zelazko, the steel claws tipping her rows of appendages clattering softly over the tiles.

Eyes screwed shut, Zelazko roared.

In the next instant, Dvart was on him. She wrapped the massive warrior in the embrace of her servo-arms and pulled him close.

'Hush,' she cooed, pressing her hooded forehead against Zelazko's. She stroked his cheek with a pallid, wizened thumb, whispering something unintelligible as she comforted the blood-spattered Space Marine.

With a shudder, Zelazko finally seemed to relax. He attempted half-heartedly to break free of the embrace, but Dvart's servo-arms held him fast.

'Why did he not listen to me, Sylera?' Hurdt heard him whisper. 'I warned him of the risks in those foolish games of his. Had I ever misled him?'

'Numus was ever one to go about things in his own way,' Dvart said. 'Obstinacy, which your brothers have always perversely viewed as a cardinal virtue, is a blight upon the IV Legion.'

Zelazko nodded, and Dvart released him from her grip.

The Iron Warrior sighed, seeming to deflate somewhat as his breath hissed out of his nose. 'Jepthah,' he called softly into the vox-link in his gorget.

Hurdt risked a breath. Drops of perspiration beaded in his thick eyebrows and dripped from the tip of his nose. He realised he was fidgeting nervously, scratching beneath his collar and licking his lips apprehensively.

The full fury of Zelazko's grief had caught him entirely off guard. It was a side the Iron Warrior had never revealed before, and had Dvart not managed to rein him in, there was no telling what destruction he might have wrought. Mauled servitors twitched in pools of blood and shattered tiles, sprawling before smouldering banks of cogitators and the sparking hololith, unequivocal evidence of the destruction one Adeptus Astartes could wreak, unarmed, in a handful of seconds.

Hurdt's throat clenched as the heavy thump of uneven footfalls in the corridor outside announced the arrival of the second of Zelazko's brothers.

Matebos lurched into the room, his movements jerky and awkward, like a desynchronised pict feed. He stumped on uneven legs, shoulders rolling from side to side as he balanced and counterbalanced with each step. The right half of his body was armoured in a hotchpotch of components, plated in rusting iron and trimmed in weathered bronze. In ghastly contrast, Matebos' left side had been warped into something of nightmare – a twisted amalgamation of flesh and ironclad ceramite festooned with rusty iron hooks and spikes of bone. A thin trickle of foetid steam leaked from his gorget, twisting over the inward-curving horns adorning either side of his battle helm and hazing the grim sodium-yellow glare of his auto-senses. Thick dollops of treacle-thick sludge oozed from the spiked maw of his helm's vox-grille, dripping slowly over the edge of his gorget and dribbling down his rust-encrusted cuirass. His left leg was bent backwards like a beast's, capped by an iron-shod hoof, while an eighteen-inch spike of fused ceramite and bone jutted from his knee.

The Iron Warrior's unnaturally hideous mutations would render him terrifying enough, but Matebos clutched the greatest horror in the twisted mass of bone and ceramite that had been his left hand. Held fast in its barbed cocoon of warped flesh and mangled iron, the contorted Adeptus Astartes gripped a blade as wondrous as it was nightmarish. It glowed from within with an inconstant unlight, leaving foul green-and-black afterimages blinking across the vision of any who looked upon it. It filled the air around it with the silken sibilance of barely discernible whispers, pregnant with veiled threats and secret promises of knowledge and power to those willing to listen.

Hurdt refused to look at the blade. Just being in its presence was painful enough that simply maintaining his footing became a challenge. He blinked rapidly, eyes watering as he tried to focus on Zelazko – yet despite himself, he found his gaze drawn to the hideous weapon.

Matebos chugged like a steam locomotive. He coughed a thick clot of dark fluid through his voxmitter, his shoulders rolling forward and back uncontrollably with paralysis agitans. 'You called me, brother?' Matebos said. He spoke with two voices, each of which said the same words with dissimilar inflection, presenting the listener with two very different ways of understanding his meaning.

'The Foretrak Gap has fallen, Jepthah,' Zelazko said. 'Blodt is slain.'

Matebos fidgeted, stepping back and forth as if agitated. He seemed possessed of a perpetual, barely contained energy which made his movements jerky and anxious. A rising, gurgling roar emanated from deep within the twisted mass of his fused ribs.

'Killed?'

'By servants of the False Emperor. Tempestus Scions.'

'I care not what they call themselves! Only where we might find them. They will feel the vengeance of Iron.' Matebos' hooved left foot stamped impatiently. 'When do we depart?'

'I am afraid you will have the honour of vengeance alone, brother. My duty precludes my accompanying you.'

'Felg can wait,' Matebos snarled. 'What of your duty to Numus?'

'My duty to avenge Numus will be executed by your hand, brother,' Zelazko said. 'The Warsmith will tolerate no further delays.'

Shoulders rolling back and forth, Matebos shuffled from side to side. A dull, wet growl died in his throat.

'As you will, brother,' Matebos said. Another wad of oily phlegm coughed from his barbed vox-grille. 'Where will I find them?'

Zelazko closed his eyes. The Adeptus Astartes' capacious appetite for information enabled him to recall data in perfect detail even after one cursory glance, digesting and extrapolating from it with shocking accuracy.

Hurdt knew that there were three primary routes between the

Foretrak Gap and Vytrum, each with dozens of ancillary tributary roads branching from them. Weighing the advantages and drawbacks of each would take his planners weeks – it would be like predicting the trajectory of a blade of grass in a hurricane.

Zelazko had the solution within the span of half a minute. 'They will come to the depot on the grounds of the military academy,' he said.

'You are certain?' Matebos asked.

'They will need to refuel and resupply prior to striking into Vytrum proper, and the academy's depot is the only location so equipped along the way. Go there.'

He turned to Dorran and Hurdt. 'You will support my brother in this. Expect the Hundred-and-Thirty-Ninth to arrive as well, though not in support of these Scions. You will leave no survivors.'

'You don't wish to capture any for interrogation?' Hurdt asked. He hoped he kept the fear from his voice, though the sweat soaking into his collar chilled him.

'No. I care not what they know, only that they die.'

'How long?' Dorran asked.

'I anticipate the Scions will arrive at the depot within a window of six hours,' Zelazko said. 'It is more than enough time for you to plan for the operation and deploy your forces.'

'What of Zheev and his Hundred-and-Thirty-Ninth?' Hurdt asked.

'Orbital picts indicate the Hundred-and-Thirty-Ninth is consolidating after hastily splitting off its pursuit from your Two-Hundred-and-Twelfth to reclaim Pokol Armoury, so my estimation of their arrival is less precise.'

'Yes, consul,' Hurdt said, in absence of anything else.

'Given the apparent resourcefulness and adaptability of these Tempestus Scions, I recommend against a frontal assault,' Zelazko added.

'They will be provided every opportunity for comfort and succour when they arrive,' Matebos gurgled, turning his smoke-shrouded gaze towards Hurdt. 'Give them a moment's respite, then box them in while they rest and resupply. When they are reeling, rain artillery on them, then hit them with a vortex warhead. I want less than memory remaining – let the warp devour them.'

'My lord,' Hurdt began, 'is that a prudent use for our last Deathstrike?'

Matebos' head lowered, like a bull grox about to charge.

'Calm, Jepthah,' Zelazko said. 'It is a valid question.' He looked to Hurdt. 'But you will comply with my brother's wishes, general.'

Hurdt nodded dumbly, wishing desperately to find a response. 'Of course,' he choked.

'When the Hundred-and-Thirty-Ninth arrives,' Matebos said, 'I will accompany your Stygians, Captain Dorran. Their commander, this Zheev, is mine.' He turned back to Zelazko and banged his right fist against his plastron in salute. 'I will bring you his head to celebrate our victory, brother.'

'For Numus,' Zelazko sighed.

Matebos turned and stalked from the room on mismatched legs, mercifully taking his ghastly blade's whispering sibilance with him.

Hurdt drew a shuddering breath the moment the twisted Iron Warrior's heavy footfalls finally faded from hearing.

Zelazko took no notice of the general's relief. He rested his lascannon upon the hololith, freeing his servo-arm for repair work. Without a word, he knelt before the damaged projection device and began mending it.

Dvart slipped towards the plinth, her tiny steel feet clattering beneath her. The tech-priest took her place on the opposite side of the hololith, her augmetics whirring and clicking as she assisted Zelazko in his repairs.

'General,' Dorran said. 'We should prepare.'

'Indeed we should, captain,' Hurdt readily agreed. Unwilling to draw Zelazko's attention, he departed briskly, Dorran close behind.

Once outside, he closed the hatch behind them.

'What in the name of the Throne have we got ourselves into here, Celida?' Hurdt asked. All pretence of military decorum had faded from his demeanour – he was entirely demoralised and terrified. The veins in his temples throbbed.

'What a quaint oath, general.'

'You know what I mean, dammit!' Hurdt hissed. 'This is too far! What sort of devil's bargain did you strike for us?'

'Would you prefer it otherwise?' Dorran asked. 'We would be dead and gone, rotting on the pyre the Fire Angels made for us beneath Oranesca, had Consul Zelazko and his allies not rescued us.'

Hurdt shook his head. 'When the Iron Warriors rescued us from Oranesca Hive, I was relieved – grateful, even. Misery acquaints a man with strange bedfellows, after all. They gave us the opportunity to strike back at the bastards who dropped us into that hellhole and forgot us.'

'They helped us get what we wanted,' Dorran said. 'Now it's time to help them get what they want. It's a bit late for regrets.'

'Get what we wanted?' Hurdt spat. 'All I wanted was a Rilis free to pursue its own destiny, apart from an uncaring Imperium!'

'Are you so naïve that you truly believed the Iron Warriors were capable of munificence? What did you expect from a Traitor Legion? Freedom is a lie, general. Servitude or treason, the result is the same.'

'We are not traitors!' Hurdt shouted. The Stygian guards on either side of the door instinctively tightened their grips on their hotshot lasguns. 'We are the proud sons and daughters of Rilis,' he continued quietly.

Dorran laughed. She gestured towards the door behind them. 'Then what do you call that?'

Hurdt scowled. 'We are patriots,' he said unironically. 'And patriotism requires its leaders be prepared to make the most difficult decisions. Our loyalty is, as it should have always been, to the people of Rilis – not to some mythical God-Emperor shepherding mankind into some long-promised golden age from light years away, as the priests insist.'

'Your loyalty is not to the Iron Warriors, then?'

'They are a means to an end,' Hurdt said. 'As you say, without Zelazko's support, we would be dead and buried beneath Enth – would that the Fire Angels had championed us instead and not simply bombarded us from orbit and left us to rot in the depths of some stinking underhive.' He threw up his hands. 'Ah, well. Wish in one hand, shit in the other. Why are we even arguing, Celida? I thought we were on the same page.'

'We are,' Dorran assured him, though Hurdt had his doubts.

'Good, because we're wasting time here. After what happened in there, I've decided I would like to remain solidly in Consul Zelazko's good graces, at least until this is over. If we're finished, I need to make ready.'

'Of course, general.'

Hurdt walked towards the lifts, then turned to Dorran as he waited for the doors to open. 'For what it's worth, I'm glad it'll be the Stygians accompanying Matebos, and not my men.'

The lift doors slid open. Lieutenant Bayless, Dorran's second-in-command, stood in the doorway. Oranesca's abhorrent depths had left their indelible mark upon him, as they had upon every Stygian who escaped from its festering darkness. The flesh of over three-quarters of his body had twisted into a mantle of rosaceous, bumpy hide, hideously distorting the right side of his face into a gruesome, swollen parody of human features. The iris of his right eye had broken like an egg yolk and manifested two polychroic pupils, while his hair, once blond, now sprouted as an irregular scaling of short spikes resembling dirty fingernails.

'General,' Bayless said. Despite his ghastly mutations, the left side of his face remained smooth and handsome, like some grimly mocking reminder of who he was before.

'Lieutenant,' Hurdt acknowledged, wishing the Stygians would keep their damned helmets on.

Bayless exited and joined his commander outside the strategium as the lift doors closed.

Alone in the lift, Hurdt ran his gloved fingers over the Imperialis on his breastplate with a heavy sigh.

'The most difficult decisions,' he said, and wondered how long it would take his armourers to remove the sigil.

XII

'How much fuel do we have?' Traxel called from the back of the Taurox, where he, Fennech and Norroll consulted over a map Durlo had acquired within the Fortress of Iron and Lead.

Daviland had restocked her medi-kit with supplies obtained from the 139th. She had exhausted most of her issued stock crossing the Foretrak Gap and used up what little remained piecing Phed back together.

'Maybe enough for another hour's travel,' Bissot called back from the cab. 'Maybe less.'

The eradicant had emptied their last containers of the fuel they had requisitioned from the Rilisians three hours earlier. Powerful as the Taurox's engines were, they were woefully inefficient, burning through promethium at a rate that necessitated frequent refuelling.

'Enough time for the Iron Warriors to show themselves?' Fennech asked.

'We'll see,' Traxel said. 'I'd like to be out of the Taurox when that happens. When the flood comes, we stand a better chance if we aren't all in one place.'

'Then what?'

'Then we find the Iron Warriors and kill them.'

'Simple as that?' Norroll asked.

'In principle,' Traxel said. 'In practice, doubtfully so. One was more than enough for an entire regiment at Foretrak.'

Fennech made a function check of his bolt pistol. 'You expect both remaining Iron Warriors?'

'I honestly hope not,' Traxel said. 'But I admit that the one I do expect is the one I dread most.'

'The twisted one?' Norroll asked. 'With the… the sword.'

Traxel nodded.

'Why do you think he will come alone?'

'Because they each have a different purpose. The one at Foretrak was the siege master, responsible for sequestering Vytrum from the war to the west. The twisted one, the one I expect will come for us here, is the enforcer – he moves as he is required. The third, as Colonel Mawr and his officers explained, is the leader.'

'And he will not come?' Norroll asked.

'I do not expect him. He is their leader, but not their master. I expect he has more pressing matters occupying him – he did not make his presence known before Kiemchek and returned to the capital immediately afterwards. He will remain in Vytrum.'

'I'm sorry, Tempestor,' Norroll said, 'but this is a bit too much. How can you possibly believe what you're saying?'

'Are you dense, Norroll?' Rybak said, loading the last plasma flask into a bandolier. 'It's regicide. The Tempestor's playing regicide.'

Daviland checked Phed, who sat in a restorative trance to her right, his mind and body effectively switched off to heal more efficiently. She had mounted multiple nutrient and fluid feeds to the Scion's armour, the artificial intakes the sole means by which Phed remained able to hydrate and absorb sustenance. His injuries had required emergency surgery to the extent that Daviland was surprised she had managed to keep him alive. The scope of damage to his internal organs was so extensive that it was necessary for her to excise the entirety of his stomach and his upper and lower bowels. His heart had been perforated by shrapnel when a round of Reaper ammunition had shattered against his carapace armour, requiring her to install an artificial replacement.

She had kept Scions alive with more grievous wounds than these, but it was never for long. His heart rate would register as a flatline from now on, so she had to check his vitals by means of an implant which linked him to her medicae vambrace. Though Phed's physical conditioning and psychological architecture would keep him in the fight for the time being, he was effectively a dead man walking.

It comforted her to realise that she had given Phed time enough to choose the means of his ending. Ultimately, the length of his service to the Emperor and the manner of his death would be determined by the Scion himself.

The Taurox Prime ground over the shattered boulevard which wound around the Rilisian military academy on the outskirts of the planetary capital at Vytrum, the only movement apart from the overgrown grasses that rippled like the surface of a weed-choked sea. The day had dawned hot, and late-morning sunlight baked down on the transport with the promise of higher temperatures. Beside them, the broad expanse of the Hukstrom River meandered lazily from the ridges to the north into the broad plain where the academy lay, its blood-red waters still stained by the pollutants which had nearly rendered Rilis uninhabitable a millennium before.

Though the academy was nominally under the control of

General Hurdt's traitors, there was very little in the way of a permanent presence on its grounds. Little enough of value remained on the campus itself, the once pristine white stone of its architecture ravaged by artillery bombardment in the early days of the war and riddled with bullets in the months since.

According to Colonel Mawr, the academy had been deemed untenable and abandoned by the last of its loyalist defenders before he had even entered the Foretrak Gap nearly three months earlier. The only area of importance remaining was the school's supply depot, on the northern edge of the meander upon which the academy lay.

The Taurox rolled on, its quad-mounted tracks and advanced suspension allowing it to traverse the heavily cratered roadway without slowing. Rybak manned the turret in search of threats, though nothing presented itself. Already injured and exhausted, they had been rendered jittery by the vitalotox – Akraatumo, who had received two doses, was easily the tensest of the lot. He sat in the cab next to Bissot, who seemed to have a calming influence on him. He listened to her spin tales of her mother's heroism as she drove, enthralled by the volley gunner's fantastic stories of a woman she had never met, told as if she had been present.

'The cave was collapsing all around them as Calixe hit the afterburners,' Bissot said, calling her mother by her given name, 'jolting her Thunderbolt forward with a sonic boom. The rest of the squadron followed in tight formation, trusting her to lead them out.'

'A sonic boom?' Akraatumo asked. 'I thought they were inside an asteroid?'

'So did she.' Bissot smirked. 'But it wasn't a cave… It was Jeroboam the Great, a void whale of such prodigious size that it had swallowed the asteroid my mother's squadron had escaped into whole, while they were still inside.'

'We're coming up on the gate, Bissot,' Traxel said. 'Focus on the road.'

The Taurox rounded a bend, following the curve of the river, and the gates of the academy's supply depot came into view.

'The entry control point looks to be minimally guarded,' Bissot said. 'Guard shack and security barrier, route in controlled via obstacle barricades.'

Traxel called up into the turret. 'Rybak.'

The gatling cannons wailed, the fire from their twin rotary barrels chewing through the glass and steel of the guard shack to shred the pair of Guardsmen manning it in a storm of blood, sparks and shattered glass. The Taurox struck the barrier at speed, wrenching the black-and-yellow-striped armature from its rockcrete base as it ploughed forward. The barricades, intended to slow a vehicle by forcing it to zigzag around the obstacles, impeded the Taurox little enough when Bissot simply pivot-steered, slewing the transport around them. She drifted the Taurox around curves with a nimbleness impossible for ordinary tyres. The rear of the vehicle crashed into each barricade as she swerved around the next, reverberating through the armoured chassis with every impact.

The depot's quick-reaction force darted from the barracks facility to the right, and Rybak gunned them down. He pivoted forward, searching for more targets as the Taurox swept from the entry control point, gyroscopic mounts keeping his gatling cannons level despite the juddering impact with the last obstacle.

Bissot accelerated across the depot's yard, making haste to the fuel dump. The facility was built to the same specifications as tens of thousands of others like it across the galaxy, so navigating it was simple enough, despite the minor alterations made to the layout over the course of seven millennia.

She had barely brought the Taurox to a complete stop before

the Scions were leaping from the hatches. Each went to their assigned tasks silently, sprinting across the tarmac to gather the equipment they had been charged to find and return as quickly as possible before reinforcements arrived.

Phed and Bissot refuelled the Taurox. Promethium sloshed onto the pavement as they hurriedly filled the gun truck's capacious fuel tanks, then rushed to replenish their stock of five-gallon blitz cans. They finished stowing the full canisters as Daviland returned with a load of medical supplies, which Phed likewise assisted her in packing, dutifully obedient despite his injuries.

The fuel and medical supplies loaded, Bissot and Daviland ran off together, tasked to assist Traxel and Atebe in securing more items. Phed followed them part of the way, before taking up a position opposite the fuel dump where he could secure the perimeter around the Taurox.

Laden with supplies, Rybak hopped into the Taurox to receive the equipment Norroll, Akraatumo and Durlo dumped outside. They had just started passing the plasma gunner boxes of ammunition for the gatling guns as Fennech returned, carrying three heavily laden gunny sacks slung over his shoulders.

A heavy thump echoed from the south, followed a split second later by the unmistakable rush of artillery.

'Incoming!' Norroll shouted as the commissar and three Scions outside the Taurox dived to the ground.

Slightly over a hundred yards away, the supply shed Fennech had just returned from detonated in a fireball, casting shrapnel in all directions. The Scions scrambled up in time for a second round to splash down fifty yards closer, at the very edge of the shell's likely kill radius. Explosively propelled debris rode the blast wave into the Scions, knocking them sprawling as it pummelled their carapace armour.

Norroll's head rang from the force of the blast and the multiple impacts of debris against his helmet. He threw himself through the Taurox's rear hatch, grabbed Rybak and dragged him towards the exit as another shell struck closer still, near enough for the force of the blast to rock the Taurox on its tracks. Fragments battered the side armour like hail, scouring deep, irregular dents into the left side of the transport and blowing the armaglass viewports free of their moorings.

A fourth shell plunged through the Taurox Prime's cab as Norroll and Rybak dived out the back and skidded forward, face down, across the tarmac. Instinct and psychological reconditioning kicked in as the pair of Scions stumbled to their feet and pelted after the others. A second artillery round slammed into the smouldering Taurox, shredding the gun truck from the inside out in a plume of sooty flame.

Las-fire streaked across the fuel dump from the south, accompanied by the staccato percussion of heavy bolter fire as four Chimeras rumbled forward. Screened by the covering fire of their multi-lasers and heavy bolters, two of the transports dropped their rear ramps, deploying their squads of Rilisian Astra Militarum troopers. Five more Chimeras skirted westward around the supply depot, hemming the Scions in.

Norroll and Rybak caught up to Fennech, Akraatumo and Durlo, sheltering behind a tower of stacked shipping containers.

'Do we have a status on the others?' Norroll asked, dropping to one knee between Akraatumo and Fennech. Blood soaked through the recon trooper's blackened fatigues in half a dozen places where shrapnel had penetrated the ballistic fabric, though he banished the superficial injuries from his conscience with rotes. Rybak went prone on the rear corner of the makeshift bulwark, covering them from the opposite end from where Durlo scanned for threats.

'Still trying to reach them,' Akraatumo said. 'No response yet.'

'They should still be close enough to contact on inter-vox,' Norroll said. 'Call the Valkyrie.'

'Valkyrie Xi-Five-One,' Akraatumo called into the vox. 'Xi-Five-One, First Eradicant. Confirm.'

Static tickled across the vox for a handful of seconds.

'Valkyrie Xi-Five-One confirms, First Eradicant,' crackled the reply.

A mortar round burst ten yards to the right of the Scions with a percussive bang, sending shrapnel and debris tearing through the shipping containers. 'Xi-Five-One, First Eradicant requests immediate air support and evac!'

'I confirm your request, First Eradicant. What is your location?'

'Supply depot on Rilisian military academy grounds,' Akraatumo said.

'Confirm, First Eradicant,' the Valkyrie reported. *'Estimated time of arrival, forty-five minutes.'*

Norroll listened in disbelief. 'They might not even make it here in time to avenge us.'

Behind him, Durlo opened fire. 'Two squads incoming,' he reported coolly as he dropped one of the infantrymen.

'Flanking our position,' Rybak said. Plasma fire sent the enemy troopers diving for cover. A grenade burst off to his right, forcing him behind the container.

'Any Three-Six Xian units on vox, respond,' Norroll called into the inter-vox.

'Daviland and Bissot here,' Daviland replied. *'We've got Phed with us, still trying to locate the Tempestor and Atebe. Status and location, Norroll?'*

'Got Durlo, Akraatumo, Rybak and Commissar Fennech with me. We're bogged down behind some shipping containers two hundred yards south-east of the Taurox, just in front of the perimeter fence. Enemy is trying to flank around us, and we've run out of places to go.'

Rybak picked his shots with care as Akraatumo darted over to support him. 'I am red on plasma ammunition. Any chance of support, Daviland?'

'We're on the opposite side of the depot from you,' Bissot returned, the report of her volley gun reaching Norroll's position a few seconds after it popped over the vox. *'We were just about to ask if there was any chance of you fighting your way back towards us.'*

'Unlikely,' Fennech said, reloading his bolt pistol. He stood above Durlo and opened fire, dropping two enemy troopers before a salvo of las-fire forced him to duck back behind cover.

'Any contact with the Tempestor?' Norroll called.

'Negative on him or Atebe,' Daviland replied. *'Closing on their last known position.'*

Akraatumo looked south. From his vantage point, he could see the enemy artillery in the distance. 'Nice if we could make that artillery work for us.'

Rybak scowled. 'We'd be taken apart before we got anywhere close to those guns.'

'Not if we went underneath them,' Durlo said, indicating a rusty steel maintenance hole cover in the pavement, roughly twenty yards away.

'I didn't want to die up here anyway,' Norroll said. 'Akraatumo, Rybak, support us while we move. Commissar?'

'With you.'

'Move on three,' Norroll said.

The count was silent, but the Scions needed no prompting. They broke out from behind the storage containers, weapons firing into the traitors as they sprinted towards the maintenance access lid. After a moment's shock, the Rilisians on the right flank scattered in the face of the Scions' counter-attack.

Akraatumo and Rybak displaced as the left flank's Guardsmen broke through, flanking around where the Scions had been sheltering behind the containers just seconds earlier. The Guardsmen were already firing as they rounded the shipping containers, drawing Rybak's and Akraatumo's covering fire.

Durlo scrabbled at the manhole cover, but loose stone had filled in the gaps, giving him no means to achieve purchase or leverage on the heavy steel lid. Las-fire sizzled around the Scions' heads as the enemy regrouped.

Blue-white arcs of corposant hissed across Fennech's power fist as he struck the centre of the maintenance cover with thunderous force, collapsing the access point inwards with a shuddering peal of buckling steel and shattering rockcrete.

The commissar dropped boots first into the dust-shrouded darkness below. The Scions jumped after him, following his lead without question.

Atebe crawled across the tarmac towards Traxel, keeping her head beneath the dazzlingly bright lattice of las-fire sizzling through the air scant inches above. Caught in an enfilade as they burst from the bay they had been stripping for ammunition, a round had caught the Tempestor in the left side, punching through his carapace and sending him spinning from his feet. She grabbed Traxel under the arm, firing her long-las one-handed as she dragged him up and forward. The weapon had not been designed with suppressive fire in mind, but it proved adequate to the task.

A round struck her in the centre of her backpack, knocking her from her feet and dragging Traxel back down with her.

'Atebe!'

Volley fire from her right strafed across the Rilisian Guardsmen, sending them fleeing for cover as Bissot burst out from behind a cargo-8. Bissot's salvo continued unabated as she fired mercilessly into the retreating troopers' backs.

The Scions ran as well, skirting the fence with all haste as Atebe and Daviland half dragged Traxel between them. Bissot risked a backward sprint, firing on the run at a second squad of Guardsmen disembarking from a nearby Chimera. The volley gun spat a torrent of overcharged las-fire into the infantrymen, shredding their flak armour and forcing the squad to dive for shelter.

The Scions took cover behind a plasteel container near the fence's edge. Atebe and Bissot laid down suppressive fire, cutting apart any enemy who moved into view as Phed broke through the fence.

'Norroll, where are you?' Traxel called into the vox as Daviland smeared some foul-smelling compound onto his wound.

When the reply came, it was nearly inaudible over the crackling rush of masking static. *'We… barely hear… underneath you…'* Norroll replied. *'–ting to secure artillery.'*

'You're attempting to secure the enemy artillery?'

'–nfirm, –pestor…'

Traxel was the first to crawl through the breach Phed had cut in the fence, las-fire from a five-man squad of Guardsmen left to secure the gate sparking from his armour. He leapt up, his plasma pistol flash-vaporising one of the guards an instant before he cut down two others with a single, sweeping strike of his chainsword. He ran on without looking back, leaving Phed and Daviland to finish off the remaining guards. 'We are being pursued by Guard and severely outnumbered. Still no sign of the Traitor Astartes. Secure the artillery, and we'll mark a kill-zone for you when we locate him. Confirm receipt.'

'Confirm, Tem– We… contact you… we…' Static claimed the rest of Norroll's response.

The Tempestor led his squad into the academy grounds, sprinting through a broad field, now cratered and overgrown. At some point recently, the Rilisians had built a large and sturdy gallows. The scaffolds were a broad triangle, with three uprights connecting three long crossbeams. Twenty-four corpses of advanced decrepitude swayed in the summer afternoon's breeze, their mouldering flesh picked nearly clean by carrion scavengers. Large oil-black corvids, disturbed by the Scions' approach, croaked their displeasure and flapped noisily away to circle above the gallows, leaving their feasts swinging from creaking, thickly braided nooses.

The Scions sprinted across the field, making for the cover of buildings shattered during the earliest days of the Rilisian civil war. The pavement walkways surrounding the field were cratered by bombardment, surrounded in places by felled trees and the skeletal corpses of Rilisian cadets in gold-brocaded grey uniforms, their flesh long since consumed by scavengers. Shrapnel-riddled placards of corroding brass recalled the names of long-dead heroes outside the buildings named in their honour around the campus. A statue cast in weathered bronze, a general from Rilis' storied military past, stood arms akimbo atop a white rockcrete plinth outside a massive complex. The general smiled out over the gallows field, the pride of his paternal grin rendered perverse by the fratricide to which he had borne witness.

Atebe ducked into a building and leapt across a gap where the floor had been collapsed by artillery. She continued at a dead sprint when she landed on the other side, dodging around the broken and overturned remains of desks and chairs as las-fire tore through the glassless windows to her right, before scrambling up a dangling length of conduit. She clambered up to the third storey of the crumbling complex, trying to find an effective sniper hide. Traxel and Bissot took up positions on the storey beneath her while Daviland and Phed remained on the ground floor.

Las-rounds split the air above Atebe's head – the damned Guard seemed to pour fire on anyplace with an opening.

She dived behind a solid wooden desk. Above her, las-fire blasted divots from the wall to her left, filling the air with clouds of plaster dust. It was likely the enemy had a spotter of their own, advising them on the most effective areas to concentrate their counter-sniper fire.

She crawled below the las-fire into the hallway, picking herself back up and running again when the fire seemed to slacken. Though the Guardsmen lacked the indefatigable doggedness granted by the Scions' lifetimes of psychological conditioning, there were considerably more of them.

Atebe could hear the whip-cracks of Bissot's volley gun over the vox, slightly out of sync with the actual report as it reached her ears from below. Outside, a grenade burst amongst a group of Guardsmen, and Bissot scythed the survivors down as they dived for cover.

Atebe covered the distance rapidly, given space by the momentary slackening in enemy fire following the grenade's explosion, but was coming up on empty space. The building was missing a far wall, collapsed by artillery months earlier. 'We're running out of building, Tempestor,' she noted, slowing her pace.

'Then we displace again and continue to keep them occupied until Norroll takes the artillery.'

'And if he doesn't?'

'Let me be troubled by the "ifs", Atebe. Look to your training and perceive the victory as it will be. If all fails, die when and where I tell you.'

'Tempestor, aye.'

The floor ahead of her bowed downwards, and Atebe slid over the overhanging lip to drop onto the storey below. She sprang forward to bleed off her fall's momentum and landed a few yards ahead of Traxel and Bissot.

Traxel's plasma pistol flickered across Atebe for the briefest of moments as the Tempestor verified her identity. The three Scions dropped to ground level together, ducking low and forming a perimeter until Daviland and Phed caught up.

Phed limped, his movements ponderously wooden, though his

grip on his lasgun was strong and sure. The lower half of his cuirass was shattered, his abdomen held together by blood-stained wraps of tightly bound bandages. Intravenous drip bags festooned his armour, fastened to his pauldrons, chest and even his helmet, feeding fluids, nutrients, counter-pain narcotics and other substances Atebe had neither understanding of nor name for. Phed's face remained hidden beneath his visor and respirator, concealing any expression.

Bissot rose and opened fire again as Atebe took up a position in the next window. They fired into the Guardsmen blocking their path, volley gun and long-las crackling across the plain, dropping one with a wound beneath the left pauldron and sending another flopping backwards, nearly decapitated.

'A few more like that and this situation becomes a lot less complicated,' Bissot quipped.

'Still pretty complicated,' Atebe said, firing again.

They bolted out of the building and made for the cover of a Malcador Defender, chief amongst the preserved Leman Russ battle tanks and veteran Chimeras standing eternal watch over the fractured rubble of the academy's halls. Their pitted armour preserved beneath a layer of glossy green enamel, the venerable tanks brooded over the ruins from the campus' centre. Sheltering behind the Malcador, the eradicant opened fire on the Traitor Guard flanking around the ruin they had just escaped. In the face of the Scions' murderous fire, the troopers ducked back behind the cover of the building.

A bursting mortar forced the Xian Tigers from their cover. Daviland practically pulled Phed alongside her as they sprinted across a cratered and overgrown expanse of field, making for the cover of another ruin on the opposite side.

Bissot continued to fire into the advancing troops behind them, dazzling streaks of light puncturing armour and perforating the flesh beneath. With a heavy click, the volley gun ceased firing unbidden – though the specially modified barrels she had fitted it with could withstand the tremendous heat and stress of such sustained fire, the furious temperatures were sufficient to rouse the weapon's spirit to mutiny. Her weapon incensed to inactivity, Bissot turned and ran.

The Tempestus Scions burst into the ruins of another broad three-storey building, fronted by what had once been a spacious atrium. Shards of multicoloured glass carpeted the floor, and most of the structure's roof had collapsed during the bombardment, leaving it open to the sky. Despite the damage, it provided a handsome vantage point from which to defend.

Multi-laser fire burst across shattered rockcrete as three Chimeras' turret-mounted weapons opened up on the Scions' positions. Front-mounted heavy bolters roared, sending their deadly projectiles streaking into the ruins to explode in sparking clouds of shrapnel and dust.

The Scions returned fire at nearly the same moment, sending the dismounted Astra Militarum troopers ducking back behind the shelter of their transports.

'Respectfully, Tempestor,' Phed said, 'I request the Martyr's Gift.'

Traxel glanced at Daviland.

'We don't have time,' the medicae-adept said.

'How long does it take?' Phed asked.

'A few minutes, but–'

A Chimera shouldered its way onto the field, deploying a full ten-man squad of Rilisian troopers, led by a sergeant with a plasma pistol and improvised blade. A banner hung from the spiked trophy rack on his back – frayed black cloth marked with a crudely stylised eight-pointed star rendered in red paint. The squad's sergeant was bareheaded, and the same unholy sigil was carved into his forehead.

These Rilisians were no mere rebels, as had been Atebe's impression of them thus far – these troopers had truly renounced their oaths to the Golden Throne and put their faith in the Archenemy.

'Daviland, do it,' Traxel said. 'Atebe, Bissot, give them time.'

Bissot and Atebe flanked left and right, ducking and weaving between debris as they held tightly to the cover of the shattered walls. Shouldering her long-las, Atebe braved leaping up a nearly collapsed staircase to the second floor, exposing her to renewed fire. The wall overlooking the field below lay almost completely open, the sole cover a small lip of crumbling masonry protruding upwards from the first floor, but it was better than nothing. She crawled behind the shattered wall, giving the cameleoline of her ghillie cloak a few seconds to settle into the colouration of the surrounding rubble and dust.

Peeking around the fragment of wall, Atebe counted two infantry squads – seven personnel left, eight right – plus a five-strong command squad near the centre, spread out across the quadrangle.

She put her crosshairs in the centre of the scarified eight-pointed star on the leader's forehead and offered up a prayer to the God-Emperor. The traitor chieftain's skull exploded in a red mist. He collapsed in a boneless heap as his squadmates dived back behind their Chimera for cover.

The Chimera's multi-laser and heavy bolter opened fire on Atebe's position, pulverising her cover. She rolled left, tumbling back down the broken staircase and landing heavily on the rubble-strewn floor beside Traxel.

'*Nice shot,*' Bissot voxed appreciatively as the Chimera continued to pummel the second storey.

Atebe chuckled, giddy from the Scholam's Gift. Dopamine hummed in her brain's reward centres as dust rained down on her. Simultaneously, a flood of endorphins pushed aside the pain that flared in her lower back from her bad landing. 'Got me a bit more attention than I'd intended.'

Below, Bissot fired a four-round burst at the Traitor Guardsmen nearest her. It was the best she could manage with her volley gun without risking a catastrophic overheat.

'Praise the God-Emperor, Omnissiah and all the Imperial saints, it still fires!' Bissot whispered over the vox. One of the Rilisians dropped, three shots stitching up his torso. His fellows opened fire on her position, forcing her to duck behind the shelter of a cratered wall.

'Daviland, status with Phed?' Traxel demanded.

The first of the enemy's combat vehicles ploughed headlong through the wall. Stone crumbled and steel shrieked as the Chimera thundered into the building. Two others followed. Behind them, two additional Chimeras bottlenecked the gaping hole in the wall. Guard troopers poured from transport bays, cutting off any chance at escape through the lower level as they swarmed the ground floor.

'Ready, Tempestor,' Phed replied.

'Good,' Traxel said. 'Go.'

Phed dropped from above, hotshot lasgun blazing automatic fire as he plunged into the mass of enemy troopers. Las-bolts flashed in the dust, blasting the Scion's carapace armour open in a dozen places. Still firing, Phed collapsed into the rubble, brought down by a storm of las-rounds.

Almost simultaneously, Phed detonated, the implanted dead man's switch triggering the fifteen pounds of high explosives clustered about his body and obliterating the young Scion almost instantaneously. Those nearest the explosion were cut down by its force and the tempest of shrapnel hurled ahead of it. Cries of the wounded echoed through the roiling, choking cloud of dust left in its wake as the survivors scattered in blind panic, falling over one another in their haste to flee.

'Kill everything,' Traxel ordered. Chainsword revving, he dropped through the swirling dust into the crush of bloody, disoriented troops below.

The eradicant complied without hesitation.

XIII

Water seeped down the rockcrete surfaces of the walls, glistening in the faint green light of the Scions' slates monitron. It filled the network of tunnels beneath the academy, nearly knee-deep and rank with filth and the foetid remains of rat-gnawed corpses. It dripped from the ceilings, the faint splash of each droplet baffled and magnified by the claustrophobic confines to fill the entirety of the space with dribbling echoes.

Norroll led, followed by Durlo, Fennech and Akraatumo, while Rybak covered the rear with his plasma gun. They slid like shadows, silent but for the hushed purling of their legs through the water. Their monoscopes remained dark. Trusting in their training to see them through the rambling, flooded warrens, the Scions relied upon their helms' optics to pick up the faint reflection of their slates on the walls, portraying their surroundings in slightly hazy shades of green.

The artillery battery lay above them to the south. Many passages had collapsed during the war, costing the Scions valuable time when they found themselves forced to double-back and find a new way through the flooded darkness.

The enemy pursued them – they were certain of it. The sounds of seeping, dripping water masked their pursuers' presence as surely as it camouflaged their own, just as the host of swimming rats and bountiful colonies of microbial life surrounding the putrefying bodies fouled Actis' augurs.

Lapping water echoed quietly from the walls, at one point far behind them, now maddeningly close at hand, its source ever obscure. A faint scraping of steel on rockcrete whispered from one of the many side offices or narthexes lining the corridors, though whatever had caused it vanished before the Scions could locate it. A slight disturbance in the buoyant filth skinning the water's surface was the sole indication that anyone might have been there a moment before.

Norroll glanced back over his shoulder past Durlo, to where Fennech moved at the centre of the squad. The commissar's augmetic eye was almost dazzling in the darkness, bright like the first star in the evening sky. It illuminated his gaunt, lined face, rendering him in sputtering green light so that Norroll could plainly discern each detail of Fennech's taut features. A grin spread across the commissar's thin lips, growing broader with every strike and scrape that echoed from the shadows, seemingly entertained by the enemy's ham-handed psychological games.

Norroll drew a shuddering breath – the commissar's display of grim amusement was far more disconcerting than the enemy's clumsy intimidation attempts. He paused to collect his bearings, approximating where they were relative to where his internal compass told him the artillery lay.

The scraping began again, echoing down a hallway to the right as they arrived at a four-way intersection, though once again they saw nothing more than disturbed flotsam bobbing on the water's surface.

Norroll turned right at the intersection, but the passage ahead lay blocked by rubble. Around the corner, at the rear of the formation, Rybak snarled in a combination of pain and anger. Norroll glanced back to find the gunner irately panning his plasma gun down the hall they had just come from, his respirator and optics hanging askew.

'Rybak, shut up!' Akraatumo hissed.

'What happened?' Norroll whispered.

'Something opened my mask,' Rybak said, fumbling to refit the respirator and optics one-handed. 'I can't see anything.' He wiped blood from a deep laceration in the side of his face.

The Scions' formation collapsed in on itself, repositioning so that they had clear fields of fire down the hallway in three directions. Norroll and Durlo faced straight ahead and Fennech faced left, while Akraatumo faced rearward towards Rybak.

'Akraatumo, help him get his mask and visor back on,' Norroll said. 'Any way to get us through this collapse?' he asked Durlo.

'Not unless you want me to bring down a lot more on top of us,' Durlo replied.

Norroll scowled. They were terribly exposed in the junction, and he wanted them moving again as quickly as possible. 'Face about. If we go right at the next intersection, we should be able to–'

A dull thump echoed down the corridor ahead of the commissar, followed by a wet snap as a bright light smacked off the corner just above Fennech's left shoulder. The Scions reeled, momentarily blinded as their optics cut out to protect them from the glare. The magnesium flare splashed into the centre of the intersection, hissing and sizzling as it bobbed white-hot upon the surface.

The water in front of Rybak exploded, a flash of speed and motion lunging at the gunner as an attacker burst from beneath the surface of the foul murk. Rybak fired, his cry of rage transformed into a gurgling hiss as a wickedly serrated flensing blade was buried to the hilt in his throat below the chin. Plasma detonated against the opposite wall as Rybak collapsed, splashing backwards as the momentum of his killer's attack carried them both into the water.

The attacker was up in an instant, blades flashing like quicksilver as he pistoned into Akraatumo. Even blinded, the vox-operator was far from defenceless – all the Scions had been trained in blind fighting since childhood, forced to overcome murder-servitors and teams of bloody-minded penal legionaries alike in the darkened caverns beneath Abstinax. Though the traitor had surprise and disorientation on his side when he attacked Rybak, Akraatumo had more than enough time to react to his follow-up. The butt of Akraatumo's lasgun struck out like a staff, catching the wretched attacker in the mouth. The assassin's jaw shattered, sending him crashing back into the wall, spitting blood and teeth.

Las-fire streaked from the darkness in all directions, flashing with incandescent fury as it sparked from the Scions' armour. The enemy had managed to get around them, using their native familiarity with the catacombs to trap the eradicant in a T-shaped kill-zone, doubtless expecting to make short work of their trapped foes.

'Die in pain, apostates!' Fennech shouted as he charged the Traitor Guardsmen ahead of him, las-fire fizzing from his carapace armour and refractor field. His bolt pistol flashed, rocket-propelled rounds penetrating flak armour to burst in plumes of flame and clouds of blood. Lightning rippled across his power fist as he swung it at a trooper with a vox-set. The oversized gauntlet struck the man in the sternum, sending chunks of flesh, bone and shattered armour exploding back into the hallway with a resounding crash.

Durlo and Akraatumo leapt after the commissar, cutting apart the traitor Rilisians beneath a stream of rapid-fired hotshot rounds as they raked their lasguns down the length of the corridor on either side. Behind them, Norroll tossed a frag grenade into the passage to his right, sending the Traitor Guardsmen scrambling for cover in the seconds before it exploded.

Norroll swayed sideways, instinctively dodging as a blade flashed a hair's breadth from his throat. Rybak's killer was somehow back on his feet, drooling blood from his mauled jaw. His dual blades hissed through the air beneath Norroll's chin before he danced back out of the recon trooper's reach. Norroll lunged forward, feinting with his own blades, and elbowed his assailant in the face.

Knives clashed in the darkened corridor. Norroll managed to turn aside most of his opponent's onslaught, but what the Guardsman lacked in skill he more than equalled with sheer, bloody-minded intent. The vicious abandon of his attacks forced Norroll back towards the intersection and into the enemy's line of fire. Norroll jabbed with his right blade, then feinted left, noting the utter, desperate focus with which the traitor knife-fighter's attention flickered between his flashing monoblades.

Only the monoblades, though. Norroll blocked a brutal downward sweep, redirecting the energy into a riposte that cost the Guardsman half a step backwards. His enemy off balance, Norroll reversed the grip on his left blade and flipped it into the air above his opponent's head.

The Guardsman's eyes followed the blade up, and in the infinitesimal space of time between action and realisation, the Scion's empty left fist ploughed into his already shattered jaw.

Staggering backwards, the flenser's eyes went wide in momentary confusion as Norroll stabbed him beneath the chin in answer for Rybak's death, then deftly snatched his second monoblade as it fell.

Norroll was already moving as las-fire strobed from the tunnel network behind him, sheathing his second blade to draw his laspistol. Ducking low, he fired three shots in quick succession, caring little whether they struck true, so long as they gave the enemy pause. Brilliant flashes of light stuttered across the darkness ahead, flaring from the water-soaked walls as the eradicant and the enemy exchanged fire in the next junction. Water splashed around his knees as he ran, dragging at his already sodden boots. He willed aside exhaustion and pain, ignoring the screaming cramps seizing his calves and shins that would drop an ordinary man – such weaknesses were beneath one of the God-Emperor's Scions, and Norroll would sooner die than be overcome by mortal frailty. Teeth clenched, he pushed forward, water frothing as he sprinted down the corridor towards the flickering darkness.

Las-bolts streaked over his shoulder, Akraatumo's precision fire crackling past Norroll to bring down another of the traitors. A grenade burst down the corridor to his right as Norroll found his squadmates hunkering at the next junction. Durlo and Fennech poured fire into the corridor to either side of the intersection as Akraatumo shot over Norroll's head, covering the rear.

Bolt pistol empty, Fennech had drawn his holdout laspistol, though the weapon's ammunition counter already blinked amber. Norroll sloshed to a halt next to the commissar and offered him a fully charged powercell, which Fennech accepted with a quick nod.

Fennech ducked back around the corner as a salvo peppered the rockcrete wall. 'I was hoping you'd catch up,' he said. Blood dribbled from a fresh gash in his chin, though the old commissar seemed not the least perturbed by their situation.

'We need to break through this intersection and head right,' Norroll said, firing over Fennech's shoulder. A wild-eyed trooper in hastily patched flak armour, draped in some manner of pelt, splashed down into the mire with a smoking crater in his chest.

'Right seems to be where most of them are,' Durlo said. 'They knew which way we were going when they cut us off.'

'They're infidels, Trooper Durlo, not imbeciles,' Fennech chided. 'Though they have been perverted by the wiles of the Archenemy, they still retain the gifts the God-Emperor bestowed upon them, much like their Traitor Astartes masters.'

'I'm all for suggestions that will take us out of this,' Akraatumo said. He lay prone in the water, firing down the corridor behind them. A plasma bolt hissed over his head, streaking between Norroll and Durlo and bursting on the wall opposite.

'We're an eradicant,' Norroll said. 'Kill everything, figure out the rest after.'

Fennech grinned, baring his teeth. It was the first time Norroll had ever seen a smile reach the old commissar's good eye.

'Akraatumo, keep doing what you're doing,' Norroll ordered. 'Maybe try to kill the bastard who nicked Rybak's plasma gun. Commissar, head left. Durlo, follow me right on my mark.'

'Right with you, boss,' Durlo said.

Considering their circumstances, things were going better than expected.

Norroll had no idea how many traitors they had encountered in the catacombs – the darkness, close confines and mutable kinetics of the battleground were mercilessly unquantifiable. He had stopped attempting to hold the eradicant to any route or direction. He had likewise ceased any real notion of rational thought, abandoning all pretence of strategy or higher reasoning for the simple, mechanistic process of killing.

He had fallen into a dissociative hypomnesia, observing his own actions in some externalised, depersonalised manner in much the same way as he did his squadmates'. Blood sprayed from opened flesh and severed limbs as his blades cut, stabbed and parried, executing those three basic actions with the infinite variance dictated by the needs of the instant. There were times when he found himself marvelling at the simple efficiency with which the blades killed, before realising again that his own hands wielded them.

Commissar Fennech, Durlo and Akraatumo fought with the same unconscious efficacy as he did, any semblance of artistry eliminated in favour of simple, economical butchery. Whether by gun butt, blade or power fist, the eradicant epitomised its purpose as an agent of eradication. This was not battle the Scions engaged in; it wasn't even murder. Either abstraction required an emotional impetus, and the Scions fought with none, slaughtering the enemy with all the passion of abattoir servitors. The calculus of the situation had been gelled down into a simple binary equation: if the enemy came near, the enemy died.

In the confines of the meat grinder that had become the entirety of their world, the eradicant resorted to close-quarters fighting. Fennech deflected a power axe with his sword, the weapons sparking as their crackling energy fields repelled one another, before sending his power fist crashing through his opponent to paint the walls with ruptured viscera. Back to back with the commissar, Durlo used his lasgun as a staff, blocking attacks and cracking bone with savage counterstrikes to vulnerable, unarmoured areas. Slightly removed from the rest of the group, Akraatumo carved through the Traitor Guardsmen with his Scion blade. He engaged a group of traitors simultaneously, using a sequence of quick strikes to sever tendons and open veins, crippling one opponent seconds before dispatching another with the dagger.

Commissar Fennech had not been wrong – their foes were veteran soldiers. Trained and battle-hardened, the Rilisian Guardsmen had passed through a hellish crucible before their arrival at this moment. Despite their maddened glares and their scarified flesh, they remained a disciplined, well-drilled force.

They were as children to the Scions of Abstinax. Though they were biologically human, the doctrine by which the Tempestus Scions were raised had transformed them into something else entirely. Punishingly extensive developmental regimes and intensive programmes of psychobehavioural indoctrination had effectively divorced them from their parent species, leaving only the most vestigial elements of humanity clinging to them. Trained to physical perfection, mentally reconditioned to be ignorant of pain and fear and single-mindedly deadly, the Scions operated at a level so far beyond their opponents that their combat prowess might as well have been supernatural.

At range or close quarters, the expression of war was their language, for they fought and killed with the habitual fluidity of conversation. Akraatumo and Durlo attacked with effortless fluency, each strike, dodge and parry delivered with the easy aplomb of a seasoned debater arguing with children. In the elocution of war, however, Norroll and Fennech were master orators, each naturally gifted beyond native articulacy. Both were able to weigh the hostile crowd and convey an appropriate response – Fennech's audacious and brutally forthright expression complemented the canny foresight of Norroll's own discourse.

In their current state, the Scions would continue to kill until they received an order to stop, or either the enemy or exhaustion killed them. Their armour was soaked through with rank water, sweat and blood. As physical mechanisms, their bodies were bound to wear out at some point – Norroll fought to keep from shaking. His muscles cramped across his entire body, feeling as if they were shredding beneath his skin. While he could still feel the pain of his injuries and the febrile burning of lactic acid in his muscles, his psychological architecture, coupled with the lingering, nerve-deadening effects of the vitalotox, rendered him incapable of acting on it. His greatest hope was that they would soon simply run out of enemies to kill and be able to continue the mission, but the foe seemed inexhaustible.

Despite his age, Fennech appeared to be holding up best under the tremendous physical exertion. Norroll had no idea how much of the original commissar remained beneath his greatcoat – it seemed much of him was powered by the compact fusion generator he wore on his back. Fortified by the Officio Prefectus' fathomless strength of will, Fennech fought with power fist and power sword in tandem, the combination of brutal power and flickering speed ending any who came within his reach.

Fennech was shouting something and Durlo reacted, raising his lasgun as Norroll severed a Guardsman's hand at the wrist. A single Rilisian traitor darted towards them, bouncing from the walls with seemingly comical slowness as he somehow evaded Durlo's fire.

The Guardsman clenched a grenade's pull-ring between his teeth, and Norroll nearly laughed at the absurdity of it. The grenade was in his left fist, the top of the explosive fizzling like a firework as he wound up his arm to throw. Left foot planted, his right hand came up and his left arm snapped forward. He pitched backwards as one of Durlo's rounds struck him in his mouth, but the grenade was already tumbling down the corridor, vomiting a tail of smoke and sparks like a comet. It ricocheted from the wall to Norroll's right and bounced into the corridor behind him, just before the world ended in a rush of sound and hellfire.

'Keep it together,' Norroll whispered, trying to push Annigan forward.

'Cut my foot open on a stone back there,' Annigan hissed through his teeth. 'I think it sliced a tendon.'

'"Pain is an illusion of the body," remember?' Norroll said. 'Blood and sand'll clot up the wound, and we can clean it when we get back.'

Ahead of them, Actis turned around and waved for the pair to move forward. 'Come on!' he whispered urgently, though he had sense enough to not stop.

The queue of cadets behind them began to pass them by. Norroll wrapped his arm around Annigan and started to drag the boy forward through the scouring obsidian sands.

Annigan shrugged him off. 'Aiding another progenius is proscribed during the Path of Faith, Gry.'

'Then they'll have to kill us both,' Norroll said defiantly.

'Will we?'

A pit seemed to open in Norroll's stomach as the moment's recalcitrance withered.

Commissar Fennech loomed over Norroll, his face impassive as an alabaster effigy's. He held his bolt pistol loosely at his side, almost casually, the muzzle angled towards the ground.

'Forgetting oneself on the field of battle, however well intentioned, jeopardises the mission, Cadet Norroll,' Fennech said. 'If the God-Emperor smiles, it is only the transgressor who pays the price for indiscipline.' He raised a white-gloved finger. 'I have learned, however, that the Emperor rarely smiles.'

'"A round squandered is as two in the backs of your allies,"' Norroll said. The adage came unbidden – he had read it somewhere, once, but the source eluded him. 'Commissar,' he added quickly.

The other progenia filed past, their eyes fixed upon the tall dune ahead and away from the commissar and their fellows.

'So it is,' Fennech agreed. 'And so it is written, by Primarch Guilliman's own hand, no less. Very good, Cadet Norroll.'

The bolt pistol flashed up and fired. Norroll jolted as Annigan's blood spattered across his respirator's visor.

Blood dripped down Norroll's face as he gaped up at death.

'Allowances must be made for misfires,' Fennech said, and marched off.

* * *

Norroll awakened to the whine of hydraulics and the clatter of pebbles on cracking rockcrete. He struggled to breathe beneath the crushing pressure buckling his cuirass tight against his ribs and spine. The obsidian sands of Abstinax faded as sunlight streamed through Norroll's optics, washing his vision out in a flash of brilliant monochrome before his lenses could step down.

Blinded, Norroll blinked away tears as he attempted to clear his vision. The pressure on his back released suddenly and he could breathe again, sucking air through the clogged filters of his respirator. Still blinking, he looked up.

Fennech stood above him, shifting the slab of rockcrete that had crushed Norroll beneath it with the enormous hydraulic fingers of his power fist. He grimaced, his organic components straining under the tremendous weight borne by his augmetics. Fennech tossed the slab aside, freeing the recon trooper from the site of his premature burial. On either side of the commissar, Durlo and Akraatumo cleared debris.

Durlo hauled at a steel beam pinning Norroll's left shin. 'Can you move?'

Norroll rose with halting movements, attempting to assess his condition without causing himself further damage. 'Seems so,' he replied.

Akraatumo helped lift him to his feet.

Norroll tapped on his breastplate, the armour so badly dented, scoured and stained that it retained barely any of its original green colouration. 'God-Emperor's blessing,' he wheezed. His ribs, hips and shoulders burned. Though there was still little enough pain, he felt that all was not quite well with him internally. 'Are they all dead?'

'Yes,' Fennech said. 'Emperor be praised, the enemy grenadier did more damage to his own than to us. We eliminated the few remaining survivors before digging you out.'

Norroll nodded. 'Not that I'm unappreciative, commissar, but why *did* you dig me out?'

Durlo held up his slate monitron and shrugged. 'You weren't dead.'

'Would have been a waste, not having you along to draw fire for us,' Akraatumo said.

'It's good to be useful.' Norroll looked up to the sunlight streaming in through the hole above them, tapping a code into his wrist-slate. Actis awakened from where it idled in the corridor junction, its grav-impellors humming quietly as it rose up to the surface.

Norroll consulted the readings that scrolled across his vambrace. 'Emperor be praised, indeed,' he said. 'Seems that grenadier killed his friends and gave us a shortcut. We're less than three hundred yards south of the artillery position.'

'Your intent?' Fennech asked.

'We go up, kill the crews and turn this ambush on its head.'

XIV

Zheev leaned forward in his Chimera's command hatch, watching the mayhem unfolding in the ruins of the academy grounds through his magnoculars with a combination of fury and revulsion. Dust billowed from the ruins ahead, fresh insult to the injuries done there three months earlier. He could not see what was happening for the cloud but had no doubt of First Eradicant's involvement.

The lakrish root bobbed up and down between his lips as he chewed it. By defying orders, Traxel and his Scions had cost him an entire company at Pokol, and he had lost nearly two companies more trying to take it back. Strong as Zheev's desire to crush Hurdt's traitors into the dust was, he nursed a no less intense desire to see every Xian Tiger on Rilis executed for dereliction. The current battle at the academy only intensified this urge.

'Save some for me, Oleg, you old bastard,' he muttered, lowering the magnoculars. 'I intend to skin Traxel myself.'

Directly ahead, Attack Battalion, or what was left of it, led the charge down the academy's bomb-rutted thoroughfare. A column of Chimeras, with Major Raff's at its head, thundered towards the dust cloud at the academy's heart.

'Iron Zero to Attack Zero.'

'Go ahead, Iron Zero,' Raff said.

'What do you see, Attack?'

'Looks to be a major engagement up ahead, sir, but it's difficult to see what's going on through the dust. Something's got the traitors riled.'

Zheev grunted. 'Damned Scions, I'll be bound.'

'Likely. Colonel Mawr said they were heading to the academy's depot for resupply.'

'Wonder how they could want for anything, after the way they cleaned you out.'

After a long pause, Zheev felt compelled to fill Raff's guilty silence. 'I'm tempted to let Hurdt's turncoats have their way with them,' he said with a gallows bird's grin. 'But that would rob me of the pleasure of hanging Traxel myself.'

Multi-laser fire stitched across his Chimera's right flank, forcing Zheev to duck into the turret.

'Dammit!' Zheev cursed as a las-bolt crackled over his head. Heavy bolter fire hammered the vehicle's side armour.

Four Chimeras, armoured in Stygian black, roared from the motor pool, followed by twelve others in Rilisian ochre. The Stygians ignored Attack Battalion entirely, making directly for Zheev's command Chimera. The others peeled off, forcing themselves between Attack and the Stygians. Behind them, dismounted infantry poured from between the buildings, their heavy weapons teams readying mortars and missile launchers as the riflemen took their positions.

'Shit,' Zheev snarled into the inter-vox. 'Hard right, enemy Chimeras in the open.' Switching over to the regimental net, he called, 'Bear Zero, Cold Steel Zero, this is Iron Zero. Two-Hundred-and-Twelfth is making a move on Attack Battalion, and I've got Stygians inbound. Need immediate support at the south-west corner of the academy depot.'

'Acknowledged, Iron Zero,' Major Gunvaldt replied. *'Be advised, we are completing our flank action and approaching the northern bend of the Hukstrom.'*

Zheev pivoted his turret towards the Stygian Chimeras and opened fire with his multi-laser. 'It'll take you at least twenty minutes to get here, Gunvaldt.' He paused. 'Bear Zero, where are you?'

'Trying to extract three Chimeras from the river, Iron Zero,' Sarring said.

'Oh, for the love of the Throne!' Zheev shouted, shielding his face as the impact of a heavy bolter shell filled the turret with spall. 'They're Chimeras! They're supposed to be amphibious!'

'They were damaged. Took on water–'

'Leave them!' Zheev barked, wiping blood from his right eye. 'Balt and I can't manage against the Two-Hundred-and-Twelfth and a platoon of Stygians at the same time, Euri. Eat the losses and move, dammit!'

'Acknowledged, sir. Bear moving.'

A wave of nausea curdled in Zheev's belly as the black Chimeras closed. It wasn't fear – he had faced worse odds on half a dozen worlds – but something else, a vibration in the air that froze his marrow and sent his courage trickling away like water. A chill settled over him despite the heat of his Chimera, bristling the hair on his neck and arms.

The Stygian Chimeras accelerated around Zheev's vehicle, encircling it and insulating it against ready support from Raff's battalion. A ramp dropped and a team of Stygians rushed onto the tarmac, covering their comrade with the meltagun. The meltagun's shrieking beam slagged the command vehicle's left drive sprocket, bringing Zheev's Chimera to a shuddering halt.

A whisper, uttered with the hushed intensity of a secret bursting to be told, hissed at the edge of Zheev's hearing. He barely noticed it at first, distracted as he was by the Stygians surrounding his vehicle, but it persisted, a half-heard noise sibilating in his ears like tinnitus.

As it repeated, he began to understand it as a word – a name, perhaps, or a statement of intent in some foul tongue inimical to understanding.

Esh'laki'im.

'Everybody out!' Zheev shouted. 'Dekkan, Grelt, get that autocannon ready!' He punched the rear hatch's emergency release, firing his bolt pistol into the Stygian squad to their rear as the ramp clanged down.

A krak grenade bounced towards the Chimera, pinging gently as it cantered across the pavement.

'Move!' Zheev shouted, hurling himself headlong from the vehicle a moment before the grenade burst, sending shrapnel and fragmented track links whizzing from the blast.

Zheev crawled across the tarmac, keeping his head beneath the dazzlingly bright crossfire sizzling through the air scant inches above him. Behind him, a hotshot round caught his medic, Turmring, in the left side, punching through his flak armour. Firing his bolt pistol in the direction of the Stygians, Zheev grabbed Turmring under the arm and heaved him up and forward.

Autocannon fire roared from around the edge of the stricken command Chimera as Dekkan and Grelt opened fire, sending the sable-armoured troopers behind the shelter of their own vehicles.

A round struck Zheev in the centre of his back, knocking him from his feet. Burdened by Turmring's weight, the colonel struggled back up, cursing.

Something lumbered from the Stygian Chimera on uneven legs.

Esh'laki'im. Esh'laki'im.

The muzzle of its bolt pistol spat flame as the twisted Heretic Astartes fired into the fleeing Rilisians. Bolts spanged from flak armour or detonated on impact, pinning them to the ground. The Chaos Space Marine closed the gap, its horned battle helm nearly obscured by the noxious fume billowing from its gorget. Some manner of blade was fused to the twisted lump of jagged bone and barbed ceramite which had once been its fist. It keened hungrily, its hideous unlight leaving migraine-bright afterimages dancing unsteadily across Zheev's vision. The sword was a corporeal manifestation of pure nightmare, and Zheev held a hand before his eyes to block the sight of it.

The colonel raised his bolt pistol in defiance of the horror stalking towards him. The shot struck true beneath the tarnished iron of the distorted Adeptus Astartes' distinctively vented plastron. Externally mounted power cables crackled as the round bored through the more vulnerable flexible armour covering on the warp-gnarled Space Marine's abdomen and burst. Even for the genhanced physiology of an Adeptus Astartes, such a wound should prove almost instantly fatal.

The fiend staggered but did not fall, though its answering bolt-round went wide of the mark. Head down, it squared its shoulders and charged, drawing back its dreadful blade for a reaping strike.

The Heretic Astartes was dropped sprawling, punched off its feet by a salvo of autocannon fire from Dekkan and Grelt. The monster pitched over but scrambled clear with uncanny speed.

Zheev made the most of the brief respite, lugging Turmring as he dodged through the Stygians' resumed las-fire.

The heavy weapons team continued to pour fire on the warp-twisted Space Marine.

'Hold this,' Zheev said, handing Turmring his bolt pistol. Priming a grenade, he hurled it at the Stygians.

Though the frag grenade did little against the elite troopers' carapace armour, it had the desired effect, sending them instinctively ducking to avoid the shrapnel.

The monstrous Chaos Space Marine bellowed with two voices, its footfalls thundering across the cracked tarmac as it charged headlong at Zheev.

Zheev pulled a grenade from Turmring's belt pouch and sidearmed it at the furious Space Marine, bouncing it across the macadam as if he were skipping a stone across a pond. It detonated on the third bounce, practically between the twisted Adeptus Astartes' legs, though it scarcely slowed the accursed warrior's furious charge. Smoke bled from the flashing edge of the hideous blade as it parted armour and flesh, carving through two Stygians who stood in its path. The remaining black-armoured troopers fled, desperately attempting to gain space between themselves and the enraged juggernaut rampaging through them.

The heavy weapons crew pivoted their autocannon, stitching fire up the berserk Space Marine's torso. Craters burst open across the brute's armour as the force of the impacts spun it around, shattering iron-plated ceramite in bursts of black slime. The Heretic Astartes staggered and fell, skidding face first onto the ground as it collapsed.

The Space Marine vibrated where it lay, its movements appearing somehow out of phase with the world around it. A low, burbling sound, horridly reminiscent of weeping, or perhaps laughter, gurgled from it. Its body twisted and expanded, contorting unnaturally as irregular clusters of iron-shod, bony spikes speared through splitting ceramite. Power armour melted and flowed like wax, coalescing with the livid flesh and crackling bone beneath in a heaving, amorphic mass. Oily black blood flowed from rents between joints, hissing as it boiled away the pavement beneath in a cloud of rancid smoke.

Its right arm flailed, brass-taloned fingers scoring asphalt as they spasmed, knocking its bolt pistol spinning across the ground. Smoking vestigial wings tore free of the armour's backpack, twitching spasmodically as they shed blackened feathers of flame-edged iron.

Blood flowed from Zheev's nose as something burst behind his eyes. The whisper grew louder and louder, reaching a crescendo as the flickering blade pulsed and writhed in time to it like some hideous chant.

Esh'laki'im. Esh'laki'im. Esh'laki'im.

The Stygians ran in blind panic, order and discipline forgotten in the face of the incomprehensible, seething monstrousness of their erstwhile ally's transformation.

The Rilisians ran as well, sprinting into the depot's maze of containers and pallets as the monstrous Heretic Astartes struggled to its feet behind them. Zheev carried Turmring over his shoulders, at the rear of the group. The heavy weapons team abandoned their autocannon in their haste to flee.

The Iron Warrior stumbled, limping badly on asymmetric legs, its form swollen and further twisted. Its helmet fissured, drooling efflux and vapour as it split open across the front. Throwing its head back, it raised its infernal blade high and bellowed.

Esh'laki'im! Esh'laki'im! Esh'laki'im!

Zheev leaned against the warehouse wall, listening for any sign of pursuit. He could hear a formation of troops around the corner of the building and motioned the others to stay silent. It was a squad of guards, by the sound of them – several formations of Hurdt's traitors milled about the area, searching. Sticking to the shadows within the darkened warehouses, Zheev's squad had managed to evade their pursuers. It wasn't the first time Zheev had found himself hunted by a superior enemy force, and the old colonel knew that patience, stealth and silence made all the difference between discovery and death.

He waited silently for the patrol to pass by, before motioning for his squad to follow. It would only be a matter of time before the traitors subjected this warehouse to a more thorough search, and Zheev wanted to make sure they were long gone before that happened. They moved slowly, taking care to make as little noise as possible. Zheev led, followed by Trooper Egline, who carried Turmring, and Sergeant Horvich. Dekkan and Grelt brought up the rear, clutching their lasguns in white-knuckled grips.

They paused at the edge of the open bay doors, peering around the corner to see if the way forward was clear. Zheev shielded his face from the glare as the afternoon sun baked down on the depot. Heat hazed the tarmac and radiated from nearby plasteel cargo containers.

Zheev indicated they should hug the exterior wall of the warehouse as they slipped to the next one.

They had barely taken two steps when Egline, who held Turmring under the armpits, stumbled.

Within seconds, the Heretic Astartes exploded through the wall behind them, its malefic blade howling as it sliced apart Egline and Turmring at a stroke. The squad scattered, diving from the warehouse and sprinting away over the cracked pavement as lasfire split the air around them.

Behind them, the warped Space Marine roared, a gurgling bellow which seemed wrenched from the empyrean's very depths. It leapt after them, sometimes stumbling on two legs, sometimes leaping along on all four, its hoofed, misaligned limbs swollen to such an inhuman degree that its heaving musculature had ripped its armour open.

Zheev primed his last krak grenade and lobbed it towards the distorted Adeptus Astartes. The grenade bounced once and detonated almost directly in front of it. Intended for an anti-armour role, the blast tore the hulking brute's left pauldron free and fractured its plastron. The malformed beast staggered sideways in a gout of black ichor.

Claws gouged into the pavement as the Traitor Space Marine scrabbled. Armour panels rusted and split as the distended mutant laboured to its feet. The malignant warrior collapsed to one knee, black blood drooling from its wounds. The ground boiled and smoked beneath it as the monster propped itself up on its blade, using the weapon as a crutch to rise on its shivering legs.

'Doesn't the damned thing ever die?' Zheev shouted in disbelief, before diving for cover within the shelter of the next warehouse.

The Heretic Astartes steadied itself, smoke roiling from the joins in its armour as it drew up, swollen to its full height of nearly nine feet. Ceramite split and re-formed in new and twisted shapes as barbed hooks and spikes sprouted from its limbs. Ropes of black drool dripped as its vox-grille split and stretched into a gaping maw, revealing rows of blade-like teeth. The possessed Space Marine roared, the bony spars of its vestigial wings rippling the air about them as they glowed from within with a furnace's heat, smouldering the grass at its feet. The keening of the blade in its twisted left fist rose to a deafening wail.

'Do not look at the abomination!' Zheev ordered, his voice thick and wet as he fought back the urge to vomit.

Traitor Guardsmen rushed from behind their Chimera, their gleeful cries of thanksgiving mingling with the bellowing of their grim paladin as it tottered forward on mismatched, unsteady legs. They fired indiscriminately into the air or at the warehouse where the four surviving loyalists sheltered, whooping and braying as they chanted blasphemies with a joyous abandon.

'Esh'laki'im! Esh'laki'im! Esh'laki'im!'

Zheev's head swam, sparks dancing across his vision as pressure built inside his skull like a migraine. Sweat soaked through his fatigues beneath his greatcoat as sunlight blazed down from above with the sweltering heat of a kiln. His tongue swelled so he could scarcely breathe. The world began to spin.

A heavy bolter round struck the Space Marine in the chest. It stumbled backwards, crashing into the side of a cargo container. Unbalanced by the impact of the Heretic Astartes' massive, armoured bulk, the two containers stacked atop the first collapsed on the monstrosity.

Engines growled as four Chimeras smashed through the rubble at the southern edge of the facility, the report of their heavy bolters and multi-lasers throbbing across the ammunition dump. The leftmost Chimera raced across the field, closing on the Traitor Guardsmen with a feverish urgency. Its heavy flamer belched an inferno across the writhing heretics, immolating nearly half of them beneath a blazing carpet of jellied promethium.

Though much reduced, Attack Battalion had closed the traitors in its iron grip. The 212th scattered as the chatter of dozens of lasguns echoed across the depot, joining the chorus of heavy weapons from the Chimeras. On the opposite side of the complex, the Stygians withdrew and reconsolidated, quickly repositioning in the face of the new threat.

A platoon of Chimeras charged straight into the Stygians' position, weapons blazing, forcing the black-armoured troopers to withdraw towards their own vehicles. Boarding ramps dropped, and the loyalist Guardsmen ran to greet their former Stygian heroes with bayonets and gun butts.

The Chaos Space Marine staggered to its feet, clutching its chest as it shouldered its way free of the collapsed cargo containers. Oily black blood oozed between its fingers, igniting the pavement as it dripped to the ground. It sniffed the air, its horned head lolling to and fro on its cabled neck as it ignored the frantic battle raging around it. As if it had caught Zheev's scent, it lumbered forward, dragging its right leg and limping towards the warehouse where the colonel sheltered.

'*Iron Zero, this is Attack Zero,*' Major Raff called. '*Iron Zero, respond.*'

'I'm still here, Balt.'

'*Thank the Throne!*' Raff exclaimed. '*What is your position? We are– What in the hells is that?*'

'One of the Space Marines,' Zheev replied. 'If you can see it, you know my position.'

'*What is it, sir?*' Raff asked.

'Something that should not be,' Zheev admitted as he scrambled into the darkened warehouse. 'We need to bring it down or contain it.'

'Sir, run!'

Sergeant Horvich set himself between his commander and the miscreated Heretic Astartes, shouting his defiance as he unloaded his lasgun's power pack into it. Las-rounds stitched across ironclad battle plate and seared, warp-twisted flesh, all but ignored by the monstrous thing wearing the Space Marine's mutilated form.

The nightmare blade swept into Horvich's midsection, cleaving through his ribs and spine as it bisected his chest cavity horizontally.

The sergeant's sacrifice paid off, giving Zheev and the two survivors of his command squad an opportunity to escape. They ran, heedless of the battle raging about them, seeking to put as much space as possible between themselves and the mauled behemoth pursuing them.

XV

Norroll ducked behind a tarpaulin-covered steel container, narrowly avoiding the latest salvo of mass-reactives. Heavy bolter fire was relatively easy to keep clear of when it came from a fixed position. If it didn't get you when it opened up and you oriented on the muzzle flare, you could sprint and jink your way around it until you got close enough to kill it.

Crewed by veteran artillerymen who understood the importance of protecting their assets, the vehicles were not fixed. The drivers worked in tandem with their bow gunners, pivoting the artillery carriages to sweep heavy bolter fire across Norroll and the others.

Three artillery pieces, two Basilisks and a Deathstrike, laid down heavy bolter fire ahead of the assaulting Scions. While Norroll was certain they could make good use of the Basilisks' Earthshaker cannons, the Deathstrike was the real prize – regardless of the warhead employed, there was no chance that a Space Marine could survive it.

The eradicant had managed to cover the first two hundred yards without the enemy noticing, charging over the open, flat expanse of land unimpeded as the artillery platoon relaxed in the mid-afternoon sun.

If this deployment had reinforced anything for Norroll, it was that nothing good ever lasted.

The Scions weaved across the motor pool's expanse of cracked tarmac, sprinting between abandoned containers and rusting maintenance equipment as they approached their target. A round bigger than Norroll's fist slammed into Durlo's chest as he darted out from behind a flak-riddled maintenance shed, laying the demolitions trooper flat in a blast of armaplas spall and ceramite dust.

'Durlo?' Norroll called, ducking out of sight behind a rusty, burned-out barrel.

Durlo was already up and running again. He waved Norroll off. 'Fine,' he wheezed, rushing to the cover of a disabled Atlas recovery vehicle as heavy bolter rounds stitched across the pavement behind him, spanging heavily from the tank's side armour. The demolition vest he wore over his carapace armour was burst open and cratered through, slightly right of his sternum, the damage radiating out across his torso like a star. Beneath the flak suit, the ablative layers of his carapace had distributed the shock of the round's impact across his entire torso – a marvel of the Adeptus Mechanicus' art, the carapace armour was capable of withstanding multiple impacts from such strikes, even without the demolition rig.

'Only twenty yards to go!' Fennech called from the front, pulling them forward. 'Onwards!'

After the last week, twenty yards across open tarmac under heavy suppressive fire seemed no challenge at all. Fennech and Akraatumo went right, drawing the fire of the two Basilisks as

Norroll and Durlo bounded left. The artillery tank's crew stayed on them, opting to follow Norroll when Durlo peeled off and dived behind an abandoned cargo-8.

The moment the gun was off him, Durlo charged across the last few yards of asphalt to one of the Basilisks, firing on the move as the loader and commander pivoted into view. A round through the commander's cheek pitched him backwards onto the cannon's breechblock, while the loader was knocked spinning as a hotshot round blasted through the flak armour on his right shoulder. Vaulting up the ladder to the rear platform, Durlo kneed the loader in the face, smashing his helmetless head off the edge of the security rail.

Durlo clambered onto the guard plates protecting the upper track assembly, skirting around the Basilisk's tall shield along the right side of the tank as it pivoted after Norroll. With practised efficiency, he fitted a small, shaped charge to the turret – large enough to breach inside, but not significant enough to potentially damage the Basilisk's controls. Setting the timer for ten seconds, he slipped back across the track guard and behind the shield.

Durlo was moving the moment the charge detonated, leaping back over the track guard and throwing open the disabled hatch. The driver slumped over his controls, killed by shrapnel and the force of the blast directly above his head. Blood streaming from a head wound, the assistant driver clutched at his right ear, never even looking up before Durlo put a las-round through his skull and dropped into the driver's hole.

On the opposite side of the platoon, Fennech had taken a more direct approach. The commissar flanked around the right side of the second Basilisk and punched directly through the driver's front hatch with his power fist, immobilising the tank and simultaneously halting the gunner as the driver burst apart across the inside of the cab. Plunging his holdout laspistol into the hole he had just opened, Fennech dispatched the horrified gunner with two quick shots.

The Deathstrike's commander gave a strangled cry as Akraatumo leapt atop the vehicle.

'We surrender!' the lieutenant called through his open view slit.

From the hatch beneath the Deathstrike's augur system, the vehicle's fire controlman followed suit, repeating his commander's words over and over.

'Open the hatches and come out,' Akraatumo said down the barrel of his lasgun.

The lieutenant nodded his understanding and opened the hatch. 'We surrender,' he repeated.

'Thank you,' Akraatumo said, shooting the officer in the face. The top hatch clanged shut as the nearly decapitated lieutenant collapsed limply back down into the vehicle. Cursing, Akraatumo turned and shot the fire controlman as well, dropping him with a round to the throat.

Norroll finished the last two crew on the back of the Basilisk Fennech had just immobilised. The platoon's sole survivors were the driver and assistant driver of the Deathstrike.

Atop the vehicle, Akraatumo struggled to prise the hatch back open.

'I don't think I can get these two out,' he grumbled.

Fennech dropped from his Basilisk and climbed onto the Deathstrike. Grabbing the hatch with his power fist, he wrenched the aperture from its moorings and tossed it aside. He gestured down at the terrified driver within in mock invitation.

With a quick nod of thanks, Akraatumo shot the driver and assistant driver.

The Deathstrike's missile loomed above its gun carriage. Four auxiliary engines were arrayed about the main engine, providing it with more than enough power to deliver its payload intercontinentally. Though it was only a one-shot weapon, a Deathstrike with any warhead all but guaranteed that one shot was all that was required.

Firing a Deathstrike required the authorisation of a general officer. Absent that, only the sanction of the highest-ranking commissar on the planet would suffice.

Norroll glanced at Fennech – the God-Emperor indeed worked in mysterious ways.

'Durlo,' Norroll said, 'what's the warhead on the Deathstrike?'

Durlo glanced up from the hatch of his Basilisk to appraise the prodigious missile. 'Vortex,' he replied.

'Akraatumo,' Norroll called. 'Get the Tempestor on the vox!'

'Aye,' Akraatumo acknowledged. 'Tempestor Traxel, come in.'

'Akraatumo?' Traxel returned above the din of las-fire. *'Where are you? What's your status?'*

'We lost Rybak, but we've taken the enemy artillery, including a Deathstrike. Should be ready to fire in five.'

'Tell him we'll be ready to fire in three,' Norroll corrected, before he dropped down into the driver's hatch to pivot the tank towards the academy. 'And get us coordinates.'

'Norroll says we'll be ready to fire in three, Tempestor, and requests coordinates for fire.'

'The Iron Warrior is not at our location,' Traxel said.

'You're in luck, Traxel,' another voice interjected. *'Because I know exactly where the ugly bastard is.'*

Akraatumo glared suspiciously at his handset before casting a bemused glance towards Norroll and Fennech. 'Last station on vox, identify.'

'This is Iron Zero,' Colonel Zheev replied. *'I assume I'm speaking to First Eradicant.'*

'I… confirm, Iron Zero.'

'Where did they come from?' Norroll asked.

Akraatumo shrugged.

'Iron Zero,' Traxel said, 'What is your location?'

'Maintenance bays and storage sheds on the northern edge of the depot,' Zheev said. 'Saw what was left of your Taurox, so I assume you know the place.'

'I know it. Norroll, plot firing solution for our Taurox.'

'Hold your fire. He isn't at your Taurox, Traxel.'

'Do you have any means of marking the Heretic Astartes' position?' Traxel asked.

'Got a rangefinder,' Zheev replied. 'Just need to get in a position to use it.'

'Actis can relay the coordinates once the colonel's marked the target,' Norroll said.

'We have a servo-skull which can relay your coordinates, Iron Zero,' Akraatumo reported. 'With your permission, Tempestor.'

'Do it.'

Norroll keyed in a command on his vambrace, sending Actis speeding across the motor pool towards the maintenance bays on the opposite side.

A squad of Traitor Guardsmen lay between Zheev and a low tower of stacked containers at the far end of the darkened maintenance facility where he, Dekkan and Grelt sheltered. The traitors were visibly spooked, jumping at shadows in the gloom. They knelt in a rough semicircle fifteen yards away, shouting incoherent warnings to one another and opening fire at the foes they imagined lurked about them.

Their random fire proved a blessing to Zheev and his survivors, who traced the flashes back to the source to eliminate three of the traitors before they were even fully visible. When the colonel and his troopers finally burst from the shadows, the traitors were so disoriented that they could not properly coordinate a response to the close-in threat. A las-round, fired with more luck than skill, knocked Zheev back half a step as it cracked against his carapace armour. Righting himself, he lowered his head and barged into them.

Zheev came in low with his chainsword, catching a Guardsman under the midriff. He pulled the snarling blade free and continued past without stopping, drawing a section of the traitor's entrails out until the churning teeth severed the viscera entirely. Another Guardsman, a medic by the bloody helix artlessly daubed onto the ragged white cloth he wore on his right shoulder, exploded as a bolt punctured his sternum, showering his fellows with his steaming remains.

Dekkan and Grelt followed their commander, striking with gun butts, knees and elbows as they bludgeoned through the mass of traitors. They clubbed and kicked, driving a wedge through the semicircle of enemy fighters until they were clear.

Zheev's chest heaved, heart straining to burst. His breath sawed in and out of his mouth as he clambered to reach the summit of the stacked containers. The colonel had left his youth behind decades ago, and the previous six years of his retirement had softened him. Wiping the sweat from his eyes with the sleeve of his greatcoat, he willed his weakness aside and climbed higher, resolved that if he were to meet his end, it would be in the Emperor's name.

Daylight and smoke poured through the maintenance bay's gaping doors, which opened to the thunderous combat outside. The command squad climbed higher, struggling beneath the weight of their armour and gear as they strove for the topmost container.

Outside, Raff's battalion had put itself between the malignant Heretic Astartes and the maintenance bays. Las-fire cracked and heavy bolters rumbled, the din of battle all but drowned beneath the baleful howl of the possessed Space Marine as its armour turned their fire aside. That it could still move and kill despite all the damage it had suffered was remarkable. What remained of the transhuman warrior had practically melted into a lurching, bipedal mass of oozing black sludge and smoke, with only rust-encumbered fragments of shattered ceramite remaining to reveal what it had been. Its blade keened as it killed and killed again, reaping down all before it as it limped towards the maintenance facility where Zheev sheltered.

Zheev pulled Grelt up onto the uppermost container. 'This is going to have to do,' he panted. 'Mark it.'

Grelt drew his rangefinder from a belt pack and crawled towards the edge of the container. Despite his exertion, he held his breath as he would before marking a shot for Dekkan, aiming the laser marking tube towards the rampaging Space Marine and depressing the button. The marker left nothing visible on the monstrous Heretic Astartes, but Zheev knew it would be luminous to any targeting augurs.

Norroll listened to the twin battles being fought across the academy grounds and wondered why it was taking so long for Actis to reach Zheev's location. He glanced at the chronometer on his vambrace display and noted it had been less than a minute, far too little time for the servo-skull to cross the distance.

He joined Fennech on the loading platform as the commissar set an artillery shell into the Earthshaker's breech.

'You've taken charge here readily,' Fennech observed, locking the breech closed with a clank.

'Fell to me, I suppose.'

'You could have left it to me.'

Norroll scoffed. 'You'll forgive me, sir, but no. I found my last time under your command chafing.'

'Abstinax?'

Norroll nodded. He hopped down from the loading deck to grab an artillery round from the stack behind the Basilisk.

'I suspected as much.'

'You don't remember?'

The scars on the left half of Fennech's face puckered beneath his augmetic eye. 'No. I learned very quickly that it profited me nothing to retain the names of my surviving progenia following selection. The only cycle I can recall in its entirety is my first, and with Tempestor Ezl's passing, Tempestor Traxel is the last of those.'

'Traxel was one of your first?'

'He holds a grudge. I was most particular during my first cycle.'

Norroll placed another artillery round on the stack. 'I thought that was the effect you had on everybody.'

Fennech's laugh made the hairs on Norroll's arms stand up. It was deep and hollow, quite unsuited to conveying mirth.

Shaking off his trepidation, Norroll placed another round in the stack on the loading deck. 'May I ask you a question, commissar?'

'You may.'

'Do you recall Mierich Annigan?'

'No.'

'"A round squandered is as two in the backs of your allies,"' Norroll said.

Fennech's eye narrowed. 'The Path of Faith,' he mused. 'That was you, during my last cycle on Abstinax. The progenius willing to die for his friend.'

'That was me.' Norroll glanced down at his vambrace as gunfire and explosions continued to echo from the academy grounds. 'You killed him, then reminded me that allowances must be made for misfires.' Norroll's vambrace pinged as targeting data scrolled across the face of his slate monitron. He touched the data-slate, transmitting the coordinates to the others.

Behind the neighbouring gun, Akraatumo flashed Norroll a thumbs-up. 'Ready.' Per Traxel's coded instruction, the vox-operator had shifted to a different frequency so the 139th could not eavesdrop.

'Tempestor, we have received Iron Zero's targeting coordinates.'

'Use the Basilisks to soften up the target area, then fire for effect with Deathstrike,' Traxel said.

Norroll glanced up at Fennech. The commissar shook his head.

'Confirming, we are to fire on friendly forces?'

'That sounded like a question, Norroll.' Traxel's voice crackled across the signal. *'Is there a problem?'*

'No, Tempestor. Just making allowances for misfires.'

'Do you have the coordinates loaded?' Traxel asked.

'Aye, Tempestor,' Norroll replied.

'Then fire.'

Hurdt was thrown sprawling. Shrapnel clattered against his carapace as the force of the exploding Chimera knocked him from his feet. Instinct sent him back up and diving for cover.

An uncanny silence seemed to have fallen over the battlefield. When his helmet's audio filters finally disengaged, Hurdt could hear the grumbling of nearby Chimeras' engines above the high-pitched whine ringing in his ears. His guts vibrated, as if his insides had attempted to become his outsides.

Sheltering behind the smouldering remains of a Chimera, Hurdt sensed that all fighting had, for the moment, ceased. He looked around dazedly, searching for anything which might tell him what had just happened. Everything visible through the obscuring ochre dust cloud, traitor and loyalist, Stygian and ranker alike, was covered with a dense layer of dun grit. But for the patches of dark blood soaking through the powder, everyone appeared remarkably uniform.

Hurdt clutched at his fractured thoughts.

Earthshaker round. Had to be.

He couldn't see Matebos for the cloud of dust that billowed across the field. The momentary relief was quickly replaced by dread – if he couldn't see the warped Iron Warrior, there was no telling where he was.

A quick rush of air was the only hint the second Earthshaker round gave before it burst, perhaps two hundred yards away, still close enough for him to feel the blast. Flames glowed through the dust cloud as more Chimeras burned.

'General?' someone called from over Hurdt's right shoulder.

Hurdt drew his laspistol as Corporal Demitrus, his driver, rounded the rear corner of the Chimera the general sheltered behind.

Hurdt put up his weapon. 'Demitrus?'

'Sir, come on!' Demitrus said, grabbing Hurdt by the shoulder and pulling. 'This way!'

To Hurdt's surprise and relief, it seemed his entire command squad was still alive, if not wholly intact. Blood soaked through the dust coating Surges' and Hesturm's fatigues in several areas. Enterich, his medic, applied pressure to a deep wound which had rendered his own left arm useless. Captain Ketch, Hurdt's adjutant, and Sergeant Garrigo, the division's vox-operator, received status reports as they ran.

'What's going on?' Hurdt asked.

The group staggered as a third Earthshaker punched through one of the maintenance bays, tearing the structure apart in a rapidly expanding fireball.

'We're getting out of here, sir, is what's going on!' Ketch said.

Visibility improved as they fled the impact area. Hurdt could see movement now, as the surviving troops on both sides staggered to their feet and took to their heels. Nobody fought – troopers on either side with enough presence of mind to do so simply attempted to flee. Even the most fanatical of the twisted wretches under Hurdt's command staggered about in aimless disorientation.

The division's colours drooped, singed and ragged, in Hesturm's grip. Light reflected from a ragged bit of golden thread at the standard's tattered edge, catching Hurdt's eye – the general had cut the gold fringe from the flag himself following the massacre of the senate, when he had declared against the Imperium. He gaped at the threadbare remains of his once-proud banner, tasting blood and ashes as judgement fell on the Third Division.

With a lowing groan, Matebos staggered upright behind them. Smoking black ichor poured from the innumerable wounds delved deep into the foul amalgamation of ceramite and daemonic flesh. His right arm had been torn free at the shoulder, and his head hung askew, lolling limply with every tottering step he took on visibly broken legs. How the Heretic Astartes had even survived beggared belief, for surely even the Emperor's Angels had limits to their endurance.

Plumes of black smoke twisted from the Iron Warrior's broken wings. There was nothing angelic in Matebos – rather the converse.

Ketch dragged Hurdt forward. 'Come on, sir!'

Matebos swayed, oily black blood soaking through the thick layer of dust enveloping him. His form stuttered as whatever force kept him standing struggled to maintain its presence in the material universe. His semblance flickered between images – he staggered, now appearing as a blood-smeared and terribly wounded warrior of the IV Legion Astartes. A fraction of a second later, and Hurdt saw the massive chimerical beast that lay at the core of his blade – an iron-hooved horror defying any notion of natural parentage, its flaming pinions fluttering above a rippling skin of iridescent scales and bony, reptilian knobs. It fluctuated between the two aspects as materiality and unreality warred, overlapping and twisting about one another. The sword in its left talon shredded existence itself upon the ghastly singularity beneath its surface.

Matebos turned, its head lolling from its crippled neck. The Iron Warrior slewed drunkenly towards the loyalist troopers, like a broken puppet pulled along by the daemon-thing ensnaring his soul. It limped, growling in frustration at its host's mortal weakness.

Zheev's surviving loyalists opened fire, the fury of the Earthshaker's explosion forgotten in the face of the manifest nightmare stumbling towards them. Hurdt's Guardsmen likewise opened fire on Matebos with panicked abandon – it seemed there were some extremes beyond countenancing. The animosities of riven brotherhoods fell aside before the unnatural menace as traitor and loyalist Rilisians fought side by side against a foe hungering for their deaths.

The possessed Space Marine bellowed and charged, all semblance of restraint or sanity lost as the hulking brute tore into whatever it encountered with howling abandon, murdering all in its path.

'Zheev!'

The daemon's cry startled Hurdt, forcing him to stumble.

Slicing free of the Guardsmen, it staggered across the field towards the maintenance bay and collapsed. Chunks of ravaged armour and flesh rained from its smoke-shrouded mass. It crawled forward, dragging the sparking, smouldering remains of its broken-winged power pack behind it on partially fleshed lengths of conduit. Black blood drooled and sputtered from its trap-jaw mouth as Matebos pointed at a distant figure with the tip of its blade.

'Zheev! Esh'laki'im comes!'

Ketch dragged Hurdt up by the pauldrons. 'Run, dammit!'

Matebos, or whatever remained of the Iron Warrior, boiled from within as the tether holding it to this reality frayed. It disintegrated as it struggled forward, bearing the daemon blade as if it might lead the possessed Chaos Space Marine to Zheev, as a dowsing rod might take a parched man to sweet water.

The roar of powerful engines overhead drowned all other sound. Ketch was screaming, but Hurdt could barely hear him.

'Run!'

A moment later, the world behind them vanished in a flash of migraine light and fury.

XVI

Norroll and his team trudged across the cracked tarmac, towards the crater where the depot's maintenance bays had been. Though they remained alert to any threats, none moved against them – in the wake of the artillery bombardment and the detonation of the Deathstrike's vortex warhead, it seemed unlikely that any remained.

The recon trooper's feet felt heavy as he walked, his steps cumbersome. Being wounded and run ragged beyond the point of exhaustion for weeks at a time was nothing unusual for him. You got used to it, if it was anything that you could ever really get used to. This was something else.

The Deathstrike had eliminated all that lay within its blast radius. Nothing remained of the maintenance area, save for a disconcertingly precise, concave crater, perhaps two hundred yards in circumference and three yards deep at its nadir. The warp bubble had sucked the entire impact zone, including corpses, vehicles and even buildings, into the empyrean before collapsing in on itself. A wonder of destructive efficiency, the vortex had consumed all within its reach. No evidence remained that the Iron Warrior, or indeed anyone else within the vortex's circumference, had ever existed – allies and enemies alike had been cast into the warp.

Norroll was relieved the warhead had functioned properly, collapsing the vortex back in on itself following its detonation – he had heard tales where they lingered, meandering across the battlefield to devour all in their path.

On the far side of the crater, Atebe sat with her back to them, stripped to the waist but for her sleeveless white undershirt, her tight blonde cornrows stark against her ebony skin in the late-afternoon sunshine. A spinal traction machine wrapped around her midsection like a corset, intermittently giving off a burring, mechanical whine as it stretched her vertebrae apart. She rocked forward and back, side to side, working her slipped discs back into place with the machine's aid. She held her left leg out in front of her, flexing her knee and working her foot similarly to the movement of her torso.

Bissot sat cross-legged beside her, singing quietly to herself as she looked down one of the barrels of her disassembled volley gun. Like Atebe, she went unhelmed, instead opting to wear her dark green beret over her close-cropped black hair. Unlike Atebe, she still wore all her pitted, blackened and cracked carapace armour, whatever remained of its original green almost completely obscured beneath a heavy layer of umber dust and grime. She swung the barrel towards Norroll, looking through it like a telescope, and graced him with a wry smile before rising.

'Commissar,' she said coolly with a dip of her chin.

'Trooper Bissot,' Fennech said. 'Where might I find the Tempestor?'

Bissot gestured over her shoulder towards the blasted area on the opposite side of the crater, and Fennech departed.

Norroll unsealed his helmet, carefully peeling the suction cups holding his visor to his eye sockets free before lifting it off. After several days in an all-encompassing helm, smelling his own sour breath and consuming nothing but nutri-paste and reclaimed water, the simple comfort of a light breeze and daylight on his skin seemed a luxury. Despite the overpowering odours of blood, excrement and the lingering tang of explosives, he drew in a deep draught of air. He fished a protein wafer from a pouch on his belt and bit off a third of it.

Bissot licked her index finger and wiped it around the threading for her lower barrel. *'Bless the binding and the threading, that barrel and receiver join true,'* she prayed. *'Bless my hands as I twist these four and twenty turns of the barrel, as it is written in the Manual of Maintenance and Operation, that I might guide it aright and strip not the threads on reassembly. I turn, turn, turn, turn, turn…'*

Norroll stuffed the rest of the protein wafer into his mouth, chewing noisily. 'When did the Hundred-and-Thirty-Ninth show up?' he mumbled.

'Right on cue,' Atebe said over her left shoulder. 'A battalion of them, like the Emperor Himself dropped them onto the battlefield. They kept that thing occupied long enough for you to kill it with fire.'

Norroll unscrewed his canteen's cap. 'Thing?'

'The Heretic Astartes,' Atebe said. 'Or what was left of him.' She shook her head. 'I didn't see it, though the Tempestor says it's just as well most of the battalion died in the bombardment.'

Norroll took a gulp from his canteen. The tang of the chemically purified water was unpleasant, but it helped to banish the taste of the protein wafer. 'Matter of time for the others, I suppose.'

Atebe shrugged. 'The Tempestor is over there.'

Norroll screwed the cap back onto his canteen and took his leave of them.

It seemed a handful of Guardsmen had managed to escape the bombardment and the Deathstrike's all-consuming detonation. Smeared in blood, Daviland worked at a hasty field surgery station she had established on the right edge of the crater, where survivors hauled the wounded.

Durlo had joined the medicae-adept while Norroll and Atebe had been talking, fetching tools and supplies as Daviland required. While he was technologically adept, Durlo was no medicae, and Norroll doubted he provided her with much more than an extra set of hands and moral support. The surviving combat medics from Attack Battalion helped as best they could, either through triage or direct assistance, but there were only four of them, the odds stacked entirely against them by the sheer number of casualties in so small a place.

Norroll left them to their work, unsure what Daviland was trying to accomplish. Mercy, if that's what this was, was unlike her – from what he had inferred from Atebe, these troopers would be better served if the eradicant simply lined the survivors up in a row and executed them. Faster, anyway.

Norroll found Traxel and Fennech in calm discussion at the far edge of the vortex crater. Akraatumo had joined them, the vox-operator taking his position by his Tempestor's side, speaking into his unit. He shook his head and gave Traxel the handset.

Traxel stood emotionless and expressionless as Norroll approached, his chainsword sheathed and plasma pistol holstered. He listened to the handset, saying nothing. When the transmission concluded, he handed the field phone back to Akraatumo. Facing south, he stared forward, gaze flat and expression inert as he entered a micro-trance.

Norroll considered doing the same but reconsidered. From the south, a chorus of throttling promethium engines rumbled, growing louder by the moment as they approached the ruins of the maintenance depot. The mechanised column ground forward before a billowing cloud of dust, the clanking tracks and chugging exhaust of the regiment's approach echoing hollowly from the remaining, ruined maintenance bays to fill up the area. They moved at full speed, a formation of Chimeras in the flat ochre paint scheme of the Rilisian forces, crashing through debris, shouldering aside containers and battering through collapsing walls in their haste.

The Chimera at the head of the formation ground to a halt ten yards away. Heat haze shimmered above the vehicle as Lieutenant Colonel Sarring stormed from its rear hatch, shoulders squared and head thrust forward. Her gait was rapid, though she stifled a limp.

'God-Emperor damn you, Traxel!' she snarled, spittle flying from her lips. She brandished an accusatory finger at the Tempestor. 'Who in the hells do you think you are?'

Traxel did not answer.

'How many more of my people have to die for your victory?' Sarring spat. 'You lost us the Pokol Armoury and a full company from Attack Battalion. We took heavy casualties taking it back, and the traitors were able to break contact and escape back into Vytrum!'

Though she was considerably shorter than Traxel, her eyeline level with the Tempestor's clavicle, she stood inches from him, her gaze boring hatefully into the haggard, vacant mask of his face. She flung her arm out to the side, gesturing to the eerily precise crater behind her. 'And now you've wiped our regimental commander and the rest of Attack Battalion out of existence, you son of a bitch! What next?'

Traxel appeared utterly unmoved by her distress, if indeed it registered in him at all.

'Your orders were to secure Pokol Armoury!' she shouted, her voice on the edge of breaking. Several of Attack Battalion's survivors looked up at Sarring's outburst. 'And you,' she said, pointing to Fennech. 'You're no better. Where was the Officio Prefectus' vaunted discipline when a rogue element was introduced to the senior ground force commander's battleplan?'

'My orders, received via my Tempestor-Prime from Lord General Trenchard, were to secure this world by whatever means necessary, colonel,' Traxel said. 'Securing Pokol Armoury was immaterial to those orders, and Commissar Fennech concurred with my assessment. Once we learned of the Archenemy's involvement with the traitors, the extermination of these Heretic Astartes became our singular priority. Their elimination cuts the head from this rebellion.'

Sarring closed her eyes, calming herself with a long, shuddering breath. When she opened them again, she had regained a modicum of control. 'Given your track record since you made planetfall, I'm beginning to wonder which side of this conflict you're on.'

'My service is to the God-Emperor alone.'

'I'm sure He finds your methods unimpeachable,' Sarring said bitterly.

'Be careful, Colonel Sarring,' Fennech cautioned.

'Was the immolation of Attack Battalion worth it?' she demanded. 'Was Colonel Zheev's?'

'Colonel Zheev's sacrifice has ensured the destruction of a far greater threat,' Traxel said. 'We have destroyed two of the three Iron Warriors on this planet, colonel, yet that does not seem to enter into your calculus of victory.'

'What good is a victory if there are no victors?'

'Take such questions up with the Inquisition when it arrives, colonel, and rest assured it will,' Traxel said. 'The lives of the soldiers who fought here were forfeit the moment they laid eyes upon that accursed Iron Warrior. You are fortunate that you did not arrive with them, or you would join them on the pyre.'

Sarring gaped, the inhuman callousness of Traxel's words striking her like a visceral blow. Her lips drew back in disgust, trembling over her bared teeth. 'Throne of Terra, what is wrong with you?'

'I would ask the same of one so overwrought,' Traxel said. 'How can this whingeing possibly serve the martyrs here?'

Sarring drew her laspistol and took aim at Traxel's face in a single, rapid movement. 'Whingeing?' she hissed, tears flowing down her cheeks. 'You call this whingeing? You bastard!'

Fennech's bolt pistol was up equally fast, its barrel level with Sarring's head. 'Lower your weapon, Colonel Sarring,' he commanded.

Sarring glanced between the Tempestor's dead-eyed gaze and the commissar's balefully cold one. Her expression transitioned from shock, to disbelief, and finally to resignation in the span of a few heartbeats.

'I wonder if this was what it was like for the Enth veterans, when the Fire Angels brought Oranesca Hive tumbling down around their ears,' Sarring said.

Fennech's bolt pistol struck Sarring's face with a furious crack, sending the officer crashing to the ground.

The commissar kept his sights levelled on Sarring's forehead as she struggled to sit up. 'You walk perilously close to apostasy, colonel.'

Sarring glared hatefully up at him, blood streaming from her lacerated right cheek. With a defiance that Norroll found strangely admirable, she retrieved her laspistol from the ground and holstered it.

'Hold to your faith in the God-Emperor,' Fennech said down the length of his bolt pistol. 'He has abandoned neither Rilis nor you.'

Sarring wiped her bloodied face with a filthy, gloved palm as she rose. She looked out over the battered survivors of Attack Battalion, now consigned to death for whatever horrors they might have witnessed, and flexed her tightly clenched jaw. 'You can lower that now, commissar, if you please. I've had my fill of blasphemy for the day.'

With a nod, Fennech lowered his bolt pistol, though he did not holster it.

'So,' Sarring sighed. 'Where do we go from here?'

Deliberations began almost immediately.

Through dint of seniority, Sarring succeeded Colonel Zheev as Rilisian senior ground forces commander, a position she had never expected nor ever desired to hold. As planning for the operation continued, she found herself wishing more and more for the slow, sheepish grin that inevitably revealed itself from beneath the mantle of Zheev's frequent admonishments. She very much needed advice from her old mentor and commander.

Fennech held his bolt pistol at the ready, prepared to intercede should the two loyalist commanders become violent. Beyond the commissar's punitive threat, though, he proved invaluable in developing the tactical framework of an operation spanning two separate fronts.

Despite his striking her earlier, Sarring had released much of her rancour towards Fennech – she had let her emotions get the better of her, and in so doing wandered perilously close to heresy. That he had not executed her on the spot for such a transgression communicated volumes. Sarring found the venerable commissar patient, perhaps even charming, in an old-fashioned sort of way. He seemed to observe everything with that one icy-blue eye of his. Sarring noted more than once how his grip on his bolt pistol instinctively tightened when she raised her voice or her bearing became too aggressive, so she adjusted her demeanour accordingly.

She noticed that Fennech focused more upon her behaviour than upon Traxel's, likely because there was no real sense of *anything* from the Tempestor. Sarring had seen servitors with more personality than the eradicant's commander. He barely seemed to move, scarcely blinking as he delivered his recommendations and suggestions with a dispassion that appeared more mechanically scripted than developed by a human mind. The Scions flanking him, Akraatumo and Norroll, were similarly passionlessly inert – automata attending a senior construct until commanded otherwise.

There was significant contempt for the Ordo Tempestus amongst the Astra Militarum's rank and file, and Sarring was beginning to understand why. She had never interacted with any Scions she had shared the battlefield with before now. While Sarring had never met, or even seen, one of the Adeptus Astartes, she wondered whether she might find more humanity beating within the twin hearts of one of the Emperor's Angels of Death than she found amongst the Scions of First Eradicant.

Sarring's surviving cadre of officers and sergeants, along with the remaining seven Tempestus Scions and Fennech, clustered around a hasty sand table constructed by a pair of Sarring's Guardsmen, once surveyors in the capital before they had been pressed back into the Emperor's service. They had created the schematic from memory, using the abundance of scrap and rubble to build a crude but illustrative layout of Vytrum's city centre.

'Where is our Valkyrie?' Traxel asked Akraatumo.

'En route, sir. Estimated arrival time, ten minutes.'

Traxel nodded. 'That lets us hit them first and keep the Stygians off your backs while you drive into the city centre and get stuck in,' he told Sarring.

'What of the Iron Warrior?' Norroll asked, suddenly animated from his apparent torpor. 'We've been discussing ingress plans and order of battle, but we seem to be skirting around the main issue.'

'Our most recent intelligence placed him at the Stygian compound,' Sarring said. Using a length of antenna, one of her surveyors indicated the Chimera transmission used to represent the location. 'Given the challenge posed by the other two Traitor legionaries, I am granting First Eradicant specialised explosives to reduce the facility and bring the compound down around his head. Once you locate him, set the charge and get out before it goes off – you absolutely do not want to be in the vicinity when it detonates. On the extremely limited chance it doesn't kill him outright, it should certainly soften him up enough to make finishing him easier.'

'What type of charge will we be using, colonel?' asked Durlo, the Scion in the battered demolition oversuit who had been fidgeting with a gold coin the entire briefing.

'Godshaker Type-238 with a three-kilo warhead.'

The coin rolling across Durlo's knuckles stopped moving. 'We're to employ a tactical atomic weapon in your own capital city?'

'Do you want this bastard dead or not?'

Durlo shrugged. He scratched thoughtfully at the dark stubble on his chin, glancing to Traxel and Fennech before looking back to Sarring. 'And you are authorised to employ this weapon?'

'In the absence of the planetary governor or the planetary congress, as Rilisian senior ground forces commander, I can authorise pretty much whatever the hell I want.'

The gold coin pinged into the air.

'If you're certain, colonel,' Durlo said, snatching the coin. 'You can't put it back in the box once it's out.'

Sarring didn't reply immediately. A Tempestus Scion, of all people, was reminding her of the gravity of her decision.

Durlo's question left her an open door. She had as much authority to call off such a dreadful attack on her own soil as she had to authorise it. The Scion was quite right – whatever else happened, once they detonated such a weapon, there was no going back. History would recall her as the first commander to order an atomic strike on a Rilisian city area since the days before the Imperium.

Then the hatred roiled back, sweeping in and dragging her down beneath its black and bitter tide. Hatred for the traitors who had ruined her world and taken her family from her. Hatred no less stark for those weak-kneed bureaucrats who refused to recognise Hurdt's rebellion for what it was before it was too late to stop it. Hatred for the damnable Fire Angels who had driven Hurdt and his traitors into treachery on Enth, and for the Iron Warriors who had found and succoured them afterwards.

Hatred for all the failures which brought First Eradicant to her world.

Her innards shook. She wished that she could scream.

Durlo regarded her with a curious expression, his head cocked slightly to the side.

'Colonel Sarring?' the Scion asked.

She cleared her throat and nodded, if only to herself.

If history was to remember her as the one who consigned her capital city to the fire, so be it.

'I'm certain.'

XVII

Hurdt's gloves creaked as he flexed his fingers behind his back. They had been waiting for hours now. He was no longer a young man, and age and battle injuries made standing for long periods of time difficult. Despite this, he ground his teeth, flexed his fingers and fought to keep still.

He would never dream of exposing weakness in front of Zelazko. As Hurdt understood it, the Canticle of Iron, the ancient maxim of the consul's Legion, had no tolerance for infirmity, and Hurdt had no desire to discover what would happen when the iron within him became the iron without him.

Zelazko yet stood in the centre of the hololith, seemingly held fast within a scrolling green cage of continuously updating inventories, catalogues, indices and shipping dockets received from Ganspur. Hurdt wondered if he had simply been standing there since before yesterday, his ravenous amber eyes devouring every morsel of information as fast as it could be fed to him. But for the periodic, strobing brilliance of Dvart's welding across the room, the hololith was the sole source of illumination, bathing everything in its dim green glow. Never still, Zelazko followed the data, randomly turning left and right in a slow circuit about the hololithic dais as new information caught his scrutiny.

The Adeptus Astartes had not acknowledged Hurdt or Dorran when they returned, the entirety of his focus apparently bent on ensuring the shipments of war materiel would be ready for transit to his Warsmith. It was worse, in a way – while failure was always deplorable, Hurdt had learned early on that reporting failure had a purgative effect on the negative emotions surrounding the event. The longer he went without communicating it, the more the animus remained, twisting in his guts like steam in an unregulated pipe until it threatened to burst from him.

Beside him, Captain Dorran swayed slightly, hands behind her back. She periodically flexed her knees and shifted her weight between her feet. Her mutations seemed to have left her in a state of perpetual discomfort, though like Hurdt she bore it stoically. Hurdt occasionally heard the Stygian's breath catch in her throat when Zelazko turned towards them, though it seemed the Iron Warrior's position was merely incidental – his attention drawn in their direction by another data stream.

Dvart toiled, a darker shadow in the slightly green-tinged darkness flanked by servitors, her hunched, shrouded form occasionally backlit by the halcyon bright flare of her welder as it crackled over inscrutable labours.

Orbital pict feeds flickered into being about the Iron Warrior, most focused on the academy grounds, though some carried imagery of the Foretrak Gap. Hurdt noticed something moving across the feeds as the satellite's pict aperture zoomed in on the blocky outline of an aircraft. Indicators surrounding the craft flashed red, highlighting the unmistakable silhouette of a Valkyrie.

Hurdt closed his eyes and took a deep breath, mustering the courage to speak. Reporting failure was never easy, and reporting failure to one such as Zelazko was unknown territory. Another of the Iron Warrior's brothers had fallen, and Hurdt recalled Zelazko's childish rage when he learned of Blodt's death. The sheer terror at being so close to such an extraordinary display of violence was still too fresh, too real, to the general.

He subvocally modulated his voice as he prepared to speak – an old mnemonic he had learned early in his career to keep from sounding nervous during briefings – and began as naturally as he could manage.

'Consul?' Hurdt began.

'General,' Zelazko said in his deep, sonorous bass, his back still to them. 'I was beginning to wonder if you had forgotten how to speak.'

'The operation to eliminate the Scions and Zheev was unsuccessful,' Hurdt reported. It was easier to admit than he had expected, and with the catharsis of speaking it aloud, he felt the failure's maddening pressure begin to bleed off.

'I knew that the moment they employed the Deathstrike,' Zelazko said. 'Hoisted with my own petard, it seems. I hope you can forgive me.'

'Forgive you?' Hurdt said, perplexed. 'So, you aren't angry?'

Dorran gaped at him, eyes bulging.

'You ask why I have not killed you in a rage for bringing me ill news?' Zelazko folded his hands behind his back. 'I regret that rash display – it was childish and unseemly of me. Understand, Numus was my closest friend, even before our Legion shrugged off the cruel yoke of a thankless Emperor. I fear my immediate grief over my brother's death resulted in shameful overreaction on my part.'

Hurdt nodded. He had not expected the Iron Warrior to reply with such candour. 'The question stands.'

'Not angry,' Zelazko mused. 'Dismayed, perhaps. Once they secured the Deathstrike, there was really no way you could have hoped to succeed.'

He sighed, a curiously human sound, coming from an Angel. 'It is true, I was overwrought by Numus' death,' Zelazko admitted. 'But Jepthah's is probably for the best. He had been losing his battle with the daemon in his blade for years, and I had determined long ago that I would put him down before it claimed him entirely. I delayed, as one does – ever dauntless, never defeated, Jepthah had been our Grand Battalion's Champion. And he was my brother...' He trailed off, somehow seeming to sag beneath his armour. 'I suppose I held on to the vain hope he would overcome this foe, as he had all the others, and ultimately triumph.'

He turned, addressing Dorran and Hurdt directly for the first time since their return. 'No matter what they tell you of us, the so-named Traitor Legions, killing one's brother is always hard. It gives me solace, though, knowing Jepthah's struggle is finally over.'

Hurdt was unable to speak. It was difficult to reconcile how such a being, reconstructed at the genetic level to be the ultimate bringer of death, could seem so human.

It struck him, quite suddenly, that his motivations and Zelazko's were nearly identical. Like him, the Iron Warrior had repudiated his oaths to an uncaring and ingratefull Throne, casting aside all he had been out of a love for those who fought and died beside him. Though the consul remained threatening and, ultimately, truly inhuman, his threat was tempered with an unanticipated notion of kinship.

Hurdt glanced down at his chestplate, bare since he had the Imperialis removed.

'What would you have us do?'

The hololithic feeds around Zelazko went dark. The lights

overhead flickered back to life with a series of rapid clicks, forcing the general to squint against the sudden, unexpected glare. 'Return to the capitol building, general,' the Iron Warrior said, stepping down from his plinth. 'Gather your strength and prepare for a siege. This is personal for the Hundred-and-Thirty-Ninth, so have no illusions of quarter – there will be none.'

Hurdt nodded gravely. 'Very well, consul. Despite the overall inexperience of its personnel, the Hundred-and-Thirty-Ninth is now significantly better equipped than I am, since Pokol. I suppose I don't need to tell you that I can barely stand up one and a half regiments?'

'That will be remedied,' Zelazko said, 'but I need time and space to prepare. Ready the defences and soon you'll have no concerns as far as rolling stock or ordnance are concerned.'

'That's what I like to hear,' Hurdt said with a grin. 'When might I expect this resupply?'

'If things go to plan, you will have it within the next eight hours.'

Dvart clattered across the tiles on her multitudinous, tiny steel feet, the ferrule of her axe tapping metronomically as she approached. 'Where are you planning to get those supplies, Shomael?'

'From Ganspur.'

'Oh?' Dvart said. 'Have you located more equipment there that I was unaware of?'

'No.'

Dvart's servo-arms screeched as she nervously rubbed them together, reminding Hurdt of a hideous clockwork mantis. 'Shomael, it is unwise to tamper with the shipment earmarked for the Warsmith. The equipment is already loaded and ready, and the manifests–'

'The Warsmith will have to wait.'

'It is not so simple,' Dvart said, unable to fully conceal the tremulousness in her voice. Hurdt wondered who this Warsmith was, to inspire such fear. 'Having co-opted Rilisian stockage protocols, we cannot simply reallocate materiel previously earmarked for export without gubernatorial override. With the governor dead, this becomes problematic.'

'Leave that to me,' Zelazko said. 'I have located a contingency programme. Accessed through the governor's suites, it will enable me to override the protocols in place and deploy the assets here to Vytrum. This is why it is essential that General Hurdt secures the capital itself first.'

'We are already behind schedule,' Dvart cautioned. 'Preparing this ordnance and materiel again for remanifesting and shipment will be exhaustively time-consuming, to say nothing of the potentially damaged or lost items we will surely incur–'

'Then I will provide Felg with veteran systems!' Zelazko roared, sending Dvart recoiling. 'Should his shipment come out light from the battle ahead, the blooded machine spirits of the fighting vehicles he receives will provide more than adequate compensation, and he will receive half again as much with the next delivery.'

'Of...' Dvart stammered. 'Of course.'

Zelazko stared forward into nothing for several minutes, silent but for the grinding of his armour's power plant.

'I was too trusting, Sylera,' he said quietly. 'I treated this as a conventional military problem, to be solved with the simple application of military force. I trusted the Third Division could wear down the loyalist rabble through attrition. I trusted in Numus' genius to give us comfortable breathing space at Foretrak. In my keenness to see my duty to my Warsmith done, I refused to consider employing the very weapons I was providing him against a surprisingly capable foe whom I had granted too little credit. I went into battle with one arm tied behind my back, and now my brothers have paid for my damnable hubris with their lives. No more.'

Zelazko paced towards the shuttered grand window at the far end of the room, head downturned beneath the weight of his troubles. His confession had stripped the anger from him, cold water quenching the forge-heat of his wrath. When he spoke again, it was with hard-edged certainty.

'Our brotherhood is but small, and grows smaller still with the passings of Numus and Jepthah,' he said. 'The only way to accomplish my task on Rilis is through the active elimination of the False Emperor's lapdogs. Until I see that done, the Warsmith will have to wait or receive nothing.'

Dvart clattered across the floor and laid her withered right hand on the Adeptus Astartes' pauldron. 'How may I assist you, Shomael?'

Zelazko reached across his chest, taking her tiny, shrivelled hand in his massive, steel-mailed one with a tenderness Hurdt could not juxtapose with the simple purity of threat the warrior embodied. He smiled sadly at the magos with a kindness that should have been impossible on one gene-forged solely for war.

'I need you to go to Ganspur,' Zelazko said. 'Stand by for my signal. I will go to the capital to initiate the gubernatorial override, and you will dispatch the shipment to the Vanness Tether for Hurdt's appropriation.'

Dvart's hood dipped once. 'It will be done.'

'Thank you, Sylera,' Zelazko said, releasing her hand.

Flanked by her servitors, the magos slipped across the tiles, her axe's ferrule tapping on the ground at regular, three-second intervals. She paused in the doorway, giving Zelazko a long look before jangling out and away on her myriad feet.

Zelazko faced the shuttered windows, as if his gaze were somehow able to pierce them and see through to the city outside.

'What do you need of the Stygians?' Dorran asked.

Zelazko turned. 'Something very important.' He walked back to the hololith, the green glow from the projector's idling innards brightening as he approached, forming shifting data motes that floated idly in a growing sea of static. 'Come. I will show you.'

He tilted his head as Dorran approached, examining her pallid face with his clear amber gaze as if he might some faulty mechanism, laying bare any deficiencies. He turned back to the hololithic display, calling up orbital picts of the academy grounds. He tapped one, the display distorting and fizzling around his finger. The image showed the distinctive, blockily graceless form of a Valkyrie set down on the tarmac of the supply depot.

'Save for Sylera's lighter, this is the last operational aircraft in this hemisphere,' he said. 'It belongs to the insurgents. They will conduct an aerial assault on these headquarters to eliminate me and delay your aiding Hurdt at the capitol.'

'Then we must deploy to the capitol at once,' Dorran said.

'No. They are coming for me here, and I will be at the capitol,' Zelazko said. 'If they arrive and find me gone, they will make for the capital immediately. Given their talent for disruption, their intervention there presents an unacceptable risk to mission requirements. Your Stygians will give them the fight they are looking for. If it improves your outlook, I very much hope that you destroy them.'

'How can you be sure they will come here, and not simply support the Hundred-and-Thirty-Ninth's passage through Vytrum?'

'They will come.'

'And you simply inferred their battleplan from a glance at orbital imagery before?'

'Yes.' Zelazko traced his projected flight path for the Valkyrie from the academy to the Stygians' compound, then the 139th's route through Vytrum to the capitol building.

'Base probability and behavioural analysis, filtered through the lens of standard Imperial tactics. It's academic, really, once you've seen this sort of thing often enough. I regret I hadn't data enough on the Scions to glean before Foretrak and the academy.'

'Could we have won there if you had?'

'The only war that ever goes to plan is the one never fought. Though the odds are stacked firmly against them, these Scions do not seem to operate according to any normative battle standard I have ever encountered. They are unpredictable – erratic, even, finding their way to victory by whatever means.'

'We outnumber them nearly four to one,' Dorran said.

'Their destruction is your secondary priority. Your primary objective is to keep them bottled up until the shipment arrives and Hurdt's forces can claim it. After that, their eradication is assured, and we may go about our business.'

'As you say.'

'Expect the Scions to attack here within the next two hours. The Hundred-and-Thirty-Ninth's attack on the capital will begin before dawn, and I require time to access the gubernatorial override. Ensure I have it.'

The Iron Warrior departed without another word, his heavy footsteps echoing ponderously down the corridor in his wake, the tang of ozone and the heady, aromatic scent of old promethium he carried with him still lingering in the air.

'I'd best not keep my people waiting,' Hurdt said with visible elation. He nodded to Dorran. 'Good luck, captain.'

'General,' Dorran replied, dipping her chin as Hurdt took his leave.

Despite the urgency, Hurdt held back in the corridor outside for several minutes longer than he might have otherwise. For all the common ground he found with Zelazko, the general still had no desire to share a transport with him.

At length, the lift doors opened, and he departed.

THREE

FROM FAITH COMETH HONOUR

XVIII

The Valkyrie swept along the arterial thoroughfares of Vytrum, slipping beneath the roofs of blocky, flat-topped structures fronted in stained white marble and the Tarantula anti-air turrets squatting atop many of them. It weaved between buildings with a grace that defied its inelegant form, its vertical thrusters allowing it to make manoeuvres that should have been impossible in such close quarters seem almost effortless.

'Three minutes to objective,' Lieutenant Sandeborn announced over the vox. An Imperial Naval officer, Sandeborn had been attached to the 36th Xian Tigers for three years and had spent the last ten months assigned to First Eradicant. He was an excellent pilot – skilful but never ostentatious, his flying style a perfect match to his no-nonsense persona. Despite routinely ferrying Tempestus Scions into some of the most perilous combat zones in the segmentum, Sandeborn's longevity spoke to both his exceptional piloting skills and a superb sense of risk management.

Despite this, Norroll didn't know him at all. Sandeborn was

undoubtedly an asset, but at the end of the day, he was the transport, an occasional voice over the Valkyrie's inter-vox that gave them estimated arrival times. Despite how frequently Norroll encountered the lieutenant, he may as well have been a piece of equipment attached to the aircraft.

Norroll looked at the door gunner across from him as the white-faced buildings outside streaked past. He realised he wasn't even sure of the gunner's name, or if he was in fact male or female, as the full rebreather helmet, armour and fatigues entirely obscured gender. It had never mattered.

He looked at Traxel, sitting at the front of the troop bay, and wondered why it suddenly mattered now.

Norroll took a heavy pull of nutri-paste from his helm's dispenser, unnecessarily chewing the brackish glob. Long since inured to the flavour, he gulped down the nutrient-rich gunk.

He looked at Daviland, strapped into her harness across the bay from him, motionless but for the slight bobbing of her head with the aircraft's movements. Daviland had been unusually taciturn since she had first met with Fennech at the command centre and had said nothing to him before the commissar departed for the capital assault with the 139th. Had Norroll cared, he might have wondered why.

None of the Scions spoke, not even Bissot, who, save for himself, was easily the most garrulous of the lot. Next to her, Durlo sat quietly, golden thronepiece stowed in one of his pockets, leaning slightly forward from the bulge of the small atomic bomb stowed in his backpack. Akraatumo, between Norroll and the Tempestor, was equally passive, as was Atebe to Norroll's right. But for his own glances about the cabin and the swaying with the aircraft's motion, the Scions were almost entirely inert. His time with Bissot, Durlo and Daviland had left Norroll with expectations towards their behaviour – now, battered and fatigued beyond anything any of them had ever experienced, they hardly seemed themselves.

It reminded him of his first mission with his old Aquilon squad, years before his tenure in First Eradicant began. No talking outside of operations. No camaraderie. No personality – human automata, held idle in a trancelike state when inoperative. The Tempestors were the sole exception to this, and even they eschewed unnecessary conversation with their subordinates. It seemed natural at the time because it *was* natural. Fresh from their mental forging at the scholams, the Scions had not yet encountered anything to make it otherwise.

This was what it took to get out of an eradicant, Norroll realised. Every last vestige of humanity that had slipped through the cracks in mindscaping over the years, pushed back down and locked up tightly – not eliminated, but subsumed and repurposed. The Militarum Tempestus had no need for individuals, but the cultivation of certain characteristics was essential for the next generation of Tempestors.

Alone among the Scions, Traxel was working, using the flight time to perform maintenance on his weapons. He tightened the linkages on his chainsword, periodically revving the weapon to evaluate its function.

'Everybody up.'

The starboard door gunner opened up with his heavy bolter, raking fire across the roof of the Stygian headquarters building as the Valkyrie hove above it. The gunship released a hissing blast from its rocket pods, sending Stygians scrambling for cover as the ordnance burst across the rooftop.

Norroll was out the moment the first rockets streaked into the defences and on the ground a split second later, firing his hellpistol into the Stygians as he dived for cover, Actis hovering along in his wake.

Bissot was next out, gravel scattering beneath her feet as she dropped onto the roof. Levelling her volley gun as she beseeched Saint Joachim the Shootist for a portion of his immaculate accuracy, she strafed fire across the Stygian positions, before being forced into cover when the enemy displaced and returned fire.

Two squads of ten Stygians held the rooftop, fortified cover and carapace armour rendering them inappreciably affected by the Valkyrie's rocket barrage as they blocked the route to the access doors. They opened fire on the gunship, being sure to keep below the fusillade of heavy bolter and multi-laser fire that harried their every move. While their las-rounds had little enough effect on the aircraft, they did force Sandeborn to pivot his door gunners out of harm's way.

One of the Stygians shouldered a missile launcher, levelling the tube on the Valkyrie as it wheeled back around to drop the remaining Scions onto the rooftop.

Traxel leapt from the Valkyrie's rear ramp, firing his plasma pistol as he dropped to the rooftop. The spinning ball of supercharged gas struck the gunner in the seam between shoulder pauldron and rocket launcher, detonating the round within and spattering the rooftop in a broad arc as it obliterated the gunner above the sternum and decapitated his loader.

The remaining Scions hit the rooftop moving, springing for cover as the Stygians rapidly recovered from the rocket launcher's explosive demise to pour fire upon the attackers. Even with the Valkyrie's support, the eradicant was outnumbered more than two to one and forced to defend an incrementally collapsing beachhead. The Stygians took only light casualties as they worked their way towards the Scions, shielded from the gunship's fire by the reinforced barricades emplaced on the rooftop for the purpose of defending against such incursions.

Unable to move forward, First Eradicant collapsed inwards

behind a low plasteel bulwark, hotshot las-fire sizzling over their heads. Crawling prone across the roof, Akraatumo patched into Norroll's connection with Actis, using his clarion vox-array to analyse the strength and disposition of the enemy through their vox transmissions as he slipped through cover. He rose to one knee, las-fire sizzling over his head, and gestured for the Scions to close on his position.

Durlo was nearly finished emplacing the breaching charge when Norroll reached Akraatumo.

'How many charges do you have left?' Traxel asked the demolitions trooper.

'Three more, plus the big one,' Durlo reported. 'No remotes, so it's all manual.' He flipped open the detonator. 'Brace.'

The rooftop collapsed downwards as the shaped charge exploded, opening a hole slightly over a yard square. Without urging, Bissot dropped through first, bursts of light flickering through the dust cloud from below as she cleared the space with her volley gun. Covering their escape, the rest of the eradicant slipped through the breach one by one and secured the room beneath.

The Scions exited into the hallway behind Bissot. Norroll and Akraatumo both scanned Actis' augur receipts, searching energy readings and vox-traffic to locate the Iron Warrior and the most efficient route to reach him.

'Target?' Traxel asked.

'I'm using the Iron Warrior we fought at Foretrak as a baseline to track the radiant discharge from the power unit on the Heretic Astartes' power armour, but I'm not finding it,' Norroll said.

'Keep looking,' Traxel said, motioning Bissot forward.

Bissot opened fire a split second later as a team of Stygians rounded a corner. A rapid volley dropped one of the black-armoured troopers, but their return fire forced her back around the corner.

'Thy grace is my shield,' Bissot said, priming a frag grenade and tossing it around the corner.

'Bissot, wait!' Durlo called as the Stygians scattered in the second before the grenade burst.

'What?'

'I may need our grenades for breaching.'

'Bit late for that now,' she said with a shrug before rolling out from behind the corner to rake hotshot fire across the Stygians on the other side. A gap opened in the enemy line, making space for the other Scions to follow Norroll and Akraatumo through the intersection and down the corridor.

While the Tempestus Scions had arrived at the Stygians' headquarters with few preconceptions of what they would find, the compound was not at all what they had imagined. Lacking any maps or schematics beforehand, they had only their past experiences to guide them. The obviously recent addition of fortifications and structural hardening they encountered on the roof fit their rough generalisation of those expectations, but in their rawest conceptualisations of the area they would assault, they never imagined their present environs.

The Stygian headquarters was no fortress – it was an office, more suited to the day-to-day functions of the Administratum than to any military organisation. Sparsely acquitted, the building was even less ostentatious than most Administratum facilities. Illuminated by strip-lumens on the ceiling, the corridors were of simple rockcrete, worn and stained dark by millennia of use and punctuated by occasional alcoves displaying banners and other relics of the Stygians' most remarkable battles. Though solidly built, as were most structures constructed from the standardised templates for Imperial architecture, it was clearly never intended to withstand an attack. It seemed folly to Norroll that the Stygians would even attempt to do so here. Coupled with his inability to locate the Heretic Astartes, First Eradicant's attack on the building was starting to look like a setup.

Las-fire from the pursuing Stygians blasted sooty-edged craters from the rockcrete walls, shredding ancient banners and shattering the vestiges of battle honours.

'This is the least sensible headquarters building I have ever encountered,' Akraatumo complained. 'Unfortified, no organic defence systems… Why, in the Emperor's name, would a Space Marine choose to lair here?'

'Maybe it has access to features he found essential?' Durlo suggested, returning fire on the Stygians from near the back of the formation.

'Maybe it's a trap,' Norroll said, voicing his burgeoning concern.

A group of five Stygians burst from the stairwell, firing on the move as they hugged the walls of the corridor. A las-beam slammed into Norroll's left pauldron, spinning him round to crash sprawling onto the floor.

Daviland pulled him back around the corner, out from the line of the Stygians' fire. The rest of the Scions gathered around, screening her as she unfastened Norroll's pauldron and set about emergency surgery on his shoulder. Las-bolts crackled, chewing divots from the walls or hissing overhead.

'Not much cover to speak of,' Bissot said, lying prone as she fired into the Stygians near the stairwell. One of the black-armoured troopers collapsed face first.

'That's what I was saying before,' Akraatumo said, laying down covering fire on the Stygians pursuing from the other direction. 'Works both ways.'

Traxel darted around the corner above Akraatumo, took aim and fired, his plasma pistol deadly in such close quarters. His target exploded in a cloud of seething red mist and steaming offal, forcing the pursuing Stygians to seek what little cover they could find.

'How far?' the Tempestor asked.

'Two floors down. Best estimate,' Norroll said through clenched teeth as Daviland sutured his wound shut with a dermal stapler. He winced as the medicae-adept cinched his damaged pauldron back down over his shoulder. 'Is it a good sign that it hurts again?'

'That should mean you're working the vitalotox out of your system,' Daviland replied. She shrugged. 'Circumstantially, the timing might not be ideal.'

'Give me some space,' Durlo said, removing a shaped charge from a side pouch on his backpack. He configured the explosive on the floor several yards behind the squad, set the detonator cord and returned to the others, ducking before he clicked the detonator.

The floor exploded downwards in a flash and a cloud of dust as Durlo's shaped charge punched a hole into the storey below. Without prompting, the Scions dropped down to the lower level, forming a perimeter as they secured their position. Panicked staff menials darted down the dust-choked hallway, unwisely fleeing the rooms they had been sheltering within. The eradicant cut them down.

The Stygians had yet to respond to the Tempestus Scions' latest impromptu exit, though Norroll was certain the respite would not last. 'If you can get us down one more floor, Durlo, we should be almost on top of the target.'

'Have you picked up on his power armour?' Traxel asked.

'Not sure,' Norroll admitted. 'I'm keyed in for the brightest energy signature in the vicinity, so I assume it's him. Not typically too many mini-reactors in the upper levels of an Administratum complex.'

'Vox has gone haywire, so I can't corroborate,' Akraatumo said, muting the feedback screech warbling from his handset. 'On the other hand, it should make it harder for the Stygians to coordinate.'

Traxel nodded to Durlo. 'Do it.'

Durlo set the charge as the four Stygians from the stairwell above emerged through the hatch at the end of the corridor, calmly emplacing the explosive and detonator as las-fire streaked past him. Around him, the Scions laid down fire, hitting two of the Stygians as they exited the stairwell. The remaining pair dragged their wounded back inside the cover of the hatchway.

The corridor floor burst downwards, opening to a darkened space below. Without hesitation, the eradicant plunged through into the unknown.

Norroll rolled to break his fall as the Scions dropped through the ceiling behind him. The eradicant opened fire on the Stygians arrayed around the room, las-fire crackling above the lingering echo of the explosion. Blood exploded in inky blooms as it penetrated black carapace plate.

'Protect Captain Dorran!' one of the Stygians shouted as he attempted to shield his officer. He caught a hotshot round between the shoulder blades and slumped forward limply, held upright by the one he had attempted to protect.

His captain, Dorran, lowered the wounded Stygian to the ground, gently setting him down as the rest of her command squad overcame the shock and disorientation of the eradicant's violent entry.

'Close in and destroy!' Dorran snarled.

The Scions were already moving. Deeply indoctrinated combat procedures overrode conscious thought as they drew their blades and pressed forward, dividing to engage the individual Stygians in melee.

Traxel leapt at the Stygian commander, his snarling chainsword transcribing an upward arc from beneath, aimed at the captain's torso. Dorran parried with her powerblade, forcing Traxel to redirect his strike at the last instant to avoid having his own weapon sundered by the sword's disruptor field.

Duelling a power weapon with a chainsword was no simple feat, requiring nearly perfect control of the weapon to ensure it could block oncoming attacks with the flat while managing to avoid being split in half by a direct strike. Traxel had long ago mastered the art – his expertise had enabled him to hold the blows of an enormous powered axe wielded by an Adeptus Astartes headsman at bay on Tecerriot, and it served him against Dorran's lightning-quick swordsmanship now. Despite her repulsive, mutated pallor, Dorran was no transhuman butcher, and her weapon's disruptor field was not quite enough to offset the Tempestor's superior skill with a blade.

Norroll sidestepped, rolling left to narrowly avoid a heavy combat blade aimed at his throat. The blade scraped across his cuirass and pauldron as Norroll lunged back in with a high feint to the right, following up with a low strike beneath his opponent's open underarm. His left monoblade sank deep into the Stygian's right armpit, puncturing a lung. Norroll kicked out with a low, sweeping kick, knocking his opponent from his feet before finishing him with a quick stab between collar and jaw. Blood fountained up his right arm as he noticed the blinking green warning light on his vambrace.

'We've got incoming from the hallway!' he called as Actis' augur readings scrolled across the face of his slate monitron.

Traxel ducked a swing from Dorran's powerblade, following up with a counterstrike the Stygian commander barely avoided. 'Bar the door!' he ordered.

Norroll sprinted to the rear of the room, tearing open the hatchway's emergency access panel and slamming the override swich. The Stygians outside opened fire, las-fire streaking past Norroll as the hatch slammed shut.

He heard the traitors pounding on the hatchway, frustrated when they discovered they could not open it. A few moments later, the floor shuddered beneath them as the Stygians detonated something outside.

'That won't hold them long,' Norroll said, glancing at the updating streams on his wrist-slate as Actis' augurs supplied the relevant metallurgical stress data. 'Whatever that was caused some damage.'

'Krak grenade,' Durlo said, blocking an elbow strike from the Stygian he fought in close combat. He followed up with a palm strike to his opponent's chin, forcing the black-armoured trooper back. 'It'll take a few more of those for them to breach the door.'

A series of near-simultaneous detonations on the other side of the doorway shuddered the hatch in its frame.

'Oh,' Norroll said, glancing at the augurs' assessment of the blast door's increasing instability. 'Good.'

XIX

Vytrum's current state left much to be desired, so far as planetary capitals went. She had been the seat of both the Imperial governor and the Rilisian Grand Senate, a prima facie elected body ostensibly intended to keep the governor's broad powers in check for the benefit of the Rilisian people, while principally benefitting themselves and their entitled lineages. When the survivors of General Hurdt's Third Mechanised Division returned from Enth, no expense had been spared in making a considerable show of welcoming them home. There had been great celebrations – homecoming parades, the unveiling of a vast memorial monument celebrating the division's martial accomplishments, and grand speeches extolling the Rilisian fighting spirit and the virtue of faithful service to the Golden Throne.

On the third day, during the governor's scripted address to the senate, Hurdt and his forces massacred the Rilisian government and assembled dignitaries at a stroke. Within three more days, the 139th had crushed the planetary militia and the Stygians had eliminated Vytrum's contingent of Adeptus Arbites in their own precinct, effectively ending Imperial rule on Rilis.

That should have been the end of it.

But in short order, Zheev emerged from retirement and dug in, and Vytrum became the site of the fiercest fighting on Rilis in ten thousand years. While Mawr and his regiment had, until recently, vanished into Foretrak, the Old Dog and the handful of Imperial faithful who had answered his call from off-world had practically burned the city to the ground. Indeed, they proved so destructive that Hurdt had pulled his division out of the city, withdrawing west into the Zholm River valley, to preserve what remained.

In his absence, with so much of Vytrum already depopulated due to the most recent troop mobilisation, the surviving population who could escape scattered into refugee camps at the city's edge, picking at the once-great city's corpse like crows. Though the city's most critical infrastructure remained largely intact, much of Vytrum still smouldered, her blackened bones bearing mute witness to the civil war.

Waiting in the capitol building, where it all began, Hurdt could not help but remember. He glanced at Ketch, his adjutant, and Hesturm, his division's standard bearer, giving each a nod of acknowledgement and a quick smile of reassurance he did not in the least feel.

He thought about what lay behind the door of the governor's office at the end of the corridor.

Not for the first time, he wondered what manner of devil's bargain Captain Dorran had made for them all back on Enth.

Sarring jolted as the Chimera thundered over streets of grey brick, shaking as the dozer blade shouldered through debris, burned-out vehicles and even an enemy combatant too arrogant, or too stupid, to get out of the way. On the turret, Troopers

Temmet and Rawl had somehow found time to christen the vehicle *Bear*, after the battalion Sarring had commanded a few hours before. Rawl, an inexplicable polyglot, had written in High Gothic, *Virtus, non copia vincit* – 'Courage, not multitude, wins' – across *Bear*'s dozer blade.

She thought it would make a fine epitaph.

When the Old Dog brought Sarring back into the 139th's regimental staff during the first battle for the academy, she brought the troopers from her old manpower shop in Cold Steel Battalion with her. Temmet and Rawl, the two who had decorated the command Chimera, had both been with Sarring for years.

'What do they have?' Sarring called over the transport's intervox, teeth clenched against the steady agony the Chimera's constant rocking and vibration inflicted on her augmetic interfaces. Ever since the grateful tech-priests had rebuilt her following her conspicuous gallantry and near death during the Defence of Blackforge Gate, she had been in at least minor discomfort at all times, as though her augmetics hadn't been installed with human comfort in mind. She ground her teeth irritably and tried to ignore a sensation like sandpaper being dragged back and forth, slowly and continuously, across her nerve endings.

'*Stub autos, mostly,*' Sergeant Zoldana, the driver, called back, his face bleeding where some spall had cut into it. '*One's shooting at us with a stub, but that heavy bolter…*' One of his hands was on the drive stick, the other managing the controls of the turret-mounted multi-laser. He tried to keep a solid sight picture in his targeting reticule while he was driving, before giving up and strafing las-fire across a line of enemy soldiers. Three of them dropped, and the rest ran for cover.

Trooper Goshtelo mowed them down with a burst from the Chimera's bow-mounted heavy bolter, the large-calibre mass-reactive shells rendering the turncoats manning their heavy bolter emplacement into meat and sprays of blood. *'They got nothin' that'll stop a tank!'* he said, laughing.

'It's an infantry fighting vehicle,' Sarring grumbled. 'It's not a tank.'

Goshtelo kept firing.

'Coming up on the target, ma'am!' Trooper Diez called. 'Five hundred yards!'

'Autocannon turret up front!' Zoldana called. *'Buttoned up behind a barricade.'*

Sarring sighed. 'Rawl, kill it.'

Rawl unfolded a battered topographic map across his lap, struggling to read the chart over the Chimera's constant sway and bounce as he attempted to orient himself on his surroundings. Failing, he called over to Diez, 'What's our position?'

Reviewing the display on his data-slate, Diez transmitted the coordinates.

With a nod of thanks, Rawl started talking into his vox-array. 'Firepower, need Earthshaker at following coordinates…'

Zoldana sprayed with the multi-laser as Goshtelo opened up with his heavy bolter, striking the barricade in front of the emplacement. Their fire pummelled debris and sandbags ineffectually, drowning out the rest of what Rawl said.

The autocannon fired, but its aim was low, coming in far to *Bear*'s front. The cannon's crew adjusted, stitching a line of tracer and puffs of rockcrete dust from the pavement up over the Chimera's dozer blade and front glacis. A moment later, a battered promethium regulator station less than sixty yards to the autocannon's left exploded in a bloom of flame, forcing the autocannon crew to duck.

'Splash, over,' Rawl called.

The autocannon crew's spotter looked up, swatted his companion in the head and pointed emphatically at the oncoming Chimera. The autocannon started up again, heavy rounds chewing into *Bear*'s front armour. Goshtelo cursed, shielding his eyes as spall cut his face.

Behind him, Rawl consulted Diez's tactical display. 'Gotcha,' he said with a smile. 'Firepower, sixty right, fire for effect!'

Three seconds later, the autocannon's position ceased to exist as an Earthshaker round landed just behind it and exploded in a fireball. Proximity to the shockwave slewed *Bear* to the left before Zoldana could regain control of it.

'That was close,' Sarring said, scowling.

Rawl grinned at her with impish pride. 'Yes, ma'am.'

'I told you they got nothin' to stop a tank!' Goshtelo exclaimed. *'Or an infantry fighting vehicle,'* he added as an afterthought.

'Brace, stairs!' Zoldana called.

The capitol building stood at the top of a quarter-mile-wide square pavilion reached by a low pyramid of stairs surrounding it. Representing the classically enlightened notions Rilis' leaders claimed to espouse, it was a three-storey edifice, fronted in white marble and classically styled ionic columns and topped with a magnificent rotunda which rose two hundred feet into the air. Papers and ash swirled about, stirred by winds from the sections of Vytrum that yet burned.

Bear lumbered up the southern steps, followed by the rest of Impetus Company's five Chimeras. Heavy bolters and multi-lasers strafed the insurgents outside the building as they ran for cover.

Commissar Fennech's voice crackled across the battalion vox. *'Iron Zero, this is Fennech with Impetus. We lost contact with Bellum Company. Have you any communication with them?'* The commissar had attached himself to Impetus Company's command squad and rode with them in their Chimera.

Sarring gave Diez a pointed look.

Diez held up his index finger, indicating she should wait a moment, and attempted to contact them.

'We're here,' Sarring grumbled to Diez. 'Where in the hells is Bellum?'

'Iron Zero?' Fennech requested again.

'Bellum Company reports they were forced to divert, ma'am,' Diez relayed. 'They redirected around heavy fighting – three Chimeras bent. They're sending their mounted forces to reinforce us, dismounts trying to drive a wedge for them through the enemy.'

'How long?'

'Five minutes?' Diez said uncertainly. 'Give or take.'

Sarring cursed. 'Relay that to Commissar Fennech,' she ordered. 'Damn it. Five minutes is too late. Tell Bellum to push into the capitol building as soon as they get here. Fragging Bear Battalion's all over the place...' she muttered. 'What happened to Pugna Company?'

Diez scrolled through information charts on his slate. 'I don't know, ma'am. I haven't got anything from them since we crossed into the city. I've been trying to contact them–'

The entire squad jolted forward as Zoldana rammed *Bear* through the capitol building's southern wall. An ionic column crumbled atop the vehicle as the crash hurled chunks of rockcrete and marble bursting into the corridor beyond.

'Sorry,' Zoldana called out over the inter-vox.

'Forget it,' Sarring interrupted. 'Everybody get up!'

Goshtelo and Zoldana laid down a blanket of fire, searing through the enemy within the capitol as they attempted to flee down the corridor, multi-laser fire and heavy mass-reactives cutting men down as they ran.

'Yeah!' Temmet whooped. 'Save some for the rest of us, G!'

'Ignore him, G,' Sarring said. 'If you have the chance to kill everybody in this building before we dismount, do it.'

Goshtelo cackled.

'Sergeant,' Sarring called. 'Back us out a bit and drop the ramp.

Diez, on my order, give the rest of Impetus the command to dismount and get in.'

The squad moved into position as Zoldana lowered the ramp. Outside, Rilisian troopers were already streaming around *Bear* to get in through the hole the transport had punched into the wall.

'What the hells is this?' Sarring asked, gawping at the troopers as they flowed around the transport. She turned to Diez. 'Did you give the order to dismount?'

Diez shook his head. 'No, ma'am.'

'Commissar Fennech, what's going on?'

'Three squads from Impetus did not wait for the order to–'

'Damn it, we're going to be at the back!' Sarring growled. She pointed at a sergeant running past with his squad and snarled, 'Stop!'

The sergeant, wide-eyed, reared back as if he'd been shot. Several members of his squad piled into him, nearly knocking him forward into the commander.

'Make way, dammit! I need to get through!' Sarring turned to her squad, drawing her laspistol as she started down the ramp. 'Come on!'

Entering the building against *Bear*'s right flank, Sarring discovered that the corridor was completely bottlenecked with friendly troopers. She tried to pick her way through the milling crowd, but it was slow going. Most of them simply stood about idly, a few chatting. Some looked warily at the enemy corpses strewn bloodily about the floor. None of them made any headway.

Sarring pressed her back against the wall as she checked the ammunition for her laspistol, an old trick she had learned to distract herself from acting out of anger. She glanced down the corridor, her view completely obstructed by the densely packed troopers. Her curse was drowned out by the thunder of an artillery volley outside that dropped a shower of plascrete dust on their heads. Getting anywhere fast, including out, if it came to it, was impossible.

She pushed her way through the press of grimy bodies, smelling the reek of sweat-stained fatigues of troopers who hadn't been able to wash in weeks. After forcing her way forward for a few more yards, she became frustrated and pulled up Diez, who was struggling through the press half a yard behind her.

'Put out an all-call to Impetus. Tell the squad commanders to get these idiots up against the wall – squad to a side, stacked up alphabetically, I don't care. We can't get anywhere with them standing around stopping up the damned place.'

Diez nodded and raised the handset to his vox-caster to transmit, then stopped short, listening to an incoming transmission.

'Ma'am, they think they've found the target.'

'What?'

Diez continued to listen. 'Someone said General Hurdt is located behind the door at the end of this hall, but it's sealed. They want to go in.'

'Why would Hurdt be down here?'

Diez shrugged. 'They sound convinced, ma'am.'

Sarring gritted her teeth and took a deep, exasperated breath – this was what command of the Astra Militarum's ash and trash looked like.

'Tell the squad commanders to get everybody up against the wall. Then have the point squad clear the door and wait until we're ready to go in.'

Diez relayed the command and listened to the acknowledgement. 'They're clearing the door, ma'am.'

Sarring's right eye ticked. 'What? No. Tell the point squad to stack up and wait before entering so we can coordinate, make sure the way in is clear. They *need* to *wait*. Who's in charge of that squad?'

Diez licked his lips nervously. 'Sergeant Daffern, ma'am.'

'Oh. Damn.'

Sarring had served with Sergeant Daffern for seven years. She knew the man as a proficient administrator, with a solid grasp of regulation and procedure – not the best she had seen, but good enough. Truthfully, Sarring believed Daffern was more interested in maintaining his physique than doing his job.

Sarring was certain the sergeant wouldn't know to check for booby traps, let alone how to breach and clear a room.

She felt the explosion rather than heard it, a concussive blast that roared down the hallway, given greater potency by the tight confines of the corridor. Sarring instinctively raised her augmetic arm, shielding her face from the detonation as she twisted sideways to present her bionically augmented left side to the hail of shrapnel and fragments of armour and body parts scything through the air. Before her, the force of the blast knocked troopers over like ninepins. Sarring lost her footing, collapsing backwards onto the sprawling Diez.

A cloud of dust and smoke fogged the hallway, choking and blinding. Sarring felt a sensation in the upper part of her throat not unlike being throttled as the filters placed there during her reconstruction cycled into place, separating air from the roiling fug of particulates all around. She breathed through her mouth, powdered plascrete gumming her tongue. The chalky flavour, combining the mordant tang of explosive residue and the coppery taste of blood, nearly made her gag. Blind, eyes burning, she fumbled for her goggles, hastily wiping her eyes several times before lowering them into place. It took many long, teary blinks to clear her vision – and made no difference in the haze.

The audial receiver in Sarring's left ear returned to life with a brief screech and a pop, having automatically cut out in the explosion. She struggled to listen, but it felt as if her brain had just somersaulted in her skull. Sarring's right eardrum had ruptured, stabbing blade-like pain into her ear canal, throbbing in time to her heartbeat. With the implant in her left ear, she heard the screaming of the wounded and dying alloyed to coughing and cursing, calls of dismay and confusion, and the fading echo of the explosion ringing from the walls.

Gritting her teeth as she struggled to shake off the concussion, she turned to Diez to issue orders, hoping that would give her focus.

'Situation report!' Sarring barked, the filters giving her voice a peculiar, almost vibrato resonance.

Diez cradled his head in his hands, moaning and coughing. Blood flowed from both ears, soaking into the dust that coated his skin and the collar of his flak vest.

'Diez?' Sarring called. She jostled his shoulder to get his attention. 'Diez!'

Squinting up with panicked, tear-filled eyes, Diez gestured frantically at both his ears, flapping his hands as if he were trying to fan air into them.

Sarring snatched the handset.

'Any station, any station, this is Iron Zero. Situation! What casualties?'

Multiple broadcasts rippled across the vox-network as various stations stepped on one another, rendered incoherent by panic and desperate for information.

Sarring pulled Diez closer and hit the command override switch on the vox-caster.

'All stations, this is Iron Zero. If you are not a zero element or occupying, get off my net.'

The link immediately fell silent.

'What elements on vox?' Sarring asked. Troopers filtered up behind her as she spoke into the handset. Her command squad picked themselves up from the ground. Sarring began to push forward into the fog of dust, stepping over the fallen troopers collapsed in the corridor as she dragged Diez by his vox-rig.

It got worse as she progressed further up the hallway. Shell-shocked troopers, coughing on dust that blanched them ghost white, gave way to troopers with progressively more severe wounds as she advanced. Closer to the doorway, more than a dozen corpses lay on a carpet of blood interspersed with disarticulated appendages and broken weapons and armour. Sarring could not hope to identify Sergeant Daffern amongst the dead nearest the door, which had itself been blasted into a broad hole in the wall and through the ceiling above.

'Iron Zero, Cold Steel Zero.'

'Gunvaldt,' Sarring breathed with a sigh of relief as the Death Korps commander's voice hissed from the vox. 'Where in the hells are you?'

'Outside target area, Iron, but Bellum Company's got the way in bottlenecked.' Gunvaldt's voice fizzed with static. *'Setting up perimeter around target area to make sure nobody gets out.'*

'I confirm, Cold Steel,' she said. 'Prepare to send up your Two-Hundred-and-Twenty-Second and Extremis companies to backfill Bellum if the main assault looks like it's going to fall through. Break. Bellum, what are you doing?'

'We're behind you, ma'am, but Impetus has the entrance to the capitol all stopped up,' replied Captain Grosht, former commander of the Mordian 832nd, now Bellum Company commander. *'Apologies for being late. What was that explosion?'*

'Booby trap, heavy casualties. Displace, go around the capitol and come in from the other side, Grosht. You'll not get in this way. Coordinate with Cold Steel Zero while you're at it.'

'I confirm, Iron Zero.'

Back to the wall, Sarring inched towards the gaping hole so

that she could try to see what lay within the room beyond. She readied her laspistol and drew her power sword. A mechadendrite power conduit spooled from its housing in her left tricep, snaking down her sleeve to couple with the blade's pommel. Energies played over the blade as the sword ignited, its glow washing out in the haze of dust.

As she was about to peer around the corner, a hand from behind tugged gently on her right arm. Trooper Yues, blood soaking down his dust-white cheek where shrapnel had lodged beneath his left eye, pulled Sarring away from the opening. He gave Sarring a nod, the pilot light of his heavy flamer glowing blue in the haze.

Sarring stepped back as Yues spun round the corner and washed the room in burning promethium, but there was no need – piecemeal corpses littered the floor, victims of their own trap, now crackling away as the jellied fuel consumed them. Either they had built the explosive too strong or they had misjudged the Rilisian troops' lack of competence and assumed they would stop to clear the door. Sarring assumed a combination, heavily weighted to the latter.

A bolt weapon's report echoed down the stairwell entrance at the far end of the room, followed by the rippling crackle of las-fire.

'Any station this net, Iron Zero,' Sarring called. 'Identify who is fighting in the upper storeys of the capitol.'

'Iron Zero, this is Commissar Fennech.' The commissar's transmission was punctuated by the bark of his bolt pistol from above. *'Impetus Zero and I entered the capitol from an alternate location during the bottleneck. We have encountered heavy resistance on the third storey.'*

Sarring's command squad entered the room behind her, once a vestibule to the inner offices. Ahead, Yues led with his heavy flamer, Sarring and Diez just behind him, with Temmet, Rawl and Arys following. A squad followed, and Sarring indicated they cover the hole in the ceiling. She heard the report of las- and stub-fire open up outside, muted through the wall of the building.

Grosht and Bellum had contacted the enemy on the opposite side.

'Hold position, commissar,' Sarring ordered. 'We are coming to reinforce.'

'Negative,' Fennech replied. *'We have located General Hurdt and are pursuing.'*

'Commissar!' Sarring shouted into the vox as she darted low across the vestibule, dragging Diez by the cord of his field phone. 'Fennech! Wait, dammit!'

She received no further word beyond the percussive report of Fennech's bolt pistol two storeys above.

On the far end of the room, a hatch of battered plasteel led to a stairwell, wheezing partially open and shut on malfunctioning hydraulics. Through the haze, Sarring could make out heavy-gauge steel railing and rockcrete steps. Yues entered the stairwell and looked as far up as he could, covering the stairs with his heavy flamer.

Enemy stubber fire chattered from above, striking the floor around Yues. One shot glanced from the flak pad on his right shoulder, pitching him sideways, while another skipped down his armour's front, striking him in the left side of his abdomen. He released a gout of flame up the stairwell as he fell backwards out the door, past Sarring and Diez. Suppressive fire from the floor above scattered the squad following Sarring's, sending the Rilisians scrambling for cover and leaving the command squad exposed.

Sarring rushed into the stairwell, found a target two levels above and fired, striking one trooper in the stomach. Behind her, Diez fired two shots, dropping another combatant and wounding a third, who reeled out of sight.

A moment later, a frag grenade dropped down the stairwell. Sarring pushed Diez against the wall, turning her augmetic left side towards the grenade and ducking her head as she shielded him.

Sarring's refractor field flashed, taking the brunt of the explosion, the bubble of force slowing and redirecting much of the shrapnel as the grenade exploded. Her augmetic leg and shoulder caught the worst of it, shredding her overcoat and trousers. Shrapnel struck her helmet, and a few fragments slashed into the rear of her right thigh, slicing into the meat beneath, though the field blunted the force of the debris enough to render it painful, not fatal. She spun about rapidly and shot the bastard who had dropped the grenade full in the face with her laspistol.

She turned to Diez, who gaped at her in shock. Satisfied that the vox-operator was uninjured, Sarring spared a glance at Yues, who lay outside the stairwell on his back, being treated by Arys. Las-fire from the squad in the vestibule behind her cracked into the enemy above. Sarring bolted up the stairwell, hoping the others would follow her lead.

Rapidly clearing the door on the level above and unwilling to take time to fight the insurgents who engaged the squad on the floor below, Sarring continued up the stairs to the third storey. There, she found the two she and Diez had killed as a survivor attempted to flee through the door. The rebel collapsed into the room beyond as Sarring shot him in the back with her laspistol.

Still picking themselves up from Fennech's assault minutes before, the enemy in the room were unprepared for a second wave. Sarring cut down the two nearest the doorway with her power sword, shearing off the head and right shoulder of one and severing the arms of another mid-bicep. Behind her, Diez and Rawl charged in with bayonets. Grasping the regimental standard in his left hand, Temmet sprayed the room with his lasgun one-handed.

The room they fought in was like the vestibule downstairs, situated two storeys up on the opposite side of the building from it. A bank of shattered windows lay along the left side, facing east. Outside, huge and red, rose the lazily climbing sun, occluded by the haze of smoke which clung to Vytrum like a shroud. Corpses in Rilisian uniforms lay sprawled across the floor in pools of blood, two of them burst from the inside out with the unmistakable violence of a bolt weapon. Fennech and his squad had moved on, continuing their pursuit of General Hurdt.

More enemy infantry stormed into the room from an outer corridor, lasguns flaring as they fired on the move into Sarring and her squad. One of them, an officer by his tattered leather greatcoat and blood-spattered cream trousers, came at Sarring with a long-bladed combat knife, slashing at the colonel's chest. Blocking with her left arm, Sarring caught the blade between her augmetic forearm and bicep. With a quick twist to the right, she pulled the weapon from her opponent's grasp. Sarring's riposte sliced into her assailant's head below the left ear and exited just above his right, the sword's energised blade cutting neatly through his skull in a spray of blood, sending the top of his head flying.

Despite their relative lack of training and experience, instinct, rage and pain drove Sarring's squad forward into the enemy. Sarring hoped it would be enough to get them through this. Behind her, Diez stabbed his prone opponent repeatedly with his bayonet. Temmet reeled, right arm limp from a gunshot wound to his forearm, his lasgun fallen to the ground. With a snarl, the colour bearer kicked his opponent, skewering him on the standard's ferrule one-armed. He stabbed again, blood gurgling out around the wound as he jammed the spike up through his adversary's diaphragm.

The strange stillness that always seemed to follow such desperate engagements was broken by the sound of a bolt weapon being fired, carrying over the muffled whip-cracks of las-discharge further down the hall. Exiting into the corridor, Sarring found the hatchway leading to the opposite end of the hallway shut, blocking their path.

She cursed. She had visited the capitol building before but was unfamiliar with the layout of the level they were on. Doubling back, she and her command squad slipped through the door the traitor officer and his subordinates had appeared from only minutes before, hoping it would take them around to Fennech's location.

XX

Norroll stood before the blast door as the Stygians in the corridor outside attempted to batter it down.

'How do I slow them down?'

'Shoot the controls,' Durlo shouted from across the room, his right arm locked in a stranglehold around a Stygian's neck.

Norroll's laspistol clicked empty. Breathing a curse, he dropped the magazine and slapped another in.

'For Throne's sake, Gry!' Durlo grunted as his opponent powered backwards, breaking the choke and dropping heavily to slam onto the demolition trooper's chest. Durlo managed to squirm halfway out from beneath the Stygian, who spun round and grappled the trooper's neck in a leg triangle hold. 'Stab it or something!' Durlo wheezed as he struggled to break free.

With a shriek of grinding metal, the Stygians outside prised the blast doors apart, splitting a half-inch gap between the reinforced metal doorplates.

Norroll jammed his monoblade through a plastek panel and

cut through the network of wires beneath. With a hiss of sparks and a heavy clang, the doors slammed shut. 'Will that do it?'

His throat constricted in the vice of the Stygian's knee, Durlo could not answer.

Running back across the room, Norroll stabbed the Stygian's neck beneath the jaw and flicked forward, the monomolecular edge effortlessly sliding out through the trooper's throat and showering Durlo in a gout of arterial spray. 'Will that do it?' Norroll repeated.

Durlo nodded briskly, shaking himself free of the blackout that had threatened to claim him. 'Sure,' he croaked, wiping the Stygian's blood from his visor. 'For a little while, anyway.'

Norroll moved on to assist Bissot before Durlo had finished answering, aiding the gunner against the Stygian command squad's standard bearer, who was attempting to rally his squadmates near the hololith.

He slid in low, ducking beneath the Stygian's defences as Bissot exchanged knife blows with the black-armoured trooper. Three Stygians remained of Dorran's command squad – with Durlo occupied keeping the others out and Akraatumo bleeding and unconscious on the floor, the odds seemed to favour neither side.

Traxel yet battled the Stygian captain. Dorran's defences opened little by little as the clash continued, her tactical patience gradually being eroded by the Tempestor's superior skill as a duellist. Sweat stung her eyes, forcing her to misjudge her reach, and Traxel's chainsword snarled across her armoured abdomen, chewing through layers of carapace as it gouged shallowly into her flesh. She retreated several paces backwards, flexing her cramping wrist.

'Norroll, with me,' Traxel ordered. 'Durlo, keep the doors shut!'

'Tempestor, aye,' Durlo said, working to ensure the sparking hatch controls were still sufficient to prevent entry as the Stygians outside again attempted to force it open.

Traxel went low and Norroll went high, the recon trooper's left monoblade slicing towards Dorran's unarmoured armpit. At the same instant, Traxel's chainsword swept up into the Stygian captain's midsection, its snarling adamantine teeth carving through the gouge in the carapace armour it had cut before. Partly eviscerated, Dorran collapsed onto her back, both hands clutching at the grievous wound in her belly as she attempted to hold in her bowels.

The blast door at the back of the room shuddered with a percussive thump, the metal shrieking as the Stygians on the other side detonated a powerful explosive.

'It won't hold!' Durlo warned.

Traxel lowered his chainsword to less than an inch from Dorran's chin and revved the blade, spattering the captain's ash-white skin with her own blood. 'Where is the Iron Warrior?'

Dorran winced, her sharklike teeth stained red. It took her a few seconds to collect her breath to speak. 'Zelazko figured out what you were doing, set us to slow you up while he coordinated an ordnance drop for Hurdt's forces from the capitol building.' She gurgled. 'Guess it worked, because here you are.'

Traxel lowered his chainsword fractionally closer and throttled it again. 'What is in this ordnance drop?'

'Everything,' Dorran wheezed. 'Everything he was going to send to his masters. Transports, artillery. Enough ammunition to take a whole damned world.' She looked pointedly at the flickering image on the hololith. 'Seems you have less than half an hour before you find out the specifics the hard way, Tempestor. It's already left the Ironspire and entered the atmosphere.'

Norroll and Traxel followed her gaze. Through the flickering static, the shuddering image projected by the hololith depicted the flight path of a vessel departing from the highest levels of the miles-high iron spike that served as Ganspur's principal port. The

Astra Militarum drop-ship's avenue of approach indicated it was to dock with a similarly tall spire on the eastern edge of the city.

Norroll glanced across the room as Bissot disengaged from where she and Daviland fought the last Stygian, racing to where Akraatumo lay. The volley gunner heaved the vox-operator onto her shoulders, snatching his field phone as she did so.

'Valkyrie, this is First Eradicant,' she called. 'Need immediate support and evac on the sixth floor of the Stygian compound, north side of the building.'

'First Eradicant, repeat. Did you say evac from the sixth *floor?'*

'Get to the sixth floor, north side, and start shooting!' Bissot shouted. 'Further instructions to follow!'

'I… confirm, First Eradicant. En route.'

'When you see the Valkyrie outside the window,' Bissot shouted to the squad, 'hit the floor!'

The door shuddered, bulging inwards as the Stygians in the hallway detonated another string of explosives. The blast doors peeled in from the centre like an opening seed pod.

'How many krak grenades do they have?' Akraatumo mumbled weakly.

'More than we do,' Bissot said. 'When the Valkyrie shows up outside the window, we're hitting the deck. Are you ready for that?'

'Do I have a choice?'

The doors buckled open, heavy-gauge plasteel rupturing inwards in a cloud of dust and smoke. The force of the blast sent Durlo sliding face first across the floor, his lasgun dragging alongside him by its power cable.

The Stygians pressed through the breach, hellguns to shoulders as they searched the roiling fug for their targets. Already downed by the explosion and obscured by the smoke, the Scions crawled towards the sides of the room.

The air began to clear, smoke venting through the shattered windows. The Stygians opened fire on the Scions.

In the instant between the first shot and the second, the Valkyrie appeared outside the window, dropping down on plumes of vertical thrust. Its front-mounted multi-laser strafed the room, the rapidly fired storm of las knocking the first wave of Stygians from their feet. Simultaneously, each time the gunship strafed to a side, a door-mounted heavy bolter would fire on the Stygians, forcing them back into the cover of the hallway. The hololithic dais erupted in a shower of sparks, its crew of servitors reduced to shells of fractured components and shredded meat, sending blood and oil bursting across the floor.

Along the sides of the room, the Scions sprang to their feet, pelting for the window as fast as their legs could carry them. Traxel dived past Norroll, braving the storm of the Valkyrie's fire as he darted low across the floor, plasma pistol at the ready, to where the Stygian captain lay.

Norroll tackled him to the ground before he could get off a shot, the stream of las-fire searing through the space just above their heads. 'Are you mad?' he shouted.

'Get off me, Norroll!' From the ground, Traxel aimed a kick at the recon trooper's head.

Norroll blocked the kick, immobilising the Tempestor's leg in the crook of his arm. Traxel's plasma pistol flashed towards him, and Norroll found himself looking directly down the barrel.

For the span of a few heartbeats, the plasma pistol encompassed Norroll's entire world. He released the Tempestor's leg.

Traxel lowered the weapon. 'Let's go.' He slid onto his belly, crawling towards the window with Norroll close behind, leaving the albino mutant writhing in her agony.

'Now what?' Norroll asked when they reached the window. Multi-laser and heavy bolter fire had opened up the entire storey.

The Scions stood, bunched up on opposite walls, Norroll, Traxel, Atebe and Durlo on the left side and Daviland and Bissot, hefting Akraatumo, on the far right.

With the Scions clear, the Valkyrie launched a salvo from its rocket pods, sending the last of its frag warheads spearing through the door to burst where the Stygians had taken shelter in the hallway.

'Valkyrie, drop a level,' Bissot shouted into the vox handset.

'Understood…' Sandeborn replied, complying despite his uncertain tone indicating his actual lack of understanding.

The Stygians surged back through the doorway, their black armour now chalk white from the showers of dust and debris from the Valkyrie's assault, hotshot lasguns blazing after the Scions.

'Jump!' Bissot shouted, hurling herself and Akraatumo through the window.

They landed heavily on the Valkyrie's left wing. Akraatumo's greater weight crushed down across Bissot's shoulders and they bounced, sliding off over the wing's forward edge. Catching hold of a stowage tiedown with her left hand as she slid past, Bissot snatched Akraatumo's wrist in her right, leaving her volley gun dangling from her backpack by its power cabling.

The Valkyrie shuddered, jolting slightly as each of the remaining Scions landed on it. Above, the Stygians peppered the craft and the Scions atop it with fire. One jogged forward with a meltagun.

'Shit fire!' Sandeborn cursed as he gave power to the engines, nearly dislodging the Scions as he heaved the gunship back up to the sixth storey on its vertical thrusters. He brought the multi-laser to bear, strafing it once more across the Stygians firing from the window and forcing them to dive for cover.

The meltagun shrieked, shuddering the gunship as its starboard engine ignited in a plume of black smoke.

'Climb!' Traxel shouted into the vox from where he clung to the fuselage. At his command, the Valkyrie shot straight upwards, rotating as it powered away from the Stygian compound on one engine.

Finding handholds along the top of the fuselage, the Scions locked their grips and held tight until the Valkyrie's ascent levelled out. Breached in multiple places, their carapace armour was unable to pressurise or regulate temperature as they climbed, forcing them to employ rotes to consciously elevate their metabolisms.

Akraatumo's wrist gripped in one hand, Bissot dangled from the wing, straining to pull herself up with one arm. It was something she was ordinarily capable of, even in carapace armour with a full combat load, but with another Scion attached, it proved impossible.

'Let me go, Favae,' Akraatumo said as Vytrum rapidly fell away beneath them.

'We've lost enough since we came to this stupid world,' Bissot spat, straining as she strove to pull them up. 'If I can swing you towards the door–'

'Second time's the charm,' Akraatumo said. 'I always knew being in an eradicant would be the death of me.'

'It's that damned vox-set,' Bissot said. 'It kills everybody!'

'Best I take it with me, then,' Akraatumo said, chuckling weakly.

'Just…' Bissot arm-curled Akraatumo, screaming as she strained to pull the fully armoured Scion up. She managed to bring him nearly to the level of her belt before her bicep failed. It took all her strength to maintain her grip on his wrist. 'Can you pull yourself up?'

'I can barely breathe. I can't feel anything below the neck.'

Howling with the strain, Bissot tried again to lift him, shuddering as the muscles and tendons in her upper arm began to shred. Her grip on Akraatumo's wrist began to falter.

'I just wish I could have heard the end of your mother's story,' Akraatumo said. 'I never found out how she died.'

'Something like this,' Bissot said.

'You can tell me the rest when we meet again.'

The Valkyrie hit an updraught and Bissot's grip on Akraatumo's wrist failed. He fell leadenly towards the streets far below, his signal vanishing from the eradicant's wrist-slates as he dropped out of range.

Slipping past Norroll, Daviland slid down the wing, gripping the fuselage with her left hand as she grasped Bissot's wrist and dragged her up.

With the aid of the door gunners the rest of the Scions had managed to clamber around the wings and climb inside. Norroll and Atebe helped Daviland and Bissot as the gunners closed the bay doors.

Sitting next to Bissot, Daviland examined the volley gunner's right bicep through the shredded sleeve of her fatigues. Bissot's upper arm was already red and swollen as the medicae-adept began to treat the injury.

'Destination, Tempestor?' Sandeborn asked over the vox.

'Check your scanners for the biggest thing flying,' Traxel replied.

'Oh,' Sandeborn breathed. *'That's a Devourer-class drop-ship!'*

'Do we have anything that can bring it down?'

The lieutenant laughed. *'No,'* he said. *'Not even close. Unless I could somehow manage a direct strike on the bridge, not even crashing us into it would be enough.'*

'What about the rocket pods?' Durlo asked.

'Assuming I had any rockets left in them?' Sandeborn said. *'Frag warheads only. She's equipped for an anti-personnel role. Heavy bolters and a multi-laser are no threat to a Devourer.'*

'Other options?' Traxel asked.

'I've still got the Godshaker,' Durlo said.

'Can you get us close enough, Sandeborn?' Traxel asked.

'You're going to…' Sandeborn began. *'Of course you are.'*

'You've seen us do crazier,' Norroll noted, slumping heavily down on one of the Valkyrie's side benches.

Sandeborn's scoff came across the vox as a puff of static. *'Yes, I can set you down on top of the drop-ship, Tempestor. Just have to come in behind it to avoid its weapons systems. They're not terribly manoeuvrable, so it should be no trouble.'*

'How long?'

'Five minutes. Less, maybe.'

'Not sure if five minutes is going to be enough to patch our armour enough to seal it,' Norroll said.

'We won't be exposed long,' Traxel said. 'We breach in, get to the engines and get out.' He turned to Durlo. 'Are you ready?'

'Aye, Tempestor,' Durlo said, nodding. 'One breaching charge left, and the Godshaker.'

'Good.' Gesturing to the cases stowed beneath the benches, the Tempestor addressed his squad. 'Primary objective is to get Durlo to the engine compartment and get back to the Valkyrie. Failing that, we bring the drop-ship down by any means necessary.' He lifted his head, addressing the unseen pilot in the cockpit. 'That means *any* means, Sandeborn, so if we are unable to evacuate the drop-ship, it's on you to bring it down.'

'Very good, Tempestor,' Sandeborn said. *'I'll spend the intervening time planning appropriately destructive ways to end my life in the God-Emperor's service.'*

Traxel nodded. He grasped hold of one of the hand straps suspended from the ceiling above as the Valkyrie accelerated towards and around the drop-ship, giving the Devourer's lascannon turrets and rockets a wide berth.

Nothing said equated to no questions, at least as far as the mission was concerned, so the Scions occupied their time in preparation. Norroll watched abstractly as Daviland continued to work on Bissot's arm. The medicae-adept had flensed it open to micro-suture the muscle tear and tendon damage to the gunner's right bicep – neither spoke. Bissot stared blankly ahead, eyes unfocused, as Daviland cinched her flesh shut again.

Replacing the equipment in her medi-kit, Daviland stretched her neck, twisting her head from side to side before slumping back into her seat. It was impossible for Norroll to know what she was thinking beneath her helm's featureless facemask, but the medicae-adept projected weariness.

Next to them, Atebe replaced Bissot's and Daviland's capacitor batteries before turning her attention to her long-las. Apparently satisfied that it was in working order, she checked the rest of her kit before lapsing into a silent immobility of her own.

Durlo sat to Norroll's right. Having already replaced his capacitors, the demolitions trooper inventoried his remaining equipment – a shaped breaching charge and the Godshaker Type-238 tactical atomic bomb with a three-kilo warhead. He ran his hand admiringly over the Godshaker's smooth black casing. Returning it to his backpack, Durlo settled in for the remainder of the journey. He produced his golden thronepiece as if from the ether and sent it gambolling forward and back across his knuckles.

Norroll slouched against the Valkyrie's bulkhead as he replaced the magazines for his laspistol. He had never been so exhausted in his entire life. Even his earliest days at the scholam could not match the sheer depletion he felt at this point. There was a haze at the edges of his vision, and he could not remember when he had last actually slept. Only the faintest recollection of what life devoid of pain resembled remained to him. He looked to Daviland, Atebe and Bissot across from him, and at Durlo trancing next to him, somehow still rolling the coin across his knuckles, and wondered which of them was going to die next.

He felt like a machine left running indefinitely without benefit of fuel or maintenance, juddering on the verge of total collapse. He tried to focus on the moment, but when focus tumbled beyond his grasp he simply sat there, staring vacantly into space.

Traxel knelt in the centre of the Valkyrie, patiently screwing a plasma flask into his pistol – had to be patient when a simple mis-thread could result in a fatal overheat.

'Would you have shot me?' Norroll asked.

Traxel made a final check of the fit of his plasma flask and tapped the bottom.

'Yes.'

'First Eradicant, we are coming round the drop-ship,' Sandeborn announced. *'Matching speed. Prepare for insertion.'*

Norroll stood up and grasped the overhead strap. Anything else would have to wait.

XXI

Fennech darted through the doorway at the end of the corridor, followed closely by Lieutenant Morlitz, the Impetus Company commander. The pair burst into a large, broken-down administrative area, accompanied by the surviving three troopers of Morlitz's command squad. An overturned table lay on its side in the rough centre of the room.

Five men in heavily patched Rilisian flak armour huddled behind makeshift barricades of broken lexographs, their lasguns and stub pistols trained on the door. They opened fire the moment Fennech and Morlitz barged in, forcing the Guardsmen into cover.

Fennech saw the target at the back of the room, half obscured by overturned steel repositoria and furniture. Hurdt's hair was longer than he had seen in the picts, his uniform a bit more dishevelled and his overcoat a bit more worn, but he was unmistakable.

'General Hurdt!' Fennech shouted, levelling his bolt pistol at the traitor. 'The God-Emperor's judgement is upon you!'

Hurdt looked directly at Fennech in surprise, then turned and darted through the door at the back of the room. Fennech's bolt went wide, bursting against the doorframe.

Fennech ran after him, stub-fire spanging from his carapace armour and refractor field as he ploughed straight through the centre of the room, leaving Morlitz and his first sergeant in the doorway. Fennech dropped one of Hurdt's men on the other side of the makeshift barricade with a round from his bolt pistol as he vaulted the overturned table. Another came at Fennech as he landed, blade raised. The commissar punched him in the stomach with his power first, reducing the man to a mass of shredded meat and viscera oozing down the near wall.

The commissar hurled himself through the door, heedless of what may have been on the other side. It was a stupid thing to do, the sort of recklessness that got you killed, and he knew it. Head down and leading with his bolt pistol, he crossed the threshold, trusting Morlitz and his men to keep the enemy off his back.

Fennech sprinted across a long, narrow passageway with three partly opened doors on his right, once likely administrative suites, and a row of shattered windows lining the entirety of the wall to his left. Firelight flickered in the room at the end of the hallway, and Fennech made for it.

He felt renewed – young, even. The notion of bringing down a traitor to the God-Emperor invigorated the commissar more than simple food or sleep ever could. His breath was metronomic, his bionic respiratory system pumping oxygenated blood through his system far more efficiently than the one he had been born with had ever been capable of. He ran tirelessly forward on augmetic legs.

The ammunition counter in his augmetic left eye corroborated what the red indicator flashing on his bolt pistol meant – he had only one shot remaining. He would just have to make it count.

Behind a battered hardwood desk in the office at the end of the hall, General Hurdt scoured every surface with a hand flamer.

Charts and books blazed in the flames, and data-slates scattered across the desk's surface crackled in the heat. Hurdt ignored Fennech, focused instead on destroying intelligence.

Fennech stopped in the doorway and lined up a shot between Hurdt's shoulder blades.

'Drop the weapon, general.'

Hurdt raised his hands, letting the flamer fall limply from his grip. He moved smoothly, almost casually, as if utterly indifferent to the situation.

'Turn around,' Fennech ordered.

Hurdt did as he was told, his hands still held up loosely on either side of his head. His dark, heavily hooded eyes regarded Fennech with practised nonchalance.

'Looks like you got the drop on me, commissar.'

'This goes one of two ways, general,' Fennech said.

Hurdt glanced at Fennech's bolt pistol and grimaced. 'You mean, either you kill me now, or we can wait until the Inquisition shows up, puts me to the question and then eventually kills me in some public and vindictively appropriate manner.'

Fennech's chin declined a degree.

Hurdt sighed. 'That's a tough one,' he said. 'Might be better if you just shot me now and got it over with.'

Fennech hesitated, eyeing the general suspiciously. 'Is this a desire for atonement, general? For absolution?'

'Absolution, absolutely.' Hurdt nodded. His tongue flicked nervously across his lips. 'Fire away.'

Iron sights of his bolt pistol over the general's left eye, Fennech squeezed the trigger.

Hurdt recoiled, starting backwards and involuntarily raising his hands over his face as the round detonated less than a yard from him. The amplified refractor field enveloping him flashed with sudden incandescence.

Slowly, Hurdt lowered his hands. Reaching beneath his plastron, he quickly withdrew a smouldering golden device not much larger than a pack of lho-sticks. He cursed, dropping it swiftly as it burned his hand through his glove.

'They assured me it would work, but I wasn't sure,' Hurdt admitted, shaking his singed hand. 'For what it's worth, commissar, I never meant for all this to happen. I never expected Zheev and Mawr could put up this much of a fight.'

Fennech glared at the general from the other side of the smouldering desk with unvarnished disgust.

'I have always been a proud son of Rilis,' Hurdt said. 'I did what had to be done so that my world could chart its own destiny, apart from an uncaring Imperium that plunders its resources and betrays its children.' He drew his power sword. 'I hope you believe me when I say that I never intended to take up with the Iron Warriors – that was a line I never expected to cross.'

Fennech's lip twisted in a cold sneer as he holstered his empty bolt pistol.

'General,' he said biliously, 'I don't care.'

A split second later, he vaulted the desk, power fist crackling.

Hurdt ducked to the side as Fennech cleared the desk, narrowly avoiding the blow that would have taken his head off. The fist's disruptor field sizzled as it swept past, singeing his hair and left ear. Pivoting around the commissar, Hurdt sliced his sword upwards, severing the power conduit to Fennech's gauntlet. With a deft turn of the blade, he swept it towards the commissar's midsection.

Fennech narrowly blocked Hurdt's strike with his power fist, though without a power field to deflect it, the blade sliced through the gauntlet's housing and into the augmetic arm beneath. Inconvenienced but otherwise unharmed, Fennech backhanded the general with the oversized fist, drawing his own power sword as Hurdt tumbled backwards across the desk, spitting blood.

Fennech walked around the desk, sword raised. He loomed above the stricken general, power sword crackling as he raised it to strike the deathblow.

It never fell.

Intended to protect Rilis' lord governor from harm, the defence guns in the corners of the room sprang from their concealment, the storm of high-calibre solid shot from their servitor-manned stubbers tearing through Fennech's greatcoat and shattering the carapace armour beneath. Instinctively, Fennech hurled himself behind the cover of the desk. Blood leaked from multiple wounds as he waited for the automated stub-fire to relent.

By the time it had, he had nearly bled out.

'You commissars,' Hurdt said through bloodied teeth. He spat, massaging his swollen jaw as he picked himself up. 'Every damned one of you is a showman. You just had to make this into some fragging lesson, even without an audience.'

Out of ammunition, the servitors idled on either side of the room, burring noisily as they tracked the slowly rising commissar. Fennech retrieved his cap from the ground, placed it back on his head and straightened it. He swayed where he stood, fighting to maintain his balance and his grip on his power sword. He took a step forward and nearly toppled onto his face.

Hurdt backed away slightly, his own powerblade raised. 'Sadly, you're not the first commissar I've run afoul of. Adekwane was my division commissar for years.' Hurdt shook his head sadly. 'He was the best, Adekwane. The best. We'd been together since Cadia. Killing him was the hardest thing I've ever had to do in my life,' he added with a sigh. Hurdt lifted his own cap, exposing a broad, livid scar that cut through the thinning iron-grey hair atop his head. 'Gave me a final lesson, though. You can bet I'll never underestimate a commissar again.'

He replaced his cap. 'When I first enlisted, I had a sergeant who used to say, "If you ain't cheatin', you ain't tryin'."' Hurdt chuckled. 'I took that to heart. I'm pushing ninety-five sidereal, commissar, and the juvenat treatments just aren't cutting it any more. I had to bring you down to my level.'

'You think your duplicity will save you,' Fennech said, his voice still strong despite his wounds. 'It will not.'

The general took a step forward, angling his sword to strike. 'You know what they call someone who plays fair, commissar?'

'The Emperor's retribution is upon you,' Fennech spat through bloodstained teeth.

Hurdt's expression soured. 'A loser, commissar. They call him a loser.'

'The Hundred-and-Thirty-Ninth is coming,' Fennech said, undeterred. His hand trembled as he raised his power sword. 'Do you think your deceit will spare you from their wrath?'

'It's like talking to a recording,' Hurdt muttered.

Something beneath Fennech's carapace armour gave as he stepped forward, sending blood sheeting down over his greatcoat. Head high, he lunged at the general.

Hurdt parried, the energised blades clanging together briefly before the power fields repelled each other. He reeled back in a burst of incandescence as his sword glanced from Fennech's refractor field, before blocking the commissar's blade with a clumsy parry. Rebounding, Hurdt's crackling blade sliced off three of the thick fingers on Fennech's gauntlet, but that did not slow the commissar. Narrowly dodging the cut Fennech had aimed at his neck, Hurdt fell backwards.

Fennech swatted Hurdt's blade aside and rammed his own weapon down. It stabbed deep into the floor and stuck fast as the general rolled aside.

'Even dying, you're better than I am,' Hurdt gasped, scrambling upright against the door at the rear of the room as Fennech wrenched his sword free. His breath sawed in and out through his mouth. 'Like I said, not as young as I used to be.'

Fennech took a step forward, trusting his augmetic legs to keep him standing. His head swam, dots blinking across the tunnel vision that threatened to swallow his sight. The old rotes from the scholam banished the disorientation, bestowing a red-tinged, crystalline clarity to his eyesight.

Hatred, his oldest ally, was with him – it sustained him, driving him forward. Pain and doubt fell away as the world around him slowed. He looked upon his enemy, his perception hyper-focused so that he could see each bead of sweat gleaming on Hurdt's forehead, the dark stains on his greatcoat, the scars on his face and neck. Lightning arced across his power sword's edge, its hungry blade poised to scythe the traitor's head from his perfidious shoulders.

General Hurdt's power sword plunged through Fennech's chest below his breastbone as the commissar struck, running him through. His augmetic pulmonary system compromised, Fennech collapsed limply over the general, chin resting on his shoulder.

'Just because I said you were better than me doesn't make me a slouch,' Hurdt whispered in Fennech's ear. 'I just have to take my opportunities as I get 'em.'

Hurdt rolled Fennech off him, withdrawing his power sword from the commissar's chest. Fennech wheezed, scrabbling at the desk as he struggled to rise.

'No more pronouncements, commissar?' Hurdt asked, gasping. 'No more promises of retribution?'

Fennech glared at him, his human eye narrowed against the sheer brilliance of his hatred. His augmetic ear caught the whisper of footfalls from down the corridor behind him.

'All of your achievements will be as nothing,' he wheezed through a throatful of blood. 'I die satisfied in the knowledge that you will be stricken from history.' A thin, bloody grin stretched Fennech's lips taut. 'Such is the fate of all heretics.'

Hurdt shrugged. 'Everyone knows who Abaddon is,' he said, and struck Fennech's head from his shoulders.

The fusillade of las-fire burst from the doorway before Fennech's head had even stopped rolling. Sarring entered the room just in time to see Hurdt dive across the desk.

'Hold fire,' she commanded, though Diez continued shooting. Sarring jostled him to get his attention, then raised a clenched fist. Nodding, he stopped.

Sarring could hear Hurdt rummaging through something behind the desk, cursing several times, his movements rushed with panic.

'Surrender, general,' Sarring said, struggling to keep herself from panting. 'We have you cut off. Make it easy on yourself and come out.'

'Makes it sound easy on you,' Hurdt called back.

'Would it reassure you if I told you I've a vested interest in seeing you brought to trial?'

Hurdt barked a bitter laugh.

'I won't give you the option again.'

'You have me over a barrel, Euri.'

Sarring refused to dignify Hurdt's condescension with a reply.

'I'm coming out,' Hurdt said. 'Don't shoot. I surrender.'

'Cover me,' she ordered Rawl and Temmet, who assumed covering positions from either side of the doorway. Diez, getting the idea, followed suit, taking up a prone, supported firing position at their feet.

Cautiously, Sarring limped into the room, laspistol raised as she stepped over Fennech's decapitated body.

'Come out slowly, general. Hands where I can see them.'

Red-faced and sweating, Hurdt did as he was told. He rose

from behind the desk, arms casually upraised. His deactivated power sword hung on his thumb by its crossguard, dangling loosely behind his head.

'Drop it, general.'

The power sword fell to the floor with a resounding clang.

Hurdt ducked back behind the desk.

Sarring fired on instinct as Hurdt dropped, her shot going wide and striking the armoured hatchway at the rear of the room. Their commander positioned between them and General Hurdt, Sarring's troopers held their fire.

Hurdt lunged around the desk at Sarring, coming in low and easily getting inside the younger officer's defences. A blade flicked out of a scabbard hidden inside the general's sleeve, and he plunged his dagger into Sarring's left side, under her flak vest. The envenomed blade hissed as it burned through Sarring's leather greatcoat and lodged in her plasteel ribs.

The general breathed a curse.

Sword in hand, Sarring punched Hurdt in the face. Her steel fist crashed into his jaw like a triphammer, sending him pitching backwards over the desk in a shower of blood and teeth. He thumped to the floor, coming to a rest against the blast door at the back of the room.

Sarring plucked Hurdt's dagger from her side and tossed it away.

'What's behind the door?' she asked, looking up from Hurdt to the heavy plasteel hatch he lay before.

Hurdt struggled to sit up. He mumbled wetly.

'What?'

Hurdt spluttered through his mashed lips and broken jaw.

'I said, don't open it. Leave it alone,' he slurred.

'Open it,' Sarring ordered Rawl. 'The rest of you, cover him.'

Temmet signed the command on to Diez, who complied.

Warily, Rawl stepped past Hurdt and accessed the hatch's control panel.

'Access code's already been entered,' Rawl said.

The general trembled. 'Don't,' he mumbled to Rawl. 'Please.'

With a contemptuous scoff, Rawl flipped the door control. Hydraulics hissed as the blast hatch slid open.

A giant in burnished iron stood before the clattering cogitator array inside, his helm's glowing amber optics hungrily devouring the information scrolling down the display screen. The Adeptus Astartes turned to face Rawl, his battle helm fashioned into the visage of an iron skull with a blunt, shallow V-shaped wedge protecting the vox-grille.

The helm's speakers distorted the Heretic Astartes' irritated growl into the snarl of an angered beast as he drew his chainsword.

Hurdt's gurgling moan died as the Space Marine's heavy boot stamped down, crushing the general's chest.

The giant was through the door and among them before any of them had a chance to react. His chainsword swiped out, bisecting Rawl at the waist with enough force that each half of the trooper was sent cartwheeling across the office in a tangle of severed viscera and spraying blood. His bolt pistol roared, bursting open Temmet's chest and blasting his internal organs free of his ribcage. At the same time, the Heretic Astartes' servo-arm drove his lascannon onto Diez's helmet like a piston, pulping the vox-operator's skull and driving the remains into his chest cavity.

Sarring watched as the events around her seemed to occur in almost comically slow motion. Shocked beyond any conscious understanding of the action, she raised her powerblade to intercept the Space Marine's chainsword by reflex alone. Bolt pistol in hand, he struck her with a vicious backhand, the force of the blow crushing her left pauldron and sending her flying from her feet.

Las-beams erupted from the doorway as Lieutenant Morlitz opened fire, accompanied by at least one other squad.

By the time Sarring had recovered from the fall, the giant had already slaughtered a path through her troopers in the doorway. His chainsword snarled, limbs spinning and offal spilling in his wake as he thundered down the corridor, a blur of lustrous iron streaked in blood.

Unable to respond to a threat which struck them down with the fury of a thunderbolt, the Rilisians ran, tripping over one another in their haste to flee. Those who retained the presence of mind to fight fired upon a target seemingly invulnerable to their las-fire, who rewarded their bravery with death.

Picking herself up, Sarring pursued, her body responding to a half-formed impulse to halt the armoured juggernaut's rampage through her men. She bounded down the corridor at an awkward limp, stumbling forward as her bionic leg far outstripped the capabilities of the organic one, half tripping over the mauled corpses of her troopers lining her path.

Always, the Space Marine was just slightly ahead, his butchery so efficient that it barely slowed him as he pushed through the Guardsmen. He seemed to kill with each step, the act as mundane to him as simply running down the hallway might be to a normal man. Chainsword revving, bolt pistol firing and servo-arm bludgeoning, he delivered death with a practised economy of movement that ensured he could continue forward at pace – a consequence of his retreat, rather than the objective.

The Heretic Astartes cut down any who stood in his way as he made his escape. Most of the Guardsmen were unable to even react to the colossus carving through their comrades. The more fortunate collapsed against the walls, blood-spattered and shuddering, unable to process how they had been spared. Mere happenstance separated the living from the dead.

Sarring had nearly caught up to him as the Space Marine smashed into a narthex at the end of the corridor, opening fire on the far wall with his lascannon and shouldering through it to burst out into open space beyond. Momentum carried her after him through the breach, power sword extended to strike as the two plummeted towards the ground.

Armoured boots hammered into the pavement three storeys below, shattering it with a resounding crack. The Space Marine's power armour absorbed the fall, and he was on the move again, sprinting eastward.

Sarring struck the ground behind him. Her innards lurched, jarred by the fall – though her augmetic leg took much of the impact, the human body was not intended to experience such force. Tumbling sideways, she collapsed, struggling for breath.

'Hold it together, Eurydice,' Sarring hissed to herself as she scrambled to her feet. Her breath sawed in and out of lungs that were still only human as she continued after the Space Marine, power sword sparking. She stumbled – the fall had damaged her augmetic leg, and the searing pain in her chest and abdomen suggested she had broken something vital internally. Her heart hammered behind her ribcage, throbbing so rapidly it felt it might burst at any instant. Sweat sheeted down her face, stinging her eyes. 'Just get the bastard.'

The Space Marine's lascannon pivoted on its servo-arm, opening fire on the move. An incandescent streak of focused energy sizzled through the air, close enough for her to feel its charge prickling the skin on the left side of her face.

Sarring flinched but continued forward, desperation and anger rendering her heedless of the danger. Her sole focus was given to catching up to the Heretic Astartes and meting out whatever small measure of vengeance she could – for her family, her world and her Emperor – before he slew her. He owed her at least that satisfaction. Sparks licked eagerly across the blade of the power sword clutched in her steel fingers.

He was only a few yards ahead of her now, lining up another shot with his lascannon.

Sarring felt the blow in her chest. Her left arm continued forward, spinning end over end, still grasping her power sword. Carried onwards by her momentum, she collapsed face first into the pavement.

'No,' she mouthed through numbed lips. 'No no no.'

Sarring writhed in agony, right hand clutching at the smoking hole bored cleanly through the augmetic left half of her upper torso. She couldn't breathe. She could barely see through tears and sweat.

Straining to keep her eyes open, she realised the ironclad giant stood above her.

He had holstered his bolt pistol and lowered his chainsword, silent as he regarded Sarring where she lay. He looked her over slowly, his gaze lingering on the smouldering crater punched through her torso before appraising the augmetics which replaced nearly the entire left half of her body. The thick, shallow-V wedge of his skull faceplate dipped slightly.

'See what they make of us,' he said, his voice soft despite the distortion of his helm's voxmitter. 'The zenith of mankind's art. They manufacture gods, then use us as nothing more than weapons. How perverse our species is.'

He turned and walked away, his thudding footfalls fading gradually, until Sarring could not hear them any more. Her vision faded with them, darkness encroaching from the edges until only a small, bright spark at the centre remained.

Then nothing.

XXII

'Standing by, First Eradicant.'

Sandeborn's announcement prickled in Daviland's ears as the Scions rappelled onto the Devourer drop-ship. The Valkyrie had approached the landing craft from behind, matching speed to effectively hover between the twin lascannon turrets mounted just below the vessel's bridge.

Norroll was first out, as usual, followed by Bissot, Durlo and Traxel. Daviland and Atebe were last, sliding down the relatively short distance to the ship head first. By the time they reached the top hull, Durlo had already finished emplacing his final breaching charge. They had all employed the Rote of Flame to raise their body temperatures before the Valkyrie opened its doors.

The rote had been one of the earliest and most vital lessons they learned at the scholam – a harsh lesson that claimed many young aspirants during the first days. While the Scions' omnishield helms and specially crafted carapace armour could be hermetically sealed to withstand many hostile environments, including even the hard vacuum of the void for brief periods of time, their armour was far too damaged to do so. More than forty thousand feet above Vytrum, the air was practically unbreathable, even with their armour's oxygen feeds. Beyond the very real risk of hypoxia, the Scions were fully exposed to low pressure and cold, enduring temperatures driven far below freezing by altitude and windshear.

The Valkyrie rose, ensuring it was safe from potential debris ejected by the breaching detonation, though it remained in the same position relative to the drop-ship. When the Scions were safely behind the cover of the Devourer's lascannon turrets, Durlo detonated the charge. It exploded with a brief flash, its smoke rapidly swallowed by the howling wind, leaving only a small hole punched through the fuselage. Through this hole the Scions dropped, one by one.

The interior was dark, illuminated only by red emergency lighting and the cyclic amber pulse of rotating signal lights. Servitors tromped lethargically between columns of Leman Russ battle tanks and Chimera armoured transports, packed bumper to bumper through the cavernous hold. There were no visible tech-priests, or even Militarum escorts, as the Scions crept low around the armoured vehicles. Drop-ships of the Devourer class had two decks for the rapid deployment of an entire regiment's worth of personnel and equipment from orbit. In a Munitorum-standard loadout, the upper deck of the craft held the infantry, while their vehicles were parked below, ready for occupation and rollout the moment the vessel landed.

The interior of the vessel was far too densely packed with vehicles and supply crates to hold any infantry, and Daviland had to assume that the entire space had been given over to vehicle and ammunition transport. If a standard Devourer was large enough to carry a fully manned and equipped regiment from orbit, it stood to reason that this one carried enough vehicles and materiel to equip a small division. Battered and broken as the traitorous Rilisian forces were, this drop of fresh vehicles and supplies would give them the edge to finally break their long-running stalemate with the loyalists.

Atebe said what Daviland was thinking. 'Tempestor, would it not be better for us to take this ship for the loyalists?'

'Undoubtedly,' Traxel replied.

Atebe's next question lingered unspoken for several long seconds. 'So, why don't we?'

'Who would pilot it?' Traxel asked. 'You? Durlo? He is quite technologically proficient, after all.'

'I've no idea how to pilot a drop-ship,' Durlo admitted.

'It's the reason the Militarum Tempestus relies upon the Navy to ferry us about,' Bissot said, pointing up to the Valkyrie above.

'Who is piloting it now?' Atebe asked.

'Servitors, judging by the way it's flying.' Norroll shrugged. 'I can't imagine any pilot worth his salt would dream of letting a Valkyrie park above his ship.'

Traxel motioned Norroll forward with a nod of his head.

A few minutes later, the recon trooper reported back. *'This is unusual.'*

'What do you see?' Traxel asked.

'More what I don't see,' Norroll said. *'This is a ghost ship. No crew, no security, no tech-adepts. Just servitors. Menial type – not even gun servitors. I've been giving them a pretty wide berth, but I practically just ran into one. Didn't even look at me. Just stepped aside and kept going like I wasn't there.'*

'Where are you?'

'Lower level, heading back towards engine maintenance. Hatch to the bridge is welded shut. Keep your wits about you, just in case, but I think you can safely pick up the pace.'

The eradicant crept forward, keeping low as they filed through the narrow corridors between armoured vehicles and military bulk shipping containers. Norroll's assessment seemed accurate enough – the only other biological entities on the drop-ship beyond the Scions themselves appeared to be the complement of servitors. Graceless on their metal-shod feet or clanking, industrial-grade augmetics, the monotasked cyborgs executed their preprogrammed functions, checking each vehicle they passed and utterly ignoring the Tempestus Scions.

'Where are the tech-priests?' Atebe wondered as she slipped between a pair of tandem fuelling servitors.

'Here,' Norroll said over the vox. *'There's one here, just outside the engine room. Some assembly required.'*

The recon trooper waited outside the engine compartment, kneeling above black-robed, piecemeal remains soaked through with blood and unguents. It had been a tech-adept of Stygies VIII, judging by its robes and the badges adorning them – Ganspur's relations with the secretive forge world were long and oftentimes fractious, largely due to the occult, acquisitive nature of the world's tech-priests.

'Grace of the Throne, protect those worthy of your light,' Bissot whispered, the rest of her prayer muted by her respirator as she shielded her eyes from the unholy binharic scripts scrawled across the bulkhead outside the enginarium.

'Don't look at the symbols on the walls,' Norroll warned belatedly. Sigils daubed upon the bulkheads and decking in blood and oil distorted the Scions' perceptions with the hallucinogenic blight of warpcraft. The visual assists of their optics stuttered, and the sibilant static that hissed in the audio speakers of their omnishield helms seemed to bear an almost sentient malevolence.

There was a maliciously calculated methodology to the cruelty inflicted upon the carcass. Nearly all the unfortunate tech-priest's augmetic systems had been forcibly removed from its organic base and sorted around it, though the logic used in the sorting was lost upon the Scions. The only bionic components which remained still anchored to the mutilated remains were the optical and audial systems, indicating that whoever or whatever killed the adept had wanted it to witness and understand its suffering.

Daviland and Bissot approached from the narrow avenue between vehicles as Durlo whispered prayers to the God-Emperor and Omnissiah both. Given the sacrilegious desecration of the tech-priest, Daviland wasn't certain prayers would be enough.

'Is this the only tech-adept aboard?' Traxel asked.

'Only one I've found,' Norroll replied.

'No tech-priests, no pilots, everything servitor-run and automated,' Durlo mused. 'Reduces the risk of outside interference. Factor in the desecration of this adept, and it could indicate Ganspur is not allied with the traitors. Perhaps they thought this was business-as-usual production, until it was too late?'

'Leave such questions to the Inquisition,' Traxel said. 'Move.'

The eradicant deployed as ordered, though they discovered only more servitors occupying the engine compartment. The lack of hostility aboard the drop-ship was deeply unsettling. The creaking of the vessel, the bass rumble of the engines, even the leaden tread and periodic mumbling of the servitors set them all on edge. It felt as if unseen foes must surely lie in wait, about to strike from an unexpected quarter at any moment, yet none did.

The sole exception to this hyper-alert state was Durlo, who seemed perfectly relaxed. Entering the engine compartment, the demolitions trooper set to work preparing the detonation site for the Godshaker Type-238 with a number of tools he had likely found on-site.

Durlo nestled the bomb within the network of pipes forming the engine's central fuel feeding system and adjusted the flow of several critical promethium arteries around the compartment. The golden thronepiece played across the knuckles of his left hand as he worked, pinging into the air and slapping back into his palm at regular intervals before resuming its dance, back and forth.

'What are you doing?' Daviland asked, the disagreeable combination of monotony and acute watchfulness finally wearing down her behavioural barriers.

'Re-routing and pressurising the fuel feed,' Durlo answered. He had removed his helmet and was thoughtfully chewing on his lower lip as he regarded a fitting he had just changed out. 'An atomic bomb can do a lot of damage, but I want to make sure there's nothing salvageable when this ship hits the ground.'

'Where did you learn how to do this?' Like his coin juggling and other sleights of hand, Durlo's gift for destruction had always fascinated Daviland.

'Reading, watching, doing,' Durlo said, loosening an elbow fitting with a heavy spanner. 'Some of it's just innate, I suppose – hip bone's connected to the thigh bone. This goes to that.' The coin pinged into the air, and he snatched it without looking. 'Mostly, though, I just like blowing things up.'

Durlo chuckled as he twisted the ends of a wire together. 'Me and my silly coin. Favae and Gry always arguing. Actis always trying to be smart. And you, coming from outside of the Xian Tigers with your different ideas and Ultramarian sensibilities. Courage and honour, and other such things that the Thirty-Sixth knows nothing about.'

Daviland grinned, though she knew Durlo was unable to see it for her mask. 'I don't know what you mean.'

'Favae, can you hand me the–' Durlo began. Before he could finish, Bissot handed him a soldering iron. 'Oh, thanks.'

'How long?' Traxel asked.

Durlo looked over his work. The Godshaker was tied into a cage of jury-rigged pipes and linked to the ship's power systems through a network of pressurising valves feeding from the main fuel lines. 'Skipping over the technical bits, I'd say this should be sufficient to knock this ship out of the air.'

'Not destroy it?'

Durlo scoffed. 'And then some.'

Traxel nodded and gave Durlo's left pauldron a heavy clap. 'Good man,' he said. 'God-Emperor speed you.'

'Thank you, Tempestor.'

Atebe gave Durlo a nod and followed Traxel out of the enginarium.

Norroll approached Durlo, helm tucked under his left arm. Between his broken nose, heavily bruised face and unwashed ginger beard and hair, which had grown out to nearly an inch long, he was scarcely recognisable from when the deployment to Rilis began. Norroll's tawny eyes glittered as he headbutted the demolition trooper – not hard, but there was a noticeable knock when their foreheads collided. Norroll turned and departed without a word, leaving Durlo with Bissot and Daviland.

Bissot hugged Durlo tightly, then followed it up with a headbutt of her own.

'What?' Durlo asked.

'I'm jealous,' she said.

'Don't be.' Durlo smiled. 'See you at the Throne.'

Bissot clenched her fists and gave a sharp nod.

'Emperor's light shine on you, Favae.'

'What in the hells is going on?' Daviland demanded.

'Valkyrie's waiting,' Durlo said. 'You should get going.'

'You're not coming with us?'

'Oh, for the love of Terra, Salenna!' Bissot exclaimed. 'You're just figuring this out?'

'No remote detonators,' Durlo said. 'One of us has to make

sure this works properly. No offence, but that's out of everyone's field but mine.'

He was correct, of course. Short of beatification, martyrdom in the line of duty was all any Tempestus Scion could hope for. Though she might wish otherwise, there was nothing Daviland would do to stand in the way of Durlo's duty.

Bissot departed, leaving Daviland and Durlo alone.

Daviland slung her lasgun and crossed her hands over her chest in the sign of the aquila. She reverently declined her head.

'Courage and honour, daughter of Macragge.' Durlo smiled, returning the salute.

'Courage and honour, son of Abstinax. Die well.'

'I will.'

With a final nod of farewell, Daviland turned to leave.

'Hey, Salenna?' Durlo called.

Daviland looked back.

'Here.' Durlo's thumb popped forward, his golden thronepiece arcing as it spun end over end through the air.

Daviland caught it.

'God-Emperor bless you,' Durlo said. 'Go.'

Coin in hand, Daviland turned and left, jogging past oblivious servitors and the armoured vehicles and containers they mindlessly attended. Above, the wind howled through the hole in the upper fuselage. Tucking the coin into an interior pouch beneath her carapace breastplate, she leapt up through it and clambered into the gale that swept across the top deck, before climbing back up the thick length of rope to the Valkyrie.

Located fifteen miles east of the capitol building, the Vanness Tether served as Vytrum's link to the orbital ring above and the stars beyond. A slender spar of iron spearing through the nearly perpetual haze of smoke that had clung to the capital since the start of the Rilisian civil war, the tether was nearly two miles high.

The exterior of the tower was studded with landing platforms – parking for atmospheric craft was provided at the lower levels, while fortified Skyshield platforms for military aircraft ringed the mid-levels to the upper spire. The tower was crowned by a network of bulk craft umbilicals, capable of tethering the void-capable ships which provided Rilis with much-needed supplies in exchange for the planet's exports.

The Devourer-class drop-ship descending from the moon above was bound for the spire's crown, a more secure location to offload the supplies for the traitor Rilisian forces than a direct ground landing. While touching down in the heart of Vytrum would have no doubt made for a faster resupply, it also increased the risk that the shipment might be intercepted by the loyalists. Having thrown in with General Hurdt in the earliest days of the civil war, Vanness' staff would ensure the general's forces received the resupply crucial to their victory.

Far outpacing the slower transport, First Eradicant's Valkyrie dropped from the low stratosphere, its sole engine burning hot as it approached the Vanness Tether.

'Visual on the Iron Warrior,' Sandeborn announced when they were half a mile from the spire. *'Telemetry identifies his location as Skyshield Four. Throne, he's big!'* the lieutenant gasped. *'I can see him from here! Permission to engage.'*

'Permission granted,' Traxel said. 'Let us off above Skyshield Four. I want solid confirmation he's dead.'

'Acknowledged, sir.'

Wind howled into the crew compartment as the Valkyrie's door gunners slid open the side hatches and manned their heavy bolters. The gunship's multi-laser spun up, sending crimson streaks of las-fire strafing across the landing platform to stitch over the Iron Warrior where he stood near the centre.

Shallow cherry-red dimples smoked upon the Heretic Astartes' burnished armour as he watched their approach, his lascannon idling at his shoulder.

'For Throne's sake! Die already!' Sandeborn snarled, still firing. The multi-laser's muzzle glowed hot from the continuous fire, the radiance gradually creeping back over the spinning barrels.

Amidst the relentless hail of multi-laser fire, the lascannon on the Iron Warrior's servo-mount snapped to life. The morning sunlight flashed on the yellow-and-black hazard stripes adorning the weapon's muzzle cowling as it swivelled menacingly towards the gunship.

'Shit!' Sandeborn exclaimed. *'Evading!'*

The Valkyrie's pilot jerked the stick hard to evade – though the door gunners' restraint tethers kept them from falling out, the manoeuvre threw them from their feet. Standing ready to deploy, the Scions clutched at the safety straps hanging from the ceiling, straining to maintain their grips as the lieutenant jinked the aircraft from side to side, desperate to avoid being struck by the lascannon.

None of the Scions saw the lascannon fire, but all felt its impact. The armour-reducing las-bolt pierced the gunship's remaining engine, rupturing it in a plume of oily black smoke. Dead in the air, momentum carried the Valkyrie forward, its graceless form still airborne despite its lack of engines.

Klaxons wailed as the Iron Warrior lined up another shot.

The heavens shuddered as a massive detonation rippled from high above. Though the Devourer had only been visible as a tiny speck in the clear blue sky, the Godshaker Type-238 exploded with the brilliance of a second sun. The remains of the drop-ship tumbled planetward, trailing coils of smoke from the larger black cloud of the explosion spreading behind it as sudden darkness devoured the morning's light.

It took a few seconds for the blast wave to strike the Valkyrie, forcing it into a nosedive. The gunship's wings nearly shredded off as it tumbled headlong towards Skyshield Four.

Every window from the top to the mid-levels of the Vanness Tether shattered in a cascade. The bulk landing tethers at the crown shrieked, protesting as the blast snapped several from their moorings and sent them crashing to the streets two miles below.

In the Valkyrie's cockpit, Sandeborn worked with what he had left, fighting to bring the stricken gunship in over the Skyshield.

'Prepare for contingency insertion, First Eradicant,' he called. *'We'll make it interesting for him.'*

The Valkyrie pitched right as Sandeborn threw all power into the gunship's vertical thrusters. Power failed and the semi-controlled pitch became an uncontrolled spin, sending the aircraft corkscrewing down.

'Out!' Traxel ordered. Fighting gravity, he leapt from the Valkyrie's left door, timing his exit to be nearly parallel to the ground, with space to clear the craft's ragged wings.

Norroll was out directly behind him. Bissot and Atebe escaped through the craft's right door a split second later, leaving Daviland struggling against the force of gravity. She heaved herself towards the door, past the hapless gunner flailing in his safety harness. Another second and she was out, dropping head first from the left door after Traxel and Norroll as the Valkyrie continued its twisting nosedive towards the Skyshield.

Daviland barely got her grav-chute to activate before she crashed awkwardly into one of the umbilical ports at the top of the Vanness Tether, bouncing from the surface at approximately one-third of her weight. Buffeted by the wind howling from the atomic blast above, she scrambled, frantically clawing at the plasteel with her fingertips as she fought to keep herself from sliding over the edge. Drawing her blade, she wedged it between two metal joins. Her fall was arrested with a sudden jolt, leaving her feet dangling out into space as her grav-chute crackled at her back.

She felt the Valkyrie's impact ringing through the tether's superstructure, juddering through the swaying spire. Sliding backwards as her blade slipped, she fumbled frantically through her pouch until she found a mag-tether. She managed to clamp it to the bulkhead just before she slipped over the edge and off into space, the rope pulling taut as it halted her fall.

Buffeted by the fierce winds of an expanding nuclear explosion less than six miles overhead, Daviland dangled from a length of rope nearly two miles above Vytrum, spinning as she struggled to eject her grav-chute. A plume of black smoke rose from where the Valkyrie had smashed into the landing platform below.

She finally managed to decouple the grav-chute, sending the twin fins fluttering listlessly to the ground. Her weight returned, along with the control it gave her in the wind. Hand over hand, she began to climb up the rope to the umbilical gate.

'First Eradicant,' she called into the static-laden vox. 'First Eradicant, this is Daviland. Can anybody hear me?'

She received no response as she pulled herself up over the edge. Feeling the relief of a solid surface beneath her feet once more, she drew her laspistol and dropped down onto the steel gangway.

Daviland activated the umbilical's hatch, taking care to stay close to the side of the gangway as the door hissed open on wheezing pneumatic hinges.

'First Eradicant, if anybody can hear me, I'm at the docking crown at the top of the spire. I am en route. Can anybody give me their position?'

Her vox signal fouled by the electromagnetic pulse of the explosion above, only static answered.

Solid shot rushed past her as stub-fire stuttered from the other side of the door. Readying her laspistol, Daviland charged inside.

XXIII

'Does anybody have contact with Daviland?' Traxel called across the vox.

'*–tive, Tempes–*' Bissot replied, her signal awash with distortion.

Norroll knelt next to Traxel behind the cover of a cogitator terminal, his knee resting on the carpet of broken glass from the window they had smashed through minutes before. 'She was still on the Valkyrie when we jumped,' he said.

Traxel nodded. His vambrace displayed no information regarding Daviland's status, meaning she was either too remote for her signal to reach or dead. Status readings for Bissot and Atebe came in stuttering bursts, desynchronised and distorted by electromagnetic distortion.

'*Mid-lev– somewhere,*' Bissot continued. '*–tered lots… enemy troops. Looks… got more …way. Garrison–*'

'Can you hold them?' Traxel asked, trying to make sense of her broken transmission. 'Norroll and I need to get to that Skyshield platform and verify the Iron Warrior, the one that Stygian captain called Zelazko, is dead.'

'*–stor, aye.*'

Traxel cut the link.

'Certainly easier with a clarion vox,' Norroll said.

Traxel grunted his agreement. 'Skyshield Four is three levels above us,' he said, slipping out from behind the cogitator station.

'Did Bissot say something about a garrison?'

'She did.'

Passing Traxel, Norroll picked his way through the empty administration suite, an unlovely, unadorned space beneath its glistening carpet of glass. Crouched low with his laspistol raised, he scouted ahead without augurs – he had lost track of Actis following the emergency bailout from the Valkyrie and had been unable to establish a signal lock with the errant servo-skull since. He moved forward carefully, looking and listening as he had been taught years before.

A low scuff of shoe leather on flooring from outside the office's door caught his attention, and he signalled for Traxel to halt. Motioning for the Tempestor to come around to the right side of the door, Norroll crept around to the left of the desks and their gently rattling cogitators.

Facing each other, Norroll indicated that they move on a three-second count. The Scions burst through the door, firing into the grey-robed office menials lined up on either side of the hallway, stub pistols drawn. Four workers fell immediately, while the others shot wildly at their attackers, shouting in uncoordinated fear and snapping off blasts from their guns as fast as they could pull the triggers. Even in the close confines of the corridor, not one round hit its mark – though one of the unfortunates managed to shoot himself in the leg.

The screaming began in earnest as Traxel's chainsword slashed through three of them at a stroke, the revving adamantine teeth spattering the walls and nearby workers in blood and viscera as he sprinted past them. Norroll was forced to be more selective with his targets, sweeping with his monoblade and firing on the move with his laspistol, though he was no less deadly for it. Untrained and unprepared, the workers were mere speed-bumps along the Scions' route and only delayed them slightly.

At the back of the formation, the workers' black-robed overseer pressed his charges forward, flabby jowls quivering as he shouted commands, exhortations and curses. He fired his double-barrelled shotgun into the press, shooting one of the grey-robed personnel in the back and striking Norroll in the upper chest and left shoulder.

Norroll pelted headlong into the overseer, barely slowed as his carapace armour absorbed the shot's impact. He plunged his monoblade into the man's right eye socket, shooting him just above his expansive belly for good measure before twisting past him and away, Traxel at his heels. Shouldering through a steel doorway, the pair entered the stairwell and began to climb, taking the steps three at a time.

The planetary militia trooper's helmet snapped forward over his face as the back of his head exploded. Lying prone along a steel catwalk, Atebe lined up the crosshairs of her long-las on the next target.

Her position overlooked a well-lit concourse, into which six separate arterial passageways converged. There were five levels of civilian transport concourses stacked atop each other in the mid-sections of the Vanness Tether, each with six separate passageways branching off from the central atrium to the docking berths that studded the spire's exterior.

Atebe and Bissot defended the fourth of these levels, containing the planetary militia troopers so that they could not interfere with Traxel and Norroll's mission in the higher reaches of the complex. The level above, where Atebe and Bissot had dropped into the facility during their emergency evacuation from the Valkyrie, had a hole bored straight through it, as if some manner of large projectile had penetrated it on one side and crashed out through the other. The skeletal remains of the travellers who had died there remained where they fell, forgotten and undisturbed through the more than three months of fighting.

The three arterial passages lying to the south and south-east were thronged with planetary militia troops, bottlenecked in place by Atebe's long-las and Bissot's ceaseless volley fire. They huddled at the edges of the corridor, their caution learned from the dead troopers littering the entrance to the concourse ahead of them. An officer in a peaked cap towards the front of the southernmost arterial brandished his chainsword in an attempt to rally his men.

Atebe shot him through the forehead.

'There doesn't seem to be any shortage of them,' she called.

'Certainly doesn't,' Bissot said, raking fire across any who sought to brave the open expanse of the concourse. There was an edge to her voice, a barely suppressed joy that carried over the vox-link. Atebe knew Bissot's approximate location below her, based upon her pattern of fire, but the sniper's position on the catwalk kept Bissot outside her field of view.

'These are planetary militia troopers,' Atebe said. 'I'd heard that nearly as many defected to the traitors as remained loyal, but I didn't expect we would find them *all* here.'

'They are not very courageous,' Bissot said derisively. *'They have us outnumbered at least ten to one, and still they don't come out and fight.'*

'Be careful what you wish for,' Atebe cautioned, a moment before the first wave of troopers from the southern junction rushed forward. Atebe picked out the squad leader, a thickset, silver-haired man with a tapered white beard. The front of his skull collapsed inwards as Atebe's high-powered las pushed it out through the back of his head, splashing his blood and brain matter over the trooper behind him.

Bissot fired, her volley gun shrieking as it filled the air with an arc of effulgent las-bolts. Four troopers fell, their flak vests nearly useless against the penetrating fusillade.

'Ask, and the God-Emperor provides!' Bissot exclaimed, never letting up on the trigger. *'O God-Emperor, I beseech thee lend thy sword, that I might spill enough of their blood to be seen as worthy in thy immaculate sight!'*

Atebe brought down another trooper charging Bissot with a shot to the head. Though the trooper's flak helmet miraculously withstood the shot, it pitched her into Bissot's line of fire, where she was dispatched.

More troopers charged as the remaining three survivors of the first wave crashed into Bissot's position. Focused on the second wave as it pushed out of the passageway, Atebe had no means to see how Bissot fared. Another trooper fell, missing the top of his head, and yet another dropped with a las-wound burned cleanly through her chest, but there were too many for Atebe to account for all of them. Some stopped, seeking cover behind the steel seats once used by travellers passing through the air transfer hub as they began to fire on Atebe's position, while others dodged between planters of black marbelite and abandoned food vendor carts as they made for Bissot.

Bleeding from a head wound, one of the first wave of planetary militia troopers staggered back into Atebe's field of view and was cut down half a second later by Bissot's volley gun. Below, Bissot was singing, her voice carrying even over the volley gun's near-continuous report:

'Through fields of flame that burn the sands,
Through pyres banked high by unclean hands,
Through hate and night and fog and death,
No foe shall stand while I draw breath!
Come all! Come all! I bring your end!
My soul, my will, my life forfend.
With righteousness, my soul entwined
With thou, O Master of Mankind!'

The entire concourse echoed with a tumult of weapons discharges. A grenade burst amongst a group of enemy troopers, fallen from a dead man's hand as he caught a round in the throat while preparing to throw it. Their lack of proficiency and discipline was more than made up for in numbers. Officers ruthlessly herded their charges forward into the Scions' fire, determined to push through the eradicant's strong point.

There was a desperation to their action – fear, not duty, drove them forward. Through the scope of her long-las, Atebe could see the panic in their eyes. They feared something more than the Scions. As she brought down another aged officer in too-tight fatigues and ill-fitting flak armour, she realised these troopers must be more afraid of the Iron Warrior than they were of the Xian Tigers. It seemed these troopers fancied their odds against a pair of Scions over the reprimand of their master should they fail.

A labour servitor trundled forward, the vicelike metal claws replacing its lower arms raised offensively. Atebe put a round through its lifeless left eye, but many more of them lumbered out in front of the planetary militia troopers. Someone had been clever, repurposing the facility's servitors to soak up the Scions' fire. She brought down two more with a single, well-placed las-bolt, penetrating through one servitor's pasty-fleshed skull and into the next one behind it.

Something interrupted Bissot's stream of fire below, snapping

Atebe back to the present – she had been in the Killstate, her thoughts elsewhere as she killed automatically. Bissot being overrun meant their position was in danger of collapsing, which meant failure. Without interrupting her methodical extermination of individual targets, she called Bissot over the vox just as the volley gun growled back to life.

'What's going on down there, Bissot?'

Bissot's immediate answer was a series of grunts and snarls. *'Just handling things manually,'* the gunner replied breathlessly. The volley gun's report pulsed from below like an engine. *'Some inventive soul has repurposed the servitors.'*

Atebe smirked. 'You said you wanted a fight.'

'Like I said, ask, and the God-Emperor provides,' Bissot said, laughing. *'I think I'm heading for an overheat or a burnout, though.'*

A fresh wave of militia troopers pushed forward behind the wave of servitors, dodging between the automata as they attempted to escape her volley gun's unrelenting fire. These were not combat-hardened troops – they were sweating and wild-eyed, their fervent gazes clearly under the influence of narcotics. At their backs, officers executed any who showed a moment's hesitation. One squad turned on their erstwhile leader, killing him and trampling his body into the floor as they fled the slaughter, but still others continued forward.

'We only have to buy Norroll and the Tempestor time,' Atebe said as a shot struck her left vambrace. Her long-las dipped, slipping from fingers left instantly numb by the impact, though the armour saved her arm.

'Tadia?'

Atebe adjusted her position, bracing her rifle on the back of her left arm. 'Yes?'

'Do you think my mother would be proud of me?'

Looking down at the dozens of dead and wounded planetary

militia troopers scattered across the blood-soaked floor of the concourse, Atebe grinned. 'Yes, Favae. I think your mother would be very proud of you.'

Bissot sighed quietly. *'Good.'*

The volley gun seemed to laugh, its report bursting across the atrium with drawn-out, manic joy as the planetary militia troopers before her fell or fled. With a final burst, the weapon stopped firing, its indomitable spirit finally overburdened as its mechanisms failed. Singing unintelligibly, Bissot lunged forward into the attackers, swinging the red-hot barrel of her faithful volley gun like a heavy iron brand as she smote the impious below. She had affixed her bayonet and reaped a terrible tally as she clubbed, stabbed and stomped her enemies to death. She laughed as she killed, singing Imperial hymns as she battled free of the press of troopers attempting to claw at her, liberated by her own righteousness.

Unwilling to risk hitting Bissot, Atebe fired into the troopers further back before they could close in and engage with the furious gunner. Dropping a pair, she risked a glance down.

Bissot's struggle was the most breathtakingly perfect melee Atebe had ever witnessed. A ray of sunlight had broken through the nuclear cloud above, streaming through the windows to form a halo of radiance about Bissot's head, as if she had been suffused with a fragment of the Emperor's manifold divinity. It took all Atebe's willpower to tear her focus from the glorious slaughter below and release her awareness enough to re-enter the Killstate.

The explosion beneath her registered but held no particular significance to Atebe as she swept the floor of hostiles. By the time the vibration of running footsteps on the stairway to the catwalk she lay upon snapped her partially from the Killstate, Atebe had lost all track of how many she had killed in the concourse below. She rolled, repositioning her long-las as she moved – at Atebe's will, the target's head came apart. Her sight picture adjusted, and she fired again, striking another trooper in the lower jaw. They flopped lifelessly to the ground a split second apart.

Atebe took a deep breath, relaxing the Killstate just enough to exist in the present. She lifted her cheek from her rifle and listened to the screams of the wounded echoing through the concourse. An unidentifiable, high-pitched monotone squalled from close by, seemingly all around her. She ran her scope across the entire concourse, picking out movement here and there, but nothing that registered as a concerted threat against their position.

'Bissot?' she called. 'Bissot, are you there?'

The only reply she received was the thin sprinkling of static returned by the vox.

She glanced at her vambrace, where the flatline of Bissot's vitals stuttered beneath her own.

She rose, keeping low as she stepped over the pair she had just killed, and descended the stairs. Thin tendrils of smoke twisted from the centre of a heap of the intermixed corpses of planetary militia troopers and servitors which lay spread across the blood-smeared floor. The bodies radiated from the centre, like the rays of a rising sun. Three of the casualties towards the far edge of the pile moved, and Atebe shot each one in quick succession. Holding her long-las with her right arm, she covered the area to the south as she used her left hand to dig through the pile of corpses at the centre for Bissot.

She found the volley gunner lying face down beneath three enemies in a pool of blood, smoking beneath the exploded capacitor unit on her back. Lacking the Martyr's Gift, which Daviland had already bestowed upon Phed, Bissot had manually overloaded her capacitors, killing the enemy as they finally managed to bring her down.

'Your mother would be proud,' Atebe said, rolling Bissot's corpse over and lightly wiping away some of the blood smearing the gunner's face.

Beneath the blood, Bissot's visage wore an expression of beatific serenity quite incompatible with the violence of her death. There was no pain in her closed eyes, and a soft, benign smile turned up the corners of her mouth. The strange radiance Atebe had noted before seemed yet to linger upon the volley gunner, and the sniper found herself returning Bissot's gentle smile.

The three levels Norroll and Traxel had to climb to reach Skyshield Four were easier to access than they had anticipated. The air was filled with the reek of promethium smoke and the tang of heavy metals, growing thicker and more opaque with each storey they climbed. Administratum adepts, labourers and servitors blocked their path. Some resisted.

Norroll stopped counting how many he had killed at thirty, and it had become steadily more monotonous since. The corridors were awash with blood and viscera as he and Traxel butchered anyone foolish enough to stand in their way, irrespective of whether they were attacking or fleeing. There was a sense of retribution to the massacre, Norroll thought, a final comeuppance for those who had turned from the Emperor's light, but it was far from satisfying.

Smoke filled the stairwell, obscuring their sight as they rushed to the third level. Their respirators were still sufficient to filter out the toxic fumes.

Clearing the hatchway at the top of the stairwell, the Scions were fired upon by a handful of grey-robed adepts choking on the smoke. A bullet flattened against Traxel's armour below the sternum, and the Tempestor decapitated the shooter for his accuracy. Norroll cut down two more, then another as Traxel wrenched his chainsword free of a ribcage. As the ruptured corpse dropped limply to the ground, they found themselves unopposed, their path to Skyshield Four finally open.

Six servitors, armed with high-pressure hoses connected to the bulky tanks of fire retardant mounted to their backs, stumped towards the hatchway. Utterly indifferent to the Scions, the servitors babbled to themselves as they halted at the platform's closed hatch, unsure how to proceed when they discovered their way blocked. Traxel and Norroll passed them by and accessed the door's controls.

The hatch opened with the smooth hiss of well-maintained hydraulics, and the Tempestus Scions shoved past the firefighter servitors and onto the landing platform.

The Valkyrie's tail was twisted up over the back of the fuselage while the nose of the gunship was flattened into the ground – despite his aircraft's being dead in the air, Sandeborn had somehow managed to nosedive it directly onto his target. The heat of the blaze consuming the gunship had further warped its frame, causing it to buckle beneath its own weight.

The fire's heat was nearly unbearable, singeing the hair from skin where the Scions' fatigues had been torn open. Traxel and Norroll studied the flaming wreckage, searching for evidence that their quarry had somehow managed to survive.

'It could be hours before this has burned out enough for us to mount a proper search,' Norroll said.

Nodding, Traxel sighed. 'I'm debating whether it's better to let the fire do its work or let the servitors do their jobs so we can get on with it.'

As if in answer, the framework towards the front of the conflagration crumpled with a shriek of twisting metal. An armoured panel collapsed, ringing from the landing platform's deck as a flame-wreathed figure rose from the heart of the pyre. The Iron

Warrior pushed through the wreckage, tearing through it with his bare hands or smashing it aside with his servo-arm.

Dropping his damaged lascannon to the deck as he extricated himself, the Heretic Astartes drew his bolt pistol from its hip holster, taking aim on the momentarily dumbfounded Scions.

'From Iron cometh strength!' the Space Marine shouted, firing his bolt pistol. The round glanced from Norroll's helmet, knocking him from his feet.

'From strength cometh will,' the Iron Warrior continued, flames wreathing him like some malevolent fiend stepping free of the inferno. Traxel dodged as he fired another shot. The round creased the Tempestor's left tricep and detonated in one of the servitors behind him.

'From will cometh faith.' Zelazko's left leg was clearly injured, but he was moving now, dragging his foot as he approached the Scions. Another round burst against the rear of Traxel's right pauldron in a puff of shrapnel.

'From faith cometh honour.' Two rounds spanged from the platform where Norroll had been knocked prone a split second before. 'From honour cometh Iron.'

Hobbling towards the Scions, Zelazko drew his chainsword and thumbed the ignition.

'This is the Unbreakable Litany,' the Iron Warrior bellowed over the chainsword's roar. 'May it ever be so.'

XXIV

Zelazko burst from the smoke, his armour smouldering and soot black from the flames which had engulfed him. His chainsword snarled in his grip, the hungry animus of the blade's corrupted spirit clamouring in its keenness to feast upon the Scions' flesh and blood. Even limping, the Iron Warrior was incongruously fast for his bulk – the dichotomy between expectation and reality stymied Norroll's ability to understand what he was seeing as the transhuman charged them.

Norroll's forebrain worked on the sheer improbability of the situation he found himself in, rather than focusing on the animal part of his brain screaming for him to flee. Statistically speaking, any given Imperial citizen's chance of ever encountering even a single Adeptus Astartes across the breadth of the galaxy in a single lifetime fell so far into the realm of extreme improbability that it should be impossible. The one charging him was the third he had encountered in under two weeks, and before that there had been the ones on Tecerriot. Traitors all.

It was comforting to focus on such trivialities in moments like this – far better than accepting the reality that there was simply no way he would ever be fast enough to avoid the avatar of death charging headlong towards him.

Traxel's chainsword struck the Iron Warrior's aside in mid-swing, a direct hit to the side of Zelazko's blade that turned the killing blow into a glance that chewed down the length of Norroll's left pauldron, spitting armour plate and ceramite. With the grace of a born duellist, Traxel diverted the energy of his swing, angling his snarling blade to glance up the length of the Heretic Astartes' weapon to strike at Zelazko's less-armoured throat.

Zelazko swayed backwards, his artificer-crafted armour's fibre-bundle musculature and servomotor augmentation in the joints granting him an impossible level of dexterity, enabling him to simply avoid the chainsword's spinning teeth. Flicking his own chainblade around, he slapped Traxel's weapon aside with a casual upward strike, then punched the Tempestor in the side of the head with his free hand.

The blow spun Traxel into the air, cratering his helm and sending him careening backwards. Against an unarmoured opponent it surely would have been a decapitating strike, but the ablative microlayers in his helm held, distributing the force about the whole of his head. The Tempestor flailed as he slid to a halt, struggling for orientation.

Acting on instinct, Norroll stabbed upwards, driving his right monoblade into the softer, ribbed armour of Zelazko's armpit. The Iron Warrior's servo-arm swung out from above, smashing into Norroll's flank and crushing his carapace. Pain flared in his side as his ribs buckled and the world spun around him. Norroll twisted through space, tumbling over the side of the landing platform. He reached out, desperately grasping at a section of raised blast shielding at the Skyshield's edge.

His fingers hooked on a length of power cabling on the underside of the platform, narrowly arresting his fall. Norroll dangled beneath the Skyshield, swaying in the wind near the upper reaches of the Vanness Tether's mid-levels. The outskirts of Vytrum spread out nearly a mile beneath him, entirely obscured by the boiling haze of dust kicked up by the blast wave of the explosion above.

Taking a deep breath, Norroll pulled himself up with one arm, pushing away the searing pain in his ribs to reach out and take hold of the cabling with his other hand. He kicked a foot over it, fumbling for a handhold on the platform above.

He had lost both monoblades when the Iron Warrior struck him, and doubted whether his laspistol would prove sufficient to bring the Traitor Astartes down. Carefully, he managed to secure a fingerhold against the blast shielding, balancing on the cable as he prepared to free-climb back up to the platform.

The thump-and-hiss discharge of Traxel's plasma pistol quickened his pace. Norroll dug his fingertips into the tiny lip of metal at the bottom of the shielding and pulled, feet swinging beneath him as he scrambled upwards and secured a grip on one of the small shrines to the Machine God decorating the blast shielding at regular intervals. He heaved his right foot onto the bottom lip of the platform and rose, stabilising himself enough that he could look over the shield.

No sooner had Norroll managed to peek over the barrier than his right foot slipped, dropping him down and nearly pitching him from the Skyshield. He snatched reflexively for a handhold, halting his fall as his fingers closed around the blast shield's upper lip. Grunting, he struggled to right himself. He strained to climb over it, his battered and fatigued body protesting as he managed to hoist himself high enough to look over the edge once again.

The Heretic Astartes clutched Traxel in his servo-arm, holding the Tempestor inverted mere inches before the soot-blackened skull visage of his battle helm. Arms pinned in the servo-arm's clawlike grip, Traxel spat a wad of bloody phlegm onto the Iron Warrior's visor as he struggled to free himself. Blood dripped down the right side of Traxel's head, sheeting from where his ear had been torn off when the Iron Warrior had forcibly removed his helmet.

The Tempestor's plasma pistol lay at Zelazko's feet, while his chainsword was on the deck of the landing platform, several feet in front of where Norroll scrambled over the defence barrier.

To the west, the remains of the Devourer-class drop-ship smashed down onto the capitol building, ejecting a plume of flame as it eradicated the structure. The drop-ship's blackened corpse teetered for a few seconds before collapsing, the vessel's fuselage seeming to wilt as it buckled and collapsed over the length of the capitol mall in a titanic shriek of protesting metal.

Distracted by the fury of the drop-ship's destruction, Zelazko glanced away from his captive.

Traxel wrenched his left arm free of the servo-arm's grip and snatched the last krak grenade from his belt, priming the explosive and stuffing it between the Iron Warrior's gorget and helm.

Driven by some atavistic impulse, the servo-arm snapped open, dropping Traxel head first to the deck. Zelazko clutched frantically at the grenade wedged behind his gorget, fumbling at it with scrabbling fingers before it exploded in his hand.

The Traitor Astartes swayed, the gyroscopic stabilisers in his boots snarling as they struggled to keep him upright. A plume of smoke twisted from between his shoulders, obscuring much of his head. Crippled by the blast, his servo-arm dangled limply from its mount on his power armour's backpack. He reached for his helmet with his right hand, staring bemusedly at his mangled limb before seeming to realise that the extremity was missing.

He released his chainsword from his left hand and pulled the ruptured battle helm from his head, dropping it heavily to the ground.

Traxel grabbed at his plasma pistol, his fingers wrapping around the grip before Zelazko planted a hard kick into the side of his head, sending the Tempestor rolling and skidding across the deck.

Norroll clambered over the blast shielding, firing his laspistol on the move before slipping face first onto the platform. The shot went wide, streaking past the bleeding nub of the Iron Warrior's right ear, though it managed to draw the Heretic Astartes' attention from the Tempestor.

Zelazko hurled himself at Norroll. His injuries made him clumsy, and he collapsed onto his chest with a peal of metal on metal. He was up in an instant, propelled forward by inhumanly responsive reflexes.

The delay was enough. Fuelled by desperation and adrenaline, Norroll snatched up Traxel's chainsword, thumbing the activator stud and swinging for Zelazko's neck as he shambled towards the limping Space Marine.

The Iron Warrior blocked the strike with the vambrace of his truncated right arm. The chainsword snarled, biting shallowly into the flesh beneath as it lodged within the iron and ceramite of Zelazko's armour.

Traxel's krak grenade had torn the flesh from most of the right side of Zelazko's head, along with his nose and lips, reducing much of his face to a glistening crimson skull. Glaring hatefully with his remaining bloodshot eye, Zelazko struck Norroll with a vicious backhand. The recon trooper crashed backwards against the platform's blast shielding and collapsed in a limp heap.

Yanking the chainsword from his vambrace and tossing it aside, Zelazko lunged after the stricken Scion.

* * *

Atebe dived to the deck at nearly the same instant Norroll hit the ground on the other side of the platform, entering the Killstate and taking in the scene before her through the obscuring cloud of thick black smoke. Traxel was sprawled out on his back, no more than fifteen yards from her, while Norroll lay face down across the landing pad in the lee of the blast shield. She felt the heat radiating from the Valkyrie's wreckage through her carapace armour and smelled the burning reek of promethium fumes through her respirator's filters.

Even limping, the Iron Warrior crossed the deck with uncanny speed. His bare, bloody jaw worked, though his words were lost to Atebe. Reaching Norroll at a run, the Space Marine grasped the recon trooper by the head and lifted him from the ground.

Drawing in a deep breath, Atebe lined up her crosshairs over the right side of the Traitor Astartes' flayed head.

The las-bolt struck Zelazko two inches above where his right ear had been, blowing a chunk free from the top of his reinforced cranium. The Iron Warrior swayed, dropping Norroll limply to the deck as he pivoted to face the new threat. He stared bemusedly at Atebe, drooling blood from his slack jaw.

His remaining eye blinked once, and Atebe shot him through it.

The flatline screamed from Daviland's vambrace as she sprinted over blood-smeared tiles, past the dead and cowering wounded in the corridor. Laspistol raised, she raced pell-mell for the hatchway to Skyshield Four.

Atebe lay prone on the floor in the doorway – she was fine, and Daviland ignored her, rushing past her onto the landing pad. The Iron Warrior's nearly headless corpse smouldered, face down on the deck, and she ignored that as well. She headed for Traxel, holstering her pistol as she ran and readying her medi-kit.

She trusted Atebe to cover her as she slid to a halt on her knees next to the Tempestor.

Traxel gazed skyward, all the traumas and uncertainty which had plagued him since Tecerriot finally released. She glanced at her medi-slate, though she didn't need it to know what her senses already told her – Tempestor Traxel was dead.

'Emperor light your way, Tempestor,' she whispered, rising to her feet.

Gathering her medi-kit, she trudged to Norroll's side. Her legs and back were stiff, her feet leaden, as she slumped down beside him. His pulse registered clearly on her vambrace, rapid and shallow but steady.

'Atebe,' she called, 'are we clear?'

Atebe shut the blast door behind her, cutting off any interruption from inside. 'Yes.'

'Come here and hold his head. This is easier with two.'

Atebe complied, though she made sure she continued to face the doorway. 'What now?'

'Hold his head steady.'

Daviland unclasped the seals on Norroll's helmet and gently lifted the fractured armour free. The entire left side of his face was unrecognisable where severe blunt-force trauma had shredded the flesh to the bone and burst his eyeball. Beneath the swelling and discolouration, his cheek buckled visibly inwards. Blood drooled from his slack, puffy lips.

Daviland removed a brace from her medi-kit and snapped it into place, immobilising Norroll's neck with Atebe's help. She unfolded a stretcher from its compartment beneath the kit's armoured housing directly beside Norroll before unbuckling his cuirass. 'I need your dagger.'

Atebe handed Daviland her Scion blade without comment.

Cutting open Norroll's fatigues, Daviland reached back into

her medi-kit and produced a stimm injector, loading it with a heavy dosage.

'Hold him steady,' Daviland said. 'He's going to jump.'

Atebe pressed down on Norroll's shoulders. 'Ready.'

Immobilising Norroll's legs with her left arm, Daviland jammed the injector between his ribs, directly into his heart.

Norroll gasped, kicking and flailing as the cocktail of medicinal compounds coursed into his bloodstream. Daviland and Atebe strained against his thrashing, struggling to keep him secure as his muscles spasmed. After nearly half a minute's writhing, the convulsions subsided, leaving Norroll gasping on the landing pad's deck. He groaned, burbling unintelligibly for a few seconds through his broken jaw and missing teeth.

'Stay still,' Daviland said.

'S'lenna?' he slurred, opening his watering right eye. He looked up at Atebe. 'Tadia?'

'Best you don't move,' Atebe said.

'Did we win?' Norroll murmured.

'We won,' Daviland said wearily. 'Don't talk. He fractured your mandible and your left maxilla and zygomatic arch.'

Norroll winced as he probed the damage with his tongue. 'My what?'

'Your face, Gry,' Daviland explained. 'He broke your face.'

'Oh,' Norroll mumbled. Atebe pushed down on his shoulders as he suddenly struggled to sit upright. 'Where's the Tempestor?'

EPILOGUE

'Thank you for your account, Tempestor,' the interrogator said. He rose from his folding chair on the opposite side of a simple Munitorum-green field desk, steadying himself on his walking stick of decoratively twisted black iron. 'As ever, the dedication of the Militarum Tempestus and its unwavering devotion to the Throne are appreciated. Your duties here on Rilis are discharged in full, and we do not wish to further delay your departure.'

'Of course,' Norroll said. His words were still slurred, though he was getting accustomed to speaking through the right side of his mouth. The left half of his face was swathed in bandages and his jaw remained wired shut. Daviland had implanted the augmetic grafts for his left eye a month before and had assured him they were taking well.

A wave of nausea struck him again. He had felt queasy for weeks, a side effect of the counter-radiation tonics the medicae-adept had subjected them all to.

He and the interrogator stood face to face in the makeshift

headquarters which had served as the 139th Mech's command centre. Half a pace behind Norroll, Daviland and Atebe silently flanked their Tempestor, lasguns held across their chests. Their armour had been patched and functionally repaired, but still bore all the scars accrued months earlier.

A squad of five Scions in the halved red-and-black carapace of the 32nd Thetoid Eagles stood behind the interrogator, their right pauldrons emblazoned with the Warwing, the stylised eagle symbol of their regiment. Utterly immobile, they mirrored Daviland and Atebe, hotshot lasguns held across their chests and the lenses of their battle helms glowing with a faint green light. Neither group of Scions had spoken so much as a word to each other in the months since the 32nd Thetoid's arrival.

'If you don't mind my asking, sir, what will happen here next?'

The interrogator rapped his cane on the ground thoughtfully, scrutinising Norroll with deep-set eyes as forthcoming as knapped flint. He was an older man of middling height and build, swathed in a heavy greatcoat of black leather, with thinning sleet-grey hair and a hard-worn, craggy face. The edge of his left eye was deformed by a long scar which marred his features from brow to jaw. He appeared physically robust, despite his advancing years and what appeared to be a debilitating injury to his left leg.

'As you know, Lord General Trenchard has taken direct command of the military reconquest of Rilis, and three Rilisian divisions have been recalled from across the segmentum to secure their planet,' the interrogator replied. 'Along with the contingent of Tempestus Scions from the Thirty-Second Thetoid Eagles who accompanied us from Enth, I am confident in the inevitability of this world's return to the Emperor's light. I fear it will be some time before we complete our investigations here, but rest assured, my master's intent is to get this system back up and running in service to the Throne as quickly as possible.'

Norroll nodded stiffly. He didn't know what else to say.

'I hope that satisfies your curiosity, Tempestor,' the interrogator said with a thin smile. 'Return to the Thirty-Sixth Xian Tigers with honour. You have accomplished great things here.'

'Thank you, sir.'

'You are dismissed.'

As one, the eradicant turned on their heels and left. Traxel's chainsword thumped against Norroll's left hip.

'It felt like that would never end,' Atebe breathed as they walked through the jumbled corridors of the complex which had served as the 139th Mech's command centre. The Xian Tigers themselves were never maltreated during the interrogation process, simply kept sequestered from the other internees for the duration. 'Three weeks of inquiries.'

A tent city had been built outside the headquarters, the entire area walled up and transformed into a massive processing centre. Survivors of the Rilisian civil war on both sides had been brought here for incarceration, interrogation and, frequently, execution. Norroll had heard of another such centre on Ganspur.

Autumn had come to Rilis in the three months since the civil war's end, and the ridges rising to the east of the Zholm River were ablaze with orange and crimson in the late afternoon's golden sunlight.

Passing without comment through a gate guarded by a pair of Scions from the 32nd Thetoid Eagles, First Eradicant made for the field which had once served as a makeshift motor pool. The area had been converted into a landing zone housing four separate landing pads, and the Xian Tigers crossed to the far side of the field, where a black Valkyrie, marked with the thrice-crossed 'I' of the God-Emperor's Holy Inquisition, awaited them.

'Any idea what's next, Tempestor?' Atebe asked as she and Daviland boarded behind Norroll. One of the door gunners slid the passenger hold's door shut behind them.

'None,' Norroll admitted as he sat down. 'I'm to meet with Tempestor-Prime Bassoumeh as soon as we arrive on Sindral-Beta, but I've no clue what she wants to speak to me about, or what she's got in mind for us afterwards.'

'Probably another operation,' Atebe said as the gunship rose into the air on its vertical thrusters and pivoted westward.

'Probably,' Norroll agreed neutrally.

Bound for the Inquisitorial frigate parked at low anchor above, the Valkyrie climbed into the upper atmosphere. Within, as Rilis fell away beneath them, the Scions lapsed into quiescence, readying themselves for their next deployment.

ABOUT THE AUTHOR

R S Wilt made his first foray onto the battlefields of the Dark Millennium during the early days of *Warhammer 40,000: Rogue Trader*. His previous works for Black Library include the short stories 'Eradicant' and 'The Guns of Enth'. A retired United States Army officer who spent most of his career bouncing around Europe, he lives with his family.

YOUR
NEXT READ

THE FALL OF CADIA
by Robert Rath

Cadia – a bulwark against the forces of Chaos that reside in the Eye of Terror. This proud world stood defiantly for centuries, until it was targeted for destruction by Abaddon the Despoiler in his Thirteenth Black Crusade.

For these stories and more, go to blacklibrary.com, warhammer.com, Games Workshop and Warhammer stores, all good book stores or visit one of the thousands of independent retailers worldwide, which can be found at warhammer.com/store-finder

YOUR NEXT READ

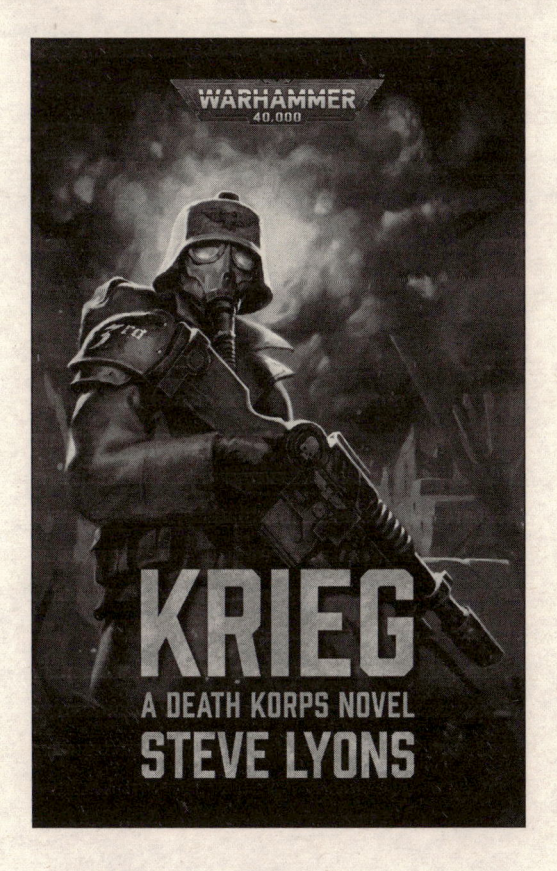

KRIEG
by Steve Lyons

The Death Korps of Krieg lay siege to a hive city on the outskirts of Warzone Octarius, desperately trying to prevent untold masses of orks and tyranids spilling out into the Imperium. How far will the ruthless Korpsmen go to achieve victory in a seemingly unwinnable war?

For these stories and more, go to blacklibrary.com, warhammer.com, Games Workshop and Warhammer stores, all good book stores or visit one of the thousands of independent retailers worldwide, which can be found at warhammer.com/store-finder

YOUR NEXT READ

MINKA LESK: THE LAST WHITESHIELD
by Justin D Hill

Cadia has stood in grim defiance against the enemies of the Imperium for ten thousand years, an indomitable bulwark against the forces of Chaos… but now, the 13th Black Crusade has come, and there will be no victory. Here, Minka Lesk will be tested in the very fires of a world's destruction.

For these stories and more, go to **blacklibrary.com**, **warhammer.com**, Games Workshop and Warhammer stores, all good book stores or visit one of the thousands of independent retailers worldwide, which can be found at **warhammer.com/store-finder**